GIDEON'S WARRIORS

GIDEON'S WARRIORS

DOUGLAS MULLIS

TATE PUBLISHING
AND ENTERPRISES, LLC

Published by Tate Publishing & Enterprises, LLC
127 E. Trade Center Terrace | Mustang, Oklahoma 73064 USA
1.888.361.9473 | www.tatepublishing.com

Tate Publishing is committed to excellence in the publishing industry. The company reflects the philosophy established by the founders, based on Psalm 68:11,
"The Lord gave the word and great was the company of those who published it."

Book design copyright © 2014 by Tate Publishing, LLC. All rights reserved.
Cover design by Jim Villaflores
Interior design by Caypeeline Casas

Published in the United States of America

ISBN: 978-1-63185-640-2
1. Fiction/Action/Adventure
2. Fiction/Christian/General
14.05.27

This book is dedicated to my loving Mother and to all the English teachers that encouraged me to become a writer. And to all my brothers and sisters in the Christian Motorcycle Association, winning souls for the Son.

With a special thanks to all those who have served and especially to those who made the ultimate sacrifice.

SEMPER FI

FOREWORD

Although this is a work of fiction, all of the spiritual things experienced by the characters have come from my personal life; including astral travel, meeting demons, witches, and shape-shifting. The experience of Joseph in prison is my own testimony using circumstances that better fit his character as an indigenes American.

I have never experienced combat in the battlefield, but I have done battle with the forces of the spiritual world. I can testify that the only way to stop demonic possession is to call upon the name of the Lord—Jesus the Christ. If you are having the same problems that Tom has with nightmares, anger, and guilt there is only one way to get healing; and that is through prayer. He said, (Jesus), that he would never turn away someone who seeks him. May you find him now and know the peace that can only come from above.

Blessed is he whose transgressions are forgiven

Psalm 32:1

Forgive them Father for they know not what they do: Except these guys know exactly what they are doing. And what they are doing is the will of the Evil one. Draped in black leather, their bodies covered in kabalistic tats, they roam the Kingdom of Light in service to the Lord of Darkness.

Vultures in the distance reveal their trail of destruction, while my steel horse waits, patiently thumping out its heartbeat—potato-potato, waiting for its master to take up the reins once again and face eternity in the cause of Light. Throwing my leg over the saddle of my '64 Panhead, I settle my six foot four inch frame and get ready for what lies ahead. Pulling mirrored shades down over pale blue eyes I drop the tranny into gear and pull out onto the black gash of macadam leading to either road kill or glory!

Feeling the road slipping under me I start to think back to where it all started and the fantastic journey that has brought me to this place. An ordinary childhood with loving parents who took me to church every Sunday, but who know nothing of the enemy or his nature. Sixteen years in the Marine Corps with two tours in Iraq taught me how to kill and I was very, very, good at it.

"Gunny, front and center," boomed out the voice of my LT. "You and your squad will take the front door. Use flash-bangs to get in and fer Christ's sake try not to kill any non-coms."

"Non-combatants, yeah. The only non-com's I've seen here are under the age of two LT." Too often that was true, you could not be sure who the bad guys were since few wore uniforms and even kids as young as ten were used as mobile I.E.D.'s (Improvised Explosive Device). 'Kill'em all and let God sort 'em out', had become my motto. I was on my second tour and determined to go home not only alive, but in one piece.

I had been the hometown hero and looked the part: tall, lean, blond, with penetrating blue eyes, square jaw, and a voice that was somehow resonant with authority.

Even though I was scared most of time throughout my first tour, when I found I was going to have to make a second, something in me died. I made up my mind that, no matter what, Gunny Sergeant Tom Harper was not coming home in a Hefty bag.

As we came to the courtyard door I had my point man, Cpl. Armstrong, put a small C-4 charge on it. "Fire in the hole," he shouted and there was a bang followed by the rest of us throwing flash-bangs to disorient anyone inside. I directed two of my men to the right, two to the left, and Cpl. Armstrong and I went up the center, weapons ready.

I heard the distinctive sound of an R.P.G. (Rocket Propelled Grenade) and dived for cover behind a fountain in the central garden. It went off about three meters behind me, throwing Cpl. Armstrong up and over me like a child's broken toy. I knew right away he was dead and so were the rest of us unless we moved fast. As the smoke cleared the AK-47's started their deadly chatter from what seemed like every opening in the house, sending gravel flying in little explosions everywhere and making that distinctive hypersonic crack as they flew past my head.

Two more of my men went down with cry's of "Medic" and "Sarge, I'm hit." We were taking too much fire so I screamed at my radioman to call in re-enforcements, but he was hit too.

I threw two grenades at the house where we were taking the most fire and my last squad man, a private by the name of Jack Kellogg, tossed a smoke grenade as well. I was up and moving before the dirt hit the ground, headed for the double windows on the right side of the front door, and calling for Jack to follow.

With both of us squatting under the window I tossed in my last grenade. After the blast we both went in guns blazing. There was blood and body parts every where and the floor so wet I slid half-way cross the room before coming up against a pile of bloody rags which was all that was left of what had been human beings only seconds before.

With Pvt. Kellogg in tow we started sweeping the rest of the house killing anything that moved or looked like it still could. I did not care whether they were non-com's or not by that point. My people, four good men, were dead or wounded and somebody was going to pay!

On the upper floor I sprayed the final room with fire and with Kellogg following close behind me the world, as I knew it, changed forever.

Something seemed to hit me all over like a giant hammer and at once I felt like I was being squeezed down to the size of a grape; then just as suddenly expanded out to infinity—then nothing. Not just nothing, but NO-THING: Then a voice, gentle and kind, a voice I seemed to know said, "I have need of you Tom Harper."

I don't know why, but memories of sitting in church looking at pictures of Jesus suddenly came back to me and I knew…I knew. "Yes Lord," I said, "I am here."

Dust and smoke choked the air of the upper room where I lay on my back surrounded by the bodies of a dozen men. All were dressed strangely for the area. Tight black outfits covering them from head to toe, like Ninja warriors, and armed with weapons not usually found in Iraq: Tech 9's, Mac's and assorted hand guns.

I sat up looking for Kellogg who was back out in the hallway unconscious. I looked myself over and saw no wounds: no wounds on the men around me either. My ears were ringing and I felt a warm trickle of blood coming from my nose as I struggled to my feet. I glanced out the window and saw a man on a rooftop across the street aiming an R.P.G. my way. With no time to think

I jumped up, threw Kellogg over my shoulder, and plunged down the stairs with Hell following.

There were three or four bad guys at the bottom of the staircase, but I was moving so fast and screaming bloody murder, that they must have thought I was a 'djin'. I went through them like a bowling ball hitting a strike and kept right on going out into the street all the way back to our lines. I was told I collapsed there suffering wounds to my back from the R.P.G. and a concussion.

CHAPTER 2

After two weeks in hospital I was awarded a Silver Star for meritorious bravery under fire and sent back home with an Honorable Discharge to join the ranks of the unemployed. During my recovery though I kept remembering that dream of Jesus speaking to me and it left me wondering if it was all real or not. What did he mean by "I have need of you?" What could He possibly need me for? I sure wasn't no Jesus freak and wasn't trying to live a Christian life.

There was a feeling though that I just could not get away from, a sort of empty gnawing in my spirit that just would not go away. For now though I was free and had about twenty K in my pocket so I was thinking…ROAD TRIP!

I had always wanted to see some of the U.S. and this seemed like a good time to do it. I could look for a job later and frankly, I still had some demons I needed to shake off. I couldn't think of a better way than on my old '64 Panhead with the breeze in my face and the open road in front of me. I had done a lot of work on it with my dad before I went into the Corps. With bobbed fenders, six inch over front end, Mustang tank, high bars, solo saddle with a sissy pad, and painted in Midnight Blue she was a real beauty.

Home was in Jonestown, Texas where everyone was sad to see me leave again so shortly after returning, especially my mom. My dad seemed to understand though, maybe because he was a vet from the Nam and understood what I was going through. I had been home about a week and was working on the bike out in the barn when he walked in with a bottle of Jack Daniels and two glasses. I had not known my dad to drink much and was a little surprised to see him pour us both a good stiff three fingers of the golden liquid.

We sat sipping the Tennessee firewater and looking over the rusted primary chain on the bike, but I could tell that something was on his mind. I decided to wait knowing that he would tell me when he was ready. After two more glasses of tongue lube he finally looked at me and asked, "Are you ready to talk about it son?"

I just looked at him with my best little-boy-lost look and said, "Talk about what dad?"

"About the dreams son," he said. "The ones that wake you up in the middle of the night. Those dreams," he said with that thousand-yard look in his eyes.

It was a look I had seen before when I was a kid and the Nam was still coming out of his pores like some toxic poison.

"I'm not sure dad," I said suddenly feeling very small. "I'm not sure I can. Some things happened over there, terrible things, and I just don't know if I can talk about it yet. Maybe never dad, I just don't know."

The bottle was about empty and there were tears in his eye's that spoke volumes to me about his own pain, a pain I knew was there, but we had never talked about.

"Son," he said drawing in a deep breath, "I carried my pain from the Nam like my own personal cross for decades after coming home until it almost ruined my marriage and destroyed my spirit." He took another sip of J.D. and lapsed into silence for a while.

Not knowing what to say, but remembering those days, I just waited.

"Son we all do terrible things in war. We are called upon to participate in an un-Godly act of inhumanity while people still expect us to act in a civilized way. The fact is, war is kill or be killed, no mercy, no quarter. Kill that other S.O.B. first so you can come home. It's that simple for those who have been there and impossible to explain to those who sat at home watching it on the five o'clock funnies."

A long speech for my dad, but I could see he was working his way up to telling me something that, at least to him, was very personal and very painful.

"Son, I killed your Uncle Bob."

Just like that. Then he looked me in the eyes, and I saw in those windows to the soul the pain that had lain hidden there for so many years.

CHAPTER 3

"We were on a mission in Cambodia that did not exist. We weren't supposed to be there you know. It was part of Nixon's private war.

"Bob had been wounded by a pongee trap, one of those little holes you step into and boards with nails close on both sides of your foot. It was bad, real bad, because we could not call for help and we could not afford to be caught. We knew the danger going in, but somehow in that moment it all took on a reality that had only been abstract up to that point.

"We gave him some morphine and tried to keep him quiet, but the nails had gone right into the bone and he was in terrible pain." Dad got up then obviously feeling agitated and walked around a bit. "Charlie was real close. We were there to call in B-52 bombing runs on the HO Chi Min trail you know.

"At one point a V.C. stopped to take a leak and got my boots wet; that's how close they were. Bob was crying from the pain and we had no more morphine; nothing to help him. We all knew that we were going to die if Bob gave us away. We would be tortured in some camp until we were dead or the war was over. The only other choice was unthinkable.

"We had been working our way out carrying Bob; traveling by night, resting by day, dodging patrols, and praying for a miracle." Again he was silent for a while as the cobwebs covering the old wound were brushed away leaving it as raw as the day it was made.

"Miracles were in short supply in those days and we were getting desperate. Bob's wounds were festering and the smell of death was on him. I knew that gangrene would kill him soon if we did not get him to hospital, but we were still in Charlie's backyard and that was a world away.

"Our extraction point was still about five klick's away when we walked right into a V.C. patrol of about thirty men. They did the unthinkable and started making camp with us right in the middle of them."

Again, a long silence full of pent up emotion passed before he could go on. "I was holding Bob, trying to keep him quiet, but the fever from the infection, and the pain, were just too much for him. He started making these little mewling sounds and trembling from chills. I knew that if I could not keep him still and quiet we were going to be in a world of hurt. Thirty against five just ain't good odds son. So I put my hand over his mouth and held him tight as I could, but he was becoming disoriented and fighting me.

"I tried to knock him out with the butt of my pistol, but I was so scared that I must have hit him to hard. I did not notice right away, so relieved that he was quiet now; he was not breathing."

My dad drained the last of his whiskey with tears streaming down his cheeks and for several minutes I watched as his body was wracked with deep sobs. I could only watch, because I was crying too, like a five year old who has been caught breaking his mom's favorite china.

"I knew he was dead son and I was also aware that I had killed him. I know that I did what I had to do to survive, but that does not make it any easier. We hid his body in some thick brush where we hoped he would not be found then we slipped out during the night with the sound of bombs going off to cover our escape. After two more days in the bush we made our way to the L.Z. (Landing Zone) and home."

He paused again to take another drink, but finding the bottle empty, he threw it in the corner and just seemed to disappear inside himself. I grabbed him tight as I could and that night we joined a fraternity as old as man himself: THE BROTHERHOOD OF THE WARRIOR.

I slept that night better than I had in a long time. The faces of the women and children in that little room were still there, but no longer seemed to be accusing me. I still felt I owed them something, there was still a debt of guilt, but I did not feel I was bearing all that weight by myself anymore. I was not alone or unique in any way. I was in the brotherhood and we all bore these same feelings. I was not free yet, but no longer suffered as much as I had.

CHAPTER 4

Off the road just ahead is a little bar calling itself the *Last Chance Bar and Grill*. In the parking lot are about a dozen bikes and half a dozen or so cars and pickups. The cages look local, but the bikes are all sporting out-of-state plates and the sort of mods that say outlaw.

Inside, the place is like hundreds of other little waterholes: poor lighting, stench of stale beer and unwashed bodies, and a bartender with big boobs and a cute smile. Citizens were on the left and bikers on the right where the pool table was. There were also a half dozen ol' ladies at the bar.

I stepped up and ordered a beer from the attractive bartender. She put my brew on the bar top and said, "You best watch your back Honey, this is a rough looking crew."

I had to agree. They were wearing Pagan Colors and bulges here and there suggested concealed weapons. I took my beer and moved to an open table where I had the wall to my back, citizens to my left, and outlaws to the front.

They didn't seem to be interested in me; I was just another Lone Wolf. I was looking at the pictures over the bar showing the place and its patrons in a better time, when a couple of the bikers started beefing over the pool table. Looking over at them I had the sudden impression of having seen them somewhere before. It was that Déjà-vu thing again, but this time it was a flashback to a little room and a dozen men in black.

They suddenly got up at the command of one greasy looking individual and—this is where it got really freaky—he looked at me as they were leaving and gave me a wink, as though we shared some secret. Then the rest caught up slapping each other around and the spell was broken.

I finished my beer and went out to my bike. They were gone by then, but on my bike, hanging from the handlebar, was something that sent a chill right through my soul. A black silk hood with eye-holes cut in it, just like the men were wearing in a little room, in a place far away, and a lifetime ago.

Down the road a few miles, I came to a little town and stopped for gas. After filling the tank, I asked the gap-toothed old man running the place about food and lodging in the area.

"Only'st place close is the *Cactus Inn* about three miles down the road. Don't knows as ya might be partial to it though," he said in a cryptic manner.

I packed beer and chips in my saddlebags and headed out for this oasis-in-the-desert. The old man was right, the place made the phrase 'Roach Motel' come to mind as soon as I pulled up.

It had probably been built back in the early 60's when the highway was new but was now reduced to a few working units just this side of condemned. The A.C. in the office sounded like it needed a complete re-build about ten years ago, but still looked better that the proprietor sitting behind the stained and often repainted counter.

She looked like something out of an old time sideshow carnival. She was about five-six and had to mass at least two hundred kilo's, with porcine eyes that sized me up like a pork-chop. They were like two black holes in a bottomless pit and if you weren't careful they drew you in to a place you did not want to go. The flower print muumuu hung on her sweating body like a flag in a dead calm. I was tired though and decided to go ahead and get a room.

"What can I do for ya handsome?" squeaked out of a mouth that looked like a red gash cut into a pink marble slab.

"A room for the night with A.C. that won't leave me with permanent hearing damage, if ya got it," I said.

"Why shore honey," dripped out of her mouth. "Number four has good A.C. and a clean bath. Twenty dollars for the night and just let me know if you want anything else. Okay?" One of those black pits winked at me in a truly terrifying way.

"No thanks," I answered, "just the room. It's been a long day."

"Okay sweetie," she said, "You know you sound just like Sam Elliot?"

"Who?" I said, even though I had been told this before. I did not wish to encourage her.

"Sam Elliot, the actor." she went on, "He does a lot of westerns."

"Sorry," I said backing out the door, "I've been out of the country for a long time. Marine Corps you know."

I headed out the door into the blast-furnace heat of a July Nevada evening and turned down the drive to the row of rooms. Room four looked like all the rest—about as inviting as a dentist chair in Tijuana. A bed, a side table with lamp, and a closet that doubled as shower and toilet. There was a small chair next to the window unit that was laboring to keep the room just under the boiling point of lead.

I tossed my gear on the bed and headed for the shower, popping open a beer on the way. Plenty of rust stains and calcium deposits everywhere, but the water was cool as it rained over my body washing away the road grime and sweat of the day's ride.

By the time I finished the shower, the room had cooled down some. Taking a seat next to the bed, I found a Gideon's Bible on the table. I picked it up and started thumbing through it. A small tract fell out into my lap showing Jesus on a motorcycle and saying, "Jesus would have been a biker." Funny I thought and tossed it on the bed without opening it or the Bible. Instead, I went out into the courtyard and had a look around.

On a hill about two hundred meters behind the motel something caught my attention. A man dressed in black was looking at me. I had a sudden feeling of panic as my warrior instincts were aroused. While I watched, he raised his hands up, bringing what looked like an R.P.G. to his shoulder. I looked around quickly for some cover, looked back, and he was gone.

I stood there trembling; going back again to that little room in Iraq, but the strident voice of the innkeeper suddenly broke the spell.

"Looking for something sweet thing?" in a voice that nearly gave me a cavity.

"Thought I saw something," was my lame response. I decided it had been a mirage and changed the subject, "You know of somewhere around here where I can find a cold beer and a good steak?"

"Jim's down the street," she said, raising up an arm that could have fed the Donner Party for a week and pointing out the direction. "They got good food, cold beer, and live music tonight."

"Thanks, I'll check it out," I said and headed back to my room before my trembling legs gave way under me. I sat down trying to convince myself that I had seen nothing, but somehow, I knew what I had seen was real; not an illusion.

Gideon was back in its place on the table with the tract neatly on top. I stepped into the bath and looked at the window, but it was way too small for anyone but a two year old to get through. There was no way anyone could have gotten in that room and out again without me seeing them—but there it was where I had not left it.

I had a sudden feeling of panic growing in me because this was getting too strange. I was beginning to doubt my own sanity. I turned for the door to get out but...I am in that room again. The bodies are all around me, except this time there is someone new: An old man with long white hair, piercing yellow eyes, and a real Mona Lisa smile. There seemed to radiate from him a sense of peace that was as palpable as it was invisible. He spoke two words to me, "GET OUT!"

I was back in the motel room when a sound from outside awakened a distant memory—**R.P.G.!**

I picked up my gear and ran straight across the parking lot into the room across from me and as I hit the door the pressure wave from the exploding round caught me and that, as well as my momentum, took me through the door and head long into the far wall.

I bounced off and fell onto the bed much to the surprise of the local mayor and his wife-for-the-night. I made a hasty apology and backed out the broken door to see unit four was no longer there: Or units three and five for that matter.

My first thought was to get away since R.P.G.'s are not something I am used to having fired at me in small-town U.S.A. I jumped on my bike and lit off into the gathering darkness leaving a very upset motel operator screaming at me unintelligibly and shaking a large chicken drumstick at me as pieces of meat flew out of her mouth.

On impulse, I turned onto a dirt road and headed out into the desert hoping to find a place of refuge where I could just sit down and figure out what was going on. Too many things were happening to me that could not be explained. Books don't move themselves or people appear out of nowhere. Was it P.T.S.D. (Post Traumatic System Disorder)? Or was it that I was slipping over the edge into madness? I had to find some answers and find them fast. Who wanted me dead? Was it terrorists chasing me for something I did back in Iraq? That might be a good place to start since I had done some pretty bad things back there.

For now though I needed a safe place to hide and the open desert seemed like a good spot. I drove until the dirt road became two ruts and then finally just faint wagon tracks.

I was in an area of canyons and mesas so far from city lights that I suddenly felt as though I was the last person on earth. The only thing I saw to remind me that I was not alone was the slowly moving red and green navigation lights of an airplane moving across the open celestial bowel above me.

I pulled the bike into the time worn walls of an old Indian pueblo. It was a good spot with walls on two sides and a sheer cliff behind. The ground in front was uphill with a view that was open for at least a klick. Nobody was going to sneak up on me here even if they were on foot. I broke out a blanket from my bags and settled in for the night hoping I would stay warm enough without a fire.

After a few minutes the insects took up their song again, punctuated by the eerie yips of coyotes. Except for the sounds, it was a lot like Iraq.

Several times I nodded off only to come awake, gun in hand as insurgents were charging me. Each time it was so real it left my heart pounding and the urge to run so strong that it took an enormous amount of self-discipline to remain still and quiet. I held onto the thought that I was in America and it was just my imagination working overtime.

Somewhere around midnight, I finally gave in to a deep, sound sleep, brought on by exhaustion from the day's stress.

CHAPTER 5

"Sergeant Tom Harper. Report!"

The words rang in my ears as I snapped to attention looking for the source of the command. I hit my head on the low ceiling of what looked like a Kiva, a circular underground room used by Indians for ceremonial occasions, although I was not aware of how I knew this.

There was a fire burning in its place on the floor with smoke dancing its way out through a hole in the roof and a white haired old man sitting across the fire from me. The smoke was burning my eyes and I could feel a knot rising on the crown of my head as the old man burst into laughter.

"You again!" I said. "What's going on? Who are you?"

I reached for my pistol only to discover that it was not in my shoulder rig, in fact, I was not even wearing the same clothes anymore. I was dressed in black leather from neck to foot: Leather jeans over heavy black boots and a leather shirt as well. I felt as though I had been turned into another person. I had never really liked the outlaw look and had stayed away from it as much as possible.

"Sit down," he said gently, but with that tone of command which causes a person to obey without thinking. "There is much you will need to learn and little time to teach you. You have answered His call and you must now decide."

"Hold up there old thing," I shot back. "Whose call?"

"The one who said, 'I have need of you'."

"But that was just a dream. I don't believe in Jesus or all that religious crap," I shot back angrily.

✝ ✝ ✝

I came awake with a coyote not two inches from my nose. His yellow canine eyes boring into mine imparted a feeling of intelligence. Then, with a snort, he tuned and trotted off into the desert night leaving me to wonder about all the Indian legends I had heard as a kid about coyotes being messengers; supernatural creatures.

Those eyes haunted me as I fell back to sleep. Was it just a dream or coincidence? The way the old man had laughed reminded me of the coyote's yipping. 'Course that would be crazy; it really would be time to check into the Prozac Palace.

✝ ✝ ✝

A series of clacking noises woke me up. A large Crow was looking at me from the Adobe wall and tapping his beak against the wall like some kind of Morse code. It could have been, but never having learned Morse code, it was just so much noise.

"Piss off," I mumbled and tossed a rock at him. In turn, he lifted off leaving me a gift on my jacket. Cursing his entire species, as well as his Creator, I got out some T.P. and wiped my jacket clean.

My warrior instincts kicked in at that moment with the hairs of my neck standing up. I feinted to my right, then jumped over the adobe wall to my left as a round kicked up the rocks where I had been. I stayed down listening for the shot so I could place the sniper, but he must have been using a suppressor because I heard nothing.

To make things worse all I had was a handgun with limited range and no idea where the shooter was. All I could do was sit tight and hope he would move in and maybe, make a mistake. With walls on three sides my only option was to run toward him and that would be suicide. At least I would be in the shade until noon and he would bake in the sun.

After a while I heard a Jeep laboring its way up the basin toward me and risked a peek over the wall to see who was coming. I saw a generous cloud of blond hair behind the windshield, but the vehicle was still about a hundred meters away. Too far to see who was driving and, not wanting to draw fire, I pulled my head back down behind the wall to wait.

When the Jeep came to a stop, I leveled my pistol over the wall and ordered the driver to freeze. She, just as politely, told me to drop my gun. She was standing to the right of me and pointing a rifle at me. There was no one in the Jeep, so I turned my head slowly to look at the Amazon who had taken Gunny Sergeant Tom Harper prisoner.

She was about five-eight, with honey blond hair over a face that, no doubt, had broken a thousand hearts: Green eyes that spoke to my heart like a wildfire in dry California brush, and a body that would grow wood in the Petrified Forest.

"Were you the one that shot at me?" I demanded.

"No," she said, "but if I wanted you dead you would be, so drop the pistol and put your hands on your head."

I had been so preoccupied by the Cadillac bumper bullets under her blouse, that I hadn't noticed the badge there that said U.S. Department of National Parks on it.

"Yes Ma'am," I said, "I didn't mean any harm. I didn't know I was in a restricted area."

"That Pueblo you're squatting in is protected under park law," she said. "You better have a real good reason for being there."

I knew I would have to think quick, because there was no way she would believe the truth. Or worse, I would be thrown into some lockup until they figured out who blew up the *Cactus Inn* and why.

I was saved from this problem by the sight of a man on top of the mesa about three hundred meters away. It was the glint of a scope that caught my eye and I dropped down to my knees behind the wall and hoped he wasn't using a .50 caliber that would go clean through the wall, and me.

"Lady," I said. "There is a man with a scoped rifle on that mesa out there and he is aiming at us. He took a shot at me about an hour ago and he's getting ready to shoot again, so you better take cover."

"That's a good one stranger, but I happen to know that you would need a 'copter to get on top of that mesa. Besides, I would have heard the shot."

"He's using a silencer," I said.

She was about to make some reply, when the cliff wall exploded just above her head and sent her scrambling for cover. Unfortunately, she was startled and jerked the trigger of her Winchester 30/30 putting a bullet across the right side of my neck. It was not a serious wound, but it did hurt like being slapped with an old fashioned Hickory stick.

She jumped down beside me and, seeing me bleeding, she started freaking.

"This is not happening," she shouted. "Who's shooting at me?"

I just looked at her and pointed at the wound on my neck indicating that I could not answer.

"I got a first aid kit in the Jeep," she said and started to go for it. I grabbed her, pulled her down, and got on top of her to shield her, as well as keep her still.

"Don't move," I growled into her ear in my best sergeant voice. "He can't get us here behind the wall. Let me have your rifle and I will try to spot him. Maybe I can get him. Gunny Sergeant Tom Harper, Marine Corps, just back from Iraq," as though that was all that needed to be said.

"You spot, I'll shoot," she said. "I'm the law here."

"Okay," I answered, "I seem to be his real target anyway."

I moved to a new position and quickly had a look along the ridge. I saw him looking back at me, then he turned with a wave of his hand and disappeared.

"Show's over," I remarked and sat with my back to the wall. "I could use that first aid kit now if you don't mind."

"Where did he go? Did you see him?" she asked. "And what do you mean you're the real target? Did you have something to do with that incident at the *Cactus Inn* last night?"

She asked all these questions rapid fire without letting me answer while still searching the ridge for any sign of the shooter. In answer, I pointed at my bloody throat once more.

"Oh yeah," she said, picked up my .45 Colt Auto, and turned to go to her Jeep throwing in, "Just don't move till I get back Gunny Sergeant Harper?"

I could not help but enjoy the view as she walked away. To say it was nice, was to say that the Golden Gate Bridge is just 'okay'. With some effort I turned my attention back to the mesa ridge looking for a 'chopper or sounds that would give some clue to the shooters position when I heard her say, "Radio's out. Looks like he put a bullet in it before leaving. Any idea who he is or why he's trying to kill you?"

"No I don't." I said, feeling a bit better as she knelt down to clean the wound. "Who are you?"

For a moment she just looked at me and then went back to work on my neck.

"Dakota Walsh, park ranger," she answered finally.

"Pretty name for a pretty woman," I said, which got me a shot of antiseptic on my neck that burned like cheap whiskey.

"Sit still soldier," she grunted. "You ain't hurt bad, I've done worse shaving my legs," which at least gave something else to think about.

"I can tell you this much, he missed on purpose. Only an armature would miss two easy shots like that." I went silent then, thinking back over the previous day and everything that had happened. There was something that was working at the back of my mind; worrying me like a Chihuahua trying to have his way with a Great Dane—It was just out of reach.

"That may be so, but it ain't gonna stop me from tracking him down and slamming the cage door on him." There was a look of fire in those jade eyes now and I honestly felt sorry for the poor jerk that had held us pinned down for the past hour.

"You still ain't said why you were out here last night," she said.

"The same guy shooting at us fired an R.P.G. at me back there at the *Cactus Inn* and I just wanted to find someplace safe for the night, ya know?" I felt I could trust this woman as she turned back to finish bandaging my wound and I saw around her neck a beautiful copper and turquoise cross nestled in between her ample breasts.

"I drove blind, just going as far into the desert as I could; hoping no one would be able to follow me." I told her about what had happened the day before, the bikers, the nut job that kept following me around shooting at me, the attack at the motel, but not the dreams; not yet. I even told her about the incident in Iraq in the upper room.

While I was talking, we got into the Jeep and started driving around the mesa to look for signs of the shooter, but as I had told her, we found nothing. This guy was a pro. There were a few footprints that ended at the cliffs edge and nothing else—no brass, cigarette butts, nothing.

By the time we made it back to the bike, it was well past noon and we were both getting hungry.

"I ain't gonna arrest you," she said. "But I do want you to come into town with me. There is someone I think you should meet."

"Okay but let's get something to eat first, I'm starved," I said without trying to whine too much.

"Sure," she said. "We'll stop at Mom's: Great food and nice people."

CHAPTER 6

Mom's was a bright spot next to the highway with a large paved parking lot and a huge homemade pie on the roof. One of those old roadside attraction kind of places that were popular in the 60's, with souvenirs and cheap jewelry, most of which came from China nowadays. There was a lot of Indian stuff too and some of it looked pretty good. Inside, past the counters in the cool rear, were the tables and booths of the restaurant.

We stepped up to the counter and were greeted by 'Mom' in a loud booming voice.

"Hey Dakota, long time no see."

'Mom' was six feet four inches tall and at least one hundred twenty kilo's, with black hair in braids to his waist in the traditional Sioux style. Behind his greasy apron, I saw that he wore a Shamans charm, which was ornately worked and looked very old.

"Hey Jason, see your still in business. Health Department hasn't caught you serving road kill again have they?"

"Hey, it was only that one time and nobody would have known if the license plate hadn't left numbers on the meat," he said in a mock tone of hurt. "Don't be poisoning new customers on me Chica," he said looking at me. "Looks like you caught a big one. You wanna feed him or skin him?"

"Oh, feed him I recon. Then I will decide what to do with him."

"Thanks a lot," I said trying to look suitable hurt. "Tom Harper from Texas and lately the Corp: Glad to meet ya."

Jason leaned over the counter to shake my extended hand and I saw the Anchor tat on his arm.

"Semper Fi," I said.

"Semper Fi," he returned. His handshake was firm, his black eyes clear above high cheekbones. I felt that this was a man I could walk into Hell with, kick ass, take names, and make even Satan himself run for his momma. I would soon find out how prophetic those words really were.

After a great meal of chicken fried steak, mashed potatoes, fried okra, and corn on the cob, I set my mind on dessert, as well as whether I should talk about my dreams with Dakota and Jason.

The roar of a dozen Harleys pulling into the parking lot and lining up in front of the restaurant interrupted us. I recognized them right off as the same bunch I had seen at the Last Chance Bar and Grill two days before. Jason heard them too and came out from the kitchen to have a look. Glancing at me he asked, "Friends of yours?"

"Saw them two days ago, but they are no friends of mine. Pagans from their colors and hardcore. Well armed from what I saw too."

The group paraded in; twelve men and six women. Their leader looked around as the others spread out looking at the souvenirs and came toward us in the dining room. He was about five-eight with long brown hair tied back with a tube and a red bandana wrapped around his forehead.

Taking off wrap-around shades he revealed gray eyes that had a feral look to them, over solid cheekbones and dark skin. He was solid under his open vest, no shirt, and no gun that I could see, but that could not be said for the others in the gang. Their women were often used to hide weapons in their purses and clothing and they usually stayed close to the men for that reason.

Stepping up to the leader Jason said, "You folks are welcome to eat, but you gonna have to wear a shirt." He pointed out the sign taped to the register that bore the old refrain: NO SHIRT—NO SHOES—NO SERVICE.

For a moment time seemed to stand still as these two forces of nature faced each other. Then one of his gang stepped up and said, "What's up Handlebar?" This was apparently a reference to his greased up mustache.

"Nothin' bro, just gonna see if we can get some food to go. That be alright with you Tonto?"

For a moment I thought Jason was going to go off, but he just smiled and said, "That'll be fine. Hamburgers and fries for all of you?"

"That'll be fine Tonto," laughed Handlebar as though he had said something really funny. Before stepping away his eyes shifted to mine and I had the feeling that evil had found a home behind those dark lenses.

He turned away to rejoin his friends and said, "Pay the man Maggott."

Dakota looked at me and whispered, "Get your hand away from the gun, too many people in here."

I whispered back, "It's his play, but your right. Not here, not now. Let's hope he knows that. The way he looks at me though, it's like he knows me and has some kind of score to settle."

"You sure you never met him?" she asked.

"I would remember those eyes, believe me."

Jason returned to the kitchen to fill their order and they went back to the front looking for beer and chips. One of the ol' ladies separated herself from the others and headed for the restroom behind us. She gave Dakota a look as she passed and a moment later, she excused herself and headed for the john too.

Inside, the first thing she noticed was how frail and scared this girl looked. Somehow, she just wasn't the one-percenter type. She was five-six and about fifty-two kilo's, with mousy brown hair, porcelain features, small breasts, and a nice figure.

"They are after your friend," she started. "They are gonna kill him if they get the chance."

"Any idea why? He says he's never seen you people before."

"Got something to do with a gun deal that was supposed to go down in Iraq. Don't know anything else 'cept that, if you wanna keep your man alive you better get him outta here."

With that said, she walked out and went back to the front to join the others.

Dakota came back to her seat, relayed the cryptic message to me, and suggested we take off through the back door of the kitchen rather than risk a shootout. I had been watching them and had noticed that there was always at least one of them watching me.

"No way darlin'," I said. "Too many eyes on me. Does Jason have a weapon?"

"Yes, a shotgun behind the counter. What you got in mind?"

"Go tell him to put it on the counter when he brings out the order. Let'em see yours as well. I will put mine on the table here. You stand over there at the corner of the counter where you can cover the others and have cover for yourself. If he's smart he won't try anything knowing we have a good field of fire on him."

"Okay," she said and went into the kitchen. She came out a few minutes later, helping to carry the orders and taking up her position as planned. As Handlebar came over to get the order, he held one of the ol' ladies close to him—her bag easily within reach of his right hand.

I opened my jacket on the left side revealing my service .45 while Jason reached under the counter to place his old double barrel Greener on the bar. Handlebar's eyes glommed onto the ten gauge and I saw just a glint of fearful respect in his eyes.

Jason remarked, "Really need to do something about that coyote that's been raiding the trash cans out back. Anything else ya'll might be needing?" he asked. "If not, that comes to twenty dollars and ya'll come back anytime."

With a growing smile that said 'next time,' he began to collect his order, moving slowly as he took us all in. Picking up the last bag, he shot me a glance and, this time, I winked at him.

As they were pulling out of the parking lot I took note of the leaders tag number and watched them until they were out of sight. Jason, Dakota, and I then took a seat in a booth and heaved a communal sigh of relief. I passed the tag number on to Dakota and said, "See what you can get from California D.M.V. on this guy. A name and picture if you can."

"Will do, meantime you need to find some place safe to stay."

"You are welcome to stay at my place out on the reservation," said Jason. "No way they can sneak up on us out there man."

"Thanks Jason, but I don't want to put you or your people in harm's way."

"It's them what will be in harm's way Tom. Nobody hunts on my land unless they have permission."

"Okay, sounds good, and to be truthful, I need some rest. I have been having some really intense dreams lately; very weird stuff."

"Well, we can talk about that too," said Jason. "Dreams are something we Indians know about."

"Follow me Tom and I will take you out to Jason's place. You'll like it out there. It's very peaceful with lots of good people and open sky."

"Okay, let's go," I said. "Just let me fill my tank first."

CHAPTER 7

The road out to Jason's was just graded dirt, complete with pot-holes that threatened to pound my kidney's to pâté after only a couple of miles and the dust kicked up from Dakota's Jeep was so thick that I had to drop back a hundred meters just so me and the bike could keep breathing. The land was as dry as a politician's promises and as barren as a Nun's womb. Except for the occasional Saguaro cactus, sagebrush, Piñon pine, and a few Joshua trees, there was not much to break up the monotony.

Lizards and Roadrunners were the only signs of life other than the ubiquitous Turkey Buzzard patiently waiting out the cycle of life hoping to get lucky, as we blazed a trail through the heat-shimmer of late afternoon.

The occasional rotting remains of traditional Indian Hogans, abandoned for more modern homes, could be seen at the side of the road; empty of life, but simple and elegant in their design.

We finally rolled into Jason's homestead heralded by dozens of mongrel dogs and boys dressed in jeans and T-shirts. There were the usual abandoned cars and appliances lining the side of the road and parked in back yards behind broken fences. It may have looked like no one was about, but the occasional glint of light on optic glass said otherwise. People had been watching us by our dust trail for the last twenty minutes. No way was anyone going to sneak up on these folks.

We pulled in amidst the yips of dogs and the excited cries of children to park in front of a rather simple looking modern three bedroom ranch house that you could find in any suburb in Middle America. It was cleaner than most of the other places and painted yellow, with purple trim, to keep away evil spirits, as

Dakota informed me a little later. There were the usual front lawn decorations for the area: bicycles, toy trucks, a few cactus plants, and a grass carpet with large brown holes worn in it.

In the doorway stood a pudgy little girl of about eight and behind her a woman who filled the entire door. She was almost as big as the woman at the Cactus Inn, but she had a light in her eyes that seemed to spread out across everything in her sight. I could feel her joy-de-vive from where I stood and I knew that Jason was truly blessed.

As I cut the motor and dropped the side stand I was engulfed by barking dogs and squealing children all gathering around to look at the stranger Dakota had brought and his Iron Horse. I got the impression that they did not get many guests here, except for the occasional government bureaucrat who probably wasn't welcome anyway. And there is something about a motorcycle that draws kids like a sale on shoes will draw women to the mall.

Dakota got out of the Jeep and started toward the big woman in the house with a shout of, "Eh-Yat-Tah-Hey Helen."

"Eh-Yat-Tah-Hey Dakota," she called back in return. Helen wore traditional Navajo clothing, along with a lot of silver and turquoise jewelry that was nicely offset by her nutty-brown skin. She had a wonderful smile that said you were truly welcome in her home. She turned her gaze on me as I approached and spoke aside to Dakota, "Don't tell me you have finally found a man Dakota?"

"It's not like that Helen, though I did find him in Coyote Canyon."

"Yes, Jason called to let me know you were bringing him here. You must come in and tell me everything that happened. There was something Jason said to Samuel that sent everyone on alert. Is it bad?"

"Maybe, maybe nothing. Someone did shoot at us this morning in the canyon and then some outlaw bikers at the restaurant were acting like bad-asses. Might have something to do with

Tom here. Anyway, you know Jason, always a sucker to help a fellow Marine."

Dakota was minimizing the whole thing to keep Helen from worrying, but the way she was holding herself betrayed her words. I pulled myself away from the kids and walked up to meet my hostess.

"Hi, my name's Tom Harper," I said extending my hand to her. She took it with both hands, as though she too were a veteran.

"Blessings on you Tom Harper, welcome to the Hogan of Jason Longbow. I am his wife Helen Walks Far. Please come in where it is cooler and have a seat."

Inside, the house was tastefully furnished with throw rugs on the hardwood floor and native tapestries on the walls. Candles seemed to be everywhere, but not lit yet. A large screen TV stood to one side decorated with pictures of Helen, Jason, the kids, and Jesus. In fact, Jesus seemed to be everywhere. There was not a wall that did not have his picture, a cross, or some homily from the Bible on it. This seemed a little odd since I figured them to have some sort of Native American religious belief. Well, it really was none my business.

We all headed into the dining room where Helen had us sit down and offered us glasses of ice tea. "Is anyone hungry? I've got roasted Piñon nuts if you like," she said.

Taking a few Dakota said, "I love these things Helen, some-time you are going to have to show me how you make them. Unfortunately, I can't stay long. I have to get back to the park, you know."

"Yes, yes," Helen said. "Duty calls. You work to hard Dakota. You should take more time to watch the wildflowers grow. There is more to life than busting people for littering."

I got the feeling this conversation had gone many times before. Helen looked at me and said, "This one is strong Chica, he has good eyes," meaning I guess, I would make a good husband.

Women—I guess they are the same everywhere; just can't stand to see a man single and happy.

Dakota laughed at that; a clean, happy sound, that came out unfettered, with a musical quality.

"You know me Helen, no time for that. It's just me and Sparky from now on."

"You should let go Chica," Helen soothed. "That was over two years ago and Sparky is a nice cat, but he won't keep you safe at night out in those hills."

"You're right, that's what I have my .44 Remington for."

Helen burst out in laughter that left her whole body shaking like a giant Jell-O mold, so genuine, so full of joy that I found myself envious of her.

"Chica," she said with a sly wink. "There are some itch's that rifle just won't scratch." Then even more laughter, as to some private joke.

Helen walked Dakota out to her Jeep and I stepped out the sliding doors to the backyard to have a look at the terrain. A large freestanding swimming pool was there with several of the neighborhood kids splashing around in it, and beyond that, only scrub brush and arroyos for maybe four or five klick's to the mountains. The land gently sloped upward from here and downward from the front of the house. An easy place to protect and difficult for an enemy to sneak up; especially with all the dogs they had.

I turned back to the house, smiling at the kids splashing in the pool and flashing back to my own carefree distant childhood and the Martin's pool next door. Those were good days. Kind of makes a man wish he could turn the clock back sometimes.

Back in the kitchen, Helen was working on dinner as I walked in. There were cooking odors and smoke in the air from chicken frying, flat bread baking and other dishes I was unfamiliar with, but which brought rumbling reminders of how long it had been since lunch. I sat down taking up my tea and having some of the

Piñon nuts that were something new to me and very tasty. I made a note to look for them back home.

Helen turned back toward me saying, "You have dreams you can't explain don't you?"

"Is it written on my face or something?" I replied. "Everyone seems to be asking me that lately."

"My husband is a Shaman and a man of God," Helen said. "For several months now he has been seeing a powerful man of Spirit coming who will do battle with the forces of the Evil One."

She came close, bending over and looking me in the eyes. "You may be the one. There is an aura about you that even I can see, but you don't know yet. You are still asleep."

She went back to cooking again as though that explained everything. I suddenly felt a headache coming on and went out to the bike to get some aspirin out of my saddlebags, as well as some fresh air.

Things were moving too fast for me in directions that were totally unfamiliar. I was feeling like I had been dropped into the wrong L.Z. and told to fight an enemy I knew nothing about. After digging out the aspirin I straightened up and saw a little girl to my left staring up at me with little almond eyes and a dirty face that needed a mother's attention.

"Are you the One?" she asked in such a forward and innocent way that I was taken back for a moment.

"The One," I said, not really understanding the question, especially coming from such an angelic little face. "I don't know what you mean darlin'," was all I could muster for an answer. She ran off giggling and repeating herself over again, "The One, The One."

In the distance, I could see a dust cloud approaching and looked around to see if anyone else had noticed; which of course they had. From another ranch house came a voice, "It's okay Tom, it's Jason."

It was strange having all these people knowing me, but me not knowing them. Still, I did feel safe for the first time in several days. The voice emerged from the shadows and took on a face. He was short, only about five-six and heavy set, but moved with the grace of an athlete. He walked up to me and I could now see long braids, slanted eyes that were Indian black, and features that showed him to be in his late twenties or early thirties.

"John Little Bear," he said with a laugh and extended his hand to me. He was wearing the old familiar anchor tat as well.

"Semper Fi," I said.

"Semper Fi, little brother," he returned. "Jason will be here in about twenty minutes. Don't worry about the kids, they are all worked up about the legend, ya know. They think everybody on a bike is 'The One', he said as though I knew what he was talking about.

"You are safe here bro. Nobody can sneak up on us here. We have been working on a perimeter warning system for a while now. We included some nasties that will really put a hurt on anybody stupid enough to show up without an invite."

"Thanks," I said, but I was still curious. "What is this business of 'The One' all about?"

A shadow passed over John's face as though he had been caught with his hand in the cookie jar.

"Guess I said too much, seems I just can't keep my mouth shut," he said nervously looking away. "Jason will bring you up to speed when he gets here. Guess I better get back to my post." He sped off before I could get anything else out of him.

Feeling confused, I turned back to the house, and headed in before anything else could happen. As I reached for the screen door a crow perched on the roof over the front door swooped down and attacked me. It actually clawed me on the forehead and screeched like a soul from Hell as it took off into the sky.

Helen banged open the screen door and shouted, "Be gone in the name of Jesus!" and grabbing me by the arm she jerked me into the house. "You're bleeding," she said handing me a kitchen towel. "That demon bird has marked you."

"It's only a crow," I said, only half believing it though. There had seemed something almost demonic in its cry and its choice of target. "Thanks Helen," I said. "He almost got my eyes."

She was headed for the first aid kit that was kept in the kitchen. "Yes," she said, "he was sent to blind you if he could; to make you more vulnerable. You will have to be very careful from now on about animals—and people. Jason will be able to tell you more." She busied herself with cleaning and dressing my wound. As she was finishing, Jason came in like a whirlwind from the desert; his face full of concern and worry.

"What happened," he asked Helen looking at the bandage on my face. "I felt something attack our house as I was driving up."

Helen quickly filled him in on the crow attack while I sat wondering how I had managed to find myself on the wrong side of Alice's looking glass.

Looking at me, Jason finally said, "I think we may have to move tonight. They are closing in faster than I anticipated."

"Would someone please tell me what the hell is going on?" I demanded, sounding a bit hysterical even to myself. "Who is closing in on what? Who is 'The One', and why do people seem to think it's me?"

"In good time Tom," said Jason. "But right now we need to move fast. They have found us through the crow and whether you are 'The One' or not they think you are, and they will be coming for you. You will not be the only one in danger; everyone here will be."

Jason began collecting various kit bags from the closets in the hallway and bedroom as he spoke. "You must prepare for battle or else we all may be killed." He threw me a large military backpack as he pulled on night camo's. My own clothes were dark enough for night op's, so I just pulled on the backpack and smeared on some black camo as I waited for Jason to finish getting ready.

"Take the AR-15 and an ammo bag, unless you would prefer the 12 gauge."

"I'll take the 12 gauge if we are going to be in close quarters. I've got my K-bar, too."

"We will be face to face if it comes to it, but I am hoping they will hold off for a couple of days to see what our next move will be. They may come at us tonight with a small patrol though, just to see what we're made of, so be ready."

I picked up the military spec. Mossburg pump and jacked in seven rounds, including one up the spout. Also, a bandolier of ammo holding twenty-four rounds and a box of loose ammo for a total of fifty-five rounds. They were all double-ought shot and guaranteed to drop anything out to about sixty meters.

A very nasty weapon for in-close fighting and one the insurgents in Iraq really hated. The sound of the slide jacking in a round was often enough to make them surrender. Being a martyr was cool, but not if you were blown in half. Vestal virgins, it seemed, weren't interested in half a man, or worse, surviving with arms or legs blown off and unable to enter paradise at all.

"Where are we going," Jason went on, "anything that moves may be the enemy, whether it has two legs or four; my advice is—shoot first, ask questions later."

"I hear ya bro," I said, shoving my K-bar down my boot top. "Can I ask where it is that we are going?"

"Better not to say," he said pointing to his ears. "You never know who might be listening."

CHAPTER 8

"Keep close to me and maintain trail discipline at all times," Jason said to the little group of men gathered by a junked pickup. There were three shadows beside our own; one I had already met, John Little Bear, and two I had not. It was too dark to make out much, but I could tell by their silhouettes that they were big men, not the kind you would want to have on the wrong end of a back alley brawl.

They introduced themselves as David Long Bow and Simon Bright Star. I did not know it at the time, but these men would soon form the core of our elite Band of Brothers.

As we moved off into the darkness, Jason took point with me right behind, David to the left, and Simon to the right. John fell back to cover our rear, all without a sound, as though each man instinctively knew where his place was. I had only experienced that kind of unit awareness a few times even in Iraq and it left me feeling very secure about going into harm's way with these men. This was something that transcended the physical and took me into the spiritual. How far it would take me, and where, is the thing legends are made of.

Moving silently across the desert floor at a quick pace, we covered maybe a mile before Jason raised his right hand to signal a stop. I moved up next to him and took a knee as the others blended into the brush and became invisible. Somewhere in the distance a pack of coyotes were calling down the moon with their age-old song. Jason turned to me and spoke in a low whisper, "They are looking for us brother, but they are not close yet."

With another hand signal, we started to move out again. As we rose up, we found ourselves face to face with a large coyote with big yellow eyes. I put my hand on Jason's arm and whispered, "I know this one." I leaned closer to him, almost nose to nose, then with an almost silent yip he turned and trotted off a few yards, then stopped and looked back at us as though waiting for us to follow.

"I think we should follow him," I said to Jason.

"Yes little brother, he is your guide."

So we set off after him at, forgive me, a dogtrot. After another mile or so, the coyote stopped, then went down on his belly indicating we were to stay low and quiet.

A few minutes later, we could hear the pack as they cut back and forth looking for our trail. We stayed quiet for a good ten minutes before the coyote finally stood up, sniffed the air, and then moved out again. Silently we picked up and began to follow. At the base of a mesa we entered a canyon and followed it through twists and turns that left me lost in no time.

We finally came to a spot where the coyote went to ground again and Jason spoke, "We're here, though it beats me how he knew where we were going."

"He seems to have a connection with me." I said. "I saw him as an old man in one of my dreams."

"That would explain a lot," said Jason as he reached down and pulled up a trap door cleverly disguised as a big rock. It was made of fiberglass and painted to match the surroundings so well that no one would likely spot it. He went down a ladder and motioned for me to follow. Once inside one of the others said, "God bless," and closed the hatch over us.

Jason turned on a small camp lantern that threw out a weak yellow light that was just enough to illuminate our little cave. It was about ten by twelve by five meters and crammed at one end with boxes of M.R.E.'s (Meals Ready to Eat), ammo of various calibers, an M-60 machine gun, grenades (both frag and smoke), and even a case of claymores. On some shelves I saw flares and medical supplies that could outfit a small surgery, and some more modern stuff in the electronic range.

"Quite a stash here Jason, you must be expecting a real war."

Turning to me, his face becoming very serious, he picked up a Bible from one of the shelves and said, "You have no idea Tom. There is a war going on out there and, has in fact, been going on since the universe came into being. The forces of Light and Dark, Good and Evil, Heaven and Hell; however you want to phrase it brother. We are at war and to paraphrase Jesus in Mark chapter nine, verse forty: 'Anyone who is not for us is against us'." As he was reading, I noticed that the bookmark he was using was the same one I had seen back at the Cactus Inn: '*Jesus would have been a biker.*'

"The war has always been in the spiritual world, but has now crossed over into the physical world in a big way; the world we live in brother. And we are going to have to take up weapons, not only to defend ourselves, but to overcome the enemy if we are to survive."

This was the longest speech the big man had made yet and was followed by an equally long silence during which he seemed to be organizing his thoughts.

"You say you have been having dreams, tell me about them little brother."

I told him about the little room in Iraq. The white haired old man, the coyote, my uncle Bob, even the little biker chick, and the gun deal she referred to. I talked into the early morning, pouring out my feelings of confusion and frustration, my lack of belief in this God of his and how he could possibly want me in this spiritual war since I was not a spiritual man. I sure was no Jesus freak and told him to his face.

"Maybe not little brother, but like they say, 'there ain't no atheists in a foxhole.' You answered his call in that upper room. You knew whose voice it was, so you can sit there and deny him if you want too, but the fact is—you answered the call. That is why you are different; why you have that pain inside of you that just won't go away. That pain you feel is your separation from God."

"Wait a minute big man, how do you know what I feel." I said, even though I knew exactly what he was talking about. It just kind'a ticked me off that everybody around here seemed to know way too much about me. It was creepy, ya know and I said as much to Jason, but instead of backing off he just smiled and said, "Been there little brother, just where you are now. The difference being, I guess, that you are under more pressure now, because the bad guys are coming after you before you have been properly prepared."

"What if I refuse, will they go away?" I asked thinking that, if I refused, somehow they would find someone else to hassle.

"'Fraid not bro. If you are 'The One', then it is a matter of destiny not choice."

"Now would be a good time to tell me what 'The One' is."

"He is someone I saw in my dreams. A mighty Warrior of God sent to conquer the forces of the Evil One."

"How do you know I am the one in your dream?"

"I don't yet. But I do believe you have been called."

"But I thought we all had the freedom to choose, isn't that what the Bible says? We aren't puppets right?"

"Were you ever baptized little brother?"

I thought back to that little Baptist church in Jonestown. The preacher asking me for my confession of faith and pushing me under the water. I remembered a sound like Angels singing and a feeling of overwhelming love that brought me to tears. I was fifteen and, though I believed, I did it because it was something I just thought I was supposed to do. It was like peer pressure, ya know.

I thought it didn't take, because years later I began to fall away. I started chasing girls, drinking, and raising hell as fast as I could. I was out to have fun and Jesus just wasn't part of the equation.

"Yes I was, but that was a long time ago and I really have not lived a Christian life since then. There ain't no way I could be forgiven after the things I've done Jason. You just don't know man, you just don't know." But even as the words left my mouth I knew I was wrong; he did know. Something in those gentle black eyes said, 'been there, done that, got the t-shirt to prove it.'

"Tom, a long time ago a man named Paul persecuted the early church. He was even present at the stoning of Steven. He killed Christians in his zeal to serve God, as he understood him. On the road to Damascus Jesus called him out, just like he is calling you. He went on to write half the books of the New Testament you know. If Paul could be forgiven, so can you little brother."

I sat there thinking about the things I had done in Iraq: the kids I had killed, innocent lives I had taken, and even if it was war—it was still murder.

"Brother," he said. "The hardest thing you gotta do is forgive yourself."

"I don't know how Jason. How can I ask God to forgive me? I knew what I did was wrong and did it anyway."

Jason opened up his Bible again and turned it to John 3:16 and read, "For God so loved the world that He gave his only begotten son, that whosoever believes in him shall not perish but have eternal life."

"I know that one Jason, I've seen it a hundred times at football games, ya know. The guy with the tie-die wig and the sign saying, John 3:16." I was trying to make a joke of it, but Jason only gave me a little smile. The kind that says, 'I know and so do you.'

"The Bible talks a lot about forgiving, but it also talks a lot about vengeance and judgment," I said.

"Yes it does little brother. It speaks of judgment for unbelievers, but forgiveness for those who are covered by the blood of Jesus," Jason answered. He sat for several minutes looking lost in thought while I went over my memories of sermons about vengeance and the 'Wrath of God' that I had listened to on so many Sunday mornings in my youth.

"Tom, have you ever heard of Augustine, the Christian scholar?"

"I believe I've heard the name, but honestly, I don't think I've ever read any of his stuff."

"He gave one of the best illustrations of what forgiveness is that I have ever heard. He stated that man, in God's sight, is no more than a pile of excrement. Because of our sin and self-will, we are un-holy. He is so holy on the other hand that he can't even bear to look at us just as most of us would not care to sit around looking at piles of shit all day, 'scuse my Irish. But the blood of Jesus is like a layer of pure white snow that falls from heaven and covers that disgusting pile of crap, so that God no longer sees what is beneath—he only sees the pure white snow."

I sat thinking about this example for a minute, and then he went on with another.

"The Bible talks a lot about sheep and shepherds ya know?"

"Yes," I said.

"My grandpa raised sheep and I remember, as a kid, a little 'God trick' he taught us. Now and then a Ewe would die giving birth and the lamb would too if we could not get another Ewe to adopt it. Now, what my grandpa would do is clean that lamb up real good washing away all trace of its mother; all the blood and everything ya know.

"Then he would go out to the flock and find another Ewe that had just given birth. He would collect the placenta and then rub it all over the orphan lamb. After that he would take that orphan and present it to the Ewe. She would sniff the orphan, smell her own blood, and accept the lamb as her own.

"You see Tom, it's kind of like that with us and God. We get covered by the blood of Jesus so that God sees his blood and accepts us as his own. 'By his blood we are made perfect in the sight of God and joint heirs to the kingdom' (Romans 8:17)."

"You've given me a lot to think about Jason," I said, "but I am feeling really tired and hungry right now. How 'bout we have a couple of those tasty M.R.E.'s and take a nap?"

"Okay little brother, I'm kind'a tired too. We can talk more after we rest."

With the light turned off, I lay on my cot thinking of the things Jason had said when I felt an overwhelming conviction to get on my knees and ask God to forgive me. Jason's breathing had fallen into that soft cadence that indicated sleep so I rolled onto my knees and reaching back through the years, I began to pray.

"Father God, I don't know how to pray to you anymore, but I am going to try. I ask that you would forgive me my sins, that you would make me white as snow, and restore me to a loving relationship with you. Please Father, I have sinned against you and only you. Please forgive me."

At that moment, I felt something deep down inside me like a huge dam bursting. Waves of emotion began to wash over me like some huge tidal wave. I began to shake so hard that I lost control and could not hold myself up. A sound seemed to be coming from somewhere, like a lost child crying for his mother. That cry was coming from me and I realized I could not stop it. All those years of pain were coming out in a torrent of emotion that could not be stopped anymore than a freight train can be stopped by a sheet of paper stretched across the tracks.

I felt someone holding me and a voice whispering in my ear, "Its okay son, let it out, let it all out."

And I did, with tears pouring down my cheeks in cataracts like Niagara Falls. Great sobs racked my body that probably registered a good nine on the Richter scale until all the baggage I had carried for all those years was washed away.

The last thing I remember was another voice, one I had heard before somewhere saying, "Welcome back my son." Then came the kind of sleep that swallows like the grave; deep and restful.

CHAPTER 9

I was looking at a landscape devoid of life stretching for miles in all directions. I seemed to be on top of a mountain, but I couldn't tell where. It is an open desert, but not like in Nevada—different. No plants to speak of, only a few low bushes and no trees. On the plains in front of me are armies with numbers like the grains of sand on the beach. They look like some obscene monster from an opium dream, constantly in motion without moving, preparing for battle at the end of Time.

"What you are seeing is the destiny of man," came a voice from behind me. I turned and standing behind me was the old man, looking like Charlton Heston from the 'Ten Commandments'—complete with long robe, white hair, and staff in his right hand.

"What can I do old one? No one man could stop such a war. There must be at lest a hundred million men out there," I said.

"You are right. You can't stop them; nor should you. This war will bring the End of Time."

The scene shifted, we were still high on a hill, but now we overlooked the Nevada desert once again. In the distance I could see the outlaw bikers riding the highway, leaving death and destruction in their wake, like some mad band of berserkers.

"Those men are evil my son, they are in the service of Lucifer and they do his will. They come to kill, steal, and destroy all that is good in the world. It is in the destiny of a few chosen men and women to stand against them, that good might triumph over evil, and the Hand of God be stilled from bringing about that final battle for a little while longer."

"Are you saying I am the one to lead this battle?" I asked. "Who am I to do such a thing? I am just a poor weak sinner who doesn't even know how to pray. You should find another; maybe Jason. He would be a better choice than me."

"Father uses those he wants to use for reasons that are His own. He knew you before you were formed in your mother's womb (Psalm 139:13) and he knows your strengths and weaknesses better than you or anyone else. It doesn't matter if you believe you are the one—only whether you will answer the call."

Smell of earth, clean, with a touch of mushroom and—omelet? I opened my eyes to the dim light of the lantern and saw Jason holding a plate under my nose.

"Denver omelet with hash browns little brother," he said, with a real twinkle in his eye. "Not as good as what I make in the restaurant, but not bad as survival rations go."

I sat up and took the plate from him feeling like I had not eaten in days instead of only a few hours. I dived in without regard to good manners and wolfed it down in a few quick mouthfuls.

"Easy little brother, I will need those fingers when I get back to Mom's ya know."

"Sorry bro," I said as I licked the plate. " I was feeling really starved for some reason."

"Have any more dreams last night?" he asked as he cleaned up.

"I sure did," I said. "It was really weird too." I went on to tell him about it as we sat and drank coffee.

"You know Jason, I really felt like a great weight was pulled off me last night and now another has been thrown on to take its place."

"Don't worry little brother, you wont have to carry it alone. There are more of us out there; people you have not met yet."

"Oh yeah?" I replied. "I don't suppose Dakota is one of them?"

"I think she may be little brother. I saw that the two of you bonded right away, though that may not be a good thing in a combat situation you know."

He was right of course; it isn't good to be distracted by someone you care for in combat. It's too easy to make a mistake that gets somebody hurt or killed. You got to keep your wits about you in a firefight. 'Course I always cared about my men when we were fighting too, but I could see how this might be different.

Jason was talking again, "You met David, John, and Simon last night, and there will be others Tom. I have seen twelve in my visions—a nice Biblical number, just like the apostles right?"

"Yeah brother, just like the apostles," I said, as I suddenly remembered that one of them was a traitor.

"What next Jason?" I asked. "We can't just stay in this hole, nice as it is. We will have to go out and take the battle to the enemy. How are we to know who the bad guys are anyway? And since we are commanded not to kill, what are we going to do with them when we do find them?"

"Those who raise their hands against us are our enemies Tom. They wont be hard to recognize and yes, the sixth commandment states that 'thou shall not murder.' In war we kill because we have to. It is up to us to judge whether it is a just cause or not."

His eyes seemed to look back into the past for a moment before he went on.

"I believe we were wrong in Vietnam Nam. I believe it was not a just war and we paid a heavy price for that decision. Saddam Hussein was a madman and needed to be taken out, but again, I do not believe it was a just war. Those decisions are made at a higher level little brother. We, as soldiers, fight and kill as we are ordered, because we are not the ones in power. However, it is our duty to make sure that the innocent are protected as much is possible. There will always be collateral damage in war and it is our duty to limit those casualties when we can."

He took a break here to let me consider his words while he communicated with the men outside. Each reported that the area was all clear.

"So killing bad guys is okay, is that what you are saying? Wouldn't it be our duty to convert them or lock them up instead?" I asked.

"Sure little brother, but that is going to be up to them. They always have a choice, but these guys are fully in the service of the Evil One and most will choose to die just like the murder-bombers back there in the Middle East. Their motto is 'Better to stand in Hell than serve on my knees in Heaven.' There are others out there who take the word to the outlaws, like Herb Shreve and the Christian Motorcycle Association. However, these guys are looking to kill us because we are trying to stop them from bringing on the Apocalypse."

I had to think about that one for a minute and then asked, "How can they do that? I thought only God could do that."

"That is true bro, only God knows the day (Mt. 24:36) and only he has the power. But the Evil one has deceived these people into believing that they can bring about the end of the world. I don't know what their plan is, but they think they can become the rulers of the world by removing all the followers of Christ. They don't believe there will be a final battle of Armageddon (Rev. 16:16). No Christians: No battle. They have fallen for the lie, just like Eve did back in the Garden of Eden."

"So it is up to us to keep them under control. But keep them from what exactly? The law would handle them if they just went on a killing spree wouldn't they?" I asked.

"Yes Tom, the law would as long as it is against the law to kill us. But what if it was legal like it is in a lot of those Middle Eastern countries? Under Islamic law, it is not illegal to kill unbe-lievers. They are commanded to kill anyone who does not submit to Islam. All they have to do is change the law, then it's open season, and believe me the day is coming. The media already treat us as though we are a bunch of intolerant bigots bent on making everyone believe what we want them to believe or else they are all going to Hell.

"As usual with the Devil, it is partly truth and partly fiction. If they don't believe, they will go to Hell, but it is not our job to make anyone believe. We couldn't even if we wanted too. God does not want lip service, so such a conversion would not help that person or keep them out of Hell. As Jesus said in Mathew 7:22-23, 'On judgment day many will tell me. Lord, Lord, we prophesied in your name and cast out demons in your name and performed many miracles in your name. But I will reply. I never knew you. Go away; the things you did were unauthorized.'

"The world is headed for this belief: 'It does not matter which road you take because they all lead to the same place.' You and I know they don't and that is why they will have to kill us. We are the witnesses who will not be silenced except in death (Rev.11:7-10)."

"Okay brother, I think I am beginning to understand, but I really need to take a break and think on all this for a little while, if that is okay with you."

"Sure, you got the gist of anyway, the rest is just details and strategy. I need to go out and check the perimeter anyway. When I come back, I will knock exactly three times on the cover and say 'Jesus loves you.' The others are also aware of this code, so if you hear anything else be ready to shoot.

With that, he lifted the cover and slipped out into the bright daylight leaving me alone with my thoughts and my doubts.

CHAPTER 10

I must have dozed off because I found myself standing in the Souq (a marketplace) with people all around me, but looking closer I saw they were all women. Suddenly they stopped what they were doing and turned toward me. All their eyes were on me, as though I had suddenly appeared naked as a child.

As one body they started producing weapons, from shopping bags, from under their clothes, from baskets holding fruit, it seemed from everywhere. All these weapons came to bear on me and I was the only one in the whole place that wasn't armed. I was paralyzed and could only scream out sounds that I could not understand. Just like us shouting in English at the Iraqis—it could only have been meaningless noise to them.

They began to shoot at me and I woke up.

I could hear gunfire from outside and shouts too muffled to understand in this underground sanctuary. I grabbed the shotgun, flipped off the safety, and moved to the hatch just in time.

The sudden burst of sunlight blinded me, but I was able to make out a shadowy form in front of me. I reached up with my left arm, grabbed the guy by his vest, and pulled him down into the hole with the lid falling down over us.

Now that he was taking a nap, I kicked his Ingram automatic away and took a quick peek out of the entry cover to see what was going on outside. I could not see anyone and it had gone dead silent, so I turned my attention back to my new house-guest.

He was wearing a Satans Slaves patch, whoever they were, and I quickly stripped off his jacket to search for more weapons. I found a nice collection: several knives, two small handguns, some vials of white powder, probably speed, and an ice pick taped to the small of his back.

Sounds of someone approaching drew my attention and I grabbed up the shotgun, moved to the back of the cave again, and got ready for a fight. Three firm raps followed by the recognition phrase relieved the tension and I said, "Come on in, I have already made our guest comfortable.

The lid popped up and Jason's face appeared, big toothy grin on his face as he looked down at our guest and said, "He gonna be able to answer questions little brother?"

"Soon as he wakes up. I only gave him a little headache bro. Anybody else hurt?" I asked.

"No, we're okay," he said with a smile. "Can't say the same for these punks though. I know we wounded two of them, then they turned tail and ran."

"How many total?" I asked.

"There were six including him." He said pointing to at the unconscious man. "I would be interested to know how he knew about our hidey hole."

"Yeah, looks like we're going to have to move unless you want to set a trap here."

"The trap would be good, but we're gonna have to move everything out. I'm gonna call for some transport and in the meantime, let's see what sleeping beauty here has to say."

I had already used some zip ties to secure his hands behind his back and Jason reached down to roll him over onto his back. I stopped him saying, "Careful bro, I've seen this before," and used my foot to flip him over. Too many times I had seen someone get the crap kicked out of them by somebody trussed up this way. As he came over he spit at us, but I was one step ahead using my boot to block his spray. It also had the advantage of directing his spittle back into his own face.

"Thanks little brother," said Jason. "You just saved this heathen a beating."

"Na, just put it off for a while."

I turned my attention to the man on the floor who was still spewing a steady stream of obscenities at us.

"Shut up or I'll pull your lower lip all the way over the top of your head," I said as I picked up some pliers from the shelf with the medical supplies. "I haven't done this in a while, so if I miss the first time and grab your tongue just be patient. The last Iraqi I did this to was very patient; it only cost him three teeth and part of his nose. It really improved his looks though, all the women chased him, some of the boys too."

I poured some hot, but not too hot, coffee on his face making sure that some of it went up his nose with satisfying results. The effect is somewhat the same as water boarding, but much more painful.

"Let's start with your name bad boy and go from there."

What came out of his mouth wasn't his name and would have required an entire troop of side show contortionists to accomplish, so I decided to try a different approach. I got out one of the flares on the shelf and got Jason to help me get him out onto the ground above.

We dragged him over to a large boulder, pulled his pants down to his ankles, and draped him over belly down. I had Jason hold his head as I squatted down beside him so he could see what I was doing.

"This here is a magnesium flare that burns at around two thousand degrees Fahrenheit and is almost impossible to put out once it gets going. What it can do to human flesh is something you don't even want to think about; then again, you might want to start thinking about it real quick 'cause my patience is almost gone."

I stepped around behind him greasing the end of the flare with some Vaseline and continuing to talk, "You can start by telling us how many of you there are and who your leader is. Last chance dude. After I light this thing off, I ain't gonna try to pull it out."

The thought was too much for him and he finally caved in.

"Okay, okay, you bastards. I'll tell you everything I know."

"Where are the Pagans that were out here two days ago?" asked Jason.

"I don't know man, we got a call from our president, said to do whatever we was told. Our chapter enforcer took the call, okay man? I didn't hear nothin'. He says to pack some heat 'cause we're going to trash some Tontos. That's all I know man, I swear it."

"I don't know big brother," I said banging a couple of rocks together and making a sound like the striker on a flare. "He does look kind'a stupid, but I think he's not telling us everything."

"Yeah little brother," said Jason. "He's got Pagans riding on his turf and don't know a thing about it. I say—fire in the hole!" We all laughed at the joke 'till we almost fell over.

"Okay man, gimme a chance," he said, with spittle running down his chin. "Yeah, yeah, we know about them. They some real bad-assess man. Handlebar, their leader, put a bullet in our V.P. just 'cause he wouldn't help him look for you guys. The guy is real whack man. They was staying out by an abandoned gas station near Glendale. They'll kill me man, I'm dead; just shoot me. I can't go back."

"What are they gonna do next pinhead?" Jason asked. "How many more people from your chapter can we expect?"

"There ain't no more man. They was only ten of us, two was out of town, and the other two in jail. I swear it man."

"Okay Jason, I don't think we'll get anymore out of him. He's too low in the group to know anything. I just got one more question for you. What does your enforcer look like? Make it a good description, and his name?"

"His handle is 'Ripper' and you would know him by the scar that runs from his right eye to his neck."

With that info in the book, we let him go. After what we did to him we couldn't give him to the police and after what he had done—he wasn't going back to his chapter either. He really was a dead man if they found him after spilling his guts to us, so we stripped him of his patch and let him go.

CHAPTER 11

We went back to Jason's restaurant and hooked up with the others for a war cabinet meeting. For the moment, we figured we were safe. The first probe by the enemy had shown him to be weak and disorganized. He would be licking his wounds and figuring his next move so this was time we could not afford to waste.

Over hot plates of Chiles Rellenos, re-fried beans, and rice, we set to the business of planning our next move.

"Dakota, were you able to get any info on that plate number we got the other day?" I asked.

"Sure did Tom," she said and dug into her satchel bag to produce a folder. "He's a bad character with a long and checkered history. His name is Steve Meronek, A.K.A. Handlebar. Here, read it for yourself."

A checkered career indeed: Over thirty-six arrests starting at the tender age of eight for shoplifting (not a candy bar or something, but over a hundred dollars worth of prime rib) to murder in the first, acquitted because the witness had a sudden loss of memory.

Over the years, he was thirty-six now, he had done fifteen years in various state institutions and had been classified as an anti-social psychopath. This guy could carve you up with his right hand, while eating a Snickers bar with his left.

He had been a Pagan patch holder since he was nineteen and had worked his way up through the ranks pretty quickly. Seems like if he wanted a position with the club, he always got it; one way or another. No one had ever proved murder on him, but it was plain that trying to could get you killed.

"Looks like he has been trying to forge alliances with several clubs including Hells Servants, Satans Slaves, and a few other major one-percenters. All within the past two years. Any idea what brought that on?" I asked Dakota and the others present.

John Little Bear spoke up, "I am not sure if it is germane, but I ran across a report at the office around that time that hinted at a major gun running effort that was shaping up between the outlaw gangs and some rogue military people out of Afghanistan. Could be they're back in business."

"What office is that John?" I asked.

"Oh, sorry Tom," Jason spoke up. "John is a field agent for the F.B.I. and David Long Bow, my little brother, is an officer for the Nevada State Police. Simon Bright Star is an agent for the D.E.A."

I was impressed by all these acronyms to say the least.

David was shorter than his older brother by maybe a foot in height, but easily had thirty pounds on him. He looked like his clothes could barley contain him. His sleeves had slits in them to allow for muscle flex and his neck was as large as one of my thighs. I had no doubt this guy could go bowling with Volkswagens for balls.

Simon was the exception: thin, dapper, with short brown hair, gray eyes, and aquiline features. He was a gadget freak and the man to go to if you needed to hack a database. He seemed perpetually down, never smiling, a real cigar-store Indian. We had a lot in common; both of us had seen too much of man's inhumanity to man and could not shake the demons of the past. All of them had proven themselves in Uncle Sam's foreign exchange program—the Marines.

"Okay, David or Simon, anything from you guys that could shed some light on the situation?" I asked.

David looked up, "We have been hearing rumors for some time about a major gun deal with the bikers. Seems they are buying up large lots of weapons, but no word on what they plan to do with them. If they are looking to sell them, we sure would like to know to who."

"How many guns we talking about Dave." I asked.

"We estimate enough to outfit at least two squads or roughly sixty men."

While Dave had been speaking, a new face walked in stopping to shake hands with Jason and the others. He was three meters, short red hair, blue eyes, and a manicured mustache. His clothes were government issue: dark blue sport coat and slacks, white shirt, plain blue tie, and oxford shoes; brown.

"Tom, fellas, this is Peter Gault, A.T.F. field agent and a damn good man. He will be working with us as much as he can. He was in the first Gulf war, Special Forces Army Green Beret, and a real asset for sniffing out illegal gun deals. Have you found anything out for us Pete?" asked Jason.

"Yeah, good to meet you Tom, look forward to working with you." He had a good strong handshake, clear eyes, and a strong sense of self. I could tell he going to be a good man to have on our side

"Reports have been coming from Interpol indicating that a large shipment of arm's left Russia about six weeks ago bound for the U.S. We tracked them as far as Cuba and then lost them. We believe they are going to try to bring them in from Mexico by air somewhere here in the Nevada desert. Our best estimate is that it will be sometime in the next four or five days. They will most likely disguise it as Agro products."

"What are the chances we can catch them at the airport Pete," asked Simon.

"Depends on how smart they are and how patient. If they send them fully assembled we should be able to spot them, but if they break them into pieces it will be a lot more difficult."

"Okay then," I said. "We know they are trying to bring in a lot of firepower, but not why. Most of these gangs are loyal

Americans and not likely to be involved with foreign terrorists, so let's stick to what they do best; drugs?"

"Maybe Meronek has decided to branch out into something new," said Simon. "They could get plenty of weapons right here in the good ol' U.S.A. and not have to take near the risk."

"Simon's right," shot back a new voice. Everyone turned to see the newcomer who introduced himself as James Hightower, N.S.A. (National Security Agency). He was five-ten and probably no more than sixty-four kilo's, with graying auburn hair, limpid blue eyes, clean-shaven, and dressed casually in blue jeans, leather C.H.I.P.s (California Highway Patrol) jacket, T-shirt, and engineer boots.

"Our friend Meronek has more in mind than a simple gun deal, but what he does want will require weapons that can't be traced back to him or anyone else."

Taking a moment to walk around the room shaking hands he finally came up to me, "Your Tom aren't you?"

"Guilty as charged," I said.

"Can you say; Area 51?"

It hung there in the air like a triple burrito fart.

"Area 51!" I repeated as though I had just been told the Vatican was really just a front for Bingo. "I thought Area 51 was a myth. What could Area 51 have to do with these jerks?"

"It's no myth, it exists. We can't be sure what it is they want there, only Meronek can answer that."

"Maybe I can help ya there partner," rumbled a voice like quiet thunder from behind a stack of magazines. "Jake Holland, F.B.I. Special Investigations Unit." Jake was an impressive looking man: six-two, close to one hundred twenty kilos of solid muscle, shaved head, steel gray eyes, hardware all over his face and ears, and tat's everywhere but his face. This guy looked the quintessential biker: leather vest, no shirt, leather jeans, big Harley boots, and plenty of chains hanging from everywhere.

"Okay," I said, "fill us in Mr. Holland."

"Call me Bones, please." He said in voice that sounded like a tiger purring over a fresh kill. "I've been undercover with the Devils Angels in Kingman now for four years. I had some contact with Meronek and his group of degenerates. Seems like he ran across some psychic type about three years ago and ever since, he's been getting more and more weird. He keeps talking about bringing on Armageddon by capturing an alien weapon system that is hidden in one of the hangers there.

"He sees himself as the Anti-Christ and somehow destined to rule the world. One of our people in his group says he has been doing a lot of speed and acid for the past two years as well. No doubt in my mind that the guy has had a total break with reality and this psychic is manipulating him.

"Nobody has ever seen her though. She calls herself Madam Blavatsky, but there is no record of her anywhere. She has some kind of agenda, but we don't know what it is; other than this whacked out scheme. Whatever it is, Meronek isn't talking about it."

"Your agent a little brunette girl, about five-six, one hundred thirty pounds?" asked Dakota.

"Yeah," answered Bones, "You met her?"

"Yes, here in the restaurant. She tipped us that Meronek was going to try for a shootout in here to nail Tom. She looked very scared."

"Maybe we should think about pulling her out," said John.

"I would rather not if we can help it," said Bones. "We need to know who this Blavatsky is and she is our only source right now. Mary Ann can handle herself, she is a top rated agent in the bureau and she knows how to get out if she needs too."

"Mind if I ask who's Old Lady she is?" I said, wondering how she could be with these guys without being asked to compromise her morals.

"She told Meronek that she was a priestess of Antoine LeVay's Satanic church and her power came from remaining a virgin. So far it has worked for her, keeping him entertained with Tarot card readings and feeding his ego," said John.

"Okay, great," I said. "But none of this explains why he is trying to kill me."

A voice from the booth behind me turned my blood to ice, "Maybe I can help you with that one Nephew."

CHAPTER 12

Somewhere, there was a voice calling my name, a woman's voice, a voice I knew. "Tom? You okay Tom?" It was Dakota's voice.

"Yeah, yeah," I said coming up out of a deep dark well. "Sorry, for a moment I thought I heard my Uncle Bob's voice. He died in Vietnam in '67."

"The rumors of my death are exaggerated Nephew," I heard as Uncle Bob's face came into focus beside me. I started to feel that sinking feeling again, my field of vision was closing in to nothing. "Hold on Nephew, don't go away now."

I started to feel anger boiling up in me, turning everything topsy-turvy. I was trying to talk, but nothing was coming out of my mouth.

"I know Nephew, but there is good reason for what happened. This was not just some cruel joke played on you and your dad. A little later on I will tell you about everything that happened, but right now we got bigger fish to fry okay?"

I was beginning to hyperventilate and my ears were starting to buzz.

"I think we better give him a few minutes guys. This is a lot for him to take in all at once," Jason said. "Drinks are on the house, everybody relax a minute."

Everyone moved over to the lunch counter for coffee and soft drinks leaving Bob and me alone. I looked at Bob the same way I imagine the Apostles must have looked at Jesus after the resurrection. I reached out, touched him with a finger, and said, "Now I know how Thomas must have felt. How can you be alive after all these years and not let us know. Dad thinks he killed you in Nam. How could you do this to him?" My voice had gotten really loud and I was on the edge of hysteria. Part of me was ready to kill him and the other desperately wanted to hug him and smother him with kisses as he had done to me when I was just a kid.

"Calm down Tom," Jason said as he tried to smooth my emotions. "Bob couldn't help it. He had amnesia about who he was and where he came from up until about a year ago. He was in deep with the program and it was felt that you, and your family, would be safer if he did not contact you."

"Who felt that?" I demanded. "Who?"

"I'm sorry Nephew, but you will just have to accept that as an answer for now. If they want you to know, they will contact you. Until then, please try to believe me, I did not do this to hurt you or Joe."

I got up, walked outside to my bike, fired up the motor, and roared off into the heat wave of late afternoon. Too much for one day, I just could not take anymore. I had to find a nice dark place with plenty of cold beer and nobody to bother me for a few hours.

Twenty minutes out of Moapa, I came to the little town of Glendale and found what I was looking for. A little place called the Iron Horse Saloon and Billiard Parlor. There were a few pickups and local bikes in the parking lot so I swung in and parked where my bike could not be seen from the road.

Inside, I found a nice spot in the rear where my back was safe and waited for some service, which wasn't long. A cute little redhead with an enormous rack walked up and asked, "What'll it be sweetie?"

"I'll have a beer and a lap dance when you get the time."

With a giggle that produced lovely waves of motion under her tank top she turned and said, as she was walking away, "Names Tracy, be right back with your beer sweetie."

When she came back with the brew, I gave her a twenty and told her to keep them coming. There were several guys and a few gals playing pool and pretty much passing away a small town evening, just as people probably were all over the country. The beer was cold, but for some reason it just wasn't hitting the spot tonight like it used too. Things just kept spinning around in my head: Uncle Bob not dead, standing in front of me, all five feet ten inches of him with the same blond hair and gray eyes as my dad.

There was a nagging itch at the back of my mind that I had seen his face more than once in the past few days. I don't know how long I sat there, but the waitress came over and set a drink in front of me saying, "Black Jack, neat. He said you would know who it came from."

The spell was broken. I looked around but saw no familiar faces. Outside it had gotten dark, but the parking lot lights revealed Bob sitting on a bike next to mine. I left the Jack sitting there and walked out, not really sure what I was going to do or say. When I got to where I had parked, Bob and his bike were gone even though I had heard no one drive away.

Suddenly, somebody hit me in the back throwing me several feet in the air and knocking my bike over too. I hit the pavement rolling and felt the fires of Hell scorching my back. I could swear I heard a voice booming, "Your mine Harper," as the world was lit in surrealistic shades of orange and red.

I came to rest on my back with my ears ringing, and smoke rising from the hair of my head. The bar was a vision of chaos; a cosmic Bar-b-que with people running through the parking lot with their bodies on fire. Vehicles were exploding in great balls of fire with gasoline spraying its pyrotechnic death in all directions. I had been spared the full force of the blast by a van I had parked behind, but I could see that if I did not get moving fast I would be caught up in the holocaust as well.

The smell of gasoline and burning human flesh was overpowering, threatening to make me throw up as I ran to the bike. Out of no where I suddenly felt super-natural strength come over me, powering me along as I yanked the nearly four hundred kilos of bike up on its wheels, threw my leg over the saddle, and hitting the starter, I roared out of the parking lot into the Stygian night, leaving a vision of Dante's Inferno in my rear-view mirrors.

I headed for Jason's restaurant and the safety of numbers. I was hitting close to ninety when I saw something in my mirrors that gripped my heart with icy claws. They looked like the bright red eyes of demons, about a dozen sets, closing on me fast. I opened the throttle all the way with the bike lurching under me, the air flowing into the carb with the roar of a Kansas cyclone, the speedo cranking over a hundred, and climbing fast.

The air pushing against me became a living force trying to push me off as I went flat on the tank to streamline myself. Even with the roar in my ears from engine and air deafening me, I could still hear those demon shrieks behind me. I screamed out, "Lord Jesus, if you care about me, SAVE ME NOW!"

The motor cut out as I suddenly felt a peace I had never known before descend upon me. The howls behind me ceased as I slowed to a stop—out of gas. I sat there for several minutes before I finally got off, fell to my knees for the second time in my life, and thanked the Lord for delivering me.

As I got off my knees, I heard the yip of a coyote in the distance and knew it was my friend letting me know he was with me. I made a note to ask his name next time we met. I turned the petcock on the tank over to reserve, fired up the engine, and pulled onto the road again toward Mom's.

CHAPTER 13

"I want to know where he is you morons," screamed Steve 'Handlebar' Meronek. "I don't wanna hear no damn excuses understand?"

The rest of the gang sat looking slack-jawed and scared. Handlebar was more than capable of killing someone when he was in one of his rages. That was one of the reasons they had not picked up a prospect in over two years—word had gotten around.

"Where's Shiloh?" he bellowed, throwing an empty beer bottle against the wall of the abandoned filling station with a satisfying crash, pieces of glass spraying in all directions to join their cousins littering the floor.

"She went out to get her cards Handlebar," said the girl named Gomer 'Bittytitty' Reaux. She was thin, too thin, and had the look of a worn out stripper though she was only in her early thirty's. She was Handlebar's 'property' for the past year, and in that time, she had aged ten years. She grabbed another beer from the cooler and brought it to him twisting off the cap before putting it in his hand.

The door opened and Shiloh walked in carrying the little bag that contained her 'magic'. She sat down at an old table and began to mumble her incantations while shuffling the Tarot cards.

"I must know where he is," Handlebar repeated. "Show me his future."

"The cards reveal what they will Handlebar, you know that. Here shuffle," she said as she passed the deck to him.

Meronek shuffled the cards and handed them back to Shiloh, who began to make the spread. Still chanting to herself she laid the cards out on the table slowly, as though each movement was somehow sacred, until she had made the full spread.

"Well witch, what do they tell you?"

"He has powerful forces watching over him. You can find him tonight at a place with pool tables. It may be the last time She (meaning Madam Blavatsky) will be able to help you."

"What do you mean? She has more power than that piss-ant coyote of his."

"Perhaps," Shiloh said, "but there are greater powers than either of them in this battle."

"Go on witch," Handlebar growled. "What powers would that be?"

"Nothing on Earth Handlebar." She left it there for him to figure out as she picked up her cards, put them back in her bag, and waited to see what would happen next.

"Saddle up you pathetic band of losers," Handlebar barked. "Let's find this Tom Terrific and Bar-b-que his ass."

As they made their way out one of them picked up a L.A.W.s (Light Anti-Tank Weapon) rocket.

The parking lot at Mom's was packed, the booths and tables filled with Saturday night customers on their way to somewhere else after a good meal. I asked the girl at the register where Jason and the others had gone and she handed me a note by way of answer. Inside was a detailed map of the local area with mile markings and directions to another 'safe' place. I just hoped it was safer than the last one.

On the TV in the restaurant the fire and explosion at the Iron Horse was being reported: Six dead with a dozen injured and no explanation as to the cause. More details at ten as they always say.

One face in the crowd caught my attention though, it was Meronek's lieutenant: tall and stooped over as if gravity and life had beaten him down. He was alost skeletal. I remembered

Handlebar calling him Deadman and I knew his presence was more than coincidence.

The thought that they had butchered those people at the bar just to get at me sent a feeling of revulsion through me. I made a resolution to track them down and bring them to justice no matter what it took. This was war now and no quarter would be given.

I went back outside and headed toward the safe house indicated on the map. I had been driving south about twenty minutes down state 168 toward I-15 out of Moapa, toward the Moapa reservation, when something in the distance caused me to slow down; a pair of eyes reflecting light back at me. My first thought was every biker's nightmare—deer.

As I drew closer, I saw it was a single coyote. He did not move, but stood facing me broadside as I pulled to a stop in front of him. I could see no headlights in either direction so I shut down the bike and killed the lights. I started to put down the side stand when he suddenly bared his teeth and started to growl in a very unfriendly way.

"What's the matter old one? Road Runner get away from you again?" I asked him. The way he was acting told me there was something wrong here. Again, I peered off into the darkness and suddenly lights appeared behind me. The coyote skittered off the road behind a dune and, pushing the bike, I followed. We both hunkered down and waited until, with a roar like a hundred banshees, the bikes passed us and disappeared into the night.

Turning back to the coyote, I found the old man sitting cross-legged and watching me.

"They seek your blood and will not be satisfied until they drink their fill Tom Harper."

"Yeah, I get that," I replied. "They just killed six people trying to get me. I've had enough of being the hunted, I must become the hunter."

"Yes Tom, but it is more important to find the one who leads them. Destroy these and She will only find others."

"Tell me more about this She old one and before you go, how about telling me your name."

"She is an old spirit and a servant of the Evil One."

"Okay, but how do I fight a spirit?"

"You can't yet, but you will learn."

A sudden buzzing behind me, the trademark of the Southwestern Diamondback, drew my full attention. There was nothing there and when I turned back, he was gone. "Old fart still didn't tell me his name."

I sat down with a pocket torch and looked at the map to see if there was some other way to get to the area indicated when I had the feeling that the others needed me. I fired up the bike and took off in the direction the bad guys had gone. It was pay back time and with seven or eight of my friends in front of them and me behind the coroner was going to be putting in some major overtime tonight.

CHAPTER 14

"They're coming," Jason said. "They should be here in about twenty minutes."

"How do you know?" asked Dakota. "Ear to the ground Kimosabe?"

"Very funny paleface," retorted Jason with a smile. "Got a call from Mary Ann. She says they found out Tom got away and was headed here. Probably got a crow working for them, so we need to move fast. These guys are packing some serious hardware. Jake, Peter, Simon, take the left flank, and the M-60 in the tower. James and David to the right on the old bus with the .50. Me, John, Dakota, and Bob, if he shows, will defend the cave here.

"Let them get close and wait for us to shoot first so as to draw them in as much as possible. Try to stay out of sight of any birds." Looking around at everyone he finally added, "Go with God." Everyone headed to their positions silently and with deadly purpose.

Jake, Peter, and Simon climbed up into the old stone tower that had been built by Native Americans somewhere in the distant past. There was a gun slit cut into it and they pulled the canvas cover off the M-60, 7.62 caliber light machine gun, which had been stationed there. With a fire rate of 550 R. p.m., it could definitely ruin the enemies best laid plans.

On the right, James and David clambered up on the top of an old British double-decker bus that had been brought over years ago as a tourist attraction in Las Vegas. Lack of parts and bad management had finally brought it out here to the desert to entertain the pack rats and prairie dogs.

On the upper deck, thick plates of steel had been fashioned into a gun tub, and a Browning AN M-2 H.B. .50-caliber heavy machine gun was mounted on a gimbal to provide a wide field of fire, covering everything from the tower on the left, to the cliffs on the right. If you have never seen a Ma Duce in action firing at 500 R. p.m., all I can tell you is the word 'awesome' describes it like 'bad' describes an F-5 tornado.

Up in the cave Jason and John busied themselves with sand-bags for firing platforms, while Dakota broke out and arranged grenades setting them in rows—flash-bangs to the front to diso-rient, frags in the middle, and H.E. (High Explosive) in the rear in case they got too close.

With the sandbags arranged, Jason and the others took up their AR-15's, which had been converted to full-auto, and read-ied themselves for the coming fight just as the bad guys pulled over a rise about a quarter klick away.

"Okay," said John, "here they come, lock and load."

Jason could be heard muttering Psalm 23: "The Lord is my shepherd, I shall not want. He makes me to lie down in green pastures, he leads me beside still waters, he restores my soul. He guides me in paths of righteousness for his name's sake. Even though I walk through the valley of the shadow of death, I will fear no evil, for you are with me; your rod and your staff, they comfort me. You prepare a table before me in the presence of my enemies. You anoint my head with oil; my cup overflows. Surely goodness and mercy will follow me all the days of my life, and I will dwell in the house of the LORD forever. Amen."

Dakota in turn, was quoting Psalm 27, "The LORD is my light and my salvation, whom shall I fear?"

John, practical as always, said, "Kill'em all, God will know his own!"

Handlebar could see the cliffs coming up by the way they blocked out the stars. They were getting close so he hand signaled the others to slow down. Again using hand signals, he directed them to fan out into a v-shaped formation. The ground here on the sides of the dirt road was smooth enough, but you had to be careful. You could find yourself at the bottom of an arroyo without seeing it coming.

At a hundred meters, he could just make out the tower and the bus, but there was no sign of the cave. By not stopping to recon the area, Handlebar was about to make a major tactical error. Arrogance, blood lust, and drugs overcame good sense. At fifty meters, he signaled a stop killing the motors, but leaving the lights on, and had everyone dismount.

"Stoneface, Cracker, Jinks, and Roady you go left and check out the bus. Ripper, Oilcan, Speedbump, and Buzzard you go right and check that tower. Deadman, Roadkill, Maggott, and Wrench, we go up the middle. Stay low, move fast, and kill anything that moves."

A sudden sharp pain on my right cheek, the feeling of liquid running back to my ear—nice juicy bug; must have been a big one. "I hate it when that happens," I muttered trying to wipe away the remains and getting my fingers all bug-gut sticky in the process.

I saw their brake lights come on about five hundred meters ahead and figured they were coming to a stop. All spread out the way they were I knew they were forming a skirmish line. I went on to get a little closer then shut off my lights and motor; coasting until I stopped. I pulled the Greener out of my saddlebag, having picked it up before leaving Mom's, and filled my coat pockets with 10 ga. double-oughts—pity the guy that takes a blast from this hog.

I headed up the road on foot keeping to cover as much as possible since I sure didn't want to catch a bullet from friendly fire.

All of a sudden, the whole night sky lit up followed by booms like jets breaking the sound barrier. I realized they were flash-bangs after a second and got down behind a mound of earth to protect my night vision.

I decided to stay put, as the area around the tower and the bus lit up like a Pink Floyd Laser show with green and red tracers. The cave continued to expel grenades and small arms fire convincing the bad guys that any designs they had on the occupants was overly optimistic. I hated sitting there, but the Greener was no good for more than about thirty meters and my .45 wasn't much better for accuracy beyond forty meters. All the targets were still at least a hundred meters away and the air was full of the angry buzz of stray rounds. All I could do is wait and watch.

After maybe five minutes of steady fighting, which seemed much longer, everything went quiet. Not just quiet but the total absence of sound that you can only find in the desert. Even the insects that provided the usual night music had been impressed into silence by the firefight.

Jason's voice boomed out breaking the stillness, "Give it up Meronek, you are outnumbered, and there is no way out for you."

It seemed like a good time for me to let them know I was here too so I shouted, "You're surrounded Meronek, you got nowhere to go." I hoped that Jason would be able to hear me after all that noise.

I heard the sound of running footsteps coming my way and waited until they were right on top of me. I popped up pointing the Greener and shouted, "Freeze scumbag," at the same time. I guess he was just stupid because he began shooting. Little starbursts flashing out of the suppressor gave away his position as he ran toward me.

The Greener split the night with a roar as both hammers fell, spitting out a total of thirty-four, .38 caliber balls, which carved their way through their victim, stopping him in his tracks by ripping off his right leg and shredding his right arm into a pulp. He hit the ground face first still running and flopped around like a fish in the bottom of a boat. By the time I had reloaded, he was dancing with the Devil in Hell.

The rest of Meronek's gang made their way back to their bikes and came barreling toward me. I popped up as they came abreast and let go the Greener again. One rider exploded in a cloud of red mist, his bike going on without him for fifty meters or so. Another left the road and crashed into a large Prickly Pear patch with screams of pain and the engine roaring at full throttle until it flooded out.

I walked over while reloading to have a look at the remains. The sun was just starting to brighten the horizon, giving off enough light to make out my victims. The first was nearly blown in half; gutted by the buckshot with only his spine to hold him together. By some twist of fate, he was still alive, his hands clawing at the air. I knelt down beside him and asked his name.

Through the gasping sounds as he tried to suck air with a torn diaphragm, I heard him say, "Jimmy Townsend" and "F—you," as his dyeing words. Remembering the list of characters Dakota had produced, I crossed off 'Buzzard', and moved on to the other guy. He lay in the Prickly Pear like some kind of oversize voodoo doll whimpering from the pain and begging for help.

"Looks bad dude," I said holding the Greener on him and checking for weapons. "What's your name?"

"Eat shit and die asshole," was his irreverent reply.

There was a strong smell of gasoline from the punctured gas tank of the bike, which was lying across his left leg. I stepped around him and prodded the bike with my foot causing more gas to run out.

"Be a shame if this thing was to catch fire," I said, as I reached into my pocket pulling out a pack of matches to play with them in my left hand. "'Specially with your bike on top of you and all. One more time knot-head," I said as I peeled off a single match and prepared to strike it. "Your name."

Fear was in his eyes, but he still thought I was bluffing, "You're a cop man, you can't do that, I got rights," he whined.

"Wrong on two counts punk. I ain't a cop and you gave up your rights at the Iron Horse last night." I struck the match against the striker just lightly enough to cause a spark but not enough to light it.

"Okay man," he shouted. "You'll blow us both up. Are you crazy?"

"No," I returned. "Just pissed off enough to light this hog up with you under it."

"Okay man, names Speedbump."

"Roger Moor?"

"Yeah, yeah, that's my name. Get me outta here man, these cactus spines are killing me."

"What good are you Speedbump?" I asked fishing for information. "What can you tell me about Meronek that would convince me to keep your sorry ass alive?"

✝ ✝ ✝

Handlebar's world exploded in white light and a wave of pressure that knocked him backward on his butt. There was a howling in his head and giant red balloons everywhere he looked that moved with his eyes. He felt as helpless as a newborn baby, not knowing which way to move. So he lay where he fell, feeling a warm wetness spreading through his crotch and smelling feces from somewhere. 'Probably one of those dummies with me,' he thought, it never occurring to him that he would load his own pants.

As his sight slowly returned, he could see the arcs of tracers passing over him, and felt wonder at the magic lights dancing before his eyes, until it finally came to him what they were. His Lt., Deadman, grabbed him by the collar and shouted in his ear to get under cover. They both crawled behind some rocks and made themselves as small as they could.

Screaming profanities, Handlebar began firing his AK in the direction of the cave until he emptied the clip in one wasteful burst. Fumbling for the clip release, he finally managed to get the empty out just as the area around him and Deadman exploded with return fire from the tower. Tracers bounced around them like an orgy of drunken fireflies and Deadman screamed at him to stop drawing fire.

Those shooting at them found new targets, allowing them time to skittle back toward the bikes and better cover. Firing up his machine, gunning the motor as a way to recall the group, but not waiting for the others, he launched himself down the road with Deadman following and the rest not far behind.

As he rolled past my position, he heard the Greener go off, and felt a sharp pain in his right butt cheek that nearly knocked him off the bike. Looking in his mirrors, he saw two drop out leaving only five lights following him now. He screamed out his rage and anger loud enough for the others to hear over their motors as they rolled into the rising sun, leaving their dead behind like so much garbage after a rock concert.

Looking out from the mouth of the cave Jason saw Handlebar and his minions spread out before him. He let them get to within eighty meters before tossing out three flash-bangs and opening up with the AR-15's. With all the excitement it was a wonder there were not more casualties on both sides. The tower and the bus both opened up, seeding the dry Nevada night with flowers of red and green. The occasional blossom of orange from a frag or white from a flash-bang, the earth shaking booms of H.E., and over all; the cloying odor of cordite mixed with fear and blood.

There was sporadic fire being returned, but it was obvious that the Pagans were outgunned and this firefight was not going to last long. The shooting came to a stop as everyone took a break looking for targets.

A sudden burst of fire from down in front of the cave chopped up the hillside doing no real damage, but was returned by the guys in the tower a hundred fold. That seemed to take the fight out of them as they broke and ran for their bikes.

In the distance, the familiar bark of the Greener told Jason that Tom was settling the score with someone. Then the roar of the bikes leaving and one more shout from the Greener announced another Pagan dispatched to his master. That would bring the score to roughly six Pagans down.

It was time to check for casualties and assess the body count on both sides. Looking first to those who were with him he asked, "Dakota, John, you okay?"

"I'm okay," from Dakota, although sounding on the edge a bit.

"Think I may have been grazed by one Jason," from John. "Right across the cheek, burns like Hades bro."

"Doesn't look too bad," Jason comforted. "Might even leave a little scar. I hear the chicks love that."

"Yeah, too bad I'm already married. Hope the wife don't mind."

Dakota was moving at once for the med kit and tending to John while Jason left to check on the others. "In the tower, report," he shouted.

He heard three okays from the tower and two more from the bus. One minor wound was pretty good for all the shooting that had gone down. "Fan out and have a look for any wounded. Report back as soon as you have something. Be careful, Tom's out there somewhere."

As soon as the words left his mouth, he saw Tom coming up the road with somebody in front of him. "Good," he said to himself. "At least one prisoner and maybe some answers."

CHAPTER 15

"Please man, just shoot me. I can't take no more," whined Speedbump.

"Keep moving dirtbag, you ain't hurt that bad," I answered. We were coming up to the cave entrance as Jason was coming out.

"Eh-Yat-Tah-Hey little brother," he called, "What have you brought us?"

"I found a dog in a cactus patch big brother. Got any pliers?"

"What for? They will fall out on their own in a week or two."

"Yeah, but I don't think I can put up with the whining that long, be better to shoot him I think."

"Let's see what he knows first, we can always shoot him later. Plenty space out here to bury him; looks like we got six to bury anyway. That .50 sure makes a mess out of a man, ya know."

"Yeah, don't much matter where you hit him either, almost always fatal."

"At least we can let him put some names to what's left," said Jason.

"Get him up here and let me have a look at him," shouted Dakota from inside the cave. "Looks like John is going to live, his wound was no fun at all." She came walking out with some twelve-inch pliers and a hacksaw in her hands, along with a most evil grin on her lovely face.

"Move it knot-head," I said, giving him a boot to help him along.

"Ahh," a lovely cry of pain. "Please man that hurts!"

"Do try to be gentle with him Dakota," I said with a laugh.

Jason and I went out in an A.T.V. that had a trailer and picked up the bodies. We got them laid out and waited patiently for

Dakota to finish so we could get some ID's on the stiffs. Some were so mangled that not even their mother's would recognize them.

"Give us some names punk," Jason ordered after Dakota waved us into the cave. "Tell us who your friends are."

"No way man, I ain't telling you pigs nothing more," he said looking nervously at me.

"Sound familiar big brother?" I asked. "Lemme get another flare out and you make our guest comfortable."

"Wait, what are you talking about? What flare? What do you need a flare for?"

The results of our interrogation were predictable. Six names were crossed off the list of Handlebar's minions: Cracker, Jinks, Roady, Ripper, the Satans Slaves enforcer, Oilcan, and Wrench. At this rate, Meronek was not going to be able to carry out his plan for Area 51 anytime soon.

He would have to find replacements before going ahead and according to Speedbump, Meronek was making a lot of promises to some of the local gangs: money, dope, and guns for anyone who would ride with him, but still no info on who was backing him or who the mysterious She was. We did have the location of his hideout though and everyone was preparing to go there as soon as the bodies were taken care of.

I walked over to Jason and called the others together as well. "Anyone willing to bet he'll still be there?" I asked. "Chances are we won't find anything but empty beer cans and cigarette butts. So I suggest we split up; half of us go to the hideout and see what we can find, the others question the local clubs."

"Good idea Tom," said David. "I've got some sources on the street I can check."

"Me too," added Bones. "Besides, I gotta check in before the club starts missing me."

"Right Bones," I said, "and thanks for your help. Keep us posted, okay?"

Handlebar didn't bother with going to the hideout in Glendale, figuring correctly, that the God-squad would sweat the location out of one of his fallen comrades. Trust was for suckers and he was no sucker. He stopped only long enough to pick up the women and the supplies he had left at the turnoff to the canyon, then headed for a backup location only he knew about. The pain in his right leg was getting real bad and the whiskey he was downing for the pain was making it hard to drive, or even see the road for that matter.

They were about five klick's from their new hidey-hole when a trooper pulled out to follow them. He did not know if a B.O.L.O. (Be On The Look Out) had been sent out or if the Pig was just hoping to get lucky by harassing him, but after about a klick the gumballs went on and he knew he would have to pull over or risk him calling for backup. He knew he could not outrun them, especially with the old Jeep carrying their supplies and ol' ladies. He gave a signal to Deadman as he came to a stop at a pullout with a scenic overlook.

As the trooper got out of his cruiser, Deadman pulled out a sawed off, let him have it with both barrels and no warning. Maggott tossed a lit Molotov on the unit and everybody burned off without looking back.

Very neat he thought, all done in under sixty seconds, no witnesses, and no way to recover the video from the Pig's unit. What a crew he had, too bad he had lost so many back at the canyon. He would have to settle-up with that bitch Shiloh for that one after he took care of his leg. Stoneface had some shrapnel in his shoulder and back from a grenade to take care of as well.

That had been a bad scene. She had told him the battle would be his, so what went wrong? Could he have a snitch in the group?

The guys had been riding with him for several years and he felt he could trust them to keep their mouths shut, but you could never be a hundred percent sure of anything. Everybody but Speedbump was accounted for and he saw him get blasted by Harper with that damn Greener. That left the women and he had never trusted bitches. That was one thing his mother had taught him—the hard way.

They rode down a side road into a valley following the old wagon tracks and there, hidden by shadows, was the opening to an old silver mine. "Maggott, go back and cover our tracks, those Pigs'll be looking for us real quick."

"Sure Handlebar, but the drag behind the Jeep looks like it did a pretty good job."

"Stay back there by that old shack and keep watch. You see anybody coming, you call me on the cell."

Inside the old mineshaft, they pulled out some camo netting to cover the bikes; it wasn't great, but good enough for a flyover.

CHAPTER 16

"Hey Charlie, Tom here…Yeah, Tom Harper, your old Gunny Sergeant. Hey, look partner, I need ya to cover my back…Think you could reach Bill Travers and Dick Rogers? Okay, call me back at this number as soon as you can. Thanks bro." I put down the phone and turned back to the others. "Charley, Dick, and Bill were some of the best of my squad back in Iraq, all Christians too."

We settled back into a booth at Mom's waiting for our food. Jason was in the kitchen doing the cooking and sitting next to me was Dakota, James, and John, the rest were out working their sources for any clues they could turn up, or were trying to get some rest and clean clothes after the firefight. I knew I needed to. It felt like it had been a week since I had a bath and a good nights sleep and no way of knowing if I ever would again.

"Tom, Tom," a voice was calling my name from somewhere, distracting me from something that was terribly important. I tried to answer, but there was no sound—to open my eyes—but they would not. I screamed in my fear, reached out for purchase, and finally called out for the LORD.

Light—faces around me that I knew—familiar sounds. "Tom, you okay little brother?" The face of Jason moved in front of me. "You had us scared man. You just fell out face first in your soup."

"Come with me Tom," Dakota directed. "Time for a little nap. You can sleep in the back room."

I started to protest, but the soup dripping down my face cinched the argument. I went along without any further protest. I was asleep before my head hit the pillow.

A blue lake stretched away over the horizon, fluffy white clouds forming vaguely familiar faces, soft green grass under me, and a gentle breeze smelling faintly of pine and honeysuckle.

"Nice place huh, Nephew?"

I turned to see Bob seated next to me on the grass. "Where are we?"

"I don't know Tom, It's your dream."

"Oh yeah," I said. "What's going on Bob? Why am I important in all this?"

"Because you have found favor in the eyes of the LORD Tom. There does not have to be any other reason. The fact is, you have been chosen, as I was chosen, and it is an honor. He does not do this for everyone you know."

I looked back to the lake, to the clouds in the sky once again forming a face, an old man with long white hair. I looked to Bob again, but he was gone, and in his place, a single rose. A voice from above? Or maybe just thunder? "Follow Me."

✝ ✝ ✝

"You ever notice how snitches rhymes with bitches?" mused Handlebar aloud. He was pretty stoned on a mixture of cheap whiskey, Oxycontin, and several joints of good weed. He was looking around at the ladies and trying not to scream as Roadkill, the official ex-military medic and enforcer, dug around in his thigh looking for the hunk of buckshot that was embedded there.

"I know it's one of you sluts," he slurred through clenched teeth. "I can smell it on ya."

Bittytitty slinked over to him bending down and wiping his face with a wet towel. "Come on baby," she cooed in his ear. "You know I wouldn't do that. I love you baby. I would do anything for you. It might be Shiloh baby. You know I have never trusted her."

Handlebar put his hand in her face and shoved her onto her backside. "Get away from me bitch," he shouted as he fumbled for his gun, but Deadman had taken it knowing how Meronek's temper flashed when he was trashed.

"I'll kill you, you lying bitch. I'll kill all of ya."

The sudden movement sent a wave of pain through the psycho's body that hit his brain like a runaway freight train, sending him into unconsciousness.

"Lucky for you Bitty," said Deadman. "You better make yourself scarce before he comes to. He might just kill you for this. You getting kind' a wore out anyway."

She knew it was true, but where could she go? She couldn't go to prison, not with her expensive tastes in chemicals. The D.T.'s just weren't for her. She withdrew to a dank corner near the exit of the mine and started making her plans.

Handlebar dreamed again of his mother calling the police and turning him in. He had killed the neighbor's Doberman for taking a crap in their yard and soiling his brand new Converse sneakers in it. He had called the dog over using some steak from the 'fridge and cut its throat with his switchblade. It had cost him one year in the C.Y.A. (California Youth Authority) and he was still mad about it. He had been only ten and swore that someday, she would taste steel too.

CHAPTER 17

I woke to the smell of coffee and...honeysuckle. Getting my eye's open took a lot of effort, but it was worth it. Dakota was looking at me with a sweet smile on her angelic face and a cup of hot black mud in her hand. "Welcome back Tom," she said.

"How long have I been out?" I asked as I took the coffee and slammed down a big gulp. It burned all the way down igniting pangs of hunger as it spread through my belly.

"You've been out for ten hours. Didn't figure there was any big hurry to wake you though. The bad guys are hurt too and holed up somewhere. They have not hit the radar anywhere yet. Probably hiding in the desert somewhere."

I sat up sucking down more of the caffeine laden life-water and again smelled the honeysuckle. I realized it was coming from her. She smelled clean and in my sleep-dazed eye's she was suddenly far more than a companion-in-arms, she became the desire of my life. But that would have to wait for a while; we still had other business to take care of.

"Any chance of getting some of Mom's famous breakfast?"

"Whatever you want Tom. There's a Hero's plate spread out for you in the dining room. Thought you might like a shower first. As a matter of fact, we took a vote on it. Showers over there, clean towels, and a change of clothes too. See you shortly."

She left and I got up off the cot finishing the coffee and stumbling toward the shower. As I took off my t-shirt, I could swear a buzzard fell out the sky and I could hear people running and screaming out into the street.

As I entered the restaurant, I saw David, John, Dakota, and Jason, still dressed in his white cook's apron, sitting in one of the booths. They all looked pretty grim-faced as I approached. "Did I miss a spot or something?" I asked. "You all look like something stinky just walked in."

"No Tom," said David. "We just got a report in about a trooper that was killed. Took a shotgun blast in the chest and his car was set on fire; probably to cover up who did it. They left tracks in the pull out area though: five bikes and a jeep, which sounds like our bunch. We've got choppers in the air and off-road patrols looking for them but nothing so far."

"Damn Dave, I am sorry to hear that. Did you know him?"

"Yeah, Carl Latham, been in uniform for eight years. He leaves behind a wife and two beautiful daughters."

"How far away did this happen?" I asked.

"About thirty miles south, close to the restricted military site outside Las Vegas. They may be hiding in the hills there; probably in an old mineshaft.

"Yeah, especially if one or two of them are wounded," added John.

Jason came back out of the kitchen and served plates of Huevos Rancheros, hash browns, a stack of buckwheat pancakes, and plenty of Maple syrup. "You need anything else little brother you just call."

"No thanks Jason," I said. "This'll be plenty."

They were heading for Area 51, but they would have to find more soldiers to replace their losses. "Didn't I read somewhere that the former head of the Devils Angels was living just across the border in Arizona?"

John Little Bear spoke up, "Yeah just outside Kingman on the way to Phoenix. He opened up a Harley shop there; had to co-opt a local club for his own protection. Might be Meronek is looking to pick up some soldiers there."

"Be a good place to look John. Can we get somebody there to keep an eye on them?"

"Better than that," said Jason. "That's where Jake is. He's riding with them. I'll see if we can get word to him. Anyway, if they hear from our boy, I'm sure Jake will let us know. Just hope Meronek's psychic contacts don't smell him out."

"Yeah, we will have to pray a hedge of protection around him."

✝ ✝ ✝

"Get over here bitch," growled Handlebar. "Roll me another joint and pass me that bottle if you know what's good for you."

"Sure baby," Bittytitty said moving over next to him. "Here baby." She handed him the bottle and began rolling him a number. "Like we're almost out of weed baby. Like, you want somebody should go out and like, get some?"

"How we doing on meds, Deadman?"

"We're getting low on Oxy's and weed both, but we got plenty of anti-biotics and booze. We can send Maggott and Bittytitty over to Hardcore's place to get some more if you want. Take the jeep so's they can pick up some food and water too."

"Okay, okay, how long I been out anyway. Last thing I remember is Bar-b-quing that Pig."

"You been out for two days Handlebar," said Stoneface. "Cop's have been all over the place searching."

"Yeah," Deadman went on, "they ain't giving up, but they have started searching further away from here."

"Okay. Maggott, you and Bittytitty take the jeep and get us whatever we need. Leave your colors here and take the cell phone. If they need an ID call me and don't screw this up."

As Maggott and Bittytitty pulled out, neither of them was aware of the Eagle watching them from its place on the mountain.

"We got a snitch in here. Who you think it is Deadman?" said Handlebar.

"I ain't for sure bro, maybe Shiloh can tell you with her cards, she ain't been much use any other way lately."

"Got a point bro. Get over here Shiloh and bring yur cards."

With Maggott and Bittytitty gone, Shiloh sensed her opportunity. Bittytitty had been a major source of problems for her from the beginning, always looking over her shoulder and constantly being suspicious of her. "Okay Handlebar," she said. "Shuffle the cards."

"Thought I would give you guys a call," said Jake. "Seems Maggott and Handlebar's old lady came by the club looking for drugs and supplies. They picked up some Oxy's and weed. They also talked about killing a state trooper and burning his unit. Handlebars orders, but it was his Lieutenant, guy by the name of Deadman, that pulled the trigger."

"That's real good Bones," I said. "Did they give you any idea where they were hiding?"

"No, and I couldn't get away to follow them either. I did get the feeling that this chick, Bittytitty they call her, might be willing to come in. She looked scared."

"Alright, we will keep that in mind. If you get the time to ride out on the highway where the trooper was killed, see if you can spot anything okay?"

"Will do buddy. I will get back to you tonight."

"Sounds like one of Handlebar's women might be wanting to get out," I said to the others gathered. I told them the rest of what Jake had said and we settled onto a map to start referencing known caves and abandoned mines between Moapa and the place where Officer Carl Latham was murdered, which was near the military reservation on US 93 just off I-15 in a desolate spot.

"In the meantime, do we have anyone we can talk to about what Area 51 might have that these guys want?"

"I might be able to make some calls that could turn something up," said James Hightower, the N.S.A. man.

"Okay good, because I hate to go at this without some idea of what they are after. Some kind of Super Weapon? How big is it? How destructive? You know what I mean?"

"Yeah I see. Small enough to put on a jeep?" said Hightower.

"Exactly, or will they need something bigger? By the way," I went on, "Has anybody heard from Bob or know how to reach him?"

Blank looks on every face said, 'No'. "Okay maybe I just need to take a nap, that always seems to work."

I looked outside through the window and felt the need to ride, too much sitting around waiting. If this woman was willing to come in, she could be a real help.

"Can we get in touch with Mary Ann, Peter?"

"Only through a drop or in person. But if they come out we can try making contact. What's up?"

"Maybe put a little pressure on Bittytitty to come in, make her out to be a snitch you know?"

"Could work," he said, "if it doesn't get her killed first. You know their motto? God forgives—Pagans don't. The only good snitch is a dead one."

"Yeah I know. But we really need to get some good Intel on these people whatever it takes."

I went out back of the restaurant feeling the July heat beating down on me like a living blanket, smothering in its intensity. There were just too many unanswered questions at this point and answers were what I needed to form a strategy. I needed the security of a plan.

"Sometimes you just have to trust in someone greater than yourself Nephew. That he has a plan and you are part of it."

"I don't even want to know how you got on the roof Bob, or why. But I do need some help."

"He knows what you need Tom and he knows when you need it. Trust in him youngster, he has the strategy all worked out, and he will reveal it as you need it. The main thing is patience and trust."

"Okay where do we go from here?"

"Look for a flat chested girl."

"Yeah Bittytitty, we're working on that now."

I left Bob on the roof and walked around to where my bike was, really wanting to go for a ride, but feeling that I did not want to try it alone this time. I was frozen in thought, looking in the restaurant through a window, when three bikers pulled in with whoops and plenty of horn blowing. It was the guys I had called earlier come to join the fight!

"Charley, Dick, Bill! Great to see ya buddies. Semper Fi!"

"Got here soon as we could Tom. What's up?" said Charley, as he wrapped his arms around me in a big hug.

"Hold up bro, lemme get a look at ya first."

Charley was five-eleven and built like an English bulldog. He had the biggest arms I had ever seen on anyone. He could bench five hundred pounds and had such an easy going spirit that you just had to like him: brown hair, blue eyes and in every other respect just an average looking guy. Except for those guns and his chest, it gave the impression of being top heavy.

Bill Travers had been our specialist with the M-79 grenade launcher, known as the blooper. He could drop a 30mm party favor in your shirt pocket at seventy-five meters and he did not know the meaning of the word fear.

Six feet and eighty kilo's with fire engine red hair that he kept cut close, he had the kindest looking brown eyes I've ever seen, but there was some real Sheffield steel behind them. He could use a Bowie knife like Michelangelo used a paintbrush.

Dick Rogers was six feet one and eighty-eight kilo's, black hair, and, due to a childhood accident, had one blue eye and one red eye. It looked strange and sometimes gave the impression that he wasn't quite sane. He had been our squad gunner and knew the M-60 Pig better than some guys know their wives. He could strip it, change barrels, and have it firing again in sixty seconds. He was another guy that did not know what fear was.

I saw him walk his M-60 into a squad of insurgents in Mosul one time, taking them all out, and receiving two wounds in the process. He saved the lives of a Hummer crew that day and earned himself a Silver Star in the process. As I greeted him though, something did not seem quite right, there was something different in those eyes—something I could not quite put my finger on.

"Let's go inside guys and I will introduce you to the posse."

We headed inside laughing and slapping each other on the back but Dick hung back saying he needed some gear from his bags. As we went in the door, a crow landed in the parking lot and exchanged a long look with Dick—a look that was more than casual.

✝ ✝ ✝

"Did you get everything?" demanded Handlebar; meaning the Oxycontin.

"Yeah boss, got the Oxy's, a brick of good weed, food, water, everything," answered Maggott as he nervously handed the pills over to Deadman.

"Where's the slitch Maggott?"

"I swear I don't know what happened to her boss. I stopped to get gas and while I was pumping, she went in to use the can. When I finished and went in to pay, I couldn't fine her nowhere man. She must'a went out the back. I drove around looking for her like almost an hour, but she wasn't nowhere. So I came back man, I didn't' know what else to do."

"You could'a called you useless shit-for-brains," said Deadman.

"I would have man, but she got the cell when I wasn't looking. I was scared she might call the Pigs or something, that's why I got out."

"It's okay Maggott," soothed Handlebar. "You done the right thing."

This caused Deadman to look over at Meronek quizzically, as this was not like him at all.

"Bitches is that way man, you can't trust them."

"Yeah Handlebar," said Maggott. "How could I know man, she's your woman right? How could I know she was gonna split, right?"

"Bring me one of those bottles of whiskey Maggott," said Meronek with an evil glint in his eye.

"Sure boss," answered Maggott, but as he reached the whiskey case, he saw Meronek reaching for his favorite knife. It was a Buck sheath job and he broke into a run for the exit.

"Get him Deadman and bring him back alive," he purred, in a voice like a tiger after eating a gazelle.

"Call just in from Boulder City guys," said David Long Bow. "A girl claiming to be Meronek's ol' lady just got picked up trying to steal a car. Says she's willing to tell us everything if we will put her in witness protection."

"Tell them to hold her until we get there," said Jason.

"Yeah," I joined in, "have them put her in P.C. (Protective Custody). Anything happens to her and heads will roll got it?"

"Will do Tom," replied Dave as he turned back to the phone.

As we headed out to the parking lot, Dick Rogers came up and asked, "Can I come along? Get a taste of the action, ya know."

"Don't see why not bro but we're only gonna get her and come right back. Sure you wouldn't just like to wait?" I asked.

"Well yeah, I guess so. I still need to catch up on stuff here I guess, huh?"

"Yeah and you just rode three hundred miles to get here man. Relax; there will be plenty for you to do. Get some rest, we'll be back in a couple hours."

David, John, and myself got into Jason's van and the four of us headed toward Boulder City to pick up our package.

CHAPTER 18

She sat on the swing hanging from the porch of her cabin nestled in the Redwood forest of Northern California. Reddish-blond hair flowing in the gentle Pine scented breeze, her face a study in contradiction. Pale green eyes, aquiline nose, high cheekbones, and a squared jaw showed her great beauty. She looked to be around thirty, her ample breasts still firm, as though defying gravity, narrow waist above well-rounded hips, and legs like Sharon Stone.

But it was behind those lovely eyes, those portals to the soul, that ugliness lived. Like the line from an old Eagle's song: 'A pretty face don't mean no pretty mind.' Her full lips even now softly chanting a summoning spell, calling upon her Dark Master; compelling him to come into her presence.

From the trail into the woods where her hidden alter lay, came the sound of a thousand tortured souls, sending birds and squirrels to search for cover; for something wicked this way comes.

A dark form came into view on the trail leaving in its wake things disgusting in odor and appearance, skittering away in search of dark places to hide. He is as tall and handsome as she is beautiful, with long jet-black hair down to his shoulders flowing in the breeze of his passing. His face chiseled from some fine piece of marble by the hand of a master, but the eyes are two black holes sucking all light and life into them to a place of no return. Face to face, they regard each other and the world waits; afraid to move or speak as though all life might be silenced forever.

"Why do you call me woman?" he asks in a voice smooth as oil. "Why do you disturb my sleep?"

"He grows in strength and is favored with help from Him," she replies.

"You knew this would happen, that is why you were given power over the animals and my servants. But I see you have wasted many of my servants and have gained nothing in return. Perhaps I made an error by putting my confidence in you." At this, the wind whirled leaves and detritus around his feet, and his eyes glowed an unearthly red.

"I beg of you Master to be patient with your servant," she groveled. "The plan is in motion, all will be done according to your will. Even now my servant is on his way to bring about the Great Deception."

"Your servant is an idiot bent upon his own destruction. I have sent another to remind him of his purpose and whose servant he is."

He turned to leave but she was not finished yet. "Master," she spoke imploringly, "can you not destroy the old dog who helps him?"

"You do not know what you ask woman." He spoke harshly to her like a simple-minded child. "He is a Power too. You must outwit him if we are to succeed. This is a battle of wits as much as it is a battle of flesh and blood. To succeed you must use all your female guile. I remind you: Failure is not an option!"

"I will not fail you Master," she replied meekly.

"See that you don't.

She sat in the interrogation room geeking around with one ciga-rette in her hand and another burning in the ashtray. Maybe ten years ago she would have been pretty, but now she looked like a used up, dried out, crack-head. She couldn't have weighed more than forty kilo's and at five-ten she could slip between the cracks in the sidewalk and not even touch the edges.

"She's seen better days," I said to Jason.

"Yeah," he replied, "a life of sin takes its toll."

"Okay fellas, she's all yours and welcome to her," said the trooper who poked his head in the door. "Name's Mike Benton, Cpl. Mike Benton. She doesn't smell very nice, kind'a like an ashtray made from Roadkill, and she seems to be coming down off something. She hasn't been very talkative other than telling us she's Meronek's old lady."

"She'll open up to us or we'll drop her off at the Devils Angels clubhouse," I said.

"Yeah," Jason added. "They would get her talking."

I opened the door and stepped in along with John, since he was authorized to put her into the witness protection program. I introduced the two of us and we took a seat.

"What is your full name?" I asked her.

"Gomer K. Reaux," she answered in a defiant tone. "Like, how long you people gonna keep me here? My life is in danger, ya know? Like, I can be a real help to ya, ya know? Like, I know where Handlebar is, ya know? Like, I can help ya, but you like, gotta get me in that witness program, ya know?"

I could see this was going to be a long evening; like ya know?

"Settle down Ms. Reaux," John interjected. "We will get you out of here to a safe place, but first we want you to tell us a few things, like where we can find Meronek and the others in his gang okay?"

On the drive back, after dispatching half the state militia to Meronek's last known position, Reaux began to tell us about the demonic forces that were working with him. She told us about Shiloh, even though she did not know Shiloh, A.K.A. Mary Ann, was one of ours, and about the mysterious She, Madam Blavatsky, and how he was able to receive messages from various animals including crows and coyotes. No one else had ever met this woman or knew what she looked like, but when he wanted to see her, he would drive up into northern California to the Redwood forest near Truckee.

He would always go on alone from there so no one could have contact with her. That was the way She wanted it and She always got what She wanted

She told us the names of those still riding with him, Maggott, Speedbump, his lieutenant, Deadman, and Roadkill, his enforcer.

"He sent us to Hardcore (Jack Shepherd), to get supplies, but also to tell him that we like, needed some replacements."

"How did Shepherd respond?" John asked. "I know Shepherd's crew isn't very big, only about twenty guys. They're more like his personal bodyguard and he's not likely to give them up."

"Yeah, like that's what he told us, ya know? Like, he says he would have to make some phone calls to some people. Like, he said it might take a few days to get them here, ya know?"

"Okay," I said. "We can work on that John. See about getting taps on Shepherds phones and e-mail. Ms. Reaux, where else is Meronek likely to go? He's probably figured out you ran out on him by now, so he will have to move to a new hideout."

"Like, I ain't sure. He spent about a month riding around out here, just him and Deadman ya know? Handlebar's like a psycho ya know, but he ain't stupid."

"What's the deal between him and Hardcore Ms. Reaux," asked David. "Hardcore isn't helping him out of the goodness of his heart."

"It's like Hardcore belongs to She, has for a long time ya know? Like he's to old and sick now to be of any use to her, so Hardcore introduced Handlebar to her, ya know? Ever since he met that bitch he's like, getting really paranoid, ya know? Like, he's gonna start whacking anybody he thinks is snitching on him, ya know? Like when Handlebar holds court, nobody' safe man, ya know?"

We were approaching Moapa and John suggested that Reaux be put in the safe house straightaway rather than stopping at

Mom's first, for security. Jason agreed and we took some back-trails to avoid any prying eyes, two legged or four, to get there.

We left David there with a couple of Jason's men to stand guard and then headed back toward town.

"Look here Handlebar," pleaded Roadkill. "There ain't but four of us left man. It ain't like Maggott did this on purpose ya know? Bittytitty took off on her own. Nobody could'a predicted it. I didn't see it coming neither and we need every man we got."

"Roadkill's right man," joined in Deadman. "Maggott's always been loyal and one less bitch ain't gonna hurt us none. She don't know enough to hurt us anyway. We're better off without her. You said yourself she was a lousy lay anyway."

Meronek lay on his back looking at Maggott and drawing his finger along the razor sharp edge of his Buck knife. "Yeah, yeah, okay," he finally spit out. "But you screw up one more time Maggott and I'll tie your guts to the back of my bike and drive off with'em, ya understand?"

"Yeah boss," Maggott said with evident relief in his voice. "I understand. You can trust me Handlebar, you know that man. It's them bitches ya can't trust man, they're all jealous of Blavatsky man, ya know what I mean boss?"

"One thing he's right about," spoke up Deadman. "We should'a never brought along the bitches for this job. We should'a left 'em at home."

"Deadman's right bro," injected Roadkill. "We should put 'em all on a bus and send 'em home right now before they get us busted. Keep Shiloh if ya want, but get rid of the others."

"Yeah okay," Meronek gave in. "We'll do that on our way to the rez (military reservation). Pack up and let's get outta here before the Pigs get here."

As we pulled into Mom's the parking lot was full. Mostly tourists picking through the trinkets and baubles, with plenty of kids running around outside in the play land that Jason had put in a couple years back in answer to McDonalds challenge. What drew my eye though was a solitary crow strutting around the roof watching the parking lot and, I could swear, us in particular.

"Everybody sit tight," I said as I picked up my cell phone and called Dakota. "Hey, there's a crow on the roof and, I know this may sound kind of weird, but I want you to chase it away. Shoot at it with an air gun or something. Kill it if you have to, but get rid of it so we can come in."

"Getting paranoid Tom," she asked. "Would you like me to blindfold the garden gnome too? How 'bout Barney the Dinosaur in the plays-scape, should I hit him with a tranq dart just to be safe?"

"Trust me Dakota," I said, trying not to sound angry. "This is serious. I will explain once he's gone. Okay?"

"Okay Tom, but it better be good."

I saw her come out the backdoor with an air rifle in her hands and look around at the roof until she spotted the crow. Taking careful aim, she fired off a pellet hitting the crow and causing it to jump into flight. It did not get far, slamming into the desert floor about twenty meters from the van. She went over prepared to deliver the coup-de-grâce, but that was unnecessary and she gave us the high sign to come out.

Jason and I walked over to the crow, while David went inside the restaurant to confer with the others.

"Good shot Marshall," I joked. "One less deadly crow in the cornfield."

"I'm serious Tom, you better have a good reason for this. I don't like killing animals if it isn't necessary."

"I had good reason Dakota, let's have a look at it."

Jason bent over the bird checking it over. Using his pocket-knife, he slit it open from crop to anus. Out of it came a stench that would have choked a buzzard off a gut wagon. As Jason pulled back trying to avoid the odor he said, "This one has the mark of the Evil One on it for sure."

Backing up quickly, I thought Dakota was going to feed the ants with her lunch.

"You okay?" I asked her.

"Yeah that smelled a lot like de-comp, but how? The thing wasn't dead, was it?"

"Yes it was," replied Jason. "Been dead for at least three days, see the maggots in the stomach? This bird was acting as eyes and ears for someone."

"Tell me I did not shoot a dead bird. I saw it fly, it could not be dead!"

Dakota was beginning to sound a little hysterical, so I grabbed her by the arm and started walking her toward the restaurant. "I know it sounds crazy, but there it is. Somehow this Madam Blavatsky character can animate these creatures for a while and use them to spy on us."

I got her inside where we took a seat in the back with the others. Everybody but Jake Holland, who was still at the Devils Angels clubhouse, was there. Dakota took a seat and exclaimed, "How can that be? How can someone do a thing like that?"

"Maybe I should answer that one," came the voice of my Uncle Bob as he walked in through the back door. "The crow was being kept in a state of pseudo-life by a demon. That demon is a servant of Madam Blavatsky, who in turn, is a servant of Lucifer.

"Blavatsky stays in touch with Meronek and keeps him informed of what's going on around here as well as where everybody is located. Always be suspicious of any animal that is alone and spends too much time in the area around you. Crow's are favorites because they like to hang around almost everywhere, especially where there is food. But, and this is important, you will seldom see just one. Other crows will not hang around when a zombie is present. Same with coyotes."

"Wait a minute," I said. "I thought the Devil didn't have the power to raise the dead to life."

"You're right Nephew he doesn't. But, technically they aren't alive. They only look like it. They are rotting from the inside out and are only good for a few days before they fall apart. He is the master of lies and that sort of resurrection is just another of his fake miracles."

"What else should we watch out for then Bob," I asked.

"Watch out for anything that does not fit—for people whose motive is not clear. For us, we must be careful of everyone. Do not trust anyone, not even your friends. Be suspicious of everyone unless they have proven themselves. The best way of course, is to ask them if Christ is LORD, because only those who freely confess him, belong to him."

"This does present some problems for us," I said. "Since most people are not Christians and many who say they are don't really know him, we could find ourselves surrounded by agents of the Evil One without knowing it. I'm afraid Bob is right. We will have to treat anyone we don't know as a possible agent of evil. Don't give out information concerning our movements and undercover operations to anyone not in our core group—that being the twelve of us here right now."

"Good advice Nephew," Bob said. "Now, I need to go out and see if I can pick up Meronek's trail since this woman has no idea where he has gone. He had already pulled out of the silver mine by the time the troopers got there."

"Okay Bob, good hunting, but sometime I would like to talk to you about some things okay?" I said as I walked out the back door with him.

"Such as Nephew?"

"Such as a room in Iraq and a fella that looked a lot like you firing an R.P.G. at me through the balcony doors."

"Yeah Nephew, I will make time to bring you up to speed on many things as you are able to understand them. Don't get in too big a hurry. I'll see you soon, maybe tonight or early tomorrow."

CHAPTER 19

On a mesa about a mile outside the restricted zone of Area 51 stood four greasy, dirty, sorry examples of humanity. Looking out across the flatland toward Area 51, the sorriest of the four was speaking.

"Out there man, across the plain, through the fence and we are in. We grab the gizmo, creepy-crawl back out and the rest is history."

"How we gonna get through security man?" asked Maggott. "I heard they got ground sensors and lasers along the fence, probably some other shit too."

"Absolutely my moronic friend," he replied. "Some of the most sophisticated sensors in the free world. That's why we have Madam Blavatsky on our side. With her help and the people she controls, we will be able to walk right in."

The sky suddenly took on an ominous color, the breeze shifted direction carrying the sharp tang of de-comp on it. A growl announced the presence behind the group of a single coyote, saliva drooling down his exposed fangs, one eye missing and filled with the dancing children of death, a few falling from the animals open mouth to squirm on the ground.

Meronek approached the animal kneeling down in front of it and taking on a reverent tone he said, "I am listening Mistress, what message have you brought me?"

In a voice that only he could hear, She spoke her words into his mind. "The time is near Steven, my darling. Soon we will carry out the battle for the World and you will become the Master of all I have promised."

"Yes Mistress, thank you. Have you seen where the enemy is? How can I defeat them as long as they cheat? They know where we go and are ready for us. Last time we met they killed six of my men."

"Fool! You attacked without consulting me—that is why you failed. They are stronger than you because their minds are clear of the poisons you are so fond of putting in your body. They are not fools; if you had waited, I would have told you of their defenses. Perhaps I should look for another; one whose mind is clear."

"Please Mistress, I have done all you have asked and I swear my mind will be clear as soon as this wound heals. It will take a few days for re-enforcements to arrive anyway. Then we will be ready Mistress, and the victory will be ours."

"See to it then or your place in Hell will be the lowest, most foul place of torture that even your limited intellect can imagine."

With that, the coyote collapsed to the ground and burst open releasing such a nauseating odor that Meronek and his three companions spent the next few minutes on their knees puking. To escape the foul odor they finally had to pour their stock of cheap whiskey over themselves, as well as into, and jump fully clothed into a muddy waterhole to wash away the stench. Afterward, they set out for a cave not far away where they could hide until they were ready to attack the base.

"I don't know about you Tom, but I'm starved," announced Dakota. "I would like a nice juicy steak cooked just enough to stop the bleeding."

"Okay," I said. "Where would you like to go?"

With a sparkle in her eye she leaned toward me bringing the scent of honeysuckle my way. "How 'bout my place. I've got a couple Rib Eyes that need to be eaten soon or they're going to spoil. You any good with a grill?"

"Let's see; I'm male and I'm from Texas," I said with a wink. "I was born with a meat fork in my hand."

"I'll bet you were. Must have been hard on your momma though."

"She gave it to me. Put in my hand six months after she got pregnant."

"I'll make a salad and we can grab a couple of baked potatoes from Jason. I've got wine in the fridge or we can get some beer if you'd rather."

"Actually, wine sounds pretty good. I haven't had a nice romantic dinner for way to long."

"Who said anything about romance cowboy? This is just dinner, okay?"

"I hear ya," I said with a grin. "I wouldn't have it any other way."

Dakota's house was a nice little two-bedroom cottage on five acres of forestland out by the Lake Mead National Recreation area. It was on state 169 close to Overton, but far enough out to be private.

We set out for her place which was about ten miles away, stopping for a few items at the local convenience store. I spent most of my time watching the sky for birds as I was feeling really paranoid now that I knew we could be watched at any time and nearly anywhere.

With every bike that roared by, I found myself reaching for my .45 and wondering if my life would ever return to normal. No doubt about it, Dakota was a beautiful woman and any man would fall all over himself to make her his own. She was pretty enough to be Playboy's Playmate of the Year and that is putting it mildly. Still, the timing just seemed all wrong, but maybe the Lord would fix that too.

As we pulled out into the gathering dusk, a bike passed us with a rider that looked just like Dick Rogers, but I couldn't be sure. It set me to remembering our time back in Iraq and some of the things we had been through.

The four of us had been out on patrol one night in a little neighborhood in Baghdad when Charley got the bright idea of having an impromptu bar-b-que in the backyard of a house. There was a real brick pit there with charcoal and everything. Charley had snagged some steaks from the Officers Mess and thought this would be a good time to cook 'um up. All we needed now was some lighter fluid.

I had some C-4 in my pack and next thing ya know we got a nice little fire going. C-4 makes a good fire starter. I got the charcoal going and Charley got the steaks out as Dick was throwing some more charcoal on the fire. All of the sudden the place lit up like the Fourth of July.

Seems the place belonged to a fireworks maker and what we thought was charcoal was really a bag full of homemade black powder. The flash was tremendous, you would'a thought a small nuke went off from the mushroom cloud it sent up.

Poor Dick got his eyebrows singed off, as well as some of his hair. He freaked out bad that night, screaming and firing his M-60 blindly. Later, we had a good laugh about the whole thing even though we ended up giving the steaks to the guy that owned the house since we kind'a messed up his back yard and all. Dick was the only one that never really seemed to see the humor in the whole mess.

As Dakota went into the house, I took a moment to survey the area looking for possible lines of attack and defense. Somehow, I was falling back into a combat-zone state of mind, even though I wanted to have a romantic evening. I chuckled to myself with that thought as I pulled out the Mossburg 500 12 gauge and turned to go into the house. Before going through the door, I had one last look for crows or other critters.

"Set the bag down on the counter," Dakota instructed. "Grills out back if you would care to get the fire started. I'm going to change into something more comfortable. Be back soon."

Out back was a nice little Weber Grill with a cover on it. I cleaned the rack, put in some charcoal, and got the fire going just as she came out with a cold beer in hand.

"Here ya go cowboy," she said in a very sultry voice. "A nice cold brew after a hot days work."

"Thanks miss Kitty," I said in my best Texas drawl. "By the way, is there some place I can wash off the trail dust?"

"Why shore," she drawled right back. "Right this way."

She led me to the spare bedroom which had a half-bath with a shower stall and toilet.

"You can take a quick shower if you like, just be careful of scorpions. They like to hide in the towels."

"Wouldn't care to scrub my back would'ja ma'am?" I asked, in as seductive a manner as possible.

"Wouldn't mind at all cowboy," she said with a coy little smile. "Soon as we're married."

The cold shower felt great and by the time I got back the charcoal was ready. As the steaks cooked and Dakota busied herself with the salad and potatoes, we made small talk about what Meronek could possible want from Area 51.

"I mean," she said. "Do you really think there is any 'alien' technology in that place? Surely if there were, we would be using it wouldn't we?"

"I have never known the Military Industrial Complex not to use a weapon it possessed. The only reason I can think of, would be if they did not know how to use it, or did not know how to power it."

"Yeah I can understand that or maybe that using it would be more dangerous than it was worth."

"That is possible too. There were a few scientists that feared the Atomic bomb would start a chain reaction that would destroy the planet. Fortunately, they were wrong, but it did not stop them from using it. The possibility that they have alien technology is pretty remote though. I don't say impossible—just not likely."

"You don't think that our meteoric rise in technology this past hundred years could have been due to outside influence."

"It's possible as I say, just not likely. Aliens would have nothing to gain unless they just like watching us kill each other and we have gotten pretty good at that without help."

"Yeah. No denying that I guess."

I brought in the steaks and we sat down to a good dinner after which we cuddled in front of her fireplace and watched the original 'The Day the Earth Stood Still'. Kind'a corny maybe, but it did get me to thinking about why Meronek would be so dead set on getting into Area 51. Something had to be there and Madam Blavatsky was the key to understanding what it was. Somehow, we would have to find her and for that I was certain that I would have to unravel the secrete behind Meronek and Hardcore. We talked late into the night, just kind of getting to know each other, until we both fell asleep on the Futon couch; it was the best nights sleep I had had in a long time.

CHAPTER 20

"He didn't seem to be interested in us," said Charley. "Just the woman."

Gomer 'Bittytitty' Reaux lay on her bed almost unrecognizable. Her eyes had been crushed to jelly, her tongue ripped out with pliers, shoved down her throat until she strangled on it, and just to make sure, her belly had been ripped open from one side to the other, spilling her guts out onto the bed.

"This was a revenge killing," said David. "The death of a snitch."

"Was anyone else hurt?" I asked.

"Tommy Crow Eyes was stabbed," said Jason. "It was a gut wound, but the Doc says he should recover all right. Looks like he was stabbed with some kind of military knife and whoever did it knew how to use it. If Charley had not been here to stop the bleeding, he probably would have died."

I took Charley to one side and sat him down. "What are you doing here Charley? You, Dick, and Bill were supposed to stay at the restaurant."

"Sorry Tom," he started and then took a deep breath before going on. "We wanted to help and just sitting around the restaurant was boring man. So when Jason said he was going to bring some food out here, we decided to come along."

"Okay buddy," I said looking around the room at the other faces there. "Where is Dick, I don't see him here?"

"I don't know Tom. I heard him holler that the guy was escaping out the window and he was going after him, but he was gone by the time I got up here."

"Okay Charley, take it easy. I'm sure he'll turn up okay."

I went over to Jason and asked, "What do you think Jason? Could it have been Meronek or one of his people?"

"I don't know yet little brother, but so far I have not seen any evidence of anyone breaking in. Either he was a pro or someone left the window in her room open."

I grabbed my phone and called Dakota. She was supposed to be going to the restaurant. We had a nice breakfast about six a.m. and split up after I got the call about Reaux's murder. She picked up after a couple of rings, "What's happened Tom?"

"Reaux was killed, looks like a revenge killing. Is Dick Rogers or Bill Travers there?"

"Gimme a minute to look around babe." After a couple of minutes of silence, she came back on. "Bill is here, leaning over a stack of pancakes, but I don't see Dick or his bike. Bill says he hasn't seen him or Charley since about nine last night."

"Okay hon, let me know if Dick shows up there will you?" I asked. "He went after the killer and so far no one has seen him."

"Sure Tom, will do. You be careful okay?" she said with what sounded like genuine emotion.

"I will babe. You be careful too and keep a watch out for animals okay?"

I hung up and headed for the door of the safe house to have a look around, see if I could find a trail or sign of what had happened here. With so many experienced men here, this kind of thing should not have happened, yet it had. Something here was not right and I was going to get to the bottom of it.

Jason caught me as I was headed out. "Hold up little brother, before you go messing everything up. I've got our best tracker on it already. Nobody is better than Sam Conner at reading sign."

"Okay Jason, but I want to know what he finds when he finds it. I'm going to go back to the restaurant and talk to some of the other guys. You might want to come along Jason. We've got to start looking into some new resources."

Meronek crept along careful to make no sound, sensitive to vibrations that might herald a predator. His whiskers in constant motion, sniffing the errant breeze for any changes. It would do no good to get this close and be picked off by an Eagle or desert fox.

He was close now, the fence only meters way, but the hanger still a long way off. It would have been so much easier if She had given him another crow, then he could have flown right to the building. This was just so slow, so dangerous. Squeezing through the links in the fence, a quick run through no-mans-land, and out the other side. Again, a quick look and sniff, then dashing from one piece of cover to the next, only stopping now and then as the little creature reflexively stopped to groom or toilet.

Finally, after what seemed like hours, he came to the building, and running along the wall he searched for some point of entry. Trace odors telling him that others of his kind had been here recently encouraged him to keep looking. Lights were getting brighter as he approached the front of the hanger, but still no opening. These Air Force people were really anal about keeping the buildings rodent free. Around the corner were odors of humans: sweat, leather, gun oil, and others unfamiliar to him—including the ammonia of urine, both human and canine.

The huge hanger doors looked like a possible point of entry, but up close he saw that they had a rubber seal set in a groove that made entry impossible. He might have been able to chew through them, but that would take too long. He needed to find a way in fast before—

Majestic bird, the Eagle, thought Bob.

Meronek came out of the trance with a start. "Arghh damn it," he screamed in rage.

"What is it boss?" asked Roadkill, leaning in toward him with a look of concern on his face.

"The bastard got me. I don't believe it. I was all the way there, right at the door looking for a way in, and the bastard got me."

"What bastard is that?" asked Maggott.

Meronek looked at him like he had to be even more stupid than his namesake.

"An Eagle, a freaking Eagle got me just as I was about to find a way in."

Meronek got up from his cot, grabbed a whiskey bottle, and took a swig that drained half the contents. Lighting a cigarette he walked to the entrance of the mine to sit, curse the fates, and the road that had brought him to this place.

One year in the C.Y.A. for killing a dog, what kind of crap is that? Other guys had done less time for robbery, but they were out to teach him a lesson. They had, but not the lesson they had intended. It was there that the learned how to hot-wire cars and motorcycles, rip off vending machines, pick pockets, defeat alarm systems, and in general to become Public Enemy Number 1.

It was also where he lost his virginity and learned that no one cares—not the authorities, not his family, not even God. Now he would get even no matter what it took, no matter who got hurt. He would get his and everybody else be damned.

After his release at age sixteen, he went back to his mother's house and set it on fire with her and that no good drunken bastard of a stepfather in it. He took the old asshole's '45 flathead and drove north from San Diego to Oakland where he began to hang around the outlaw gangs.

He proved himself adept at stealing bikes, guns, and cars, as well as selling drugs. He could take orders and soon proved himself reliable and loyal. He became a prospect for the Pagans when he was eighteen and killed a man for the gang a year later to earn his bones.

Nobody was ever more proud of his patch and he soon worked his way up the ladder to the office of Enforcer. It was here that he earned his reputation as a ruthless killer who did not know the meaning of mercy. He gutted a Lone Wolf biker just for flipping him off in a bar over some titty dancer. He did five years at San Quentin for that one, plus two more for beating his 'celly' to a pulp over the jack-off rights to some female news-caster on the TV.

When he got out that time, he had found a new religion: The Satanic Church of California with the reverend Antoine LeVey. Here he found a god he could relate to, one that would love him for being evil and encouraged him to lie, cheat, steal, and kill.

He was such a good disciple that he eventually came to the attention of a woman named Carmine Diablo Guzman, known to her disciples as Madame Blavatsky.

She took Meronek under her black wing and began to teach him the Dark Secrets that would make him a brujo (a male witch). He would be the instrument she would play in the Great Deception. However, after years of training Meronek had shown a fatal flaw—his drug use. She hadn't really wanted to start yet because her enemies were still too strong, but it was now, or possibly never. She knew that he was either going to O.D. or wind up in prison for the rest of his life, because he had no self-control to speak of.

Discipline had never been Steve's strong point, which was why most of the other clubs tried to avoid him. It was only because of Blavatsky's relationship with Shepherd that he would have the people he needed to carry out the operation. They were on the way and would be here soon and somehow, he would have to hook up with them without drawing the attention of the Gideon's, as he had now come to call them.

Me, Jason, and David had just gotten back to the restaurant when Dick Rogers pulled into the parking lot.

"Hey Dick," I called. "Did you find anything?"

Coming over to us he replied, "I had him in sight a couple of times but his ride was just too fast."

"Which direction was he going? What road was he on?" asked Jason.

"He was headed south-west on I-15 but I lost him at the US-93 junction."

"Okay buddy," I said, "go ahead and get something to eat and catch some rest, you look like you could use it."

"Yeah thanks," said Dick. "Too bad I couldn't catch him, what he did to that woman was awful. Nobody deserved that, not even a snitch."

We walked in and took a seat in at a booth calling out greetings to the others gathered there. I called over to James Hightower to join us since he was N.S.A. "Jim buddy," I started, "any way you can get us into Area 51 to talk with the authorities there? See if we can figure out what it is that Meronek is after?"

"I'll see what I can do Tom," he said looking very dubious, "but you know how tight-lipped and evasive these military people can be when it comes to their secret toys."

"Yeah. I know all to well, but it would really help to know if we are dealing with something real or not."

"Yeah, It would Tom," continued James. "It would also help to have some idea of what Meronek and company were trying to do you know? Are they trying to kill everybody or just make everybody into zombies, or what? If I don't know the right questions I may not get the kind of answers from them that will help."

"Okay, we'll just have to try," I said, "and at least we can let them know to beef up their security."

Dakota came in from the backroom, took a seat next to me, and asked, "Hey Tom, how's the search coming?"

"Dick lost him unfortunately. You look good this morning Dakota. How's the boiler room coming?" We were setting the back room up as an intelligence center.

"Thank you. Great. So far, we've got our computers on a secure network thanks to Bill Travers. The guy is a real genius with communications equipment; phone lines have been made secure too. The only thing we have to worry about is someone listening through the walls."

"Did he sweep for bugs by any chance?" asked James.

"No not yet. He says he will have to get some special equipment to do that. He headed out about thirty minutes ago to Boulder City to find whatever he needs."

"Okay cool," I said. "Did he take anyone with him? I don't want anyone traveling alone anymore. It's too dangerous."

"No Tom," she answered. " I believe he went alone."

"Tom's right everyone," Jason announced. "We need to move in pairs from now on. It's too dangerous since we don't know who all the bad guys are. John, any word from Jake on Shepherds people?"

At this question, Dick suddenly became very attentive and moved from the counter to a position where he could better hear what was being said.

"Yeah, heard from him about an hour ago as a matter of fact. He said Shepherd has put out a call for soldiers to all the chapters. He's looking for at least thirty or forty to come in. Hardcore doesn't want to use his own people of course, since they're his bodyguards, but Jake may get a clue to where Meronek is hiding after they start drifting in.

"By the way, they were told to drop their colors when they pass the state line to make it harder to spot them. I will be putting a couple of agents around their shop and the clubhouse to watch. Since he sees a lot of people anyway, it is going to be difficult to tell who is who. We have pictures of most of the made members though, so we should be able to pick them out without too much trouble."

"Okay good deal," I said. "Dick, Jason, David, let's saddle up and drive out to Area 51 and have a look at the terrain to see if we can spot any sign of our quarry. We'll leave in thirty minutes okay?"

Everyone signaled agreement and we broke up to take care of any business we had. Dick went outside to check his oil and gas, I went into the war-room with David, and Jason slipped into the kitchen where his wife was working to get us some food for the road.

James came into the back room as well to point out some equipment that he had just brought in. "This machine picks up cell phone signals and records the conversation. It can be programmed to pick-up on a particular number. Right now, it is set to grab any number calling Shepherd—his cell, home, business, even some of the cell numbers of his posse, which Jake was able to get us. It also traps the calling number so we will know who made the call."

"Sweet," I said. "Let me know if you catch anything important."

At that moment, Shepherd's cell phone recorded an incoming call.

"Shepherd here," he answered.

"You gotta fox in the hen house."

"Shit, who is this?"

"A friend of Carmine's," was the cryptic reply and then he hung up.

"Did you get the number?" I asked.

"Yeah," said Jim, "looks like a payphone. I'll get the address from the computer."

After a short wait he turned back to us and said, "It's from a phone at the convenience store across the road."

We tore out heading to the store, passing Dick as he was coming in, but by the time we got there the phone was empty. It was located on the side of the store that could not be seen from the restaurant.

"Look for cameras," John shouted.

There were none, which did not surprise anyone and no one in the store recalled anyone asking for change either.

"Dust it for prints David," said Jason, "maybe we can find something useful, though probably not."

David stayed with the phone to wait for the print crew and the rest of us headed to the restaurant. Inside, I found Dick and asked him if he had noticed anyone at the payphone.

"Lemme think," he replied looking a little startled. "Yeah, yeah I did. Some guy that was on a sport bike, but I wasn't' really paying attention ya know. I think it was a yellow Yamaha FZ. Looked like a new one too. He was wearing a do-rag and Joe Rocket leathers, but I didn't see his face. He was turned away from me."

"Jason if you would get that info to David and have him put out a B.O.L.O. on this guy right away, maybe we can catch him."

"Right away Tom," replied Jason, but as he walked away there was a troubled look on his sanguine face.

"Good work Dick," I said, but I also noticed something strange. Dick's face was a little flushed and there were beads of sweat on his forehead where there had been none when I walked up to him.

At least Jake wasn't working under his real name, so even if Shepherd heard it, it was not going to help him. But, it would raise suspicion and make Jake's job more difficult, as well as more dangerous. I would have to give Dick the benefit of the doubt for now because I just couldn't picture him working for the other side. He had always seemed such a straight shooter while we had been in Iraq, always starting the day with a prayer, blessing his food, always going to church. He would even go to the Muslim Mosque's and talk about his faith with their religious leaders. I just couldn't believe that he would go over to the Dark side. I would need proof beyond doubt.

The Mosque had been the most beautiful building he had ever seen. The artwork was exquisite, the designs almost mesmerizing, and the acoustics fascinating. A whisper could be heard from anywhere in the building. Dick found himself in awe of the architecture as well as the decoration. He had made it a habit to visit any Mosque he came across while in the Middle East, but this was the best one yet. While he was exploring the script on the walls, he suddenly heard his name being whispered, but from where he could not tell. There was no one else in the building that he could see, so he began to walk around looking for the source.

"What do you seek here young man?" asked a man dressed as an Imam.

"I seek what all men seek," Dick replied. "Truth and the will of God."

"A good answer," the man returned. "Those who seek God are blessed to find him."

"Yes, but how does a man know when he has found God?"

"You ask rightly young man. What is your name?"

"Dick Rogers sir and may I ask your name?"

"Of course, Mohammed Al Zia. I am the Imam here. It is my pleasure to meet you. I have not had opportunity to speak with many of the Americans here. I get so little chance to practice my English. I hope I am not too, how you say—rusty? You are Army?"

"No sir," replied Dick as he puffed out his chest with pride, "1st division, Marines sir."

"Excellent, please come into my office, refresh yourself, and we can discuss the path to understanding God."

As Dick entered the Imam's office the level of luxury there impressed him. On the floor were thick oriental rugs spread about with barely a spot of floor showing. On the walls were colorful rich tapestries with intricate Damask patterns worked into them. Arranged on shelves were books, lots of books, all written in Arabic and containing beautiful illuminations. On a low table, there was a bowel with fruit and nuts of all kinds, as well as a separate bowel filled with sweet dates, a favorite of the Arabic people.

In sconces along the walls, the sweet smoke of incense curled toward the ornately finished ceiling. He settled himself onto the plush cushions in front of the table, while Zia filled two cups with coffee and, setting one in front of Dick, took a seat for himself.

"Where do you come from in America, if I may ask?" Zia said as he offered the bowels of fruit and nuts to Dick.

"I come from Dallas, Texas sir," Dick replied.

"Ah, yes," Zia replied, seeming impressed. "The Wild West, yes? Cowboys and Indians?"

Dick chuckled a bit and replied, "Well, yes. But there haven't been any real cowboys and Indians for many years sir. We still have ranches and there are Indians on reservations, but we have been at peace with each other for a hundred years."

Dick tried some of the Dates and found them to be very good; sweet like prunes, but with a nicer texture.

"These are very good Zia," remarked Dick. "What are they? I don't think I've ever had them before."

"These are our most sacred fruit of Islam, the Date. They have been a staple of our diet since Allah created the world."

They sat talking about God, drinking the thick, sweet coffee, and eating from the bowels for about an hour when Dick started to feel kind of dizzy. He struggled to his feet and turned toward the door as Mohammed Zia sat looking at him with the eyes of a snake. The room seemed to spin around him and then he was falling, falling, into a dark and endless chasm without limit.

Then a voice calling him, guiding him, pulling him up to a place of light, a place of substance. A face appeared with the voice, the grateful touch of a hand, warm on his flesh, real, so very real. The face so handsome, the face of a god, perhaps the face of God? Long black hair, soft brown eyes, clear skin, flawless, lips formed into a loving smile. He tried to speak, but could only utter noises like a suckling child who had not yet learned to command his tongue.

"Be silent my son," the face spoke in a voice that was as smooth as oil and sweet as saccharine. "You have sought me and now you have found me. Listen as I tell you what will be."

He woke up sometime later, with his head still feeling somewhat fuzzy, to find himself sitting in an Iraqi gypsy cab just outside the Marine camp. The driver told him that Zia had paid for the cab ride and he should go now—Imshi—quickly. The sun was just beginning to come up and, not wanting to be late for reveille, Dick jumped out and hurried to his quarters. He wondered what had happened to him to forget the events of the night and it was only later that he became aware of what had transpired—it was only then that he remembered the face of his god.

CHAPTER 21

Hardcore hung up his cell phone and looked around the shop. His Enforcer, Carl 'Gunner' Foxworth, was sitting in the office drinking his preferred beer, Coors, and watching his favorite educational TV show; a re-run of COPS. An Enforcer did not have to be the sharpest knife in the rack, he just had to be able to follow orders and T.C.B.(take care of business).

"Hey Gunner," he shouted, "Get over here."

"Yeah Hardcore, what's up?"

"Just got a call from Blavatsky's inside man. He says we got a snitch. Any idea who it could be?"

"No way boss," came the immediate reply. "Everybody's been checked out from A to Z man. If we got a snitch, then he's really in deep."

"Yeah. Okay, we'll just have to keep everybody on a short leash. No phone calls alone from now on and everybody moves into the clubhouse until further notice. This guy could be wrong, he didn't tell me how he came across the info. Could be they've got some tracing equipment on our phones. Break out some of those throwaway cells and give everybody one of them. Take a look at their cell phone records too. Might turn up some clues. You know what to do."

"Okay boss, I'll get right on it."

Shepherd went into his office and cut off the TV. He was nearly sixty years old, would be in another month, graying red hair, gray eyes people called intense, five-ten, and sixty-eight kilo's. He was proud of his physique, the trim waistline at only thirty-four inch's, the body of a much younger man.

Too bad She thought he was over the hill just because he had had throat cancer. He was still twice the man that punk Meronek was, or ever would be. What did She see in him anyway? The whole project was doomed to fail because of him and She just couldn't accept it. Well, it wasn't his problem. At least he wasn't going down, even if she did.

He remembered the first time he had met her, he had been a L.R.P. (Long Range Patrol) in the Nam and had found an old Buddhist temple, long abandoned, after his squad had been shot up in an ambush. It had been a good place to hide, except that he was bitten by something, and it was too dark to see what it had been.

After maybe thirty minutes, he had started seeing things; hallucinating as though he were on Acid. He had found himself sitting next to a pond, just like he had known back home when he was a kid back in Idaho. Out of the water came the most beautiful woman he had ever seen. She was five-two, Raven black hair, high cheekbones, and emerald green eyes. She was nude from the waist up and had the high firm breasts of all those girls he had stared at in his dad's girlie magazines.

She had triggered an immediate reaction in his pants that was painful in its intensity and want of attention. When she spoke, the words had come out like birdsong, floating to his ears with the fragrance of Lavender. He was struck as though by lightning, straight to his heart. He knew he was in love and no other woman would ever be good enough; would ever be able to satisfy him with the promise of her love.

"Come to me my love," she cooed like a dove. "I will be yours if you will give yourself to me with all your heart and soul. You must never put another before me, for if you do, we will never be together."

"What do you want from me?" he asked.

"Serve me and no other. I am the goddess Hazaef and I will be your protector and consort in return. I will ask you someday to do something for me. If you are faithful, I will make you wealthy and powerful beyond your wildest dreams."

"I will do as you say and I will serve no other."

In the morning, he woke with soreness in his left leg where he had been bitten, and a sticky wetness in his pants, which, as it would turn out, was as much love as he would ever receive from her.

After returning to the World he joined The Devils Angels, eventually working his way up to club President and serving Carmine the witch, when and where She had asked. He grew wealthy and enjoyed great power within the gang world, only to see it all come crashing down when the government hit him under the R.I.C.O.(Racketeer Influenced and Corrupt Organizations) Act.

After spending most of his fortune on lawyers defending himself, losing his business, his home, and finally his freedom, he found himself in Leavenworth doing ten years flat and after that, five more at San Quentin on a state narcotics charge. That is where he met Steven 'Handlebar' Meronek.

At the time, Meronek was coming up in the gang world as president of his Northern California Pagan chapter. He had been good at following orders, but there was a flaw in his character that made him dangerous.

He had been raped in the C.Y.A. when he was fifteen and had a way of being extremely violent around the Mary Ann's in the unit. He would beat them down, then rape them, even though most would have been willing to have sex with him for the asking. It was the same with the new 'fish' that would come in. The younger they were, the more likely they would get a shower visit from Meronek.

Shepherd had tried to intervene, trying to keep Meronek's violence under control, telling him that, one day, he would either catch more time for assault or get shanked. He wanted Meronek to join him, since he showed a lot of potential as a moneymaker for his club, but he would have to learn to control himself.

Some new 'fish' he had raped came after him one day on the rec yard and shanked him a dozen times before the guards could pull him off. Meronek was a changed man after that; quieter and more withdrawn. When he finished his time, he went back out as an affiliate of Shepherds club.

Shepherd himself got out a year later in '87, older and wiser, and more importantly, with a new game plan. From then on, he ran the gang more like a business, diversifying the gangs into new territories. Improving their image with toy runs at Christmas and chipping in with community efforts. It was good press and drew attention away from their real money making activities—gun-running, drugs, and prostitution.

He was careful enough to make sure none of it touched him and he grew stronger through the '90's, his wealth increased, and then came the real bitch—Cancer.

His larynx was removed and he underwent radiation and chemo to the point that he was ready to die, just to get it over with. He found that wasn't the worst of it either. After all the treatments and follow up therapy, he couldn't get it up anymore.

And where had She been all that time? Cheating on him with Meronek. Now he could only hope that he would have her in Hell, where they both belonged.

He knew that he would have to get in contact with her now and see if She could sniff out the snitch. If not, the whole operation would be in jeopardy. It was time to take things up to the next level.

We were still going to ride out to Area 51, but first, I went to Jason and asked what his tracker, Sam Conner, had turned up at the safe house.

"Little brother," Jason answered. "He could find no other sign than those left by Dick Rogers and others at the house. No sign of a sport bike either."

"Thanks Jason," I said. "It doesn't sound good for Dick. I don't want to believe it, not from him."

"True little brother, but maybe we can test him. Give out some Intel and see if the bad guys get it. Make sure that only Dick hears it and in the meantime, keep him out of the loop on anything important."

"Yeah. Sounds good. We keep him on a tight leash for the time being. He doesn't travel alone until we are ready and see what happens. Keep it casual though, so we don't raise his suspicions."

David, Jason, John, Charley, Dick, and I got on our bikes with Dakota, James, Peter, and Simon following in Jason's van and headed out to the empty stretch of desert known as Area 51.

The drive there gave me time to think back over the past few days and especially to think about Dakota. A man could do a lot worse than her. She was about everything you could want; good looks, agreeable personality, and a Godly woman too. I found myself thinking of her in a way that was different from when I first met her. I wasn't looking at her with lust now, but as a companion and friend. I would just have to hope she did not become a distraction.

We approached the base by what most of the U.F.O. people would consider the main road. As we came to within about a quarter klick of the gate, we could see a dust cloud announcing the approach of a roving patrol, which would normally provide a firm escort out of the area. David, Jason, me, and the van went on in toward the gate as we wanted to talk to the M.P.'s at the guardhouse. We had only gone about halfway when the Hummer full of M.P.'s intercepted us. I let James talk to them and explain our presence.

I asked the Sergeant, a burly dark haired Irishman, by the name of O'Rilley, if he had seen any unusual activity in the past few days, or spotted any dead animals around the perimeter fence. He told us he could not say anything without the permission of his commanding officer. Jim looked him square in the eye and, showing him his N.S.A. badge, told him to get his C.O. on the phone and get permission, or find himself patrolling the airstrip on Guam for Seagulls, because this was a matter of National Security.

After a short conference on the radiophone, O'Rilley let us know that two of us could ride with him to see the commander. The others stayed at the gate entry while Jim and I waited for an escort to the commandant's office.

We did not have to wait long. A large black Government Issue limo arrived to pick us up, with a cute little African-American driver. She greeted us smartly and opened the door to let us in, then got into the drivers cabin and headed toward some of the smaller buildings on the base.

As we approached the hangers, the windows in the limo went black, to the point that we could not see out. Even the partition window between the driver and us.

"Sorry gentleman, but our security demands make this blackout necessary."

"Quite alright," replied Jim. "We aren't interested in a sightseeing tour anyway, only some information."

"Yes sir," the corporal returned. "We will be there in two minutes."

CHAPTER 22

We were escorted by two M.P.'s into the C.O.'s office and left in the front room with a Master Sergeant McGuire. Tall and polished, as would be expected of a Lt. General's aid, he offered us coffee and informed us that General Carter would be with us shortly.

"Come in gentleman," boomed a voice much larger than the man. The General was all of five-six, maybe sixty kilo's soaking wet, with a barrel chest, and close cropped salt and pepper hair. He looked to be in his fifty's, was in fact fifty-four, had steely grey eyes, a roman nose, and a mouth that somehow seemed too big for his face.

"Have a seat," he went on, pointing out two overstuffed leather chairs positioned in front of his desk in such a way that anyone sitting in them would be forced to look up at him—a clever, but subtle psychological advantage for the much shorter man.

"How can I be of service to the N.S.A. gentleman," he said, getting right to business.

"Sir," Jim began. "It has come to our attention that a group of individuals are planning to break into this facility for the purpose of stealing an object or objects, that they intend to use as a weapon against the citizens of this nation. At this time we do not know how they intend to get in, how many there will be, or even when they plan to do it, but it appears they will try soon. Possibly within the next two weeks."

"General Carter," I began. "These men are highly motivated and led by an individual that can only be described as an antisocial psychopath. He has already been responsible for several deaths and will stop at nothing to get what he wants."

"Gentleman," the General went on, in a tone usually reserved for foolish children caught trying to peek into a women's restroom. "I can assure you that no one is going to get into this facility unless we want them to. Our security is more than adequate to the task. A mouse can't fart out there without us knowing about it and my troops are armed and trained to handle any emergency."

"I understand and appreciate that General," said Jim. "We are only here to warn you so that it will not come as a surprise to you."

I looked around the office as the discussion went on. There were photos of aircraft now famous, such as the Lockheed SR-71, the F1-11 fighter, stealth aircraft, and experimental planes that, like the Ryan XV-5B, had not worked out.

There were a few books on shelves, but mostly award plaques and trophy's which had been bestowed upon the General—a man with a small body, but a huge ego. He was not going to take our warning seriously and we would just have to hope that Meronek and his merry band of psychopaths would not get what they were after.

"General," I interjected. "We do appreciate your time, but, if it is possible, could you tell us if anything with the potential for mass destruction is in one of those hangers?"

"Well, of course there are," he shot back. "We have aircraft and weapons here that could level entire cities."

"I understand that General," I soothed, "but we were thinking more along lines of something that would be small enough to be transported in a jeep."

The General seemed to go over an invisible inventory in his head and finally answered, "Nothing I can think of."

"Okay, General Carter," replied Jim. "Thank you for your time. We will be around the perimeter of the base for the next few days looking for these people and would appreciate any co-operation you could extend us."

"Of course," Carter replied somewhat hesitantly. "I will have my people extend all courtesy to you, but I do caution you to stay at least a quarter mile from the perimeter fence in order to avoid setting off any alarms."

"Very well General Carter," I replied. "We will be sure to comply. Thank you sir for your help."

"I will have the corporal return you to your vehicle gentleman," Carter said. "Have a good day and I hope you find these men before they do anything stupid. My men have orders to shoot to kill, if necessary you know."

"Yes sir," I replied. "I am sure they do, but let's hope it doesn't come to that."

We left and were transported back to the others where we discussed what we had learned, or more accurately, what we had not learned. We decided to break up into groups and recon the area for ten klick's in either direction, breaking off when we reached the point of no return. This probably would have been a better job for dirt bikes and A.T.V.s, but we would have to use what we had.

"Meet back here at 1800 hours," I said. "At 1830, if we have not heard from you, we will start a search. Be safe and good hunting."

We took off with the van following the road to the east, the rest of us on our bikes, heading into the western skyline. Mile after mile of sagebrush, Saguaro cactus, Joshua trees, and rocks that went on forever to a horizon that blazed with light from the descending sun. A landscape that only the desert fox and coyote could love.

At our halfway point we found ourselves on a mesa overlooking the valley floor with an unimpeded view for at least ten klick's in every direction. Except for a few Turkey buzzards and an Eagle, there was nothing moving.

Taking up some field glasses, I looked the area over for vehicle tracks, but there had been so many from U.F.O. nuts and recreation vehicles that there was no hope of picking out a trail from Meronek's bunch. Dark was approaching and we had to return to our rendezvous. We would have to find another way of locating our quarry.

✝ ✝ ✝

"You see 'um boss?" Roadkill said excitedly, "Up there on that mesa. That's gotta be them Gideon's looking fer us."

"Yeah, I see 'um," replied Handlebar. "But they don't see us. Get back in the cave and let's keep it that way."

They were getting close, but they still didn't know where to look since Blavatsky was able to hide them from prying eyes. They really needed some way to get into Kingman to hook up with Shepherd and his people. Maybe some sort of diversion would work, but now that they had killed a cop there would be to many people looking for them. The pigs would not be happy until they found them. He knew this game could not last forever, that he must make his move soon, or the plan would fail.

✝ ✝ ✝

When they got back to the restaurant, most of the group split up to go home or to their real jobs, the rest went in for dinner and updates on the day's happenings. Dakota went into the back room and I followed her, wanting to be with her even if it was just for a few minutes.

Bill was seated at the control console checking for messages and any calls that the Devils Angels may have gotten. He looked up as we entered and gave me kind of a weird little smile.

"Were you able to check for bugs around here Bill?" I asked.

"Yeah, I got what I needed at a little shop in Boulder City called Spy's-R-Us. Amazing the things you can get over the counter these days. I didn't find anything though, active or passive. 'Course they could have one of the newer types that can be turned on or off remotely. Not likely, but I'll sweep once a day just to be sure."

"Cool, cool," I said. "Any messages or numbers we should know about?"

"Surprisingly few actually," mused Bill. "It's almost like they went on alert for us."

"I believe they may have," I said. "I think we may have a Judas in the house."

"In that case they are probably using prepaid cell phones; use once, and throw away, ya know."

"Yeah," I thought for a moment. "Is there any way we can eavesdrop on them by area?"

"Yeah, it's possible," said Bill, with his brow furrowed in thought. ""Course, you wind up with a lot of conversations to sift through; hundreds per hour. It would take a lot of us to keep up."

"Yes, but Jason may be able to help us there," I thought aloud. "Lots of people here abouts that might be able to help. How much equipment would it take?"

"Quite a bit," he answered. "We could do it though, might take me a day or two to set it up. I'll get on it tomorrow."

"Great Bill," I said. "You're doing a great job. One thing though, for safety please don't travel alone anymore. Okay? Take at least one person along with you and make sure you stay together at all times. Everybody needs to stay accountable right now if you know what I mean."

"Okay Tom, any idea who the snitch might be?"

Having no proof yet, I decided to stall on the question, "No, not that I want to speculate on right now. Just be careful about what you say and to who. Okay?"

"Okay boss, will do," he said. Then, looking at Dakota and me and seeing how we looked at each other he asked, "You two want to be alone for a while? I need to get something to eat and clean up a little anyway, if you don't mind holding down the fort."

"Sure, go ahead and take your time buddy." I said in all seriousness.

After Bill had walked away, I turned to Dakota and said, "Guess you and I are becoming an item."

"Are we?" she returned. "So far, I can't tell." With that, she marched out the back door, jumped into her jeep, and headed out for her home like the Publishers Clearing house people were waiting there for her.

"What set her off?" I wondered aloud.

Jason, standing in the kitchen doorway, said, "Dakota's had some hard times Tom and she probably feels that you are taking her for granted. She has just come out of a relationship that hurt her a lot. The man took advantage of her good nature. Seems he was still married to another woman, but did not tell her. You will have to give her some time. Be patient with her, and she will come to you if it is meant to be."

"Yeah, okay," I said. "I've waited this long to find someone, I guess I can wait a little longer."

† † †

With tears streaming down her face, Dakota pulled into her driveway and threw the jeep into park. She sat for a while wondering why she even bothered with men. They were all nothing but boorish animals intent only on one thing—Sex!

She had learned that lesson early in her life at the hands of her Uncle Henry. He was her mother's brother and though he had never managed to have intercourse with her, it wasn't for lack of trying. He had been caught with her older sister who was ten at the time; she was six. She wasn't really sure what he was doing to her, but it reminded her of what she had seen the neighbor's dog doing to their dog one time out in the backyard.

She had asked her mom about that and she could still remember how red her mother's face had gotten. She told her that the neighbor's dog was just helping to scratch the fleas on their dog and for a long time after that she wouldn't go near the dog for fear of getting fleas herself.

It must have made her mother suspicious though, because she had caught Henry one night not long after that, and had used language that she had only heard her dad and his friends use when they watched football on Monday nights and drank lots of beer. She wasn't supposed to know about that, but she had sneaked downstairs one night to see what all the noise was about. She had thought they were fighting, but they were just watching the TV.

Her mom had hit Uncle Henry like she wanted to kill him and he had pulled his pants up and ran out of the house with her dad chasing him with a baseball bat. She never saw him again and her mom had told her and her sister to never let anybody do that to them again.

Later on, when she was older, about ten, she found out what it was Henry had been doing to them and she still felt dirty to this day. She went into the house and took a long bath, scrubbing herself down 'there' until she was raw and the tears finally stopped.

After, she went into the kitchen to make some dinner and found Chinese for two and a note that said, "Sorry if I hurt you Dakota. I would never do anything to hurt you. I love you, Tom."

She found herself smiling and crying at the same time as she rushed to the front door. Pulling it open, she found Tom sitting on the front porch swing with a fistful of Roses and that little-boy-lost smile that had been one of the first things that had attracted her to him.

That night, as Tom lay on the couch sleeping, he had another vision—a star filled night, hot and clammy, the odors of cordite, blood, feces, and fear on the breeze. Sounds coming from far off; a fire-fight, AK-47's, M-16's, the occasional crump of grenades, screams of men wounded and knowing they were dead.

A dream he had had many times. Running from 'it', whatever 'it' was, scared to death 'it' would catch him. Taking cover behind a wall waiting for the enemy, trying to jack a round into his weapon, but the bolt is frozen, unable to free it, icy grip of fear on his heart, groping for his sidearm, which is missing from its holster. Then a voice, "It's okay Nephew, it's only a dream."

"Bob?"

"Yes, it's me Nephew," he said. "I've come to answer some of your questions."

"You mean like where you've been all these years?"

"Yes, that and many more."

Suddenly the setting changed, a little coffee bar in downtown Baghdad, well lit, and crowded with people I didn't know, speaking words I could not hear.

"I have been honest with you Nephew, I had amnesia for several years. Missionaries who healed me introduced me to a world I never knew existed. A world of spirits, both good and bad, and ideas I had never dreamed of, like shape-shifting for one; the ability to see the world through the eyes and ears of animals.

"She does the same thing, but She can only do it with dead animals, because God will not let her use animals he has given life to. I am able to use live animals because I serve him in this war and believe me Tom—this is war."

"Okay Bob," I started. "I think I understand, but why did you shoot that R.P.G. at me in Mosul that day?"

"Because the bad guys in that room were there to kill you. They were servants of the Evil One. I was able to use a flash-bang to knock all of you off your feet, because it had already been revealed to me by the LORD that you would be in that room, at that time. I waited for you to become conscious, hoping that you would be the first, and then waited for you to spot me. I got to admit Tom, you move pretty quick for a big guy."

"What happened to the guys in the room? Did they make it out?

"I don't know Tom, I was gone by then."

"Who is the coyote anyway? I thought he was you."

"No, not me youngster," he said with a pensive look on his face. "He will let you know who he is, when he is ready. You will just have to wait for that answer."

"Okay Uncle, thanks for being honest. Now, please tell me where you have been all these years."

"Yes, I said I would didn't I. I can't tell you all the places I've been, there's just too many. But they were all places where the forces of the Devil were hard at work. I was in the Republic of the Congo, in Somalia, Chad, Afghanistan, and even a few countries in South America fighting against demonic forces. The Lord has kept me pretty busy Nephew, and now, he wants you too.

"Satan has become more active in the world than he has ever been before, and the need for holy warriors is growing as well. I did not choose to stay away because I wanted to; I stayed away in order to protect you. The Devil attacked you as soon as he realized who you are to me and I was afraid he would attack your parents too. I still fear that he will and I can only put them in God's hands for protection. I know they are both God-fearing people but, of course, that doesn't mean Satan can't hurt them. He will try but, as I say, the LORD will protect them."

"What about Meronek and company? What can they possibly be looking for in Area 51 as a weapon? Is there really some sort of alien technology there they could use or is it something man-made?"

"I'm not sure what that witch is after on the base Nephew. There are lots of weapons in that place. Experimental man-made stuff, but nothing I know of that could be alien."

"Could be She just wants everyone to think it's alien. Maybe some bio-weapon, but somehow I doubt that one myself. I guess they could have bio labs there, but no one has ever seen any evidence of it."

"Too true Nephew," he said. "But no one knew of the SR-71 until it was announced by President Reagan either. Crates of unmarked stuff go into that place every day, so anything is possible."

"Yeah, I suppose your right about that, and Carter wasn't very helpful either. I'm pretty sure he was lying to us about not having any kind of W.M.D.'s in those hangers."

"Yes Tom, he was lying about something, but 'what,' is the question."

"You were there?"

"In a way yes. I was there in the form of a dove, perched outside the General's window. After the two of you left, he called hanger ten and inquired about the contents of space number 10515. Assured that it was still there and unopened he hung up. I'm not sure whose side the General is on so be careful of him Nephew."

"I will Uncle," as I made a note of the location of the crate. "Think you could show me how to do that shape-shifting trick Uncle?"

"Jason will have to show you that Nephew, I can't."

I woke up on Dakota's couch with the sun just beginning to come up in the east like a Sunkist Orange. Another day dawning, another day in the battle against the forces of evil. I set about making breakfast for the two of us: eggs, bacon, hash browns, toast, and plenty of coffee.

I knocked on Dakota's bedroom door and called her to breakfast. She came out after a moment, took her coffee as I led her to the table, and pulled out a chair for her. She looked at the plate and table setting as she sipped some java and with tears already leaking down her cheeks she turned to me muttering, "You wonderful bastard." Then she kissed me.

Jason lay on his bed thinking back over the years, he was forty-five now, not so young anymore, but still strong, still young at heart. His wife Helen lay next to him sleeping. She had put on some weight since marrying him twenty-five years ago, but had given him two fine boys. Jason Jr., who was twenty and Gabriel who was eighteen, as well as a daughter, Ruth who was sixteen. There had been two miscarriages as well, but they tried not to dwell on those, though they had a memorial for them on their anniversaries.

He remembered back to when he had been ten years old and his seventy year old grandfather, Man Afraid of Crows, had taken him into the sweat lodge and introduced him into the spirit world. The old man had taught him all he knew about magic, shape-shifting, and the Great Spirit. How to make medicines, cast spells, and walk in the Shadow World—the world between worlds.

On his thirteenth birthday he set off on his vision quest and it was there he had first met the coyote that would become his mentor and guide. He went into the Marine Corps after graduating high school even though he had a promising career as a running-back in football. Many colleges had tried to recruit him, but coyote had told him that his destiny was in serving his country.

He was eventually sent to Afghanistan to fight the Taliban in a war that seemed to go well at first and then went downhill as those in command seemed to lose control of the situation because of in-fighting and jealousy among the tribal leaders. He had risen to the rank of Sergeant Major in command of a thirty-man advance platoon rooting out bad guys in the mountainous terrain near Pakistan.

They had just entered a small village looking for a handful of Taliban soldiers they had been chasing for two days. The village had been friendly in the past and they had no reason to expect that anything had changed. Jason had positioned his men around the central square where the public well was located and was talking to the village headman trying to get some Intel on where the bad guys were hiding.

A sudden high-pitched whistling brought shouts of 'INCOMING' as mortar fire rained down on the pastoral scene. Judging by the sound and spread of the mortars he was able to tell what direction they had been fired from and was about to give orders to advance on the position when the whole village seemed to erupt in small arms fire. The Taliban had been waiting for them and now they were surrounded.

Neither he nor his men could be called cowards, as many would prove that day. They paired up into teams and advanced on the enemy. Going house-to-house and spreading outward they took the fight to the insurgents. Jason found himself facing a heavy Soviet made machine gun which had been positioned on top of a roof and was heavily defended by small arms. The gunner was doing a lot of damage to Jason's team, several were already dead or wounded, and more would be trying to take that position.

Without thinking about it too much he slung his M-16 over his shoulder, grabbed up four grenades, two in his hand, and the other two in his flack-jacket, and charged. As he ran toward the enemy, he recited the 23rd Psalm, remembering it from his childhood days in the 'white man's' church on the rez. He did not really think of himself as a Christian, because it just seemed silly to him that one man could die and pay for everybody's sins. He did like the preacher though, as he had always been kind and patient with him, explaining as best he could how Jesus loved him just the way he was and someday would call him to service.

Just the ramblings of an old fool, his grandfather had said, but here he was about to give up his life, so his men could live. The point was lost on him at the moment though and would only come to him later.

He was hit in the right leg as he charged forward, throwing one grenade then the other until it seemed to rain blood and body parts all around him. He broke through the front door, M-16 in hand, bayonet fixed, and tore into the men inside the house.

He was wounded twice more, a stab wound in his lower right back and a gunshot wound through his left shoulder. They only served to make him angry though, as he fought now with K-bar knife in one hand and his service 9mm Beretta in the other, until no one was left to oppose him. On the roof, his last grenade took care of the gun emplacement and the half-dozen men that manned it.

His men found him on the roof, bleeding out his life, and it was only through the heroic efforts of the company medic and a quick medi-vac that he survived. He knew better though. He knew it was Jesus who had kept him alive on that roof that day, by touching his wounds and stopping the bleeding.

When the President had placed the Medal of Honor around his neck only he knew who really deserved it and ever since that day he had dedicated his life to the service of the one who died in order that he might live.

Back on the rez, he had taken up a job as a cook at Mom's, and when she decided to retire she offered him the place at a price that was just too good. With his VA small business loan he took over and had been happy ever since. Then one night the coyote came back telling him that his service was needed in a new war and to his credit he had simply said, "I am here LORD, use me as you will."

At some point, he finally drifted off to sleep, but it was not a peaceful sleep. He dreamed—

Blue sky, with big white fluffy clouds, grass covered plains dotted as far as his eyes could see with the brown humps of buffalo. Warriors in the distance were dancing and singing old songs, praising the buffalo, and the Great Spirit who brought the sacred animals to them. The wind carried the musky odor of the great beasts, its offal, birdsong, and the incessant buzzing of bottle flies dining on mounds of dung.

Beside him a voice was calling for his attention, a deep and thunderous, rasping voice. It came from a sacred White Buffalo. "My son hunt until your lodge poles are full."

"This is good, but I have no bow, no horse to hunt with," he had answered.

"You speak truly my child," and he snorted out clouds of steam from his huge nostrils. "The land is no longer as it was." Jason looked back and the buffalo were gone, the braves sang mourning songs. "But the land is forever and so am I."

"You are the Great Spirit, command me LORD."

"You speak wisely my son, you are doing well. The Enemy seeks to take what is mine and use it for a purpose it was not made for. You will be my instrument to return this sacred object to its rightful place. I have gathered my warriors together with you, trust in me, and you will have victory."

"Thank you Great Father, I will trust in you."

"There is one who will seek to harm you, he will hurt many if he is allowed to carry out his mission, but like the other son of perdition, what he means for evil will be turned to good. Continue to walk in my way and be blessed."

Waking up, Jason had the feeling that there was some one else in the room with him, but there was only his wife.

At the restaurant everyone was gathered in the booths having coffee and conversation. Tom, Dakota, Jason, and Bill were in the back room looking over the damage that had been done during the night. Someone had broken in and used a tire iron, or something similar, to completely wreck their whole setup.

"Recon our Judas is responsible for this?" asked Bill.

"Most likely," I answered. "Although it could have been one of Shepherd's people."

The back door had been jimmied open and the surveillance cameras were broken. What I hoped they didn't know was the location of the recorders.

"Let's see if the tape is still here," I said to Bill who went off to the hidey-hole in the closet. We used a separate VCR for the war-room, from the security cams for the restaurant. Only Bill and I knew about this extra precaution, so there was a good chance the culprit would be caught on tape.

Bill prized up the trap door and checked the recorder; the tape was still in place. A few minutes later we were watching as a hooded figure came in through the door and started smashing everything in the room. He finally worked his way to the closet where he removed the surveillance tapes and looked right into our hidden camera: with one blue eye and one red eye.

"What do you want to do Tom?" asked Bill.

"I invited him in and I will take care of it. We may be able to use him to give some misinformation to the bad guys, so keep quiet about this. Not a word to anyone."

"Okay Gunny," replied Bill. "We'll play it your way. Not a word to anyone."

"Right," chimed in Dakota. "Not a word. I sure hope you know what you're doing Tom."

"Me too," I agreed. I pulled the tape out of the VCR and put in it in Jason's office safe in case we needed it later, then went back out and told everyone what had happened in the back room—except about Dick, of course.

I sat down with Jason, David, and Jim to have some coffee and to discuss where we should go from here. I looked around for Dick and spotted him sitting at the far end of the counter by himself. The way he was sitting, I could not see his hands, nor could anyone else, and by the way he was looking down, I could tell he was doing something. I looked over to Jim and asked, "Is there anyway you can get me Dick's text messaging history?"

"Sure Tom, give me about an hour," he said as he pulled out his cell phone and stepped outside to make a call.

Dick got up after a few minutes, slipping his phone into his pocket as he did, then came over to join us. "What's going on?" he asked.

"Looks like somebody trashed the COM room," I replied.

"Damn, no way Tom," he protested. "Any idea who? Shepherds people I bet."

It was a nice try at misdirection. "No," I said. "They got the surveillance tapes and it's doubtful they would be stupid enough to leave fingerprints."

"How long till we get it all back up?" he asked.

"Probably take at least a couple of days," I replied, even though I knew it would be back in operation before the day was over.

"Was all the data lost?" he asked, definitely digging for information.

"Yeah," I lied. "Everything was lost."

Actually, everything was being backed up every thirty minutes at a remote P.C., over a secure line at a remote location. Satan is clever, but not particularly smart and for some reason he just won't accept that anyone can be smarter than he is. Live and learn I say!

CHAPTER 23

The general closed up his office after the civilian meddlers left announcing that he was headed home early, but he had a different destination in mind. The object in space #10515 had been brought to his attention three years ago just after an airman had accidentally discovered it. It had been buried out in the Nevada desert for, God only knew how long, or why. This object could have more impact on the modern world than anything since the A-bomb.

It would seem that someone else had discovered its existence and wanted to take it into their possession, but he could not let that happen of course. Especially since he was the only person who could truly put it to its true destiny. He arrived at hanger ten and entered by way of an electronic card key, as well as a retinal ID scan at the inner door. Then there was the armed MP behind his bulletproof enclosure that came to attention and, after receiving the day's password, let him enter the warehouse-like building.

"What is it the old man does in there anyway?" pondered the airman 2nd. "Nothing in here but a bunch of crates and boxes left over from WWII."

The general navigated the corridors of man-made canyons until finally coming to the place marked #10515. A nondescript crate measuring four feet wide, by six feet long, and four feet high and marked: U.S. GOVERNMENT—TOP SECRET—DO NOT OPEN.

Looking the crate over inch-by-inch Carter concluded that it had not been tampered with since his last visit. He pulled out a folding stadium chair that he kept hidden, opened it, dusted it off, and seated himself facing the crate. Here in the dim light surrounded by treasures of the Third Reich, breathing the stale musty air, the general made his plans of world conquest without realizing the irony.

He thought back to his boyhood days in Belton, MO. where his father had been stationed at Richards-Gebaur Air Force Base. The local boys had teased and harassed him because of his short stature and the asthma that had kept him from participating in sports, calling him a sissy, momma's boy, and worse.

He had sworn an oath to himself in those days, that when he grew up, no one would ever look down on him again. After high school he went to the Air Force Academy at Colorado Springs, graduating fourth in his class. But what he lacked academically he made up for in cunning. He got what he wanted by being the best at underhanded, below-the-table dealings, that others might have called backstabbing.

None of that mattered though, not after he had pinned on those stars. Now he had the object; the thing that would make him Master of the World. Would put him head and shoulders above all the rest and a maniacal little smile slowly extended itself across his aging, weathered face.

† † †

"Bones," shouted 'Hardcore' Shepherd. "Get in here bro."

"Yeah boss," Jake answered as he hurried to comply.

"I want you to get out to the old line shack at our property and meet the guys as they come in. Tell 'em how to find the rendezvous with Meronek and give 'em whatever they need from the armory."

"Okay boss," said Jake. "Where's he gonna be?"

Hardcore handed him a map with a set of directions and watched him go.

"Stay off your cell phone. If you gotta make a call use the CB or a throw-away."

"Right boss, will do."

Jake 'Bones' Holland could not believe his good luck. The map to where Meronek could be found had dropped right into his lap. He had to wonder if maybe this wasn't just a little too good to be true. He would have to be careful and tell the others to be careful as well.

He fired up his Big Dog and headed out to the property which was a piece of land the club owned about ten miles out of town and remote enough to keep out prying eyes. They had an old one room shack there with an underground bunker they had installed to hide their stockpile of weapons and any drugs they might be trying to move. The place reeked of reefer, speed, and X which they always had several kilo's of—each. He did not dare stop along the way or call, just in case anyone should be following him. The call to Tom would have to wait.

As he pulled up to the shack he saw somebody's hog tied up outside under the crumbling carport. Pulling his Desert Eagle .357 he approached the shack and called out, "In the shack, step out and identify yourself!"

"Hold up man, don't shoot, I'm coming out," a voice said in answer to his challenge. "Name's Maggott. I ride with Handlebar man. Who're you?"

"Bones—with Hardcore."

Maggott came out with his hands raised and stood where Bones could see him.

"What're you doing here man?" Bones asked. "You guys are supposed to be hiding out. How'd you even know about this place anyway?"

"Man, I helped put in the basement," Maggott said with a smile on his face. "I was prospecting back then with the Angels, but I got into some trouble with the law here and had to move away to the west coast. Hardcore set me up with Handlebar and I been out in California since then."

"Okay, but what're ya doing here?"

"Handlebar wanted me to pick up some hardware man."

"Yeah, sure," Bones came back. "'Cept I ain't heard nothin' 'bout it and I just left Hardcore twenty minutes ago."

"Handlebar was supposed to let Hardcore know man, I swear. Just call him man, I'm sure we can clear this up."

Bones was not feeling good about this and felt like someone was drawing a bead on him. "Get inside and keep your hands where I can see them understand? Do anything stupid and I'll put holes in you."

"Okay man, take it easy," soothed Maggott. "I just need to pick up some ammo for us. We had a shootout with the Gideons man and we need to restock, that's all."

Bones followed Maggott into the shack, looking carefully around before entering all the way, and motioned for him to have a seat. "You packing?" he asked.

"Yeah man," Maggott replied. "It ain't safe out there right now, 'specially since that bitch Bittytitty snitched us out."

"Pull the piece out and put it on the table real easy like," Bones ordered.

"Okay man, I don't want no trouble," came back Maggott as he slowly pulled out his Smith&Wesson 9mm and laid it on the table.

"Don't think your gonna have to worry about Bittytitty anymore, somebody scragged her."

"Yeah! No shit man," Maggott looked genuinely surprised. "Well, the bitch had it coming. She almost got me killed taking off like she done."

That statement pissed Jake off, tempting him to whack this dirtbag out of principle, but he restrained himself with the promise that he would make a special effort concerning him at a more appropriate time.

He went to the CB which was setting on a table in the corner and putting it on the right channel he started calling Hardcore. "Breaker, breaker. Panhead, this is Knuckles you got a copy? Over."

After repeating this a few times a voice finally came back. "Go ahead Knuckles, this is Panhead. What is your message?"

"Panhead, I got company here. Calls himself Maggott and claims to belong to an old friend. What do I do with him? Feed him or plant him?"

"Feed him, then release him," came the answer Maggott was hoping for.

"Guess this is your lucky day Maggott. You know how to get in?" Jake asked, gesturing at the entry to the bunker.

"Yeah, sure Bones. If it ain't been changed."

Maggott slipped up the board covering the hatch and Jake tossed him the key to the padlock securing it. The door opened releasing a cool gush of stale, drug-laden air, and Maggott lowered himself down the ladder flicking on the battery-powered lights as he went. Reaching the floor he stepped aside as Jake joined him in the subterranean space.

"Exactly what is it you need?"

"Handlebar wants 9mm, .45's, 7.62, some frags, claymores, and a couple of L.A.W.S. or R.P.G.'s if you got 'em."

"We got all the ammo and two L.A.W.S. rockets but no R.P.G.'s."

"Great man, that'll do."

"Just how ya gonna pack all this, you ain't even got saddlebags?" asked Jake.

"I got 'em man, I left 'em upstairs in the cabin."

"Okay, it's your problem anyway. Go into the room on the left, the stuff is in there."

Jake stood at the ladder and watched as Maggott grabbed the boxes of ammo, then carried them back out into the shack, finally un-boxing the two L.A.W.S., slinging them over his shoulder, and climbing back out. Dousing the lights, Jake followed him up out of the cool climate of the bunker and into the hundred-degree heat of the day.

Maggott grabbed up his saddlebags from behind a pile of junk in one corner and began to fill them with boxes of ammo on one side, claymores and grenades on the other.

"You better hope none of those loses a pin dude. There wouldn't be enough left of you to fill a Dixie cup."

"You got that right bro," Maggott said as he carefully wrapped the L.A.W.S. in a blanket. "Would save on the price of a casket though."

They both laughed at the gallows humor, then started for the door. Bones heard it first; the shotgun-blast of a Harley approaching the cabin. He opened the door and had a look motioning Maggott outside.

"Save me the trouble of giving him directions, you can show him the way out there."

"Yeah, sure bro, no problemo," said Maggott. "He could pack some more 9mm's too, if he's got the space."

The rider pulled up under the carport, shut down his old Knucklehead, and looked at them from a dirt encrusted, weather beaten face, that looked worse that five miles of bad Irish road.

"You gotta drink? And I don't mean no damn water," he spit out. "Call me Preacher man; outta Oakland."

"Bones," Jake responded pulling out a bottle of Jack Daniels black label from his saddlebag and handing it over to the new arrival. Preacher took it, twisted the top off, and draining half the fifth in one swallow. Belching, he lit up a Marlboro, and asked, "Where the Hell are we anyway? This looks like the backside of the world's asshole."

Bones laughed a bit at the joke, took a swig of the whiskey, and passed it to Maggott who drained the last of it.

"Not far from it man," Bones replied. "We're about ten miles from Kingman. This guy will take you the rest of the way; names Maggott."

"Cool," said Preacher. "Got some water here so's I can wash my face a little?"

"Yeah," replied Jake. "There's an old pump in the back. I'll prime it for you"

As they walked back toward the pump, Maggott finished tying his saddlebags and the bundle of L.A.W.S rockets to his bike.

"Any others coming with you or you come alone man?"

"We split up before crossing the state line. Some of us was gonna drive straight through, others stopping for the night, so's we don't all show up at once, ya know. They should be coming in over the next few hours though. I drove straight through the shortest way to make sure everything was cool. I'll go with Maggott and see what's up with Handlebar."

"Cool, I'm supposed to stay here and direct the others as they come in. Can you carry some ammo? Got weapons if you need 'em too."

"Let's go shopping, man."

"Just got a message from Jake," said John Little Bear taking Tom to one side. "He's got the location of Meronek's hideout and a heads up on the replacements coming in."

"Great John, fill me in."

John relayed the message ending with, "He doesn't know how many yet, as they are straggling in a few at a time. He says that as soon as he has an accurate count he will let us know."

"Cool, stay on it and don't let Dick know anything. Okay?"

"Right."

Grabbing Jason I took him to the kitchen, told him about the reserves coming in, and asked if he knew the location of Meronek's hidey-hole.

"I know the place, yes," Jason said. "It is a good location to hide; good visibility, plenty of escape routes, and close to the base. It will be very hard to sneak up on him there."

"We could just sit and wait for awhile I suppose. If they try to break into the base, they'll get their butts kicked."

"Yeah, I've been considering that myself. They will need a diversion of some kind. They aren't ready yet and we aren't either. By the way, you know what they're calling us?" asked Jason.

"No, what?" expecting something vulgar.

"Meronek's calling us Gideons."

"Gideons huh," I said turning the name over in my mind. "I like it. Maybe we could make up some patches. I'll bring it up to the others and see what they think."

Of course, we couldn't call ourselves 'The Gideons,' as that title was already taken, so I talked it over with the group that evening and Dakota suggested, 'Gideon's Warriors'.

Everyone seemed to like the ring of that and Dakota volunteered to work up some kind of design, with the help of other ladies, and make us some patches. In protest against the outlaw patches, I told them to make it a one-piece patch with no rockers, except maybe a specialty rocker for a particular ministry. I guess you could say we were officially a motorcycle gang now.

CHAPTER 24

Meronek looked over the replacements standing around the camp. Most were the real dregs of society; hardcore outlaws with the scars and prison tattoo's to prove it. Most would kill somebody just for the fun of it, having no conscious or empathy for others or any need for such weaknesses.

They were true psychopaths with nothing to live for but the pleasure of the moment. They were his kind of people and he actually felt a tear of pride well up in his eye at the thought of leading these men into the final battle between those who rightfully should rule the world and the mud races that would serve them.

The new hideout was located in a blind canyon about three miles from the northeast gate of the base. This had been chosen because it was the weakest point in the facilities security. The gate was locked and abandoned, but still had a dirt road running through it. It had no pressure sensors in it and the vibration detectors were too far away to pick up their motorcycles.

This was the key to his plan. A Goldwing with a sidecar would be used to haul away the prize and the other bikes would be used to provide armed backup. The crew would consist of thirty bikes going in, dropping five or ten at a time, to hold the trail and provide any extra firepower they might need as they retreated.

He had also secured two high-powered ultra-lights that were rigged with .30 caliber mini-guns, as well as a box of grenades. He hoped these planes would be small enough to escape notice on radar by flying low to the desert floor and hopping up only long enough to harass any forces that were in close pursuit.

Another group of riders were being led in by Maggott and were directed to where to park their machines. This brought the total to forty, including his own group. He felt this was an auspicious number, going back to the story of Ali Babba and his forty thieves; not too many to command or too few to carry out the mission.

He set Deadman and Roadkill to work mounting M-60 machine guns to the handlebars of the bikes, as well as trailers that had mortars mounted in them. He also had the bikers install baffles in their pipes to make them quiet as possible and switches to turn off their lights if they weren't already so equipped.

It would take a few days to get everything ready and the plan drilled into everybody's heads, but at least he had people who knew how to use the weapons since all of them were military vets, so no training would be needed there. He just hoped that they would be able to work as a team and not go off on their own.

They would have to be ready in three days, as that would be the time for a lunar eclipse. It would be pitch black out there and they would have to depend on their infrared and night vision equipment, but so would the wing-nuts. That would give him enough time, he hoped, to make one last contact with Blavatsky to make sure there were no changes in the plan. He also hoped that She would have the exact location of the artifact by then. It would take too long to find it without the location number and even with the number, it could take too long. What they needed was somebody that knew where it was, to lead them to it, and that was Blavatsky's job.

Hopefully, the Gideon's and that damn Tom 'goody-two-shoes' Harper would not be able to interfere this time. They had cost him more that he had planed the first time around. They had proven tougher than he had thought a bunch of Jesus freaks would be. Well, if they tried to attack him here they wouldn't stand a chance. The entry to the canyon was too narrow and all he would have to do is pick them off one at a time if they tried to enter.

Now was the time to dream of glories to come.

Warm Sun on his back, the whistling of air past his ears, the glorious feeling of freedom in flight, eyes sharp on the ground able to pick out a field mouse from a thousand feet. Able as well to spot forty people working on motorcycles and stinking up the air with tobacco, drugs, and wood smoke. These fools weren't trying very hard to hide themselves, even a blind cub scout could find them.

He would have to release himself and report to the others what he had seen.

Jason came over to me that evening and said, "Tonight little brother, you must come with me and be initiated into the sweat lodge."

I could tell by the serious tone in his voice that this was important, but I had a date with Dakota and a T-bone steak. "Could it wait until after dinner?" I asked, looking to Dakota for help.

"No Tom," she said in way that precluded any argument. "The sweat lodge ceremony is not offered to just anyone. Dinner can wait. You go with Jason and I'll keep working here on the patch with the other ladies."

Having been duly dismissed I got up and followed Jason out to the parking lot.

"Is this going to hurt?" I asked as innocently as possible.

"A little less than a sharp stick in the eye," he answered laughing.

We got into his van and headed out toward his house, but we went past it and all the barking dogs to a place as lonely as a hooker's heart. There were two young men tending a fire; Jason's sons, Gabriel and Jason Jr. Beside them was a structure that looked like a transient's tent. It was about four feet high and just big enough to hold three or four people if they were real friendly with each other. There was a hole in the ground for a fire pit with a pail of water next to it and another hole in the roof for smoke to get out.

Jason handed me some shorts and said, "Put these on little brother, it will be hot inside the lodge and everything your wearing will be soaked with sweat."

"This isn't going to involve any kind of drugs is it?" I asked.

"No, not this time," he said with a mischievous twinkle in his eye. "This ceremony will help you to see who you really are. Next time, if it is necessary, we might use sacred Peyote to release your spirit, so you can see the spirit world as it is, but only if you are not able to do it without help."

I stepped around the backside of the lodge and began to undress, saying that it was not out of modesty, but that I did not wish to blind anyone with the sun reflecting off my pale skin. The boys laughed a bit speaking in their native tongue as I came around in the shorts and ducked into the lodge where Jason was already sitting.

"What are they saying?" I asked Jason. "Hopefully, manly comments about my finely sculptured masculine form."

"No," Jason answered laughing. "They say you look like the fish who float belly up in the stream."

"Oh," I said. "Well, as long as they are manly fish it's okay."

"Boys," Jason called out holding up the flap of the lodge door, "bring in the rocks."

They brought in four melon size rocks cradled in forked sticks that had pouches made from leather strings and dropped them into the depression in the ground. In all seriousness I looked at him and said, "I hope you're not going to pour water on those. It is already too hot in here as it is."

"'Fraid so little brother," he smiled at me. "That is how a sweat lodge works."

"Okay then brother, I will try to get serious," I said.

Jason began to speak in his native tongue and after a few moments he began chanting in a repetitive tone. He poured water from the bucket onto the rocks causing great plumes of steam to rise up and spread across the top of the lodge. It caused my eyes to film over and the sudden hot moisture made it difficult for me to breath for a moment.

After five minutes I was ready to get out, but Jason was still chanting and showed no sign of allowing me to leave. Sweat was soon dripping off my face in minor cataracts and I was definitely feeling the onset of claustrophobia. The lodge was too small and getting smaller as I sat there.

Jason began to burn some powder that he produced from a bag around his neck in a bowel shaped rock that had some coals nestled in it.

The smoke rising from it had a slightly sweet pine odor to it which tickled the back of his nose making him feel like he needed to sneeze. So he did—several times. He began to feel like he was outside of himself looking in. He became lighter, rising with the smoke and gently bouncing against the roof of the lodge. All the while, Jason kept chanting, but now he began to understand the words:

"Great Spirit,
Guide us in our quest,
Protect us from the Evil One,
Guide us into all your mysteries,
Deliver us from all harm,
Forgive us for our foolishness,
Give us wisdom from on high,
Put our enemies at our feet,
Victory is yours Great Father,
Let us be your instrument,
You are perfect in all your ways,
Give us victory Great Spirit."

This song was repeated over and over and then Tom saw the coyote sitting across from him in the lodge staring at him with a big grin on his face. He began to speak to Tom, but he heard the words in his mind not his ears.

"You have done well Tom. You have learned a new secret."

"What secret is that Coyote?" he asked.

"The secret of flying," he replied.

He suddenly found himself soaring hundreds of feet above the desert floor with an Eagle flying next to him and following Coyote, who was following on the ground. Looking around himself, he saw his own wings and feathers. He was an Eagle too! For about twenty minutes he flew, enjoying his new found freedom, and then found himself back in the sweat lodge. Cold water was running down his face and chest and the shock of it was like being born again.

He looked at Jason, who was smiling and asked, "You alright little brother?"

"Yeah," I gasped out. "What just happened? I could swear I was an Eagle flying through the sky."

"You were Tom. You have just been given the ability to shape-shift."

"Wow!" I exclaimed. It had been a strange experience and I had felt as though I had been observing things in third person, but now I was back to myself feeling first person again.

"This calls for a new name Tom, it is part of the sweat lodge ceremony. Your new name will be 'Warrior With Big Heart.' Guard this name carefully, do not let just anyone know it, especially the Evil One, or it will give him power over you."

"Okay Jason, I will guard it with my life," I said in all seriousness. "Can we get out now, I'm feeling kind of faint."

Jason opened the flap of the lodge and motioned me to leave first. The temperature was still about eighty-five degrees, but it felt like stepping into a meat-cooler.

The boys slipped up behind me and dumped an Igloo cooler of cold water over me and I swear, if my heart had not jumped out of my chest and lay quivering on the ground I would have beaten the both of them to cat food. I felt much better though after seeing Jason get the same treatment.

Dakota and the ladies had come up with what they felt were a few good designs, laying them out to be inspected by Tom and the others when they returned from the sweat lodge ceremony.

Helen Walks Far, Jason's wife, was helping Dakota and suddenly asked her, "Do you love him Chica?"

It was such a blunt question that, for a moment, she wasn't sure she had heard correctly. "Love who Helen?" was the best she could manage and knew that even as she said it, it sounded totally lame.

"You know who I mean Dakota. The man you spend all your time thinking about. Your face lights up every time he walks into the room and the light goes out when he leaves. I see the worry in your eyes even now, though he has only gone to the sweat lodge ceremony. You are afraid to let your heart go little one. I see the same thing in his eyes too, you know. Do not let fear cripple your heart, he loves you, but he is afraid that you will not love him back. Open your heart to him, do not let him go without letting him know how you feel."

Dakota felt embarrassed. Were her emotions so visible and was her heart so transparent? She suddenly felt like everyone in town could see all that she was feeling. She felt like running and hiding, felt panic creep into her belly.

"Little sister," Helen was talking again. "I only say this because I felt the same way for Jason. This is a thing only a woman can know. Let him know you care for him, but not all at once. Just enough that he will not feel discouraged. I can see it in his eyes little sister, he will be a great man of God and he has his heart set on you."

Dakota knew that Helen was right, but it was still hard for her to let herself go. She had loved Ricky so much and he had turned out to be such a rat. He had used her and abused her and then left her like she was yesterday's newspaper. Thinking back on it now she wondered why she felt as she had. He was handsome and rugged in an outdoors way, smooth with his words, always making her feel like she was the only woman on earth. He was a perfect pimp she thought. Why had she not been able to see that back then?

She looked down again at the patch designs and it came to her that this was going to be war and some would not be coming home. The thought put an icy hand on her heart and she suddenly knew that time wasted would never come back to her. She would have to love him now; there might not be a later.

With darkness, the party really began to take off. They were smoking, shooting, and snorting every kind of chemical they had in their inventory. By midnight, most of them were so wasted they couldn't find the ground to pass out on.

Handlebar was riding a meth high, tempered with a good shot of morphine, and at least a fifth of whiskey. He was looking for Blavatsky and the key to Area 51, if she had found it yet. As he passed into insensibility, he felt himself tumbling into the void of the bottomless pit. Then—-

CHAPTER 25

She was sitting on her porch, sun shining on honey-dipped hair, looking as though time stood still just for her. She had not aged a day since he had known her, probably not since Hardcore had met her, or ever would. She was outside of time, like Helen of Troy, or some ancient Greek goddess.

He approached her, stopping at the invisible line in front of the steps to her porch, the line he was not allowed to cross without paying with his life. Sometimes he thought of crossing that line and taking her by force, relieving himself of the terrible aching want that her presence seemed to create in him, but he always stopped short. The fear was ultimately greater than the desire.

He knelt down before her in a position of submission, swearing his fealty to her and her master. "Drink of my blood and spirit Mistress and Master, make of me a sacrifice."

This done, he waited for her to accept his allegiance.

"Rise unworthy worm and state your pathetic request."

She always talked like that just to cover up how much she really wanted him. "Mistress," he started, looking up at her. "We must know the exact location of the artifact. The warehouse hanger is over a hundred thousand square feet. It would take days or weeks to locate the object, especially if it is boxed and unmarked. There are thousands of boxes in there Madam."

"You dare to educate me worm!" she fairly screeched and, for just a moment, the scene seemed to shift. She looked like an old hag from a B-horror movie, then it snapped back, but left a distinct odor of brimstone in his nostrils.

"No Madame," he whined falling on his face in fear and nearly soiling his pants. "I only wish to succeed, but it will be impossible without knowing where to look."

The trouble was, she knew he was right, but none of her servants had been able to locate the box among all the other boxes. That was why she had not moved before this time. It seemed that the base commander was the only one who possessed this information and she had not been able to tempt him with any of her tricks.

He seemed uninterested in sex of any kind, was not greedy, and in fact seemed honest to a fault. He had no interests outside of his job that she could find. He seldom left the base and then only to buy items that he could not get at the post exchange, which consisted of a certain brand of cognac. Since there was no definite schedule for this, she had not been able to put anyone on him.

However, it had been over a month now since he ventured into town. "The base commander loves his brandy and has to leave the base to get it. Be ready to grab him and he will give you your answer," with that, she dismissed him from her presence. "Leave me worm and do not return until you bring me word of success."

"Yes Madam," he mewled and left her sitting on her throne feeling once again, as though his soul had just been tarred and feathered.

He was also disturbed by the memory of that moment in which he had seen an entirely different vision of her. Could she be other than she seemed? Her beauty only the result of some spell cast over him? Maybe he could keep the object for himself and serve the master directly. Then, she would have no choice but to bow down to him. Then who would be the worm, bitch! After these thoughts, he drifted off into unconscious sleep, brought on by chemical excess.

Jason and I returned to his house, where we cleaned up and headed back into town to the restaurant. We both felt the need to check in and see what events had taken place in our absence. I was especially anxious to speak with Bob, if I could find him.

As we pulled into the parking lot, I saw an old '49 Chief parked in the back. I don't know how I knew, but I said, "Bob's here, I see his ride."

Jason looked at me with that little smile that said, 'you're learning.' "You're picking up on things much more clearly now brother. You are learning to listen to the spirit when it speaks. That is good, many times that ability has saved my life, yours too, though you did not know it then."

We walked in through the back door and found Bob, Bill, and Dakota drinking coffee and working on installing some of the replacement equipment.

Dakota gave us a smile that rivaled the sun in beauty and brightness and asked if we wanted coffee. We both did and she went out to the kitchen to get us some cups.

"How's it coming Bill?" I asked.

"Pretty good Tom. I got all but a few things replaced and working. We should be totally back up in an hour. John is in the dining room and says he needs to see you ASAP, okay?"

"Sure, thanks Bill. You're doing a great job here. I'm going to recommend you for a raise and a new office chair."

"Gee, thanks boss, but I was hoping for a new coffee mug with the girl that strips as you drink your java."

"Dream on McDuff, but I'll see what I can do."

Dakota came in with our coffee, giving us each a cup and, looking up at me, she said, "You look different, did you shave?"

"Ha, ha," I came back. "I thought you would never notice."

Then without thinking about it I kissed her, not on the cheek as I had been doing, but on her luscious, firm red lips. I felt her press back and knew that we had just passed through some invisible barrier.

"Thanks for the coffee and the sugar," I said.

Her face went a bit red, but then I felt mine warm up a bit too.

"I,I,I, better call John in," I stuttered, which is not something I usually do.

I opened the door and called John over and as luck would have it, Dick came over as well. I could not let him in and I could not appear to push him away either. Jason breezed by me taking Dick by the arm and led him off with a story about taking a ride out to town to find some batteries for our laptops.

John came in and pulled out a memory stick which he handed over to Bill saying, "This is Dick's messaging history for the past month and his banking records for the past two years. I hate to say it, but there is a lot here that is very suspicious."

"This confirms our reservations John. Maybe this stuff will give us a clue to who Dick is working for."

"If we give him something big he might try to take it to the top," remarked Dakota. "You know, something that might get him a big reward."

"That's my girl," I said, pulling her to me and giving her a hug. "Brilliant! All we have to do then is find some piece of the puzzle that they need."

"I know what they need," piped up Bob. "And it would be big enough to tempt Dick to go to Blavatsky."

"Okay Uncle," I said. "Spill it. What do they need?"

"The location of the object they are looking for. That warehouse has over thirty thousand objects in it and none of them are marked, except for a location and serial number. It would take them years by trial and error."

"How do you know what it is Bob?" asked Jason.

"I don't my friend," replied Bob, with a twinkle in his eye. "But the general does. He goes there at least once a week and spends an hour or more inside the hanger. He knows what it is, but he isn't telling anyone and he has destroyed all record of the item."

"So, he is the only one who knows where it is," I surmised.

"Right Nephew. That makes him a target for Meronek and Blavatsky."

"Yes," stated Jason. "A prime target for kidnapping if he leaves the base. We will have to let this information leak out to Dick in a way that will not raise his suspicion."

"Agreed," I said. "Any ideas?"

"At least one," stated Bob. "We need to warn the general that he is in danger."

"Yeah," I returned. "Can you do that John? It would be best coming from you."

"You bet Tom, I'll get on it right now."

"Wait a minute John," Bob cautioned. "Let's brainstorm this first. Okay?"

We all went silent, as we thought how to carry this off. Finally, Bill spoke up, "We could leave it as a message on Dick's cell phone. Make it look like it came from somebody he knows."

"Okay, but who?" I said. "It would have to be somebody he would not be able to confirm. Let's have a look at those messages Bill. John, while we're doing this you go ahead and call the general."

John stepped out and the rest of us started scrolling through Dick's messages. After a while we noticed one messenger that he never replied too and judging from the content of those messages, it had to be someone of authority. They were signed C.D.G. and did not have a return Internet Protocol address.

"That's impossible," Bill remarked looking closer. "You can't send a message without an I.P. address, the server won't let you."

"There is one way," Bob answered. "But it would take supernatural power. That is probably Blavatsky and the letters C.D.G. are probably from her real name."

"Okay," I said. "I'll schedule Dick to take a watch in here this afternoon, say from 1600 to 2000 hours. Will that give you enough time to set it up?"

"Yeah Tom," replied Bill. "That will be plenty of time. I will use our server to direct-cast into his phone while he is in here. He will think it came from her because there will be no I.P. address and it will give him the opportunity to get a hold of Meronek as well."

"Okay great. I'll let him know in a minute. I got something else to take care of right now."

I took Dakota by the hand and led her into the kitchen where I kissed her very deliberately on the lips. Not like a brother either!

Dick jumped at the chance to stand a watch, even though he acted like it would be a boring waste of time. Somehow, he had become transparent to me, as though some veil had been pulled away from my eyes. I did not really like doing this, so I excused myself as soon as possible and went over to where the ladies had gathered with their patch designs. As I walked up I admonished them, "Don't tell me whose is whose, I want to pick the best one on its own merit."

All of them were very nice, but one in particular caught my eye. It had a large crucifix with a Bible and two swords behind it with the words 'Gideon's Warriors' as a border around them. Names would go at the top on a separate rocker. The Bible was black, of course, the cross white, the swords silver with brown grips, and the letters were in light blue against a background of yellow.

To be fair, I got everyone to check out the designs and then we took a vote. After counting the votes the one I had liked won and I asked whose design it had been. Helen stepped forward and said, "Dakota and I put it together."

"Very nice Helen, you and Dakota did a really great job."

Helen looked up at me smiling and said, "I chose the colors, but Dakota did most of the design. She said she saw it in a dream."

I looked over at Dakota and saw her standing over in the corner looking nervous as a schoolgirl at her first dance. I went to her, took her hand, and gave her a P.D.A. (Public Display of

Affection) by kissing her in front of everyone. I felt her struggle as though to pull away, but I just pulled her closer to me until I felt all struggle cease. I knew at that moment we would spend the rest of our lives together, no matter what else happened.

Letting her go, I said, "Your design is inspired, I really like it. I will wear it proudly."

For some silly reason, tears were running down her cheeks again, and I reached up wiping them away, as she reached up to wipe away mine.

Meronek got the text message from Hardcore:

> ...mdm says look in section twenty, serial number 23204 for package...

This was the news he had been waiting for and he turned to his group of misfits to address them.

"Listen up you crow-bait sons of three-fingered whores," he shouted. "We go tonight, so make sure everything is ready. It is now one o'clock, we will go at eight tonight. No more booze as of right now. I catch anyone drinking, shooting, or popping anything but aspirin, I will shoot your dumb-ass right on the spot. Deadman get over here, pronto."

As everyone bust into cheers Meronek took Deadman to one side to give him some special instructions. "I want you to lead this operation bro. I will have to stay here and direct the diversion that will take care of their air defenses and keep them occupied while you and the others grab the artifact. Try not to screw this up, that bitch Blavatsky will have our balls in a blender if this don't work."

"Okay Handlebar, you got it. I don't see a problem. These guys are all pro's man, I would have no problem taking out the President himself with this crew."

Meronek retreated into a cave to prepare himself for the evening. He would have to gather all the crows and vultures he could find and have them come to the area.

Since that would take several hours he would have to start now. It would take all his concentration to hold them here, which was very draining on him. He laid out several lines of speed, mixed with peyote and morphine, to keep him in the trance necessary for shape-shifting.

Then he laid back, called one of the girls over, and put her to work trying to satisfy his rather unusual needs. He didn't really like sex with women and would rather rape young men, but couldn't in front of this group.

He wondered sometimes why he was that way, especially since it usually wouldn't work unless he smacked the girl around some, but mostly he tried not to think about it too much. That was for those stupid-ass head doctors and he really hated them.

Sometimes he would fantasize about raping the head doctor that had treated him at the juvie center and that always made him reach climax. That guy was such a fag, someday he would have to find him, rape him—and cut his throat.

As the clock chimed 1800 hours General Carter closed up his office bidding a good evening to his orderly and went out to his car. This was a special night. It was four years ago this very day that the artifact had come into his possession. He started his car, drove to the hanger, and, after parking, he put a bottle of his favorite Napoleon brandy in his briefcase. After the usual ritual with the post guard inside he settled himself in front of #10515, uncorked the bottle, and poured himself a generous three fingers of the golden nectar.

He sat gently warming the glass by rolling it between his palms and finally took out a nice fat heater that a friend had smuggled in from Gitmo. At least something good came out of

Cuba. He dipped one end into the brandy then clipped the other end and finally, holding the flame from his Vietnam era Zippo lighter at exactly one-quarter inch from the stogie, he puffed it into life.

Great clouds of gray smoke erupted from his mouth and roiled lazily upward in the still air making bizarre designs in the occasional ray of sunlight that filtered through the glass panes near the top of the hanger. There were only a few lights that stayed on all the time leaving the place in a perpetual state of gloom.

That seemed to suit General Aolis Chambers Carter. He could spend hours there smoking and dreaming of empires with him as the Lord of the World. One day he would open that crate and free the genie inside, but first he would have to learn how to control the power within, for he did not wish to become a victim of his own plans.

You couldn't say that General Carter wasn't a patient man though; he figured he had plenty of time. After all, the man who commanded the Ark of the Covenant commanded the God within. Getting an extension on his lifespan would be no great trick at all. There was no reason to believe he couldn't live to be as old as Methuselah. So he sat and dreamed of castles in the sky watching the smoke curl lazily up to meet the roof and sipping his most excellent brandy, believing that he was safe here in the middle of the worlds most secure military facility.

"They're making their move tonight," announced Bob as he glided through the backdoor of the war-room. Dakota, Bill, Dick, and I were sitting at the computers monitoring communications traffic and looking for messages from Shepherds people.

"You're certain of this Bob?" I asked, knowing of course, that he was.

"Yes, I saw them preparing and Jake reported the same," he told me outside of Dick's hearing. "They have all the weapons and people they need. Dick must have gotten them the message with the location we gave him."

"Okay," I said. "Let's load up and head out then."

"What do we do with Dick?" Bob asked.

"Good question," and I pondered it a bit. "We could tell him to stay here and keep an eye on the war-room, as well as protecting the restaurant. That would be important, you know."

"He might go for it," Jason joined in. "If not, we will just have to secure him. We can't take him with us, that's certain."

We were in agreement concerning Dick so I went back into the war-room and gave him the order. He did not seem too heartbroken over it, probably did not want to fight against the bad guys, or us for that matter. I would have to leave someone to watch him though, so I asked Jason who he would suggest.

"We will leave Helen and Dakota to watch him. My wife was a police officer with the reservation department for twenty years. She is not someone you want to mess with and Dakota can handle herself too, if you care to remember."

I could not argue with that and besides, I did not want my future wife going out into a firefight with a bunch of hyped up, well-armed outlaws. As I walked out to my bike Dakota came up handing me my jacket and said, "I ain't afraid that you will be brave Tom Harper, but I am afraid of losing you, so you be sure to come back you hear?"

"Nag, nag, nag," I said and gave her the longest, sweetest kiss yet.

"You be careful and keep a sharp eye on Dick. Do what you have too, don't let him leave your sight."

"Nag, nag, nag," she said and kissed me for so long I thought we would need oxygen.

A dozen bikes fired up and headed out followed by two vans, carrying extra ammo, machine guns, and medical supplies. The roar of the bikes, the smell of exhaust, hot pavement, and burning oil was enough to inspire anyone with a heartbeat above dead. We were men on a mission and Hell was trembling before us.

CHAPTER 26

Deadman lead out the parade heading for the northeast gate hoping that Handlebar would be able to carry his end. He did not like all this spirit stuff, especially the shape-shifting. Black magic just wasn't for him. He preferred things he could see and touch. They could be trusted and having never met this Blavatsky witch, he just did not trust her.

If they carried this off though they would all be richer than Midas and more powerful than God. Of course, if they failed, they would all be dead and in Hell by morning. Still, he felt that it was better to stand on your feet in Hell than to serve on your knees in Heaven.

Brothers and sisters of the air, rise and take wing, we fly to serve our master, rise and blot out the stars with your numbers. Meronek sensed the thousands of wings around him as he flew toward the base and into history. The parade of motorcycles led by Deadman was already breaching the gate and heading for the hanger, dropping off small links of the beast as it slithered along the ribbon of road which was visible only as a brighter surface among the darker vegetation.

Bright lights, like little stars, began to come into existence as the passing of the bikes tripped flares. In turn, more little stars began popping on as vehicles and aircraft began to respond to the invasion of land sacred to the Government.

Meronek began to direct the birds in an elaborate ballet against the helicopters as they rose to meet them. The first of the 'copters suddenly pitched over as birds entered the engine intakes causing them to explode and crashed headlong into the ground sending a great mushroom cloud of burning fuel into the sky, taking out another of its kind and hundreds of his avian allies as well. When the second bird of prey hit the ground, it too exploded, lighting the whole airfield in an orange, otherworldly light along with its sister.

Others in the squadron began to settle back on the ground seeing the danger in trying to fly through this Hitchcock inspired nightmare. Men on foot and even those in the HummV's were struck so violently by the birds that they cowered behind the vehicles, which had slowed to a crawl or stopped altogether waiting for the avian assault to stop.

Deadman could see that the birds were doing better than he had hoped. The 'copters were crashing or staying on the tarmac and the other vehicles did not seem to be moving either. The ultralights began to light up the night with their deadly dance as well, shooting the vehicles that were closest to the hanger and one of them firing a L.A.W.S. rocket at the entry door blowing a hole through it and making their egress possible. At this point Deadman had fifteen men with him and he had them form up into a semi-circle at the gaping hole in the hanger as he, Roadkill, and two others headed for the newly made entrance.

Peeking in carefully, he could see the guard post still manned by an airman holding his M-16 at the ready. Roadkill threw in a claymore that had been wrapped in modeling clay to make it sticky and it landed against the booth with a satisfying splat.

A pull on the string attached to the pin shattered the booth and ended the young airman's life. The way now clear they moved into the vast space of the hanger running down the cavernous aisles and looking for the number they had been given.

The general was just finishing his cigar when his world was thrown into chaos. Explosions reverberated through the hanger and hellish orange light threw his dark empire into harsh contrast.

"What the Hell?" he exclaimed as he drew out his chrome plated, pearl handled, 1917 model, Colt .45 Automatic service pistol. As he made his way toward the entrance the pressure wave of a L.A.W.S. rocket knocked him onto his back and sent his weapon skittering across the gray painted concrete.

Picking himself up he came face to face with a creature out of some post-apocalyptic sci-fi movie. He was dressed in black leather, a red bandana tied around his forehead, wild eyes looking out of black camo paint, and a twelve-gauge shotgun pointed right at his chest.

"Who the Hell are you?" demanded the general, unaware that he was no longer in command of the situation.

"Shut-up asshole," was followed by a smack from the butt-end of the shotgun that brought stars of multicolored light to his eyes.

Another man came up and joining the first. "What'cha got Roadkill?" asked Deadman.

"Looks like an officer."

"Sure does, don't it. Bring 'em along bro."

They set out at once in search of space #2304 dragging the sputtering, bleeding, General Carter with them.

"Git on yer feet General or I'm gonna blow ya in half," growled Roadkill as they rounded a corner and stepped on broken glass from the brandy snifter.

"Come over here Deadman," called out Roadkill. "Got somethin' here ya otta see."

Deadman came over and took in the scene: a folding chair, cigar butt nestled in an oversize ashtray, broken glass, and a nearly empty bottle of brandy, all spelling out the fact that this spot was in some way special. Looking at the space number, 10515, and noting it was not the number he had been given he turned to the Carter and asked, "What's in the crate General?" Carter only glared up at him in stubborn silence as blood ran down his chin from his battered nose and upper lip.

Deadman pulled out his Bowie knife and leaned close to the general's face caressing it with the cold steel of the blade he said, "We can do this the easy way or the hard way General Carter."

"Go to hell punk," shot back the defiant Carter. "I ain't afraid of you."

"Then how come ya pissed yur pants?" Roadkill returned as they all broke out in riotous laughter. "Maybe what we're looking for is right here, huh Deadman?"

"Open it," ordered Deadman.

"No," shouted the General. "You'll kill us all fool."

One of the others named Red Dog came running up to them and said, "Location 2304 ain't nothin' man. Just a big crate with a bunch of statues in it."

"Okay," said Deadman. "This is our cargo then. Get it loaded and let's get out of here."

"What about the wing-nut Deadman. Want I should shoot him?" asked Roadkill.

"Naw," he said. "Bring 'em along for a hostage. He might come in handy, 'specially if this is the wrong box."

They picked up the crate forcing Carter to help, took it outside, and loaded it onto the Goldwing's sidecar. There was a lot of small arms fire snapping around them so they wasted no time in getting away. The ultra-lights having expended their ammunition let go their loads of grenades which covered their retreat with a blanket of smoke and fire.

From his vantage point on the roof of hanger ten, Meronek watched the caravan of bikes pull out with the precious cargo and then directed the birds to continue their harassment until all the lights of the convoy were gone. After they were safely away, he lifted up on the wind currents and ascended toward the glittering stars leaving the carnage of battle below him.

Deadman was coming up on the gate thinking they were home free when he saw something that gripped him in fear. Lights were coming at them head on where there had been only blackness moments before. Smaller lights began to blink in a staccato fashion, with an occasional orange blossom to punctuate them.

He finally realized that this was gunfire and they were flying directly into it. It had to be those do-gooder Gideons. They were the only ones that could have known about the raid and responded so quickly.

The birds were too far behind to be any help now, so they would just have to open their throttles and blow through as fast as they could. The Goldwing carrying the crate was in the lead so he signaled them to floor it and with everyone flying along at full throttle shooting back, they ran the gauntlet of Gideons and roared off toward the safety of the canyon.

Meronek saw the ambush too late and could only watch as his column of men was decimated by the concentrated fusillade of gunfire. At least the Goldwing got through, though it was smoking badly and was slowing down. He counted only fifteen bikes following, out of the forty that he had started with. At least they had the crate; the men were expendable.

Bob had shown us the place where he believed the gang would try entering the base: the northeast gate. As we arrived we saw clouds of orange fire rising in the distance inside the base and knew the battle was in full boogie. We arranged ourselves evenly on both sides of the road and threw up whatever we could find for cover, which wasn't much, and prepared for a fight.

Less than five minutes later we could hear the roar of their bikes approaching and waited until they were fifty meters away before we opened fire with everything we had. As they thundered past us into the night they left over half their number scattered over the desert sand bleeding out their lives into the thirsty earth. I ran over to one of the riders and started to give him first aid only to find that a bullet had gone through his throat ripping out his spine. He had been dead before he hit the ground.

The night was punctuated by the screams of the wounded, the smell of gunpowder, blood, gasoline, and fear. People were scurrying like vultures from one downed biker to the next checking for survivors and making sure none of them were able to carry on the fight. One of them made the mistake of wounding David Long Bow in the right leg and was nearly blown in half by Jason's Greener.

After that, the rest seemed anxious to surrender. Of the twenty-five we brought down, ten died of their wounds on the spot, four more on the way to hospital, and the rest survived to stand trial down in Guantánamo bay, Cuba as terrorists.

We were too busy with the clean up to organize a posse, but I did send Bill along to follow them and let us know where they went to ground.

CHAPTER 27

When they pulled into the box canyon Meronek was waiting for them. The Goldwing made a series of knocking noises, then froze up completely with gout's of steam and coolant gushing from the radiator and oil pouring out of holes in the pan.

Stoneface was driving, but he wasn't looking good. He had taken several .38 caliber balls from a shotgun through his chest, ripping through his right lung and doing damage to his aorta. He never got off the 'Wing'. Spewing blood from his mouth his last words were, "God-damn you Handlebar."

Somehow, the general had survived without a scratch by hiding down on the floorboard of the sidecar behind the crate. Meronek pulled him out by the collar of his uniform jacket shouting, "Who the hell are you asshole?"

Before he could answer Deadman came up saying, "That's the base commander bro. We found him hanging around this crate, so I took him hostage 'cause he knows what's in it. The one we were told about just had some statues in it, so if it's the wrong one this guy will know where to look for what we want."

"Okay," growled Meronek. "Put him under guard then and give me a damage report."

After a few minutes Deadman approached Meronek who was sitting on a rock at the cave entrance smoking a cigarette and looking very ragged. "Got three with minor wounds, they're getting first aid now, one bike has a bullet hole in the crankcase that will not be fixable, the 'Wing" is trashed, and the rest are okay."

"Alright," chuckled Meronek. It was better than he had hoped for. "Gas up everyone, we pull out in thirty minutes. Trash the ultra-lights so the Gideons can't use them to follow us, leave nothing they can use. Got it!"

"Yeah bro," answered Deadman. "We won't leave 'em nothin'."

Meronek turned his attention back to General Carter. "What's in the crate old man?" he growled.

The general decided to play for time since this Meronek character would probably kill him if he gave the wrong answer, so he told him, "A power beyond your control, what is it he called you? Handlebar?"

"You can call me Mr. Handlebar jerk-face, now answer the question."

"It's the Ark of the Covenant, you hellion."

"Hellion? Who the hell talks like that anymore old school. Hey you! Yeah, you." Indicating one of Shepherd's people he said, "What's your name?"

"Preacher," he answered.

"Figures. Grab a shovel and bury Roadkill. He was a good enforcer. Get a couple guys to help you. It don't need to be deep, damn cops'll just dig 'em up anyway."

Meronek turned back to Carter, "Give me a good reason to keep you alive."

"Do you know how to use the power of the Ark? If you don't, it will kill you and everybody with you."

"If you're lying old man, I will have Deadman skin you alive and feed your guts to the coyotes."

"Go ahead, we're all dead anyway now."

Without pondering that remark any further, Meronek got his party under way.

"Where we going bro?" asked Deadman.

"We're heading for Mexico, got some friends down there that got enough guns and vaqueros to keep us safe while we figure out how to use this thing."

By the time all the wounded were packed out the sun was up and Bill could be seen rolling back toward us. The Air Force still had a lot of questions and we did not really have answers. Not the ones they wanted anyway. Some Lt. Colonel by the name of Lee kept hounding me to find out where Meronek was going with his general and the stolen crate.

"I don't really know where they are going," I said for the third time. "I am not in contact with him and if I knew I would tell you. Why don't you give me one of your cards like the detectives on TV and tell me to call you if I remember anything."

The sarcasm did not seem to appease the colonel who continued to stare at me as though that would produce the answer he wanted. Just in time, John came over showing his N.S.A. badge and leading the colonel off to an area where he would no longer be in the way. I went over to Bob and asked him, "What's in the crate Bob?"

"I heard the general say it's the Ark of the Covenant."

"Any chance they could use the Ark?"

"About as much chance as Hitler had with the Spear of Destiny. The power of the Ark can only be released by the Jewish priests and only Levite priests have the right to touch the Ark. Anyone else will be struck dead."

"Then what are we worried about? Let'em open it and the problem will be taken care of, right?"

"Not exactly Tom," said Bob, very serious now. "There could be other consequences as well. But I am not an expert on the Ark."

"Then who can tell me?"

"I don't know for sure Nephew, but you might start with Rabbi Zevi Cohen at the Jewish Studies Center in Santa Fe. I worked with him a few years ago and in the meantime, we'll mount up and see if we can catch them before they do any further mischief."

"Okay Uncle. I will call this guy Cohen and pick his brain, but if Meronek gets across the border into Mexico it's going to be hard to get at him. He's probably got some help down there."

"Yeah, I know. He's got a good head start too. We'll catch up to him though, don't worry."

I walked off to one side and tried my cell phone, but no signal. I would have to drive out to the highway to make a call. I wondered if there was a Jewish synagogue in Las Vegas, I would have to check.

As Dakota walked out of the restroom her heart skipped a beat. Helen was lying face down on her keyboard unconscious. She ran over to her exclaiming, "Helen, Helen, are you okay?" She raised Helen's head feeling for a pulse and praying that she was all right. There was a slight bruising on the back of her neck where she had probably been struck.

"Ow, ohhhh," came welling up out of her as she regained consciousness. "What happened? Who hit me?" she demanded

Feeling relief that her friend was alive and not badly hurt she answered, "I would guess that it was Dick. Let me get some ice for you honey."

"He's gone? That snake hit me and took off! I'll kill him if I have to track him all the way to the gates of Hell itself," she fairly steamed out the words.

"It's okay Helen, I'm pretty sure Jason will take care of that for you. I hate to call him with this news though. Oh, I shouldn't have left you alone with him, it's all my fault." Dakota began to cry then, as much for losing Dick as for Helen being hurt.

Now it was Helen's turn to give some comfort, "It's okay honey, we couldn't go all night without a potty break. I shouldn't have let him get behind me, I should have known better. Damn it, I do know better!" Helen picked up her cell phone and made a call to her husband leaving him a voice mail and then to Tom, leaving a message for him too.

Dakota sat down still crying. The first time Tom had left her a job and she had screwed it up. She was mad, but she was even more embarrassed. Dick Rogers would pay for this and pay dearly.

† † †

As the gang passed over the Mexican border they stopped in a little village just south of Nogales called Gordo Mendoza. They were looking for a cage to haul the Ark and the supplies they would need. The jeep had been too shot up to use and it would be a long drive between gas pumps where they were going. They also needed to hook up with the women, Shiloh, Sjana 'Lips' Herman, Sharon 'Jugs' Lipman, and Tracy 'Bubbles' Collins. They would be bringing a four-wheel drive loaded with the weapons and a supply of the drugs they enjoyed so much.

They stopped at the village cantina and he, Deadman, and because he could speak Spanish, Preacher went in. Preacher talked with the man behind the bar who produced three cold Coronas and some information.

"He says there is a guy who will sell us his 4-by pick-up for three hundred U.S. It's ten years old, not pretty, but runs good and doesn't burn oil."

"Sounds perfect," said Meronek. "Where do we find this guy?"

After a little more conversation Preacher turned back and said, "He's not here right now. He went across the border, but he should be back in an hour or so. He will send his boy to leave a message with the guy's wife."

Meronek did not like the idea of waiting around. "There ain't nothing else around here?"

"No bro. He says it's the only thing with four wheel drive in the area. The rest are just beat-up old cars."

"Okay." Meronek stepped outside and told everyone to find some shade and get a cold drink. He went to the general and told him to come inside the cantina.

"Hey Preacher, ask the spik if he can find something for the commandante to wear."

Behind the bar, the Mexican frowned at Meronek's choice of words but said nothing to indicate that he understood.

"He says yes, but nothing new."

"That's okay, just a shirt and pants is all he needs. Just so he don't look so military ya know."

Preacher passed this along to the bartender, who spoke perfectly good English, and he sent out another young man with instructions to bring back the clothes.

Meronek did not have to wait long. After thirty minutes a beat up dirt-brown, Chevy four-by pulled up to the cantina and a very large Mexican stepped out. He was only about five-ten and weighed at least one hundred sixty kilo's, but moved with a grace that belied his girth. He spoke in a voice that seemed to small for such a big man, "Who wants to buy my burrito?"

"I don't want no burrito," Meronek answered. "I wanna buy a truck."

"My little burrito is my truck, gringo," Juan said. "Burrito means little burro, my friend."

"Yeah, well I don't spik no Meskin," Meronek came back; buzzing on the six-pack he had drained while waiting.

"My name is Juan Mendoza, amigo," he went on, trying not to show his anger with this Norté Americano puerco. "You wish to by my truck or no?"

"Yeah, I wish to buy your truck Meskin," drawled Meronek. "Two-fifty American, right?"

Handlebar was hoping to haggle with him, since that was the way business was usually conducted down here. Besides, why should he pay this spik more than he had too? Money saved was more weed and beer for them.

"No senior," Juan said. "Five hundred American is the price."

Meronek was already tired of this game and reached for the Beretta hidden in his waistband.

"How 'bout I just take it and pay nuthin?"

He pointed the gun at Juan whose smile only seemed to split his amiable face even further.

"Senior," Juan said gesturing with his hands to take in the village around him. "Let me introduce you to some of my amigo's." From every rooftop and alleyway there came the sounds of weapons jacking rounds into their receivers. There were perhaps fifty or sixty gun barrels pointing at the group of bikers who were caught totally unprepared.

Meronek looked around calculating the odds and decided fifty to one was less than satisfactory, so he slowly put his piece back in the waistband of his pants and said with a big smile on his face, "I like the way you do business Juan. You take American Express?"

Juan continued to smile, but did not laugh.

"You still want my truck, the price is one thousand American. Otherwise, you turn around and get your Yankee ass's out of here pronto, comprende?"

This was not good. Meronek nervously glanced around the square, then back to Juan and said, "We agreed on three hundred man, I was just doing a little bargaining. Okay? A grand is all we got."

"That is most unfortunate gringo," smiled Juan. "You should never insult a man in his own village, it is very bad manners. But you are a stranger here, yes? And you do not know our customs. I will take your five hundred dollars and you can have the truck, but there is something you must do first."

This did not sound like it would have a happy ending. Meronek turned toward Deadman and Preacher for help, but there were men with guns standing behind them too.

"All you have to do is kiss my burro on her nagas and then you can leave."

The villagers seemed to find this hilarious, but Meronek was not sure why. From behind the cantina there came a braying sound followed by the appearance of a donkey being led by a small boy dressed in ragged shorts, a T-shirt saying, I♥New York, and a beaten up old straw hat. He came up walking the burro around Meronek coming to a stop beside the truck with the south end of the animal pointed toward Handlebar.

"Nagas is, how you say. Ass, amigo," laughed the big man.

"Preacher, Deadman," stammered Meronek. "Do something. I ain't kissing no donkey's ass."

"If you don't," said Preacher, "ain't none of us gonna leave this place alive."

Meronek looked the situation over again and saw no way out. If he went for his gun he would certainly die. If he didn't he could no longer command the gang's respect. This guy was not giving him a break and there was nothing he could do.

Deadman stepped up and said, "Boss, we ain't got much choice. Nobody's packing. We put all our guns in the supply crate remember? You start shooting; we all die. That's cool if you want, but then we lose everything we have worked for, right? See if you can buy him out, give him the grand."

"Okay amigo, I'll give you the thousand and my

"Maybe I just take your money, guns, bikes, and whatever else you got gringo. How's that work for you?" Juan said pointing to the burro and indicating that there was only one deal he was interested in now.

Preacher spoke up again, " If he does this Juan, you let us go. Right?"

"Yes, I am a man of my word. I made a deal with you and I will stand by it. You may go."

"Okay Handlebar," Preacher said. "Speaking for Hardcore, you either kiss the burro's ass or we leave you here on your own. You got yourself into this and it's your problem now."

Now it was the burro's turn to smile!

CHAPTER 28

I called the number Bob had given me for the Jewish studies center in Santa Fe and was soon connected to the Rabbi. "Zevi Cohen here, who is calling please?" I let him know who I was and what I wanted to know, using the cover story that I was writing a book and was interested in any extra-Biblical information on the Ark that he could give me. Were there any so-called 'secrets' that it might hold? And what might possibly happen if someone opened it?

After a few moments of silence, the Rabbi asked me if I could meet him face to face. I said yes, but it would be the next morning since it would take a few hours to fly there. Fine, he says, and to meet him at the synagogue where the studies center was located.

After hanging up with him, I called Dakota to see how she was doing and found out about Dick and Helen. I really wanted to go be with her, but now I had this appointment with the Rabbi. I assured her that everything would be okay. Dick would not be coming back, not after assaulting Helen. I said I would see her tomorrow and to just sit tight for now.

I called Bob's number and left him an update on his voice mail then headed toward Santa Fe.

Just before dark, Jason and the others pulled into Gordo Mendoza, the sleepy little village where Meronek and his gang had purchased the four-by from Juan that morning. At the cantina, Jason was welcomed, mainly because he was not a gringo like Meronek.

He listened to the tale of how Juan Mendoza had made the ill-mannered gringo biker kiss the south end of Juan's burro and together they had a good laugh. After buying a round of cervezas for everyone, they got back on their machines to follow the gang.

"Somebody call Tom first and let him know what's happened," said Jason.

"I don't think this is a good idea," said John. "We don't have any authority here and we are not prepared to go into Mexico on a chase. We need to go back and plan this a little better Jason. Also, we have no permission to carry weapons here."

"John's right," said Bob. "You all go back and arrange everything. I'll follow them and hang well back so they will think they got away. One guy on a bike they aren't gonna worry about. I'll keep you posted and let you know where they're headed."

It was decided then. The main group turned back and Bob went on alone.

"Hope he knows what he's getting into," said Jason. "Meronek's not going down there unless he has some protection lined up."

"He has God with him brother," enjoined John. "And we won't be far behind."

At a coffee shop outside the Jewish studies center in Santa Fe I stood looking around for Rabbi Cohen. But not knowing what he looked like I was lost. It must have shown because a man in his sixties wearing a Polo shirt, jeans, and brown loafers motioned to me from one of the tables. He was wearing a yarmulke, had short brown hair, horn rim glasses over soft brown eyes, an aquiline nose, and a pensive mouth. He was of average height and build and looked like he lived an active life. I stepped up to him and offered my hand with the question, "Rabbi Cohen?"

"Mr. Harper. Please sit down. Coffee?" I accepted a cup and he went on, "How is it you were referred to me?"

"My Uncle, Bob Harper, said you might have information that could help me."

"Humm, I see," he seemed to turn this over in his mind like a psychiatrist hearing that I had erotic thoughts about Mother Theresa and then went on. "Robert Harper, this is who you mean?"

"Yes, do you know him?"

"Yes, I knew a man by that name. Are you related to him? I know you call him uncle, but—-," leaving the question dangling.

"Yes, my father's brother, why?"

"You are not writing a book my friend, not if Robert sent you to me." Then looking around before going on, as though to make sure no one was listening he said, "You have found it?"

I wasn't sure if I should play ignorant or not, so I just looked at him dumbly.

"The Ark, young man. Have you found it or not!"

"I am not sure what they have found, but I was told that it may be the Ark. The crate has not been opened yet, but someone went to a lot of trouble to erase all history of the object from the records where it was stored."

"Aha," breathed Cohen. "Do you know where they have taken it?"

"No Rabbi," I answered truthfully.

"Please quit calling me Rabbi, my name is Zevi."

"Okay Zevi. So far all I know is they were last seen heading into the interior of Mexico. Bob is following them though and sends back reports every couple of hours."

"You hear from him? But, that is not possible. The Robert Harper I knew died in Afghanistan in nineteen eighty-six. I saw his car blown up by a Russian R.P.G."

"He does seem to have a way of coming back from the grave doesn't he?" I gave him a quick history of Bob up to this time. I suddenly had the feeling we were being watched; an itch at the back of my neck. "Is there somewhere more private we can go Zevi?"

"Yes, my office in the synagogue if you don't mind wearing a yarmulke," which he produced from his briefcase.

"No, of course not," I said, putting it on the crown of my head.

As we walked away my attention was drawn to a squirrel that was paying undue attention to us; it seemed to be following us. We crossed a busy street in front of the synagogue and once on the other side I waited for the squirrel to follow then turned back moving quickly toward it and frightened into stopping suddenly. A large green Land Rover ended his spy career and I turned back to join Zevi. He looked at me strangely as though I had sprouted an extra head.

"We were being followed Zevi. Trust me on this."

"By a squirrel?" he asked incredulously.

"No Zevi, by the Evil One."

"Oy," was his only reply. I thought it strange though that he accepted this without comment.

His office was a study in chaos, as much as General Carter's had been in order. Papers were piled all over his desk until not a square inch of the antique Oak showed through. There were the usual academic diplomas hanging on the walls, some of them were even straight. Bookcases full of well worn books attested to frequent use and more papers, magazines, and books formed aisles on the floor.

"Take a seat Tom," he motioned to a chair in front of the desk, also covered in books, which I cleared off. "Some more coffee?" he asked. The coffee machine seemed the only uncluttered space in the room.

"Yes, thank you Zevi."

"How much do you know about the Ark Tom?"

"Only what I've read in the Bible Zevi: Size, shape, and that it can't be touched unless you are a Levite priest who has been through a purification ritual. It contains the tablets with the Ten Commandments I believe, but I don't know any more than that."

"There was also a jar of Manna and Aron's staff, but that is about all that is in the written record, yes," said Zevi. "But there is a lot more in books and scrolls not included in the Torah or the

Bible. There is a record left by a man named Zelophehad, about the Ark which is very interesting, just let me look it up here."

I figured this couldn't' take more than two or three days to find, but amazingly, he went right to a large tome and started thumbing through the pages stopping with a, "Hmm, here it is. This man Zelophehad was a Dagon priest. If you remember, the Philistine people captured the Ark and placed it in a room with their fish god, Dagon.

"The story is in the book of Samuel chapters four and five. Anyway, this Zelophehad writes that one of their priests, whose name he leaves out, tried to open the Ark with some interesting results. It says, I will paraphrase here since the language is difficult:

"The (nameless) priest commanded the spirit of the Ark in the name of Dagon, Baal, Ashdod, and several other ancient gods, to obey his commands and after sacrificing a bull, some goats, and a virgin, he opened the Ark. It goes on to say that a spirit came out of the Ark and took the form of a goddess, whose name was Hazaef. She asked what it was that he commanded and he told her that she was to obey him in all things. She stated that he could command her three times only and after that, she would obey him no longer."

"Interesting Zevi," I said. "But doesn't it seem a bit odd that a goddess would come out of the Ark?"

"Yes it is, but that is not the end of the story as Paul Harvey says, there is more. This unknown priest predictably asked for wealth with his first wish and became so rich that the king noticed him, as well as the fact that the riches came out of the king's treasury.

"Confronted with this, the priest quickly made his second wish; that he was king. Well, now he was king, but had no money since that stayed in the priesthood's treasury. With the kingdom broke the army revolted because they had not been paid and set out to kill him.

"Having gained some wisdom with the first two wishes, he was sure that this time he would get it right, so with wish number three he asked to be put in a safe place where he would still be rich and powerful.

"According to the story he was placed in the priesthood's treasury vault which was sealed up in an earthquake and remains there to this day. It has never been found. After that, the Ark was returned to the Jews."

"So, if I am to believe this, there is a way to bring forth this goddess, but you have to be careful what you wish for. Sounds like an O. Henry story Zevi."

"Yes, it does. But if it is true, it means that these people are going to try to summon the goddess. If so, it may be very bad for all of us."

"Yeah, I can see that, especially if they don't do any better with their wishes than this priest did. How common would the knowledge of this scroll be?"

"Not very," Zevi said and pondered the question for a moment before replying. "Only a few scholars would know of it and I doubt any of them would be interested in trying to use the goddess."

"No, probably not, but they might know of someone expressing an interest for this ancient writing; someone with a cover story like mine maybe."

"Possibly. I will call them and see if any of them have been contacted in the past few years with such a request."

"Thank you Zevi," I said. We talked a while longer about spiritual things including the squirrel and then I excused myself for the flight back to Moapa.

Outside, I called Dakota, "How you holding up honey?"

"I'm doing okay. Helen just has a bump on her neck and a headache that a couple aspirin took care of. No one has seen or heard from Dick. Bob called in to say he was still headed south in pursuit of Meronek. Are you on your way back baby?"

"Yes darlin', I should be there in a few hours. Meet you at the restaurant okay?"

"Okay, I'll be there and I will have a nice, juicy Rib Eye waiting for you."

"Sounds good, love ya babe," and I hung up before she could say anything else. I don't know if I could handle not hearing 'luv ya' in return. Guess I'll find out in a few hours.

He knew he was in trouble after hearing that the wrong location had been transmitted to Meronek using his phones I.P. address. He didn't think that Tom would kill him, but one of the others might. Or worse, he might find himself sharing a cell in Guantánamo bay with some guy named Abdul which really wasn't in his plans.

So he had knocked out the Indian woman and took off after Meronek and his band hoping to catch up to them before they had a chance to summon the goddess and ruin all his plans. He knew Blavatsky for who she was and was not fooled by her; his allegiance to her was only temporary. The real power was in commanding the Ark and he was the only one who knew how to use it. Those fools of hers would only bring down destruction on everyone.

He had crossed into Mexico and used his command of shape-shifting to check up on Tom and found him conferring with the old Jew who knew the secret of the Ark. Fortunately the old man was not going to tell him everything. He would lie; but tell enough truth to send Tom on his way.

It would be interesting to know if Bob had discovered it was Zevi who had tried to kill him in Afghanistan and not the Russians. If Bob had, Zevi would have to be more careful. He had not found out as much as he would have liked because Tom had noticed the squirrel and killed it before he could eavesdrop fully on them.

The old Jew had power though and he would have to string him along a while longer. He would have to be more careful of Tom as well. He was picking up on spiritual things better than he had given him credit for.

Meronek was getting out of control too. The dumb-ass had nearly gotten himself killed in that border village which would have compromised the whole operation. Blavatsky really needed to do something about him and soon.

He knew Bob was ahead of him too and would have to take care of him somehow. He might just be able to salvage this whole operation yet.

King Richard did have a nice ring to it you know.

CHAPTER 29

They were about twenty miles outside of Hermosillo when Meronek pulled the gang off the road for a break and to settle some problems. A lot of grumbling had been going on since the incident with Mendoza and if he didn't put a stop to it he would have a mutiny on his hands. It was close to dark so he had everyone pitch camp, then sent Preacher and Deadman in the four-by to a village that was close by to get gas, food, and plenty of beer.

Tonight he would have to call Blavatsky to find out what his next move should be and entreat her to help him gain leadership over the gang again. Nothing fancy, but something that would impress them, like causing someone to die by just by touching them.

In the meantime, he called Shiloh over and told her to give him a card reading. He needed to know who was following him and how close they were. One of the girls called 'Jugs' came over and said, "Handlebar baby, we can't find Shiloh anywhere. The last place anyone remembers seeing her was in El Oasis. That little village about fifty miles back where we gassed up and had lunch. She either sneaked off or just got left behind. You want to send somebody back to look for her baby?"

This news sent Meronek into a rage. He hit Jugs in the face so hard she was knocked off her feet unconscious. "Who was supposed to be watching Shiloh? Who?" he screamed, frothing at the mouth like some mad dog; his anger out of control.

All of the girls were supposed to keep an eye on her, but they had gotten lazy lately because she had been with them so long. Sjana 'Lips' Herman came to Jugs aid and said, "Why would she take off now baby? We were in the middle of nowhere. She just got left behind, that's all. We can go back and get her Handlebar. She'll be there, where could she go in that rat hole?"

Meronek pulled out his pistol, pointed it at Lips, and pulled the trigger, but nothing happened. As he was in the act of pulling the slide back to jack in a round, he suddenly felt cold steel pressed to the side of his skull.

"I'll take that piece buddy," drawled an unfamiliar voice as it relieved him of his pistol and stepped away to one side. "Handlebar, you have gone plum loco dude. Hardcore says to me, he says, 'Red Dog, I want you to keep an eye on Handlebar, as he can be a bit moody at times. Don't let him screw up the mission just 'cause he loses his temper.' Well, I recon this is what he was'a talking 'bout, 'cause you have done lost your mind."

Handlebar looked at Red Dog as though seeing him for the first time. He was six-three, seventy-eight kilo's, with red hair, piercing steel-gray eyes, a Fu Manchu mustache, heavy square jaw and enough ink to qualify as a human mural. He did not look like the kind of guy you could bitch-slap without major medical insurance.

"You kill her and we maybe got Federales all over us, so you wanna whack her you wait 'till the missions over. Okay?"

Meronek felt his control slipping further away. No one had the right to slap him down this way; not Hardcore, not anyone. But for the moment he would have to calm down or these assholes would shoot him and go on without him.

"Yeah, yeah, okay," he stammered. "I guess it don't matter; leave her go. We don't need her no more anyway. You two get outt'a my sight though," talking to the women. "And you gimme back by piece," he demanded of Red Dog, holding out his right hand.

"I'll give it back to ya in a little while partner, but not just yet. Cool off some, have a brew and a doobie bro. Relax, we still got a long way's to go."

'Good advice' thought Meronek, you go ahead and relax while I put a bullet in your head. He went over to the Land Rover and got a beer out of the cooler, grabbed a joint from Lips, then dug out a .32 auto from his kit bag, which was stored in the rear.

He walked over to a big tree and had a seat. While he worked on the beer he checked the little Browning auto to make sure it was loaded and there was a round in the spout. Then he sat back to savor the thought of how he was going to kill Red Dog and any of Hardcore's buddies that stepped in to help.

First, though, it might be best to call out the goddess and get her power for himself. He could wait, after all another couple days travel and they would be in Pedro Estevez's territory and Pedro's men would be loyal to him. One word and they would all be dead. Plenty of whores there to replace these skanks too. Yeah, things would really change then. He sat there smiling at Red Dog and the others hoping it would make them uncomfortable, but all it seemed to do was amuse them even more.

In the little village of El Oasis Bob parked next to the little church and went inside to see the priest. The padre was talking to an older woman who was dressed in widow's clothes and obviously in some distress. She was telling the priest that since her husband died six months ago she had not been able to feed her children and needed help. The padre wanted to help, but had nothing to give. He told her to come back in the evening and he would try to have some food for her. After she left still looking very sad, Bob approached the padre holding out his hand and said, "Padre, may I have a few minutes of your time?"

The Padre, a small man with weary, soft brown eyes, looked at Bob with some apprehension and said, "I have no money, what little we had was taken by your friends yesterday."

"I am sorry to hear that Padre, but they are not my friends. I am a servant of the Most High and I seek them to bring them to justice." Bob reached into his pocket and brought out a twenty-dollar bill which he pressed into the Padre's hand saying, "I know it is not much, but please take it for the widow's and children."

"Thank you Señior, God bless you. My name is Father Pedro Hernandez, how may I help you?"

"Thank you Padre. I wonder if I may ask a question."

"Of course, go ahead and ask your question my son."

"I saw a young lady at the cantina as I was driving in; she looked to be American, yes?"

"Si, Señior," he replied. "She stayed when the others left."

"Could you tell her I wish to speak with her please? Tell her I am with the Gideons. She will understand."

"I will do this Señior. She has been seeking transportation north, but the bus only comes to this village once a week. Not until Monday; three days from now."

The little priest left to find the girl and Bob sat down on one of the pews looking around the old church. It was richly decorated with hand-made stained-glass windows depicting Bible scenes and Saints of the church. The old chandelier hanging from the high ceiling with its candles and the slowly fading murals on the wall behind the alter depicting the crucifixion revealed loving, talented hands, that had spent many years at work here.

The little church could probably hold about a hundred parishioners at one time, but probably saw only about half that many judging from the number of candles burning at the alter.

The door opened again and the priest, followed by Mary Ann, who looked apprehensive, entered. Bob got to his feet and introduced himself. "Hi, I'm Bob Harper, one of the Gideon's Warriors that Meronek has been running from. May I ask who you are?"

"I'm Shiloh," she said. "Handlebar's seer and tarot card reader."

"In that case," Bob stepped a little closer and went on, sotto voice. "Glad to see you got away Mary Ann Baxter."

"How do you know that name?" she said, obviously surprised.

"We know some of the same people and are both after the same thing. Please fill me in on what Meronek has been up to the past few days and as much as you know on what he is about to do. First though, let's go to the cantina and have something to eat, I'm starved."

✝ ✝ ✝

When I pulled into the restaurant parking lot I could see the bikes and the van parked off to one side and, judging from the number, I figured most everyone was there. I went in through the back door and was immediately set upon by some crazy blond who kept kissing me and calling me sweetheart, darling, and other terms of endearment.

"Dakota, it's good to see you too honey," I said somewhat surprised. "What's going on? You act like I just got back from an extended tour of duty."

She stood looking at me and I could see a hundred emotions racing across her cherubic face, then I pulled her to me and kissed her saying, "I love you too."

"Why don't you two get a room," said Bill from behind his computer monitor. "Some of us are trying to catch the bad guys you know."

"Okay, so what have you found out so far?" asked Jason as he entered from the kitchen bringing with him the inviting odors of Tex-Mex dishes.

"I will fill you in momentito," I said. "But first I want you to see if you can find out anything concerning a goddess named Hazaef or anything about the scroll of Zelophehad, Bill."

"Any idea where I should look buddy?"

"Not really. Library of Congress, Vatican, Ancient Hebrew studies, Google, for a start I guess."

"Okay, I'll see what I can find."

Out in the dinning room I filled everyone in on what I had learned from Zevi Cohen, as well as the squirrel that had been spying on us. "I bring up the squirrel because I don't think it was Meronek or Blavatsky; so who?"

"Good question little brother," said Jason. "Maybe it was Dick?"

"I thought of that too," I said. "But where would he have learned? Is there anyway we could find out Jason?"

"Only if we could catch him while he is in the act of shape-shifting. We would be able to recognize him, but that is all. He may have learned from Blavatsky, you know."

"That could be. For the time being we will have to assume that he has the ability and be careful."

Jason's phone rang and he stepped outside to take the call while we continued to discuss Meronek and the goddess. Dakota came over and set down a plate with a scrumptious looking Rib Eye in front of me and said, "Just like I promised cowboy; one steak cooked just the way you like it; pink in the middle and charred on the outside."

It smelled great and tasted better; just like ma used to make.

When Jason came back in he gave us an update from Bob, but only told us about Mary Ann when he had John Little Bear, the F.B.I. man, and me in private. "She says she got out because Meronek was getting out of control. He was either going to start killing people or get killed."

"She did the right thing," John stated. "She could not be of any more use to him anyway. As paranoid as that dirtbag is he's bound to hurt someone."

"Yeah," Jason went on. "Bob said he gave her some money to catch a bus back north, but it won't leave the village of El Oasis until Monday. Meantime he is going to go on after Meronek.

"She said his plan is to hook up with some drug dealer down there for protection. Seems there's an Aztec ruin there that he wants to perform the 'Ceremony of Awakening' at. It's supposed to be about two more days travel if the roads hold up and they don't come across any bandits."

"Okay people," I said. "Shall we load up and go after them?"

"Might just as well hold up," Bill said coming in from the war-room. "Seems that the goddess can only be called up on one particular date: That would be July twentieth, which means we have six more days to prepare."

"Where did you find that?" I asked.

"Well, I could say it was from an exhaustive search of the Internet, but the truth is, it was in an e-mail from your friend Zevi Cohen."

"Okay," I replied. "See if you can back that up from another source please."

"Sure Tom, will do. I have found at least one other source on this scroll, if you want to try it. Her name is Nora Mayer and she's a professor at Hebrew University. Got some contact info here."

"Yeah," I replied taking the slip of paper from him. "I'll give her a call this evening."

"Great. If true that will give us a couple of days to prepare and contact the proper people in Mexico to avoid any complications from entering their country," said Jason.

"Yes," said Simon, the D.E.A. man. "I can use my contacts down there to get us in. With all our operations in the area it shouldn't be a problem. They will just think we are on another drug investigation junket."

"Good," I said. "Get on that and we will need some transport too. Anyway we could fly in close to the location?"

Peter thought about it for a minute, then said, "We might get a C-5 from the Air Force, but they may want to include some troops which might make what we are doing hard to explain. Those things can land on just about any flat surface that's long enough though."

"Yeah, let 'em know we might be able to get their general back. That may give them some incentive to help," I said. "Peter, think you can outfit us with the weapons and gadgets we need? Stuff like F.L.I.R. (Forward Looking Infra-Red Radar) night vision, grenades, small arms, and such?"

"Whatever I can't find, I know where to borrow Tom."

"Cool. Okay everybody, get busy, if you need something to do just speak up, there's plenty to go around." I went into the war-room and found Dakota and Helen working on the computers and stopping at Helen I asked her, " How are you feeling?"

She looked up at me with a big smile and answered, "Fine. My neck is a little sore and I had a headache for a while, but I am fine now. Better than that snake Dick Rogers will feel if I ever get my hands on him."

"Yes, well," I said. "I can see you will make a full recovery. Anything on the scroll or the goddess yet?"

Nothing was indicated by anyone, so I sat down to one of the secure phones and called Hebrew University in Jerusalem. The answering service there was able to give me Nora Mayer's number which, fortunately was in the U.S. But all I got was her answering machine so I left a message indicating a time sensitive matter and hung up.

Then I went over to Dakota and whispered in her ear, "The steak was great, what's for dessert"?"

✝ ✝ ✝

Another little village came into view and Dick wondered what kind of reception he would get here. So far, Meronek had done more to harm relations between America and Mexico than President James K. Polk had in 1846. As he pulled in the women jerked their children back into their little adobe shacks, dogs chased him coming close to getting under his wheels, chickens darted around unused to traffic on the little road, and the men looked at him with open hostility. Meronek had definitely been here and used his usual charm on these folks.

He pulled up to the local cantina and stepped inside its some-what cooler and much darker interior. The man behind the bar placed an Indian war club on the counter; the kind that has pieces of sharpened flint wedged into its surface and several young men in the place displayed machetes, as well as a couple of antique revolvers. Stepping slowly up to the bar Dick told the bartender that he wanted no trouble, only a cold beer, something to eat, and a little information on a very bad man who may have passed this way with a group of equally bad men.

The bartender asked him why he was looking for them leaving him with the feeling that the wrong answer could be fatal. Had Meronek bought them? Or pissed them off. "I have a message for the one they call Meronek," he said hoping that it would sound neutral as he pulled aside his vest to show his Desert Eagle .357.

"You maybe tell us what the message is gringo," said a voice from the shadows at the end of the bar. "Then maybe we answer your question."

"The message is personal, very personal. Look friend, I don't want any trouble. A man gave me some money to deliver a message, that's all. He is not the kind of man you say no too or tell that you could not deliver the message."

"This man you are looking for is mucha malo, very bad. We did not like him and we told him to leave. Now we are telling you to leave, pronto."

"Okay, no problem amigo. I do not like this man either. I will go now, but if you will tell me which road he took please."

"You go now!"

The men started to get up, so Dick decided it was time to leave and walked out the door quickly, but without showing them his back. Out in the bright sunshine he could taste again the acrid Mexican dust, see the empty streets, and feel the anger of the people. He straddled his Evo and headed the last direction he could be sure of—south.

Outside the village, the road forked, but he was able to pick up the tracks of the bikes in the dirt road and follow them leaving behind any hope of fuel or food. A mile down the road he came to an old farmhouse and pulled in hoping to find shelter for the night. He dismounted and went in on foot in case he was not welcome. There was no sign of occupation as he poked his head into the broken down lean-to's where rusting farm machinery lay strewn about. He called out to the house as he approached, but saw no movement at windows or doors.

Inside the adobe structure there were a few worn pieces of furniture scattered about and the musty smell of a building long out of use. The dust motes drifted in the air where he disturbed them and he sensed that this was a place the villagers avoided. There were symbols on the walls left by someone who practiced magic, so perhaps it had been the home of a bruja.

In the kitchen he found a five-gallon gas can that still had some fuel in it. It was old, but would get him down the road for a few miles to the next village he hoped. He went out, brought his bike up to park it inside one of the sheds when he disturbed a nest of rats the size of domestic cats and nearly dropped the Harley.

Back in the house he cleared away a spot to put his sleeping bag and placed a spell that would keep the wild life out of the area for the night. He did not dare build a fire, but used a small camp-stove to heat some food and a little coffee. Just before laying down a large ugly possum came up to the edge of his spell circle, sat down looking at him and said, "The Gideons know about you, they know you shape-shift and that you are my servant."

"Yes Master. Tom has a better grasp of the Power than I gave him credit for. I will be more careful with him now. What do you want me to do when I catch Meronek Master?"

"He is no longer important; a fool who will suffer a fool's end. The night of the twentieth July, you must be ready to take possession of the Ark and call out the goddess. You must be prepared to face the Gideons as well. They prepare even now to attack Meronek and take back the Ark. You must not fail me Dick Rogers or you will suffer the tortures of the Inquisition."

"I will not fail Master, you know I am faithful and have done all that you have asked. I have refused you nothing Master."

"See that you do." The possum turned and waddled back outside taking the faint odor of brimstone with him, but not the fear that still griped his heart.

It promised to be an uncomfortable night for Meronek. The mosquitoes came in suffocating clouds that repellent seemed to have no effect on and the only relief came from the smoke of the campfire. Even the spells he knew seemed to do little good. Then bats started diving and swooping around them taking advantage of this abundance of food. Add in the snakes, scorpions, as well as other assorted wildlife, and you had a typical night in a Mexican jungle.

He finally pulled a small leather bag out of his jacket, opened it, and using a small silver spoon he wore around his neck he scooped out a generous helping of white powder which he then siphoned up his nose. This mixture of drugs included methamphetamine, cocaine, China-white heroine, and Ketamine. This was what he used for shape-shifting, as well as making contact with Blavatsky, but tonight he was using it to escape from the devil's brood buzzing around his head.

His gang no longer respected him, or even seemed to fear him. His Lieutenant, Deadman, had taken to keeping his distance from him as much as possible and even the little toady, Maggott, stayed away. If he did not take back control soon the whole mission would go bust and then She-who-must-be-obeyed would toss him aside and find another, just as she had with Hardcore. He could not let that happen, he had to possess Blavatsky, body and soul—if she still had one. She was his reward for service to the dark master and he would kill anyone who got in the way.

As the mixture of drugs kicked in, he could feel himself lifting out of his body and traveling to another place. He was being called and could not resist.

"What have you done worm?" demanded Blavatsky. "Why are you not at the temple yet?"

Meronek could feel 'things' crawling under his skin, eating away at his vital organs, and coughing, they spewed out of his mouth and began to dance on the ground in front of his prostrate body. The pain was worse than anything he had ever experienced, even the gang rape at the hands of six older boys at the C.Y.A. or the beating he had taken from Hardcore at San Quentin for raping and beating an Aryan Brotherhood prospect. This seemed to go on forever and left him begging her to stop; begging for mercy.

As suddenly as it had begun, the pain stopped, to be replaced by waves of orgasmic pleasure that threatened to destroy his mind, just as much as the pain had. Just as he felt he could take no more, it stopped, and he found himself again, on his face in front of her.

"Answer me maggot or I will finish the job the worms started."

"Madam," his voice came out sounding childish and pleading. "They no longer respect me or fear me. They will not follow my orders. Give me power to kill one or two so that they will obey us again." Meaning, of course, that they would fear him—if not her.

"Worm," the word seemed to burn into him with the fires of hell, washing over him with the sulfurous stench of brimstone. "They already fear me and if you were not such a spineless bucket of guts, they would still be in fear of you."

"Yes madam, I'm sorry. I should have killed that fat bastard Mex and been killed too," he choked out in pathetic sobs hoping she would understand that his death would have ended their plans.

"You were a fool to provoke him, he should have shot you. It would have been better than seeing you begging on your face in front of me now."

From behind him another voice spoke, as smooth as oil, a true politicians voice. "He is rather pathetic Carmine. Why don't you let me take him now."

"No mistress," begged Meronek in a voice so choked it came out sounding like a little girl. "I will carry out the mission, then they will all bow to us: To you mistress."

"What do you wish me to do with this worm Faustus?"

"Throw him back Carmine. They will not do anything to him until after the ceremony. I will see to it."

"Yes Master, as you say."

It was late by the time we wrapped up at the restaurant and I took Dakota home. Neither of us showered, we just fell into our respective beds and went to sleep. Maybe it was because I was so sleepy, but I suddenly felt myself flying up out of my body, out of the house into the night sky free to travel wherever I wished. I thought about Bob and suddenly, without awareness that I had traveled, I found myself looking down at him as he slept beside a stream in the jungle. I sensed by his aura that he was out traveling too, and seeing he was safe, I went to look for Meronek.

I found him and his group camped in a small clearing next to a river. He was out of his body too, but in great distress. I willed myself to go where he was and was transported to a scene right out of some cheap horror film.

Meronek was stretched out on the ground with a monster behind him and the ugliest old dried up crone I had ever seen in front of him. The monster was at least three and half meters tall, but very thin, like a skeleton covered in parchment. There were things crawling around on him, as well as out of him, and there was an odor of decomposing flesh, though whether it was just from him, or from both of them, I could not be sure.

The hag was about two meters tall and looked like she had been dead for at least six months. Her body was nude, her breasts dried up, and flat against her cadaverous body. Her hair seemed alive; moving even though there was no wind and pieces of skin seemed to fall off only to grow back seconds later.

I was not sure who the man was, but I was certain that the woman was Blavatsky. She appeared to be speaking to Meronek, but I could not hear her; only a chattering like dry bones being knocked together.

They must have reached some decision, because Meronek suddenly disappeared. The man turned, as though searching around the dead, wretched forest for something or someone, his eyes looking in my direction, but not seeing me. He spoke to the woman, but to me it sounded like a kid dragging his nails over a chalkboard. Then they both started to move in my direction. I decided it was time to leave and thought about Dick Rogers.

He was lying inside a glowing spell ring on the floor of an abandoned house. I could feel at least one other presence nearby and looking about I saw a 'possum that had a spell glow on it as well. Not wanting to draw attention I decided to leave.

I rose up into the sky and willed myself to travel slowly to where Bob was and found that only a dozen klick's or so separated them. I felt myself being called back to my body, so I let go and returned. Dakota was calling me with urgency in her voice as I slowly swam my way back up to consciousness.

"What is it beautiful?" I croaked out, my throat as dry as a State of the Union speech.

"There's a call for you from Nora Mayer, she says it's important."

After everyone had gathered at the restaurant and while we were waiting on breakfast, I filled them in on the events of the night before. "And lastly," I said, "I received a call from Nora Mayer of Hebrew University's department of Ancient Studies.

"She confirmed much of what we were told by Zevi Cohen, but also had more information that he did not supply. It seems Mr. Cohen has been a suspect in several illegal sales of ancient artifacts and may be a member of a secret society called the Illuminati.

"She said the Illuminate are an ancient society who seek to dominate the world by controlling finances and influencing governments. We must assume that he is not on our side and may be actively working against us.

"The information he gave us about the Ark is correct, but not complete. It seems he left out some details concerning the sacrifice of a bull, a ram, and a goat. The bull must be red, the ram all white, and the goat all black; none may have a blemish of any kind. After they are sacrificed, their blood must be sprinkled on the Ark using a Hyssop branch, and the bodies burned on an alter."

"Where are they going to get all that stuff?" asked Jason.

"Good question; I asked that one myself. The goat and the ram should be easy. The bull and the Hyssop branch may be a problem. I have to assume Blavatsky or the demon have already considered these problems. They may try using some kind of substitutes, but we will just have to wait and see."

"I'll see what I can dig up on the Illuminate," said Bill. "Although by definition, a secret society is secret. There may not be much on them."

"Okay Bill," I said. "Peter, did you find out anything on getting us some air transport?"

"Yes, but maybe not what you were thinking. One of my C.I.A. friends turned me onto a guy that has an old C-5A Galaxy that he would be willing to, uh, 'rent' us."

"Okay," I gave that some thought. "We could make that work, I guess. How about weapons?"

"No problem there," went on Peter. "We have a nice stock-pile that has been diverted from drug busts over the years. They were to be used for anti-terrorist operations in South America until the winds of politics changed. They've been languishing in storage for ten years because no one knows how to get rid of them without being burned for hiding them in the first place. We will be doing my superiors a favor and they won't be able to say anything about it."

"Great, where are these weapons and the C-5? Can we get them here ASAP?"

"The C-5 can be here within two hours and the weapons are hidden at a facility a hundred miles north of here. There is some security, but nothing our little team of experts can't handle."

"Okay Pete, take whoever you need and get on it, we will need those weapons here and checked out by days end tomorrow."

Pete got up and picked out John, Simon, and Bill to go along with him. They would take one of the vans and two bikes for the job.

"One other question Pete," Jason said. "Is this guy willing to fly the mission? I don't think any of us is checked out on a C-5."

"He said he's got somebody to fly for us. An ex-agent type who has been using the plane to deliver food, medicine, and Bibles to various Latin American countries. He said the guy jumped at the chance when he found out who we are. Don't worry though, he doesn't know why we're going, I thought I would let you break it to him."

"Okay great," I said. " Have a safe trip bro, and go with God."

I went into the war-room along with Dakota and David, who still had a slight limp from his wound, and we all set to work looking for info on the Illuminati. I also checked e-mail and surveillance data.

Jake had reported in by payphone saying he was okay and that Hardcore was getting ready to make a trip somewhere. Maybe to Mexico to be there when the goddess was called up. He suggested coming up with some kind of ruse to keep him here. I discussed it with David and we decided to put him on the terrorist watch list. That at least would keep him off any commercial flights.

Dakota called me over and pointed out that it was nearly lunchtime and neither of us had bathed in the last forty-eight hours. Dave volunteered to continue the search and for both of us to please take a bath.

"Okay," I said. "But I don't want you in here alone. Keep Jason close to you and keep the doors locked."

"Will do boss, now get out!"

CHAPTER 30

Zevi Cohen locked his office door and left through the side entrance of the school where he caught a cab that took him to an old building near the warehouse district bearing a sign which read 'WORLD LIGHTING CORP.' All the windows were boarded over and the place had an air of having been abandoned for years. Walking up to the barred and gated front door he reached in and tapped the door buzzer in a rapid code, then waited in the shadows.

After perhaps two minutes a metal grate set in the sidewalk in front of the door began to rise up on one side revealing a stairway that lead downward into darkness. Looking around one more time to make sure he was not observed he began to descend the stairs until he had been swallowed by the darkness like Jonah into the whale.

At the bottom of the stairs he waited as the grate closed above him and lights came on brightly illuminating the corridor before him. The walls were decorated in symbols and runes reaching back into man's distant history. He walked down the narrow hallway touching certain of these symbols as he went until he came to the greatest symbol of this August society, the All Seeing Eye above a pyramid.

Here he waited until a door opened in the wall where no door could be seen. As he passed into this new room he could sense men standing in the darkness that he knew were ready to kill him if he did not say and do the right things. Questions were asked, answers given, and only then did the single lamp above him come to full brightness and a further door open. In this room was a large table with a dozen plush chairs arranged around it.

The room itself was something out of a different time, perhaps the eighteen-ninety's. The Velvet walls were covered in rich gold brocade and paintings of men wearing long beards and serious expressions were hanging behind each of the overstuffed chairs.

There was the cloying odor of cigarette and cigar smoke coming from everywhere, having permeated the furnishings and becoming a permanent component of the atmosphere. He was alone for the moment, so he went to an antique bar at the back of the room and poured himself a generous glass of Glenfiddich single-malt scotch. He removed a Cuban cigar from the humidor resting on the bar and brought it to life with the gold lighter stationed next to the box.

Returning to the table he took a seat and waited for the others he knew would soon join him. They began to file in, each, as he was, wearing a mask that concealed his face from the nose up. None knew the others or even what they did for a living. Anonymity was absolute so none, if caught, could betray the others.

After everyone had helped himself to refreshments (there were no women in this society) they settled down to the business of the night. The gentleman seated at the head of the table was the first to speak. "All come to order. Anyone having new business please wait until called upon. Bravo, you will report first please."

Each chair was assigned a letter from the alphabet starting at the head with A, and going through L. Zevi occupied chair H, so it would be some time before he was called upon, and spent his time preparing his report, making sure he had left nothing out.

His turn finally came with the Alpha chair calling out his designation, "Chair Hotel, have you anything to report on project Ark?"

"Yes Alpha, fellow brothers of the Golden Light. The project is going ahead just as scheduled. There is one factor which had not originally been included though. A group calling themselves Gideon's Warriors has entered the equation and have made it necessary to re-figure the possible outcome."

"What is the nature of this group? What organization do they represent?" asked the member called Alpha.

"They appear to be religious in nature, as indicated by their name. They comprise a group numbering about fifteen to twenty, though it is difficult to tell. Many of them seem to be ancillary in nature. There are at least twelve who form the inner sanctum. They represent no organized religion or group, such as Opus Dei or Knights of Columbus, but seem to be driven by a desire to confront what they believe is an evil conspiracy."

"What do you calculate their threat level to be brother Hotel?" asked the member known as Echo.

"Since they have no previous history it is difficult to calculate. I have determined that the majority of them are military veterans, mostly Marine Corps, and all have combat experience. They are highly motivated by their religious beliefs and by loyalty to each other. I would not discount them out of hand in this project, but I would not rate them highly either since they appear to be very short on resources.

"We should be more concerned with the one called Meronek, as he seems to be declining rapidly in stability. His actions have become very erratic. We may have to terminate him and replace him with our own man."

"This can be done on short notice and without interference from Meronek's gang?" asked the member called Alpha.

"I calculate a ninety percent probability of success since Meronek presently has no support from his gang. The only reason they keep him is his sole access to the witch Guzman and to get the secret of the Ark. Once she reveals the secret to him I believe he will exact his revenge on those in the group he feels betrayed him, which is most of them, and try to usurp the power of the goddess for himself. This cannot be allowed of course, since he would most certainly misuse that power."

"Agreed," said Alpha. "Have our man ready to step in when it becomes necessary."

The rest of the evening's business was of little concern to him, so he sat in his chair sipping scotch and planning his takeover of the world. Not even his fellow Illuminati would be spared after his ascension to the throne.

As the sun rose above the tree line of the jungle its heat, like the open door of some cosmic pizza oven poured down upon the band of outlaws increasing the misery they already endured from stinging insects, biting flies, and poisonous reptiles. Meronek was already on his feet moving back and forth through the camp like some out-of-control Napoleon giving orders to break up camp and get moving toward their final destination.

They had four days left, it would take at least two to get to the temple, and then they would have to find the proper instruments of sacrifice. Everyone was just sort of looking at him, like they wished he would just shut up and disappear into some hole in the ground instead of breaking camp and of course, obeying his every command.

Deadman, Maggott, and the girls were the only ones moving at all and only because they knew how crazy he could be. He suddenly pulled the .32 auto he had been hiding in his pocket and fired a round into the air shouting, "You son's of bitches better start moving or you'll be fish-food in five seconds!"

They got moving, but some, like Red Dog and Preacher, had a bad feeling about how this ride was going to end. Meronek had the look in his eye of someone who has lost all contact with reality.

Once underway he drove at a pace that was suicidal and only slowed down after nearly hitting a mob of javelina milling about in the road. The frightened peccaries attacked the bikes and they had to kill a couple of them. No one got hurt, but it did provide some laughs and fresh meat for the evening's cookout.

Meronek showed unusual intelligence in the next village by driving through and then having Preacher go back and get gas for them in the Chevy. All the village had was low octane stuff that was only suitable for lawn mowers as Meronek put it and left the Harley's knocking and overheating in no time.

He cursed the idiot who sold them the stuff, but did not slow down since, after all he could buy a hundred new bikes when he was King of the World.

We went back to Mom's after our showers and I cornered Jason to ask him a question that had been bothering me for a while. "Where are we going to get the money to pay for the airplane bro?"

"Well little brother," Jason said. "Besides the tidy profits I make from the restaurant, I also operate a silver mine in the Black Hills. With my investments and other ventures, I am one rich red man."

"I never would have guessed bro, somehow you don't seem like a millionaire."

"That is the secret of my wealth Tom. No one knows, so they don't hit me up for money. The Lord has blessed me greatly, so that I may be a blessing to others."

"That's great Jason, but you should not have to bear all the expense. Maybe we could put this down in a book when it's all over and get rich, huh."

"Sure, little brother," he said. "But you keep it and make Dakota a nice home to live in and some horses to keep her company. She loves to ride you know?"

"I did not know Jason. Might be something to do when we find time."

"There will be time this evening little brother and I have horses at my house. After dinner I want you to ask her to go for a ride. You both need some time to relax before we go down and take care of Meronek."

"Okay big brother, that sounds like it might be fun."

My phone rang at that moment; it was Bob. "Hey Uncle, how's it going down there?"

"Fine Nephew, just thought I would let you know, Rogers passed me this morning on his way to hook up with Meronek. He did not see me, so I let him put a few miles between us. What do you think his story is anyway? He doesn't seem the type to be in the service of Blavatsky."

"Yes, she seems to be mostly about sex." I recounted to him what I had seen in the woods the previous night. Jason listened in as well as I put the phone on speaker. "There was someone else there Bob. Was it you?"

"No Nephew. It was not me, but it may have been Rogers."

"I don't think so. I saw him just before going to the woods and he had himself trapped in a spell circle."

"Who does that leave?"

"No one Uncle that I am aware of. It had to be some other player."

"Too bad you did not follow him."

"I did not see him, I only felt his presence. It did seem kind of familiar though, we may have met. I will think about it, maybe it will come to me."

"Sure Nephew. In the meantime I will keep following the merry maniacs and keep an eye on them. I will call you tomorrow and let you know where they are."

"Okay Uncle, be careful. Bye."

Bob hung up and for a moment I felt I knew who the other player was, but then it went away. I went over to Dakota who was still at the computer and gave her a little kiss on the check asking, "How's the search going darlin'?"

"Very well, thank you sir," as she returned the kiss. "I have found a lot of anecdotal stuff on them, but nothing very revealing."

"Let me see what you have got then, it's more than I know right now."

I sat down at another terminal and brought up the file she had marked as Illm. and opened it. There were several different articles that had differing positions on the society, but one in particular caught my eye. It was positive without being saccharine and just vague enough to be written by someone in the know. Somebody wanted to present the organization in a positive light without drawing too much attention or giving away any of its deep secrets. There was no name attached to the article, but oddly, it was signed The High Priest.

It described the Illuminati as a secret society organized to guide mankind to a benevolent future where all ancient secret knowledge would be revealed. In this future, there would be the usual perks—no hunger, no disease, brotherly love, everyone the same as everyone else. I suspected that part, at least, to be pure B.S. It went on to say that in each country of the world there were a dozen individuals chosen to administer this ancient knowledge and keep it alive. They would in turn pass on the knowledge to their successors keeping the secret society alive.

"This one sounds like someone familiar with the society might have written it. Is there any way we can find out who posted it?" I asked.

"Bill might, but he isn't back yet. I book-marked it though in case you needed to bring it up again."

"Good my little Cactus Wren. Please bring it up now." I sat behind her looking at the web page and smelling her musk, taking in the curve of her shoulder, the cute shape of her ear, and almost not seeing what I was looking for. "You know what Cohen means?" I asked no one in particular. There were only blank stares in return. "It means priest in Hebrew. Zevi Cohen told me that when I interviewed him. I wonder if that is a coincidence."

"I thought you didn't believe in coincidence little brother," said Jason.

"I don't bro, I don't. When are our gun runners supposed to be getting back?" I asked.

"Should be here in about an hour," answered Dakota.

"Great," I said moving back over to a terminal and going through the rest of the Illuminati postings. After a solid twenty minutes I had exhausted all the material and decided that the Illuminati had done an excellent job of keeping themselves a secret organization. I moved back over to Dakota, getting next to her, and whispered in her ear, "Dinner tonight, at Jason's house?"

"Love too," she whispered back as I stared into her jade green eyes and feeling myself falling into them, like a star into a black hole. "I think I love you Dakota," I said as I leaned in to kiss her, tasting her lips, and thinking they were better than honey.

"By the way darlin', what is your full name? I guess I should know by now."

Her face turned a bit red and she said, "Isn't Dakota enough?"

"Yes, it is. But I would really like to know your full name before we get hitched."

"Tell him or I will," Jason pitched in.

"Janice Dakota Walsh. There, now you know."

"That's a nice name. Why are you uncomfortable about it?"

"I'm not really. I just like the sound of Dakota better, that's all."

"Okay, Dakota it is then," I said.

Pete and the others came rolling in, so we went out to see how they had done.

"Hit the mother-load guys. We got enough to overthrow the government of a small Caribbean country," said Pete as he got out of the cab of the Econoline van. I looked into the back and saw a large stack of wooden crates and metal ammo boxes. Enough to stage a small war in any country indeed. "Figured I might as well get more than we need, just in case. Besides we used up quite a bit of Jason's stuff in that gunfight last week."

"Well Pete," I drawled, "you never know what we might need, especially if we keep turning up new players in the game."

"Somebody else jumped in.? Any idea who?" asked Bill as he walked up after parking his V-Star 1200.

"No, not yet. I was hoping you might be able to help. I want you to try to find out who posted a web page on the Illuminati. Dakota has it in the war-room. No big hurry, but look at it some time this evening if you can."

"Sure Tom shouldn't be too hard."

"Pete, let's talk to your friend about that airplane," I said.

"Already done bro, he's headed here now. Should be putting down at Jason's place in about two hours."

"Somehow I feel like you guys just don't need me any more."

"Chin up old thing," Pete said. "We'll always need you to show us the way."

"Har, har," I laughed. "Come on, steaks are on me."

The gang pulled into another sleepy little village about two hours before dark and parked outside the cantina. There were a few people gathered around tables having their evening meal and a heavyset woman, who appeared to be the proprietress, was hovering over them. Meronek walked up to her and asked her to provide beer and food for his gang.

She spoke some English from having worked in the states a few years as a chambermaid for a hotel chain in Oakland. After an exchange of money she served up food buffet style and plenty of beer in large tubs filled with ice.

Preacher casually worked his way over to her and struck up a conversation in Spanish. Her name was Maria Estevez and she was a widow. Her husband had been killed in a fight in Tijuana ten years ago. She had moved back here to La Colorada after that because too many people were getting hurt or killed over drugs and other gang related activities back there. It was much safer here, though she did not make as much money as she had in the states.

He discovered she had known Meronek in Oakland when she was working for the Motel Six and he was just a kid. She had met him just after his release from the C.Y.A. because he, and her son Paco, had become friends. Paco had done time for auto-theft and they had protected each other until they were released.

Paco was now a big man in Alfonso 'Gordo' Diaz's drug cartel as a chemist insuring quality control in his cocaine operation. He would be the man that would provide security for them while they performed the goddess ceremony.

She had been proud of her son getting his degree from Berkeley, but Preacher could tell she was not so proud of him now because of who he worked for. She was sad for Meronek too. She told him how Meronek and her son had tried to straighten out their lives after C.Y.A., going to church and going back to school, but Meronek wasn't very good at reading; Dyslexic they had called it.

Paco was smart and did well, but his success had only made it harder for little Stevie. Meronek had lived with her and Paco for a while, but then he discovered that biker trash, present company excepted, (of course Señora), and just stopped coming home one day. He had stayed in touch with Paco over the years and they had remained friends, but there was something wrong with Meronek that only God, she said as she crossed herself, could fix. Preacher went away then agreeing that there was something wrong with Meronek, but he was of the opinion that it would take a bullet to fix him.

Meronek behaved himself and after everyone had eaten and filled their tanks from the old hand cranked gas pump they drove out of town to camp next to some old Aztec ruins. At least the bugs weren't as bad here away from the river, but they still had to put up with critters wandering into camp. To control them they built a ring of fires around themselves and slept inside it.

Later in the evening after the sun had slipped back down below the horizon, Preacher took a spot next to Meronek and tried to engage him in conversation. "That woman in the village, Maria, she was very nice."

Meronek looked at him like he had crawled out from under a rock, that had been under something even worse, and grunted, "Yeah. Stay away from her."

"No harm, Handlebar. I meant it. She said she knew you."

"Yeah, me and her son got history back in Oakland."

"Yeah, she said you and Paco was in C.Y.A. together. I spent two years inside myself; G.T.A. (Grand Theft Auto). That was back in the seventy's man and that place was an animal farm back then. Had to carry a shiv everywhere; wasn't even safe to take a shit man. Had to have somebody to watch your back twenty-four-seven."

For the first time Preacher saw Meronek relax some and he began to open up. "Me and Paco were tight man, we had each others back. I mean, like it didn't matter to me he was Mexican, ya know? We needed each other 'cause we was both freaks in that place. We didn't fit; ya know what I mean? We was both small and the bigger boys picked on us, but together we was the bomb man. Paco would catch one of 'em slippin' and distract him while'st I would hit him in the back of the head, then we would…"

At that point he suddenly trailed off not wanting to say what they did next. "What you wanna know for anyway man," he said, getting angry. "You was ready to shoot me back there."

"Easy Handlebar," Preacher soothed. "You was out there man, ready to blow the whole mission 'cause you lost your temper. I couldn't let that happen man. I did what I had to in order to keep us all alive man. There ain't but fifteen of us and down here in Indian country that ain't very many."

"Yeah, okay." Meronek came back. "Your right. I was too wired up from the business with that donkey. I let it get to me."

"Is Paco the man we are going to hook up with tomorrow?"

"Yeah he works for Gordo, takes care of processing all his Chiba into coke, also turns his brown opium into 'China-White.' He's really good at what he does."

Preacher brought out a fat joint that he had laced with some PCP and lit it up, sharing it with Meronek as they talked into the darkening night. "Shay Handlebar," Preacher's words starting to slur slightly. "Ya mind if I ask ya how ya got yer handle?"

"Naw, is okay," Meronek's words were beginning to slur as well and he broke out a bottle of tequila taking a big swig, then passed it to Preacher. "There was this guy at a party the Devils Angels was throwing in Oakland that had a big mouth. Said our colors reminded him of something a fag would wear to a drag party. I was nineteen then and a prospect, so I grabs a set of handlebars that was laying on a bench and beat him to death with 'em."

"That must'a made your bones dude."

"Yeah, it did. He was some big shot with the American Nazi's though and we almost went to war over it. There was witnesses heard him say it, so I was okay. I did have to leave Oakland though and join the Pagans. I got no use for them Nazi's no more 'cause of him."

"Yeah, I can grok that man," said Preacher.

"Can what? What the hell is grok dude."

"Comes from an old science fiction book man, 'Stranger in a Strange Land' by Isaac Asimov. Means like, you unnerstand, you dig it man."

"Uhh, sounds really old school dude."

"Handlebar man, I am old school." They both fell out laughing like it was the funniest thing they had ever heard. "What you gonna do with that box anyway Handlebar?"

"We do some kind'a ceremony where we sacrifice some animals and then some goddess is supposed to appear and grant three wishes to whoever can answer her test question."

"No shit man," mumbled Preacher. "Three wishes huh? Just like the genie in the bottle."

"Yeah, only this genie is real. But you gotta be real careful what you wish for dude."

"Right man, like them old stories on the 'Twilight Zone' where the guy wishes for power and the genie turns him into Hitler," said preacher.

"Yeah, exactly. Blavatsky will tell me what to ask for and the goddess will give us the power to rule the world forever."

Playing for time a little Preacher asked, "You sure she's gonna include you dude? That kind of power would be hard to share ya know."

Meronek had thought a lot about it to be sure, but he was not going to let this guy know. "I will help her to get her youth and beauty back, in return she will make me her man and we will rule the Earth together forever."

"Cool man, think about me if you need a good enforcer or anything."

"Yeah, I will." Meronek curled up and passed out then and Preacher went back to his own bedroll where he lay down and stroked an ancient symbol around his neck that looked like a Sun Disk: The symbol of the Ancient Illuminati.

✝ ✝ ✝

Before dinner was served, several of us stood up and gave their testimony about how they had come to be saved, which was very inspiring. Then Jason's father, on older version of himself, got up and preached a little sermon, "For those of you that have not met me, my name is Joseph Long Bow, and I came to know Christ in prison.

"I had been locked up with a twenty-year sentence for a crime I did not commit and I was feeling very bitter and angry about that. I had seen many of the white man's gospel preachers, but I had never known Christ. I was a Shaman of the Bad Face band of the Oglala Sioux and did not know anything about salvation.

"I was in pain, spiritual pain, that I could find no help with. Booze did not help, drugs were not the answer either, nothing helped; I felt like I just wanted to die and be done with all the pain that life had brought me. Someone gave me a Bible one day and I began to read it. I learned about Jesus and all that he had done, so one night I got down on my knees and told the Great Spirit that I would go without food until he revealed himself to me in a way I would understand.

"On the tenth day of my fast, I lay down to sleep and had a vision. Before me on the ground were twenty pair of moccasins, so I reached out to gather them up when a voice said, 'You can not take more than four,' and then I woke up. I got out of bed, got on my knees, and prayed like Gideon. 'Father God, if this vision came from you, please send it again.'

"I got back in bed and as soon as I went to sleep, I had another vision. This time there were twenty ponies standing in front of me and as I went to catch them that same voice said, 'You can not take more than four,' and again I woke up. I thanked God for these visions and the promise he had given me.

"The thing was, I wasn't sure what he meant. Four what? But I held onto that promise, because the Living God, creator of all things, had taken the time to speak to an insignificant sinner like myself who did not even believe in him. The years passed, four, five, six, and parole reviews as well—three, four, and then I was called in for review number five.

"I walked into the office and the parole agent opened my file and said, 'I see this is your fourth time up.' I had been mistaken in my count. I had only been reviewed three times not four! I knew as soon as it was out of her mouth that I would be paroled and I was. God is well able to keep his promises!

"As you men go out now to fight the forces of the Evil One, I want you to know that God is with you and neither the forces of Man or Devil can stand against you. You will have the victory!"

I took Dakota off to one side after his testimony and we talked for a while about how we had become believers. She told me that in her case, it had happened when she had been baptized as a teenager.

As she was coming out of the water, she had heard a sound like Angel's singing, and felt the hand of the Lord touch her with a feeling of love that was so open, so forgiving, that it was impossible to truly describe in words. She knew in that moment that God was real and she would serve him all her life.

Then, of course, it was my turn. I told her, "My first experience with God knowledge was after a wreck on a motorcycle. I had sideswiped a car and after getting up off the pavement and sitting on the curb, I went into shock. As I lay there, I suddenly felt that same love that you had experienced, with the addition of a bright white light and a voice that said, 'It is not yet your time.'

"I came too with only minor injuries, but the memory of that experience has always stayed with me. But, I guess, my real knowledge came during my tours in Iraq when I knew that I was being watched over by something supernatural. I just knew I was not going to die, that I was destined for some purpose. Now, I guess I know what it is, and I hope it includes you Dakota."

I kissed her and felt her embrace me as though trying to pull us together so tightly that, by force alone, we would become one body. After a long time we finally came up for air and I asked her, "You care to saddle up a couple of Jason's horses after dinner and go for a moonlight ride?"

"I would like that very much Tom Harper," she said with tears of joy in her eyes.

CHAPTER 31

Back in his modest apartment, fitting for a professor of a minor research institute, Zevi Cohen seated himself at an antique Secretary worth thousands of dollars and reviewed his mail. Afterward, he went to his laptop and checked through his e-correspondence finding a message from his man in Mexico.

—-THINGS GOING WELL—PACKAGE SHOULD BE DELIVERED TOMORROW—-PROGRAM TO BE PRESENTED ON TIME—-

This was the news he had been waiting for. He picked up his phone and called a man known as Mike the Mercenary. He was the sort of person who would do anything, anywhere, as long as the money was right.

After giving Mike the go-ahead, he transferred the agreed upon sum of money to an account designated by the mercenary and then prepared a celebratory meal of Kosher beef and a glass of wine. While eating, he looked around the apartment at the 'reproduction' paintings on the walls, the Louis the 15th furniture, and other antiques worth millions which he had accumulated over his years of fruitful and lucrative service to the society. Soon he would be able to live in a palace befitting his stature, instead of hiding like this; pretending to be a mild-mannered professor of esoteric Jewish studies. He would be greater than Solomon—he was already wiser.

The steaks had been cooked to perfection and everyone enjoyed the cookout. It was good for us to have a chance to relax after the past couple of weeks; too much had happened in such a short time. They needed to blow off some steam, but the way these people did it was new and strange to me. Nobody got drunk and there were no fights, not even any cussing. Instead, there was hymn singing and praise. Altogether, it was better than what I had become accustomed too and I felt I could find myself a place with these people.

"You ready for that ride darlin'," I asked Dakota.

"You bet cowboy, got my spurs and chaps on."

Jason led us to the barn behind the house where two horses were all ready saddled and waiting for us. "Why don't you take the Appaloosa Tom, he's more used to having a man ride him. Dakota, you take the paint. Her name is Chato, which means trouble."

"What do I call this beast brother?"

"Traveler is his name. He comes from fine stock."

Before we mounted up, I put a bottle of wine in the saddlebags along with some cheese and crackers. We rode off in the direction of the mountains steering away from the roads so that we would have complete privacy. It was about seven o'clock when we left and would not be dark until almost nine. Since we would be out well past dark, I took a compass reading before we left and made sure I had an extra clip for my Colt .45 as well, just in case of trouble.

We rode along in silence for a while as we both gathered our thoughts, not yet wanting to break the gentle, rhythmic sounds of hooves, and creak of leather saddles.

The smells of the desert, creosote and sagebrush, the gentle breeze, clean by city standard, and the calming absence of traffic noise that we become so inured to made the moment very special.

"Tom, I know we have been moving pretty fast and I just want to be sure we are both on the same page. What do you want from our relationship and I will tell you what I want."

A very loaded question if I ever heard one and one I was hoping I could answer without sticking my foot in my mouth. Trying to give the impression of deep thought, instead of stark terror, I kept silent for a long moment before answering.

"First, I want a companion in this ride of life. Someone to be my friend as well as my lover. She will, I hope, be the mother of my children; loving, patient, and nurturing. A Godly woman who will bring honor to my name, as well as her own. Willing to go where I go and love me even when things may not be so good. And I would, in turn, do the same for her."

"Wow, you said a mouthful there cowboy. But you said the right things and I agree with you completely Tom. I would want you to be honest and open with me, especially about your heart. That strong but silent thing is okay, but only to a point. I would want to know how you are feeling and how we are doing as a couple."

She fell silent then and I pulled us over to an old adobe ruin where we dismounted. We tied up the horses, got out the wine and crackers, and then had a seat under the canopy of stars. We talked of little things for a while and held hands in the failing light, sipping wine, eating the cheese and crackers, and listening to the music of the desert night.

"I don't think I could handle it if you don't come back Tom, so you be careful."

"I will, because now I have something worth coming back for. I've never felt like this before about anyone Dakota and I find it a little scary."

"Me too cowboy, but I want to go a little slower because I don't want to make a mistake again. I want to be sure that God is in this too. That it isn't just lust or wishful thinking, but real love."

"I agree darlin', I don't want to rush things. We have this operation to take care of first and then, as you say, we must seek the will of God to make sure that he really wants us to be together. But if he feels what I am feeling when I am with you, then I don't see how he could want anything else. Go with your heart and your gut." I must have said the right thing because she kissed me and afterward, she put her head on my shoulder with her arms wrapped around me and just held me.

The ride back was much too short, but I felt as though I rode on the back of an angel.

About an hour before dawn it began to rain. Not like the gentle rain back home. This was a tropical downpour and it was more like having a large tub of water poured over your head. Everyone took shelter under the trees or under the stones of the ruins. Meronek found an opening in the old structure, an ancient doorway, where he was able to take shelter and watch as the lightning would briefly illuminate the surrealistic scene around him.

He suddenly felt a hand on his shoulder from the open maw of the temple behind him and it scared him so much that he nearly ran screaming into the storm. As it was, he nearly knocked himself out when he straightened up his five-eight frame in a five-foot opening.

Thinking it was one of the others in his gang he turned cursing, "You dumb-ass son-a-bitch——," but another bolt of lightning revealed the face of someone else. "Paco you dumb-shit," he shouted to be heard over the rain. "What're you dong here man? I could'a killed you!"

"Yeah, right after you cleaned out your panties," he laughed. "I came early man, to make sure you pendaho's didn't get lost."

"Paco, it's great to see you brother, it's been too long." With that said, they embraced each other and kissed.

It was an hour after sunup before the rain let up enough to venture out of their hiding place and down to the muddy ground that was the road. For a little while there would be no insects, but they would have to be especially watchful of snakes looking for a warm dry spot to bask.

Within minutes, the rain-soaked ground began to fog and the jungle turned into one enormous Turkish steam bath. Everyone was beginning to show the wear and tear of life in the tropical rain forest. Clothes were starting to mildew and fall apart and things were beginning to grow on their bodies that weren't meant to be there. Tempers were getting shorter than a first graders attention span.

A shot rang out from the bushes along with a stream of curses as Deadman stepped out of the bushes with a snake gripped in his right hand. "What kind o' snake is this?" he shouted in an excited voice.

"Paco stepped up looking at the bright colors of the reptile and asked, "Did it bite you man?"

"Yeah," Deadman answered. "Right on my ass dude. Tell me this thing ain't poisonous man."

"I wish I could my friend, but that is a Coral snake. It is most deadly."

"Gimme the anti-dote then, do something."

Meronek stepped in to look at the snake, "You sure Paco?"

"Yes, I am certain. There is an anti-venom, but we have none here and the closest would be Gordo's compound about ten miles from here. We can try to get him there, but we only have about ten minutes before the poison will kill him."

"Sorry bro, it's been good riding with you," said Meronek as Deadman started shaking from fear and shock.

"No man, this ain't right," blurted Deadman and he ran over to the Land Rover, threw open the back door, ripped up the lid on the crate holding the Ark, and reached in to touch the artifact hoping that he would be healed, like in the stories he wrongly remembered from Bible school in his childhood.

As soon as his hand made contact with the Ark his body was engulfed in an electric-blue discharge that threw him thirty feet through the air leaving him smoking and charred as though he had grabbed a high-tension power line. The smell of cooked human flesh and burning hair was overpowering and then, to make it worse, his body burst open spilling his entrails across the ground. The heat generated by the high-power discharge had cooked his body in only a second.

"Whoa dude, did you see that?" exclaimed Preacher.

"Yeah, remind me not to touch that thing," said Meronek.

"Yes, my brother," responded Paco. "Too bad he didn't know that a Coral snake could not have bitten him on the ass."

"What do you mean?" asked Preacher.

"Its mouth is to small; his fangs to short. He can only bite on the toes or between the fingers."

"You mean Deadman wasn't bit? Why did you tell him he was gonna die?" exclaimed Preacher.

"Just having some fun with him man," said Meronek. "I didn't know he was gonna do something crazy like that."

"Yeah," Paco went on. "Just having some fun man, don't you people know nothin' about snakes?"

Preacher just looked at them for a moment, then got on his bike, fired it up, and headed for the temple leaving the others behind.

Nobody wanted to touch the corpse, so they just left Jacob 'Deadman' Martin where he lay.

Bob came by about three hours later, found the body still lying next to the road, and strangely untouched by scavengers. He didn't look like a man struck by lightning, so Bob guessed correctly that he had touched the Ark. Tracks in the mud also indicated that Rogers was still ahead of him by about an hour.

He sat down upwind of the body, had some jerky and bottled water for lunch, and called in to let the others know how he was doing. He knew he was close with only a few miles to go and now he would have to be careful to avoid any traps or guards that Meronek would post. The accidental tourist thing was not going to work here.

He wondered if Rogers was smart enough to avoid capture or if he even wanted too. Bob looked at the map he had of the area. It was an aerial map provided by a C.I.A. friend that showed every trail and mud path in the vicinity. There was a trail he could take, but it was more suited to a trials bike than his Indian Chief. After scanning the map carefully he decided to drive in as close as he could and go on foot the rest of the way.

After five miles he spotted his first guard outpost, so he pulled off the road, hid the bike, and set off for the temple on foot. He did find some booby-traps and other security measures, but they were easy enough to avoid. The real danger of course, was the jungle itself. By taking his time and being careful, he knew he would make it. He had at least twenty-four hours and only needed to move about two more miles. What could be more simple?

When we got back to Jason's place the plane was already on the ground having flown over us during our return. After dropping off the horses we made our way over to where every one was gathered. As we approached I spotted a tall, lanky individual with long brown hair, covered by a gimme cap that said U.S. AIR. Jason took me by the arm and introduced me to the pilot. "Tom, I want you to meet Allen 'Crash' Boykin, your host for the run down south and that is Jonah, your ride.

"Glad to meet you Crash. Anyone ever tell you that your nickname does not inspire confidence?"

"Yeah, but the plane doesn't either, so it evens out Gunny."

I stepped up taking a closer look at the man, "Sorry, do I know you?"

"Sort of Sarge," he drawled. "You see, there was this helicopter over in Iraq that crashed and your squad pulled a crewman and pilot out. Remember?"

I did, but not the name, or the face that had been obscured by a helmet, goggles, and a generous helping of blood. "That was on my first tour, it's been a while ya know. I remember the chopper, but I didn't get a good look at the hotshot that crashed it. I was too busy shooting at the insurgents that were trying to kill him."

"Good shootin' too Gunny. I came out with a broken arm, a broken leg, and shrapnel in my back. If you hadn't come along me and my crew chief wouldn't have made it. Thank you Gunny." He drew his lanky frame up straight and threw me a salute, then waited for me to return it. Feeling somewhat embarrassed I did, and then shook his hand.

"The handle, Crash, stuck with me from that day on Gunny."

"Yeah. What was your mission that day, I never did find out."

"We were there to provide suppressing fire for another squad on the other side of the village when we took some small arms fire that lunched the tranny, I got us away from the firefight as quick as possible. The whole drive train froze up and we went down hard, that's when you came along on your white horse."

"Well, glad we were there to help. You up for this trip tomorrow?"

"You bet Gunny," said Crash. "Just one question if you don't mind. Where are we going and what can I expect when we get there?"

"Step into my office sir and I will fill you in," I said, pointing to a picnic table with a cooler of sodas and a couple of cilantro candles burning on it.

Dakota came over and I pulled her down next to me while I filled Crash in on what we would be doing.

"Seems pretty simple. You want me to wait around or pull out and let you drive back?"

"You best hang around," said Jason. "Meronek has some drug-lord down there providing security and he undoubtedly controls the surrounding area. We will probably need to get out of there pronto."

"Amen brother," I chimed in. "If we do this right, hopefully no one will get killed, but they are not going to appreciate us taking the Ark and the goddess away from them. They went to a lot of trouble to bust it out of Area 51 and they will fight to keep it. Blavatsky and her demon will certainly do what they can to keep it and I expect that their powers are considerable. That is why we are going to employ as many flash-bangs and other non-lethal methods as possible to get it back."

"Is there a chance that they may turn the Spirit of God loose on themselves, like in that Indiana Jones movie?" asked Crash.

"It is possible of course. No one really seems to know what will happen if they actually open the Ark," Joseph answered. "The only way they could safely, would be with a Levite priest who has undergone the ritual purification process and they aren't likely to find one that would be willing to help them perform such a desecration.

"I might know of one who would. Bill, were you able to trace that web page I showed you?"

"Yeah Tom. It went back to a server in Santa Fe, but that was as far as I could trace it."

"Okay. Zevi Cohen lives in Santa Fe and he is a priest, at least by ancestry. He may have in mind crashing our little party and taking the Ark for himself or for the Illuminati if he is responsible for that web page. If that is true, we may have a lot more to deal with than Meronek and the drug-lord's men."

"Alright," said Jason. "We go in, but 'when' is the question now. Do we wait for the Illuminati people to fight it out with Meronek's people first or go in hoping that there will only be his small contingent?"

"Hard one to answer bro," I came back. "I don't know how many people the drug-lord has on site or how well armed they will be. We can assume they will be carrying AK's and will have explosives; probably a couple of vehicles with machine guns mounted on them too.

"We will take at least three sniper rigs to take out any L.M.G.'s (Light Machine Guns) and any other heavy equipment they may have. They will also keep the rest of 'em running for cover while we move in. If they have the Ark uncrated, do not touch it. I can't stress this enough. We will take an empty crate with poles to pick it up and use one of their vehicles to transport the Ark, though we will take along some A.T.V.'s just in case."

While everyone discussed the details of the operation, I took Dakota with me to the C-5 where someone had strung out some work lights throwing the scene into stark relief. The tail section was lowered, making it look like the gaping mouth of some pre-historic monster, devouring men and machines into its dark void.

Holding hands we walked around the plane nervously talking about the mission, but mostly trying to hide our emotions. Inside the plane, I noticed crates of AK's and R.P.G.'s, hand-grenades, flares, claymores, and other tools of destruction. "Looks like we have enough to take on a division of bad guys," I said as I picked up one of the Barrett M107A1 .50 caliber sniper rifles, looking it over, and musing about how much damage that half-inch slug could do to man and machine.

"I wish this were not necessary Tom," Dakota said in a voice choked with emotion. "That there was some other way."

I hugged her close to me, kissed her on her cheek, and said, "We could just walk away, but then evil would win because good did not care enough to intervene. That is why people like Hitler, Stalin, Hussein, and so many others come to power. Meek should not mean weak."

We went back toward the group which was beginning to break up now as people moved off to get in some last minute preparation and a few hours sleep. I took Dakota home and the two of us stretched out on the couch, holding on to each other as though it might be the last time and praying that it would not.

Sitting in his leather, executive office chair, Moses Goldman contemplated the world in front of him. It was only a globe, but represented so much more to a man like himself. Through hard work and dedication he had ascended to the position of Alpha member of the Illuminati, but he also considered himself a good Jew. He gave generously to charities in the holy-land, supported Jewish immigration, and helped organizations like the Jewish Welfare Fund, the Temple Restoration Fund, and many others. At heart, he was a Zionist, and he did not intend to let the goyim claim the Ark or that self-serving idiot Zevi Cohen, for that matter.

He got up, poured himself another glass of wine, and looked around his multimillion dollar mansion. Everything he looked upon shouted 'class' and 'taste'. The paintings, the carpets, the furniture, everything he owned showed the world that God had blessed him above all others.

His wife had left him, not for another man, but because, she said, he no longer loved people; only things. Let the bitch rot in her little apartment, the money she stole from him in alimony would be nothing compared to the riches and glory he would receive from the Jewish people when he, Moses Goldman, returned the Ark of the Covenant to the Holy Land where it belonged.

Then Israel would finally become the world power it was destined to be and he would be there, in all humility of course, to lead the people out of bondage, just as his namesake had done thousands of years ago.

None of this foolishness with the goddess; that was only a trick. He knew there was no such power in the Ark. The power was in the belief of the people that God inhabited the Ark and would give them super-natural victory over their enemies.

Superstition wasn't all bad; it could be used to make something happen where it could not by natural means. And if it helped him in conquering the world; even better. As long as he was at the top, it was all the same to him. He leaned forward and spun the globe with a smile on his face that many like him had worn in the past.

Picking up his phone he called a number that belonged to an even older organization than the Illuminate; so old that it was said to have been organized by Moses' brother, Aaron. Translated into English its name was, 'The Army of the Golden Dawn,' and it was dedicated to preserving Jewish heritage which included every artifact of Solomon's temple. How much they actually possessed, he was not sure, but they would once again be able to start up the sacrifices and re-establish the temple where the hated Dome of the Rock mosque now stood.

The Arabs would be the first to feel his vengeance, he would wipe them out to the last little turd-pushing child. God may have promised Ishmael to make a great nation of him, but Moses Goldman would wipe his degenerate seed from the face of the earth.

The voice at the other end identified itself as Aaron; code for the A.G.D. and Moses replied in his own coded answer. With this done, he was connected to the man who was in charge of 'OPERATION ARK.' He called himself Joshua and Moses gave him the current information on where the Ark was and what sort of resistance they could expect in trying to recover it.

"How much of a threat are these Gideon's Warriors?" Joshua asked. "How many are there and how well armed? Could we make allies of them?"

"There are no more than fifteen or twenty of them, but they are well armed and all have combat experience. I don't think they want the Ark for any purpose of their own, they just want to deny these evil people from gaining control of it."

"Altruistic then is it? In that case, we may be able to reason with them. We will let you know the outcome brother. You have done Israel a momentous service."

Leaning back in his chair, Moses closed his eyes, and daydreamed of himself leading the Jews through the Red Sea to freedom with the women and children singing songs about him and throwing trinkets of gold and silver into the growing pile at his feet. It's good to be king, he thought.

CHAPTER 32

Half a world away another ogre raised its head at mention of the Ark. It was an old monster and nearly forgotten, but nowhere near dead. It had been dealt a serious blow from which recovery had taken generations, but now it was ready to make itself known once again.

The Illuminati known as Hotel, whose real name was Maximilian Von Rhome, was intimate with this old creature of evil. Sitting now in his home reminiscent of a castle, in a secret room decorated with memorabilia of that glorious time, he savored the thought of raising the Swastika in world domination once again.

Where Hitler had failed, he would succeed with the Ark to command. With God's power at his behest, no army would be able to stop him. His loyal troops stood by in the little town of Gauymas at this very moment on the east coast of Mexico to spearhead the takeover of the ancient artifact and claim it for the Fourth Reich.

He reached for the phone and made the call that would change the face of politics forever. Heil Max.

In the little town of Belen, just south of Guaymas, at the head-quarters of the Army of the Fourth Reich commandant Eric Von Strome sits idly working a crossword puzzle from the New York Times. He curses at being interrupted by the phone, but quickly comes to attention even though he is still seated.

It is Max with the long awaited call to arms. He reaches for the camp phone and calls the Eagles Nest barrack informing his second in command that they are to form up for immediate deployment; this is not a drill! The next call is to the airfield to prepare their aging DC-3 'Dakota' for immediate departure and the glider to be loaded with the ATV's, fuel, and supplies that will be needed for the operation.

Too bad they would not have the use of their C-5, due to the failure of one engine, and a lack of repair parts. They would just have to make do, though he felt that this was no way to enter an operation. He was proud of his men and felt they were the best in the world, but lack of parts and equipment could put the operation in jeopardy. At this point, they had no choice though; the command had been given and must be carried out.

Twenty men lined up at the airfield with parachutes and weapons for a final review. After a few minor adjustments to their equipment by his own hand, Eric had the men climb into the aging Douglas Dakota DC 3 that smelled of manure, marijuana, and other chemicals from its alternate job as a smuggling plane. Having already checked out the glider which was attached to the Dakota, he climbed in and gave the signal to Hans Grubber, the pilot, to begin the take-off.

The twin engines revved up slightly as they took up the slack in the glider's towline, and then, with the brakes fully on the throttles were opened to full. When full power had been achieved, the whole airframe began to shudder as though trying to tear itself apart. Eric had a moment of fear that the wings were going to rip right off the fuselage then, with flaps fully extended, Hans let go the brakes, and the old veteran of WWII lurched forward dragging its parasite behind as both charged toward the tree line in the distance.

This was one time that Eric was glad he could not see out the cockpit. At least if they didn't make it he would never know and would simply die in a huge fireball. With engines straining at full power and Hans cursing in three languages as he pulled the wheel back with all his massive strength the Dakota leapt up into the darkening sky with the glider following after. Everyone breathed a sigh of relief and tried to pretend that there had never been any doubt about the outcome, but privately many wished the old bird had a commode instead of a gallon bucket.

In the morning I woke Dakota with a kiss and a squeeze of her hand and went into the kitchen to make coffee and to say my morning prayers. I prayed that the Lord would give us a safe day and his blessing on our relationship. After coffee and doughnuts, I suggested she go take a shower and I would take mine afterward.

"Why don't we save water and shower together?" she asked with a coy expression on her lovely face.

"I would really like that, but we better wait until after we're married," I replied. "I respect you too much to mess this up darlin'."

She looked at me with an expression that bordered on disbelief, then she pulled my face down to hers and said, "You are very special to me Tom Harper, you better come home." Then she gave me a very passionate kiss.

It was a very cold shower that morning.

Bob made his way to within a hundred meters of the temple. He could not get any closer because the area around the temple had been cleared, but he was close enough to see everything. Meronek and his band of fourteen men and three women had made camp right at the base of the ancient structure. Paco and his people numbered only ten, but they had two pickups with M-60's mounted above the cabs on pylons and another on a tripod atop the pyramid. He called Tom to fill him in and, as the phone was ringing, he saw Rogers come rolling in with a big white flag fluttering on a pole attached to the forks of his Harley.

No one shot at him but there were plenty of guns pointed at him. Bob got through to Tom at that moment and gave him a running account of what was happening. Rogers stopped in front of Meronek and, after dismounting, was searched for weapons. Bob did have field glasses and was pretty good at reading lips, but they did not face him enough to make it practical. He would have given anything to have a directional mike, but that was out of the question for now. He would just have to wait and maybe catch something as they talked with each other.

After a few minutes Rogers turned his way and he was at least able to follow his side of the conversation. Dick was telling Meronek about their plans to crash the party, but that really wasn't news to him, and claiming to be on their side. He said he was a servant of Blavatsky and someone called Faustus and that he was there to help in staging the ceremony.

Meronek did not seem to be pleased with this information, probably because he felt that he should be running the whole show. They took Rogers away to one side to wait for Meronek's decision on him. Bob finished his conversation with Tom and shut off his phone to conserve the battery since he would need it later.

He pulled back into the forest and started making his way around to the rear of the temple since that area seemed to be the least protected. When it was dark he planned to move up to the top of the temple where he would be able to control the entire area with that M-60.

At 1700 hours everyone started loading into the C-5 and at 1705 the door closed. The motors revved up to full power deafening those who would remain behind and causing them to turn away as the desert sand tried to blast away the soft tissues of their faces. As the C-5 climbed skyward Dakota could feel her heart pounding in a way that it had seldom done before, then she felt an arm slip around her waist in comfort.

"Don't worry little sister," came the reassuring voice of Helen Walks Far. "God will bring him back to you."

Dakota turned to her wrapping her arms around her and said, "He better, 'cause I love him more than life itself. I don't think I could take losing him Helen."

Mike the Mercenary loaded his people into highly modified military Hummers that had been purchased as military surplus. More armor had been added, including armored glass and floor plates against mines. There were three of them carrying five men each and a 2-½ ton truck of WWII vintage fitted with an M-60 on the cab and small arms ports along the sandbagged sides. The deuce-and-a-half carried an additional five men, as well as extra fuel and supplies for the Hummers. They would be going over-land from their staging area in Belen, south of Guaymas, so he hoped they would have an easy trip. There were only a few bikers to deal with according to the old Jew that hired him, so maybe it would be an easy paycheck. He sure hoped so, because he was getting to old for this work.

He was forty-nine, with close cropped blond hair, blue eyes that were still clear, and at just over 1.8 meters he felt comfort-able manning the Browning .50 caliber H.M.G. in the turret of the lead Hummer

It would take about four to five hours to reach their target and he hoped his kidneys would survive the pounding they were tak-ing from these miserable Mexican roads.

They had debarked from a freighter only a week ago at Guaymas and had been moving ever since, trying to avoid the Federalies, drug lords, nosy C.I.A., D.E.A., and several other three-letter law enforcement agencies.

They would have to shoot their way out since they had no air support and that would be the biggest trick of all. No doubt they would have hit-squads and police after them all the way to their extraction point at Mazatlan. That was why he planned to hide out in the jungle for a few weeks whether Zevi liked it or not. Otherwise he could spring for a couple of Chinooks to come and get them. Oh yeah, he was gonna pay plenty more to get this package.

✝ ✝ ✝

Meronek did not like this stranger who had come into his camp claiming to represent Blavatsky and Faustus. It was too pat, but it was just like that two-timing bitch. He was pacing, trying to get his thoughts and emotions under control when Paco walked up and asked, "Mijo, what will we do about this stranger? If he is who he says he is, we can not kill him. But how do we find out?"

"The only way to know for sure is for me to trance-out and see her, but if I do that I won't be able to carry out the ceremony. I will talk to him again and ask him some questions about her and he better have the right answers. Bring your gun and be ready to shoot him if I say so, okay."

"Okay mijo," nodded Paco. "I will do this."

Meronek went to where Rogers was enjoying the swarming mosquitoes in the hot afternoon sun and sat down across from him on the stone steps of the temple. "You say you know Blavatsky; describe her to me."

"I don't know if that will help bro, she projects herself as the ideal of beauty to the person looking at her and what is beautiful to me may not be to you. I can tell you about the place where she lives though; that's always the same."

Meronek considered this for a few moments then answered. "Okay, tell me about her place then."

"A single level, A-frame log cabin made from Redwood logs with a front porch that has a swing suspended by chains. There are exactly seven steps to the porch, no screen door, since she doesn't have to worry about bugs, just as there are no screens on the windows. Does this sound familiar so far?"

Handlebar had to admit Rogers had all the details down. He had been there all right or knew someone who had. "Okay, I believe you've been there, but why did she send you without telling me?"

"Because she doesn't trust you man, that's why. She doesn't trust any of us dude, don't you get that yet? She wants the power for herself and she has no intention of sharing it. I know she promised you she would, but what guarantee do you have?"

Damn it, Rogers was right. He had no assurance she would share and that was why she had kept the answer to the riddle and the three wishes to herself; only to be revealed when the goddess was present. He knew this, but wanted to believe that she would keep her word.

"I don't have no guarantee, just her word. Do you have one?"

"No, but I do not want the wishes of the goddess and what I do seek my master has already given me."

This was different; this guy was here to make sure he went through with the ceremony one way or another. "You know some way to make her keep her promise?"

"When she appears here ask her to give you the ring she wears on her left hand; her wedding band. If you have that, she will have no choice. She will not want to do it, but if you stand firm no matter what she says or does, she will have to give in. She can't carry out the ceremony because she not living flesh; she must have one of us to do it. If you get the ring she will be yours to command."

"How do you know this?"

"I serve Faustus, her master."

Meronek did not like the sound of that. "You ain't gonna try to hijack this for him are you?"

"No, he has no use for the goddess as he is beyond the desire for flesh. He is a demon of high order; Carmine is just a witch of human origin. That is why she wants these wishes, so she can be renewed and made beautiful again. You would not care for her the way she really looks. That forest and the cabin aren't the way you see them either Meronek. But you know that don't you?"

He knew this was true, he had seen through the deception before; he just didn't want to admit it. "Okay, I will get her to turn over the ring and force her to honor her promise. What do you get out of it?"

"I told you bro, I already have my reward."

After hanging up with the man called Moses, Joshua went out to his command post and alerted the Special Operations team to prepare for departure. They had been on this small island, off the coast of Mexico, for a week now waiting for this call. Now the men gathered arms and equipment and made last minute adjustments according to the Intel they had just been given.

Three helicopters, two Huey's of Vietnam vintage, and one Apache combat chopper were stripped of their camouflage and readied for flight. The combat unit consisting of ten highly trained men were loaded aboard the two Huey's. The opposing forces were not considered professional soldiers and should not present any serious threat to them.

They would pick up the Ark, make their way back to a junk steamer where they would land the choppers, dump them overboard, and make their way back to Israel.

It was a good plan and that was what worried Joshua. No plan ever survives beyond first contact with the enemy and he knew it. He had a good team though and vast resources at his command, so any contingency could be taken care of. In a few short hours Israel would reclaim its greatest artifact and finally take its rightful place among the worlds Super-Powers

CHAPTER 33

A pickup hauling a cattle trailer pulled up and parked at the base of the pyramid. Two Mexicans got out to unload the trailer. First to come out was a pure black goat, followed by a spotless white ram. Last to come out was a red bull without blemish. All three were led over to an alter that had been erected out of natural stone for this purpose and tethered in anticipation of their sacrifice.

Meronek was preparing himself for the ceremony at a creek nearby with a ritual bath. Preacher was sharpening a large machete that would be used to dispatch the animals and singing an old hymn to himself, 'Shall We Gather at the River*.'

He kept glancing at the sky in anticipation of the coming forces of the Illuminati and wondering where the best place to hide would be. He did not want to be out in the open when everything started going down, but he did not want to be too far from the Ark either. And since there would be no way to identify him, he would need a place where he could hide until his forces were victorious.

Meronek had finished his purification and came over to claim the machete giving Preacher the opportunity to slip off into the thick forest surrounding the area. Everyone else was gathering at the alter and would not notice that he was missing. The sun was just beginning to dip behind the tree line as Handlebar began reciting the ancient incantations to summon the witch Blavatsky who would have to be present before the sacrifices could begin.

The world seemed to be holding its breath as he recited the words; the insects ceased their discordant noise, the birds went to roost, and animals retreated to the protection of the forest. The air itself became still as death and an odor of sulfurous brimstone came up out of a hole that appeared in the ground forming a yellow column before Meronek. The air shimmered in front of him as something began to take form; something not natural to this world and in some way not welcome in it. At first, she appeared ancient and withered, but took on form as his words continued until she finally stood as he had seen her so many times in the woods.

"Steve, you have done well my servant. Everything is in order? The sacrifices are ready?"

"Yes mistress," replied Meronek. "There is only one small matter to be taken care of before we begin."

"And what is that?" she said with a sudden flash of anger in her eyes.

"Place your wedding ring on my finger and declare us married before all these others and we will begin."

This was not something she had anticipated and it caused her a moment of confusion. How dare this lump of excrement address her as though he were the master here. To even consider having this buffoon as her consort for eternity made her feel physically ill. Her first thought was to strike him down where he stood for his impudence, but she still needed him for the ceremony.

"I will wed you after the ritual; not before. Do not anger me now my darling, let us continue," she said trying to con him into continuing.

Meronek glanced at Rogers and saw him shake his head no, as he held up his ring finger letting him know not to give in to her demand.

"I think I would rather have the ring first my love. It is not that I don't trust you, I just want us to do this ceremony as man and wife in front of all these people who will be our witnesses."

She knew then that the fool had been talking to someone. There was no way he could have come up with this on his own: She could not kill him now, but she could not allow herself to be joined to him either. She lashed out at him in his mind bringing the horrors of the damned before his eyes to torture him into submission as she had done many times before. This time though, there was little reaction behind those eyes; no terror or pain occluded his sight. He was stronger than she had given him credit for.

They both stood unyielding in the gathering gloom of evening when the air was suddenly split with the sounds of Detroit muscle and U.S. Steel. Chunks of earth leaped up into the air as bullets from Mike the Mercenary's caravan of hired guns rolled headlong into the clearing. Everyone, including Paco and his men, had been intently watching the exchange between Blavatsky and Meronek instead of watching the road leading into the site. Within seconds automatic weapons answered Mike's challenge and they were fully engaged in battle.

Bob took this opportunity to slip up the back way since the guards had moved to the front side of the pyramid and took out the gunner at its apex by clubbing him on his head with his .45 Colt auto. Then he lay down to conceal the change in personnel. He would let them shoot it out for a while, as he was more interested in protecting the Ark than who won the battle.

Looking up, Bob saw and old Dakota DC-3 pulling a glider come into view and wondered who this could be. Another uninvited guest no doubt. Well, the more the merrier.

Hans looked down seeing the battle unfold beneath them and reported to Eric that they would be dropping into a hot zone. Eric gave the go-ahead to release the glider causing the old Dakota to lurch violently. Eric and the paratroopers held on until the plane steadied and the red jump light changed to green.

The waist door opened and, one at a time, the brave men jumped out into darkness to descend upon a battlefield lit by staccato bursts of light from automatic weapons fire and the weaving headlights of Mike's HummV's as they raced headlong toward Meronek's crew who were returning fire with the fury of desperation.

The glider crew, now set free, began their decent toward the open field in front of the pyramid hoping for a safe landing. This other force had not been expected of course, and would complicate their unloading of the glider considerably.

After all the paratroopers were out, Hans started banking to starboard when he saw the unmistakable red streaks of tracers climbing toward his ancient war-bird and heard the slap of rounds tearing through the thin aluminum coating on wings and fuselage.

The port engine made a sudden clattering racket that he knew could not be good and the black smoke that began to trail out over the wing confirmed it. The oil pressure was dropping rapidly and he had to feather the motor to keep it from freezing up. Now with only one engine he got on the course that would take him home—he hoped.

Zeig Heil for the Fourth Reich," he laughed as the plane began to lose altitude. The starboard motor was losing power and would not keep him in the air much longer if he could not fix it. He had no flight engineer though and not much time, especially since he could now see a line of helicopters coming directly toward him.

One of them was an Apache and it opened up on the DC-3 tearing huge holes in the airframe with its thirty-millimeter mini-gun, doing far greater damage than the fifty calibers had. Hans did the only thing he could think of; he went to full flaps and dived for the deck lowering the landing gear and hoping for a clear spot to put down even as he felt the impact of rounds hitting the control surfaces of the tail section.

"The war is over for you Hans," he shouted over the deafening roar of the starboard engine and the air tearing through the fifty or so gaping holes in the airframe. He pulled out of the dive just in time to settle on to the nice wide road he could see moonlight reflecting from and only realized his mistake when the wheels suddenly caught on the surface of the river and ripped off the under carriage of the plane with a sound like two freight trains colliding. The sudden contact caused the plane to nose over into the river bringing its long carrier and that of Hans Gruber to an abrupt and inglorious end.

Mike the Mercenary saw his .50's tear into the plane and smoke come out of the port engine. They would not be a problem anymore, but he was taking a lot of small arms fire from the area of the pyramid. As he raked around to concentrate his fire in that direction something swooped down out of the night sky like a Valkyrie and caught his HummV with such an impact that the vehicle was thrown onto its side like a high speed car wreck at Daytona.

Through the smoke he climbed out of the turret and staggered away from the wreck feeling that he had been badly hurt. His right arm was hanging useless at his side and had a piece of bone sticking out of it. He could not help thinking—that just wasn't right.

He was also having trouble seeing from his left eye and reaching up with his good hand he could feel a wet slippery fluid streaming down his face from a small hole in his skull over the eye which was dangling by its optic nerve. At that point Mike felt very tired and decided to sit down. This was not turning out the way it was supposed too at all.

The glider hit the ground a lot harder than Adolf Miller was prepared for and something hit his starboard wing hard causing the entire plane to spin in that direction, forcing the port wing to hit the ground digging in. Then the whole glider flipped over onto its back like a turtle.

ATV's, munitions, gasoline, and men were all thrown around like crash dummies in a Hollywood movie. As soon as everything stopped moving he released himself from his harness and tried to crawl out through the broken front windshield, but he could not get his legs to help him for some reason. It took a moment for the terrible truth to sink in that his back was broken; he was paralyzed from the waist down. He would have to lie here and hope for rescue while listening to the men in the rear calling for help that was not coming.

Bullets began to rip through the flimsy fabric of the glider and he knew that it was only a matter of time.

✝ ✝ ✝

Meronek had taken a position behind the alter and the Ark to fire back at the invading vehicles which were thrown into stark outline as the glider exploded into a huge orange fireball raining down exploding ordinance and burning fabric all over the area.

Helicopters started to fly in raking the temple grounds with M-60 rounds as well as small arms from the waste doors. The Apache turned loose its three-inch rockets on the two HummV's still racing around the field blowing one into a rolling Bar-B-Que pit and sending the other into the woods on the far side of the compound as it desperately looked for cover.

The Deuce-and-a-half went up in flames from the explosion of the glider and, hearing gunfire and explosions from the forest, he guessed that the last HummV had come across his people that had taken cover there.

He looked at Blavatsky who was keeping her head down and shouted, "Take out that helicopter, that one over there." She looked up to see that he was pointing at the Apache which was still raining death on them with its rockets and cannon fire. She cast a spell directing bats from the forest to fly into the Apache's engine intakes and rotors causing the war-bird to begin shuddering like a horse shaking off biting flies and then it just dropped out of the sky going nose first into the ground. The rotors dug up huge chunks of sod flinging them through the air in all directions and then the whole thing exploded into pieces that went flaming into the night sky landing all over the compound starting a hundred little fires.

Joshua watched his gunship plow into the ground taking its two-man crew with it and was thrown into a rage. He ordered the Huey's down sending half of his twelve men toward the pyramid and the other half toward the shooting in the woods where the other HummV had disappeared. He did not realize his tactical error until much later.

I was in the cockpit of the C-5 watching our approach and could see the fireballs from the Apache and the glider lighting up the temple compound. "Fly over Crash and let's see what's going on, it looks like somebody decided to celebrate the Fourth of July early."

"Okay boss, keep your head down."

As we passed over at five hundred feet we drew some fire but not much as most of them seemed to be busy with other targets. More importantly I spotted a signal from the top of the pyramid letting me know that Bob was there which I passed on to the others in the cargo bay.

"Okay Crash," I shouted at him to be heard over the engine noise. "Set her down." He gave me a thumbs-up by way of answer and set his glide path to intersect with the ground just past the tree line.

I was glad now that we had been delayed fifteen minutes by strong headwinds, because it looked like there was quite a battle unfolding on the ground. As we closed in, one of the Huey's lit up from the gunfire coming from Bob and lifted out of the skirmish looking for a safe place to land. The other, seeing us coming straight for it, also decided to find a less crowded piece of real estate.

Work lights that Meronek had strung out for the ceremony were still working and transformed the whole scene into a sur-realistic Hollywood movie set. I could see him running for the cover of a burned out HummV that had come to a stop in front of the alter while Blavatsky stood where she had been; oblivious to the gunfire around her.

The C-5 hit the ground hard as Crash threw the props into reverse thrust, throwing us all into our restraints, and bringing the plane to a hard stop with brakes and tires smoking. We all poured out scattering to right and left taking position to defend our Striker armored vehicle, borrowed from one of Jason's friends, as it rolled out with guns blazing at the Huey which was hov-ering about seventy-five meters away. The .50 caliber mini-gun mounted in the Striker's turret chewed into the Huey mortally wounding it, but the pilot managed to lift out and set it down behind the tree line out of sight before it could crash.

The troops the Huey's had dropped found themselves trapped between us, Meronek's people in the trees, and Bob on the apex of the pyramid. This was not a position they could maintain for long, because they were taking too much fire and could not ade-quately defend themselves.

With Crash at the controls, the C-5 roared off into the night sky to remain on station until we recalled it.

Preacher saw the HummV coming toward him and jumped behind a tree for cover and as soon as it came to a stop he looked to see who was in it, but they were not his people. The HummV started taking fire from the remnant of Meronek's people who had also taken cover in the forest. The .50 in the turret opened up on them tearing up trees, bushes, and anything else that got in the way like a chainsaw on steroids. Preacher did not really care about helping the bikers, but he tossed a frag at the HummV because it was drawing to much fire in his direction. The grenade dropped right through the gun tub sending the occupants running in all directions to get away. When it went off, the .50 went silent.

He was forced to shoot the driver who had taken a wrong turn and was running right at him. The other two disappeared into the jungle likely never to be seen again. For them, this action was over as they were the only two left of their force. Preacher could see that he had the same problem. The only ones left on the playing field were Handlebar's people in the woods, the Gideons in front of the pyramid, and maybe four of five others who were right in the middle of a triangle of fire.

Ari Miller could see that any further fighting was useless and would only result in the deaths of all his men. They had no transport out and they were vastly out-numbered. Joshua was wounded badly and their only hope was surrender. He knew that Meronek's band would not take prisoners, so he called out to the Gideons, waving his hands in the air with a white cloth. The fire from the top of the pyramid had been especially effective at keeping them from moving in any direction. Very good, because the gunner could have killed them all at any time, but chose to spare them.

Now that the gunfire had stopped someone from the Gideons shouted at them to remain where they were and keep their hands away from their weapons.

Jason was on the right flank and moved up on the Golden Dawn people first, taking them under control while I gave orders for the left flank to move out toward the HummV that had crashed into the woods to look for survivors, as well as close off the avenue of escape in that direction.

I moved over to Jason and got Bob on the phone to see how he was doing. "I'm doing fine Nephew, but I need someone to close the back door."

I dispatched three men to skirt around the pyramid and watch Bob's back, then directed our medic, a friend of Jason's who was a male nurse, to help the wounded.

Who's in charge here," I asked the ragged band of survivors.

"I am now sir," came a heavily accented voice. "Ari Miller."

"Okay Ari. Who do you people represent and why are you here?"

"We represent a Jewish enclave interested in returning the Ark to its rightful place in Israel."

"Looks like you picked a bad time to drop in Ari. You're going to sit this out while we mop up, understand? Mess this up and that man up there on the pyramid will blow your ass all the way back to Jerusalem, understand?"

"Yes sir, you will have no more trouble from us sir. May I ask your name, sir?"

"Tom Harper, Gideon's Warriors and don't call me sir. My parents were married." I went over to check on the Ark and found it to be were Meronek had left it, but now there was a Jaguar sitting in front of it. The animal stared back at me out of bright yellow eyes that showed an unnatural intelligence.

I went back to where the others were and crouched down, as firing erupted in the woods again.

"Jason, you ain't gonna believe this," I said. "There's a Jaguar guarding the Ark, but I don't think it's natural. The eyes are wrong; round pupils instead of vertical, you think it could be her?"

"No doubt of it little brother; bullets wont bother her, but this will." He handed me a crucifix about six inches long and made of silver. "It was blessed by my father, so don't lose it."

"What do I do with it," I asked. "Throw it at her or threaten to bless her with it."

"I don't know Tom, I've never done this before, but I don't think she will stick around if you carry that in front of you and rebuke her in the name of Jesus."

"Okay big guy, but if she eats me Dakota is gonna kick your butt."

James Hightower, Peter Gault, Simon Bright Star, and Charlie Lyons found the HummV smoking and abandoned where the crew had left it. Preacher had decided to disappear and make his way back to the U.S. on his own. The cause was lost, but he had to make a call first.

Moses did not take the news well at all, using some very colorful language, including some words that he could not remember having heard before. Moses told him to let himself be captured by the Gideons and keep his eye on the Ark until he could get back to him.

As the Gideon patrol came close, Preacher called out to them softly, "Yo, hey man, I surrender. Please don't shoot me."

"Come out with your hands up," ordered James. "If you got a weapon let's see it real careful."

"Okay man, " answered Preacher. "Right here it is, just my pistol and a knife, that's all I got."

James took him into custody patting him down, then turned him to face him again. "Who are you and who are you with?" he asked.

"Carl Holdman, they call me Preacher. I was with Hardcore's people riding with Handlebar. I got separated from them at the start of all this."

James looked at the guy hard because something didn't sound right in his story, but he would let it go for now. He pointed toward the HummV and asked, "Your work?"

There was no point in lying, "Yeah. They almost rolled right over me. I didn't have much choice. I tossed a grenade in and had to shoot that guy over there. I let the other two run away. I didn't figure they was much danger to us now. I think they just wanted to get away."

"Okay," Hightower said. "Let's see about rounding up the rest of your people."

They spread out into a skirmish line and headed toward the last known position of Meronek's people as one of their party took Preacher back to the staging point in front of the pyramid.

† † †

The jaguar was still sitting where I had last seen it, licking its lips as I approached, and watching me like I was a juicy Porter House steak. "Madame Blavatsky," I said as I came within six meters of her. I was holding out the cross in my left hand and my Colt in the other. I could hear a low rumble from her throat as I drew closer that raised the small hairs on the back of my neck. When I was within three meters of her, she crouched ready to spring, so I stopped.

"You know this is not going to end well for you Carmine Diablo Guzman," said Bob's voice from the steps of the pyramid. Her gaze shot up at him with a snarl, then back to me as she backed up, almost touching the Ark.

"Careful Carmine," I admonished her. "You don't want to touch the Ark. The last guy that did got fried with a million volts." I didn't know that for sure, but it sounded good, and I hoped she might get distracted enough to turn tail and run. Looking the alter over I could see that the bull was down, as was the goat. The ram was streaked with blood, but I couldn't tell whether it was its own or not.

"Your sacrifices are dead Guzman, the ceremony is over. You might as well turn and go." I stepped closer extending the cross in front of me like some sacred talisman and looking her right in the eye. She backed up a little more with her tail twitching violently until: It touched the Ark.

For a fraction of a heartbeat she was outlined in electric blue light, then she was thrown through the air about ten meters with a crack of thunder that was deafening at such close range. I was thrown onto my back and could feel the God-fire burning my exposed skin. Smoke was rising off my camo's as I rolled in the grass to put out any fire. I felt like I had been struck by lightning and if I had been any closer, I guess I would have been.

Jason came over and helped me up. I could see his lips moving, but I couldn't hear anything and motioned to my ears. He nodded in understanding and mouthed, "Are you okay?"

I said I was, even though I did not feel okay. I walked over to Blavatsky's body which had returned to human form, although grotesque in appearance. Her ancient scorched flesh fell away from her bones and turned to dust even as I watched. Worms boiled out of her torso and the stench that rose out of her was worse than anything I had ever experienced: Even week old corpses in Iraq had not smelled this bad. Flesh continued to slough away from her bones and turn to dust until there was nothing left: Not even the worms.

From the woods I heard a scream of anguish like a soul cast into the eternal darkness of the deepest pit of Hell. Meronek came running, firing his AK wildly until he emptied the clip, and then threw the gun at us like some B-movie cowboy. At the spot where Blavatsky had fallen he dropped to his knees repeating over and over. "No, no, no."

Feeling revolted by his display of love for this hell-spawn I stepped over and hit him on the back of his skull with the butt of my pistol knocking him unconscious. Looking down at the spot where she had fallen I saw something shiny reflecting light in the dusty remains. I pulled out a ring that had been on her finger, as well as a few other pieces of jewelry, and bagged them for later study.

The rest of Meronek's crew having no more reason to fight came out of the woods with their hands up, followed at gunpoint by my people.

I gave instructions for flares to be strung out across the field as landing lights and called the plane back down. Bob came down from the pyramid to join us still carrying the M-60. "Hey Nephew," he said with a big grin on his face. "Nice party, didn't know you were gonna invite so many people or I would'a baked a cake."

My hearing was coming back, but my ears were still ringing. "Sorry old thing, I should'a called first."

"I suggest we get out of here before anybody else drops in Nephew."

"Yeah, I got the team out looking for any survivors that might want to give up. They don't, their gonna have a long walk home.

Meronek's people had gathered by the alter and I had a chance to look them over. "Where's General Carter?" I asked. "And which of you is Paco?"

Preacher stepped forward and spoke, "That one is Paco," indicating a thin, black haired youngster. "I don't know what happened to the general. He took off when all the shooting started, but I can tell you that the Chevy four-by is missing."

The C-5 came thundering in at that moment raising a cloud of dust and giving me other more important business to take care of.

Some of the men grabbed the poles we had brought along and slipped them through rings in the side of the Ark, put there for this purpose long ago. They raised it up to transfer it to its new crate and I gave it a quick inspection. I saw no bullet holes or other damage, so we lowered into the box and sealed it up.

I turned back to Meronek's people and took Paco to the side. There was a defiant look in his eyes as I spoke to him. "I can't take you back to the States since you are a citizen of Mexico, but that doesn't mean you should get away free. You have committed some very serious crimes here."

"Yeah, well that ain't your problem is it gringo," he sassed back.

"What you have done here tonight has made it my problem. I will have to turn you over to the law Paco, I have no choice."

He pulled a small derringer from his pocket and pointed it at me saying, "I will not go to prison. I would rather die than go there again. I will kill anyone who tries to stop me gringo."

Keeping the little gun pointed at us, he began to withdraw to the woods. When he was about fifty meters away Simon asked, "You want me to drop him Tom?"

"No, let him go for now. I don't think his boss will be pleased with what's happened here tonight and I don't want to risk any of our lives to bring him back."

"Yeah, okay Tom," Simon said. "I know what he looks like now and we can always pick him up another day."

All the wounded were gathered up and loaded into the C-5's cargo bay, as well as any weapons we could find and before midnight we were on our way back home.

CHAPTER 34

With all the shooting no one had noticed General Carter get in the pick-up and take off heading north. He was ten miles from the firefight before he slowed down to take inventory of the situation and the truck. In the back, he found two of the gangs girls: Tracy Collins, known as Bubbles, and Shawna 'Big Lips' Thackery. Bubbles was curled into a ball whimpering and Big Lips Thackery had the vacant wide-eyed stare of a corpse.

"Are you hurt?" he asked Collins. She was hysterical and had loaded her pants, but he could see no blood or wounds that looked like her own. He slapped her face a couple times trying to bring her out of it and finally succeeded in getting a response from her. "Get out of the truck. There's a stream over there to the right where you can wash yourself. I ain't riding two hundred miles with you smelling like shit. I'll leave you behind first. Get going; you got five minutes."

He pulled Thackery's body out of the truck bed and dragged her off to the side of the road into the bushes. It was not a proper burial by any means, but he wasn't concerned about that right now. It was self-preservation time and, after all, she was just a biker slut anyway. As he looked down at her in the light of the moon though it came to him that she was somebody's little girl and even looked a little like the daughter he had lost in a car accident thirty years ago. He went back to the truck looking around until he found a shovel, then went back to Thackery's body and began to dig.

Twenty minutes later, with Bubbles cleaned up, he reached to start the truck as the Gideon's C-5 flew over them headed north as well. He turned to the frightened girl next to him and looked at her for the first time. She was about nineteen or twenty as far as he could tell, she was twenty-two, had long straight blonde hair, baby blue eyes, a nice smile, and a body that awakened feelings in him that had been dormant for decades. He had been too busy pursuing power and personal glory to think about women. The deaths of his wife, daughter, and son had scarred his emotions so much that even sex had become dead to him.

Feeling his stare, she turned to him and said, "What?"

He looked away, started the truck, and drove—reminding himself that he was old enough to be her grandfather.

With the sun coming up and no phone call, Zevi finally had to admit that something had gone wrong with his perfect plan. He picked up his phone and called the number he had for Mike the Mercenary's landline. After a dozen rings, a sleepy female voice finally answered, "Mike's Merc's, this better be life or death!"

"Zevi here, have you heard anything from him about the operation he went on last night?"

There was a long moment of silence on the other end. "Nothing yet, if I hear anything I'll give you a call. What's your number?"

"It's in the file marked Operation Light," and he hung up. He sat in his office for a long time trying to decide what to do next. To inform the Illuminati that he had failed would bring about his own dismissal, or worse and he could not stand that. There was the possibility that the Gideons had managed to capture the Ark, in which case he may still have a chance.

He began to look through his files for the names of other mercenary groups that he had considered before choosing Mike on the chance that he could still pull this out. After all, this bunch of goody-two-shoes had no intention of using the Ark; they just wanted to keep anybody else from using it. He had planned too much, worked too hard, and invested too much to quit now.

He picked up his cell phone and tried to call Preacher again. There was no answer, but after a few minutes his phone chimed indicating he had received a T.M. He opened the message which read—op busted—ark ging nth w Gids—ltr. Preacher had made it, so there was still hope. He picked up a file with the heading 'Dirty Deeds Done Dirt Cheap' and opened it to a phone number.

The phone next to Maximilian Von Rhome's bed began to ring, waking him from a sound sleep. He punched the speaker button and mumbled, "Ya, vas ist?"

The voice on the other end was nervous; apologetic. "We have failed, there were too many there."

"Slow down," Max said as he struggled to sit up in bed pushing the young woman away from him and telling her to get out. He lit an English Player cigarette and inhaled deeply of the acrid smoke while the woman went out to make coffee. Alone, he turned his attention back to the phone and began to speak, releasing a cloud of blue smoke from his lungs at the same time. "How bad was it, give me a full report."

"Lieutenant Garza here sir. I got a call from one of the paratroopers. He said there were at least three other groups there. He was not able to identify them as they wore no markings. Hans went down in the river after dropping the paratroopers and the glider exploded shortly after landing. Most of the men were killed before they could fight.

"He said he was wounded and was going to try to surrender, otherwise he would probably die. He could report no other survivors. He did say that the Gideons had taken control of the Ark and then the line went dead sir."

Max cursed vehemently as he crushed out the butt of the cigarette. "Let me know immediately if you hear anything else, ya?" and hung up the phone with a curse. Pulling on a robe, he went downstairs into the kitchen and poured a cup of coffee looking around for the woman.

"Shotsi, vo bist du?" he called out in his native German. He walked into the den looking for her and found her sitting in a chair in the living room facing him with trickle of blood running from a small hole in her forehead down her nose and chin to settle into a red puddle on the waistband of her white panties.

"Come in and have a seat Max," commanded a voice in the room.

"I'm afraid you have me at a disadvantage sir," Max said, though the voice was familiar.

"Indeed I do Max, indeed I do."

Max moved as ordered to a Lazy-Boy and sat down looking at the young woman and said, "Such a shame, to waste such a good little whore my friend. What should I call you?"

"You may call me Moses, Max. Though you have called me Alpha for many years."

A feeling like being told you have terminal cancer passed through Max's gut. None of the members were supposed to know each other, but somehow Moses Goldman had managed to unmask him and the fact that he had killed poor Tashika meant that he would probably kill him too.

"What can I do for you Moses? Why have you come here?"

"I came here Max because you mounted a little operation last night that brought an and end to years of hard work and careful preparation. You know what I am talking about Max? Your little fiasco in Mexico."

Max realized that Moses must have had an operation going as well and his must have been one of the other groups that Garza had spoken of. "Moses," he said, stalling for time. "The only one supposed to be mounting an operation was Hotel, correct? What have you done?"

"You won't turn this back on me Max. Your group of bungling Nazi rejects totally blew the whole operation. I could have handled the Gideons and those fools that Zevi hired. You just couldn't stay out of it though could you? Your dreams of a Fourth Reich have cost us the lives of many valuable men and possession of the Ark."

Max reached carefully down between the cushions for the .38 special Smith&Wesson Detective model hidden there. If he could just keep Moses talking a little longer. "I don't remember you telling us that you wanted the Ark for yourself Moses, it was to be Hotel's operation for the Society. It is not too late though, we could still take it back from these Gideons. I don't care about these Nazis', I just used them to gain control of the Ark and, truth to be told Moses, you want the same thing."

It was true of course, but Moses had no intention of sharing that power any more than Max did. "No, I do not. You would use the power of the Ark to finish the Holocaust started by that madman, Hitler. It is my desire to establish Israel to its rightful place as the leader of the world."

"Such dreams Moses. But you are not the Moses of the Old Testament and your race of degenerates will never rule the Earth."

"We are destined to rule the Earth Max. God ordained it from the beginning of time and I will be there to lead the people as their King."

"Are you going to shoot me old friend or do you intend to bore me to death?"

"No," Moses said with a glance at his watch. "I intend to wait for the poison to kill you. It was in the coffee Max."

He was feeling a bit nauseous and there was an unusual tingling in his hands. Feeling death flowing through his body he went for the pistol, pulling it out of its hiding place and pointing it at Moses. He pulled the trigger and the little pistol roared out a killing shout, but the recoil knocked the little gun out of his weakened grip and it clattered to the floor where it lay useless.

Moses felt the bullet hit him in the chest knocking the wind from him and sending him to the floor as though he had been struck with a two-pound hammer. It hurt a lot more than he thought it would, as he reached up to feel the bullet that had been deformed by the body armor he wore.

He got up and walked over to Max's body bending down to retrieve the .38 and careful not to leave his own prints on it. He could see Max's eyes tracking his movements, so he continued to speak. "The police will find you here Max with your whore; a tragic murder-suicide. I don't think they will care much about your death Max since you are not a man who had many friends you know."

There was a rattle from Max as he exhaled his last breath in life and Moses put the .38 back into Max's right hand. The problem of gunshot residue on Max was now neatly taken care of and the police should have no problem in calling it a murder-suicide.

He straightened up his tie and coat, then let himself out using the duplicate key he had made to re-lock the door. He pulled a hat down over his brow which was the same type that Max habitually wore and made his way out of the building through the parking garage.

After we got airborne and Doc, the male-nurse had checked the wounded, I started going around to the prisoners to find out who they were. We had a couple German types, six Jewish, and a couple of guys who refused to give their names, but were apparently mercenaries and five who were left from Meronek's tribe.

I had Jason grab the two merc's and bring them over to the waist door while I opened it. "You two can give me your names and who you represent or our hospitality stops right here." I pointed to the door leaving no doubt to the meaning.

One of them, who was scarred from numerous fights, laughed at me and said, "Go ahead Gunny, I got nuthin to lose."

The other stepped back and said, "Names Thompson man; from Omaha. Jack Thompson. Please, I don't wanna die this way."

I turned to the tough-guy looking at him close and trying to see him without the camo on his face, "I know you from somewhere soldier?"

"Yeah," he growled. "Camp X-Ray; Iraq. You gave me this scar over my right eye."

I had to think back to my first tour; a fight had broken out between some Army Rangers and Marines from my company. I had broken it up, but had to knock one guy out because he wouldn't quit. "Hey Charlie," I called. "Come here man."

Charlie dropped what he was doing and came over. "What's up Gunny?"

"Recognize this ugly mug?" I handed the man a rag to clean the camo off his face.

"Uh. Yeah Gunny," Charlie said, squinting at the guy for a moment in the bad light of the cargo bay. "Name was Daniels, Brian Daniels. Right?"

"Is that right," I asked.

"Yeah, you got it."

"What are you doing grunting for a merc," I asked, as I led him over to a bench and sat him down with his hands still tied behind his back.

"I'll tell ya all about it if'n you cut my hands free and gimme a cup of coffee."

"You give me your parole?"

"Sure Gunny. I ain't getting paid no more, so there sure ain't no sense in me fighting."

"Uh huh, you weren't getting paid for it at Camp X-Ray either."

"Shoot Gunny, that was just for fun. We was blowing off a little steam was all."

"As I remember," Charlie joined in handing a cup of coffee to Daniels. "Two of your Rangers went to hospital, you got stitches over your eye, and one of our men got some broken ribs. That's more than entertainment Daniels."

"Okay," he relinquished. "We was fighting over some remarks that was made. It didn't mean nothin' and shouldn't have gone that far."

"You got busted back to private, six months hard labor in the stockade, and a less than honorable discharge Daniels," Charlie said.

"I would call that more than 'nothin' partner," I said.

"Hum, heard about that huh? Okay. One of your square-heads got upset 'cause I called him a sand-nigger. I was wrong, but at the time I was really mad at the indig's and all Ā-rabs in general. I lost some good buddies just a couple days before and I didn't handle it very good. I wish I could take it back Gunny, but I can't. I got this scar and my record to remind me every day, so I became a merc. Nobodies gonna hire me ya know. I already tried the straight life; it don't pay enough."

Jason had been listening and asked, "You know God Daniels?"

"Yeah, but he don't like me."

"Why would you say that?" Jason asked.

"I been too mean, too evil boss. I just ain't no good like my daddy says."

"You ever been to church Brain," I asked.

"Yeah, I grew up going to church. Even went a few times after I got back. Same little church where I grew up; same people. They made it clear I wasn't wanted in their congregation."

"That will be to their eternal shame then Daniels," Joseph said. "You remember Paul, the man who wrote the epistles in the New Testament."

"Yeah, I know of him. Who are you Pop?"

"My name is Joseph, I am Jason's father," he said as he laid a hand on Jason's shoulder. "Paul was a persecutor of the early church, he held the coats of the men who stoned Stephen and was responsible for the murders of many early Christians. God forgave him and made him into a mighty servant for the Way. He will forgive you too, if you will only ask. The only sin that God won't forgive is unbelief."

"I will think about it Joseph. Thanks."

"Don't think about it to long Daniels," I said. "You never know when your number will be called. Today was a good example of that."

"I would like to believe you, but I've grown used to the way I am. I just don't think I can change man."

"I said the same thing bro," I told him. "The thing is, you don't have to change. God will take you as you are and then he will change you from the inside out."

"What do I have to do then?" the soldier asked with tears in his eyes.

"Just pray with me. Lord I confess to you that I am a sinner and in need of your forgiveness. I confess that your son Jesus died for my sins and that he is LORD. Please Father, accept me as I am and change me into a new creature that I may bring glory to your name. I ask this of you in the name of Jesus Christ your son. Amen."

Afterward, there was a light in his face that had not been there before and tears wet his cheeks as he prayed the words with us. I could see that he meant the words he prayed and I felt a joy that I had never known before. He would be the first person I had ever led to Christ, but I pray, not the last.

"That's it. I don't gotta be baptized or sumthin'."

"Depends. Have you already been baptized?" Joseph asked.

"I was when I was a kid, but I don't think it took."

"It did, but it does not hurt to do it again. Baptism is an outward sign of your belief in Jesus as LORD. It isn't necessary to your salvation, just a way of saying that you are reborn to a new life. If you like, we can baptize you once we get back."

"I think I would like that. That last fight came to close to being my final one."

I moved over to the Jewish soldiers and seated myself next to the one who surrendered to us. "Shalom. What is your name again, please?"

"Shalom," he returned. "My name is Ari Miller—Lieutenant."

"Thank you Ari," I said. "Care to tell me who you are representing here?"

"I am here for the Jewish people who have a rightful claim to the Ark, as you should well know."

"Okay, I'm Tom Harper of the Gideon's Warriors." I did not wish to get into a political debate with him at the moment. "I won't dispute that claim. To bad you got caught in this whole battle, but we did not know who you were or who the others were either, except for Meronek and his people. The rest of you kind of complicated things."

"We expected only the bikers and possibly you as well. We were told to negotiate with you peacefully since we do feel we have a valid historical claim on the Ark."

"Maybe you do, depends on who you represent and their motive for controlling the Ark. You still haven't told me that."

"I guess I haven't at that," Ari said. He struggled with some inner conflict for a moment and then decided to tell us everything. "Have you ever heard of 'The Army of the Golden Dawn' Mr. Harper?"

"No, I can't say that I have. But I never heard of the Illuminati until a few days ago either."

"Hum, yes. The Illuminati, they are involved in this too then?"

"Yes. Someone representing them hired the mercenaries and I'm betting the Germans too. I believe they may behind your appearance as well. They seem to want the power of the Ark very badly."

"You could be right. I do not know who it was that informed us of the Ark's appearance. Joshua may have known, but if he did he took the information to his grave."

"Do you have his personal effects, perhaps a cell phone?"

"Yes, one of your men put them in that bag over there."

In the bag I found several phones and returned to Ari with them. "Which of these is his?"

One of them beeped at that moment indicating a missed call, so I opened each one until I found the missed call message. I wrote down the number displayed and asked Ari. "This one his?"

"Yes, I believe so."

I put the phone in my breast pocket, told Ari to sit tight, and moved on to the German, hoping he could speak English. "What's your name soldier?"

"Eric Von Strome, 03569, Lieutenant of the Fourth Reich, sir. May I ask your name?"

"Tom Harper, Gunnery Sergeant, U.S.M.C., retired. I am serving the Gideon's Warriors now. Fourth Reich huh? Who's commanding you?"

"I can not tell you that sir."

"Can't or won't soldier?"

"Won't," was his defiant one-word reply.

"Wouldn't be anyone connected to the Illuminati would it?" I asked him.

"I have never heard of this—Illuminati," he stated and I believed him.

I went through the bag of property belonging to his people and found another phone with a missed call. This was a different number, but same area code. I decided to check the merc's stuff and found another missed call and the same area code again.

I grabbed Jason and the others to see what they thought, but Crash called back to say we were coming in to land and we should all take our seats, put our trays in the upright position, and pray that the landing gear was still working.

Ten minutes later, we were filing down the cargo ramp and Dakota was wrapping herself around me in a very delightful way, kissing me and scolding me for not calling her. I had to apologize for that, defending myself by telling her that I had lost track of time interrogating the prisoners. I told her of my discovery of all three groups getting calls from the same area code and that I thought it meant they had to be connected.

"Let's get everyone together at the restaurant and see what we can find," she suggested.

"Good idea Chica," replied Jason. "Let's get these prisoners split up and locked away somewhere safe though first."

"Right bro," I said. "I'll let you handle that, we can probably let the other merc go since he doesn't know anything, but let's keep Daniels around for now."

"Right little brother, will do." Jason began issuing orders for the dispersal of the prisoners and I got into Dakota's jeep for the ride to the restaurant.

I gave the phone numbers to Bill when we got there with directions to squeeze out every bit of information he could from them, especially concerning the numbers from the missed calls. We settled in for an after-action dinner and praise session, with special thanks to the Lord for the safe return of all our people.

Dakota seemed to have grafted herself to my side, so I decided to give her something to do to make herself feel needed. "Honey, I want you to look at this jewelry and find out what you can about it—how old is it, where it was made, anything you can get, okay?"

She took Guzman's items looking carefully at them and said, "Sure, be a good excuse to look at wedding bands."

"Oh? Know somebody getting married?" I asked with a grin.

"I sure do," she replied with a wink of her green eyes.

It was about 0400 and I suggested to everyone that we get a few hours sleep. I was feeling exhausted and I was sure the others were too. Dakota insisted on taking me back to her place and I let her since that was where I had left my bike anyway. It was also the place I most wanted to be.

After a shower, I felt much better and laid down for a short nap that somehow lasted for six hours.

CHAPTER 35

Moses called a special meeting of the Illuminati and sat in his chair waiting for the other members to arrive. These Gideon's Warriors had caused him a lot of embarrassment, especially with the Army of the Golden Dawn. They were not happy with the loss of life: thirteen dead, six captured, and over 100 million dollars in equipment lost.

That fool Max was largely responsible because of his bungling Nazi Storm troopers. They had caused most of the casualties, according to the report he had received from his man. Somebody would pay and it wasn't going to be him.

All the chairs except E had been filled, so he called the meeting to order saying, "Brother Echo can not make it tonight as a more pressing appointment has detained him. Shall we get down to the business at hand? We will begin with the report on your special project Brother Hotel."

There was something wrong here thought Zevi. No appointment short of one with the Grim Reaper would keep a member away from an emergency meeting and if E was dead, how did A know about it? He would consider this later and go ahead with the report for now.

"The operation did not go as planned. Too many parties showed up for the ceremony. Besides the Gideons, there was a well-organized Jewish contingent calling itself the Army of the Golden Dawn, as well as a German Neo-Nazi unit complete with Swastikas and Fourth Reich insignia. The Germans and the Jews knocked out my own people to the extent that only two were left out of twenty. This was before the Gideons even arrived.

My operation was doomed from the start by outside interference, which I believe originated in this room."

This last statement resulted in several cries of outrage and a few nods of agreement from the tabled members. Alpha had to use his gavel to finally bring order to the room. At the moment he still felt in control, after all, there was no reason for anyone to suspect his part in any of this.

With order restored Moses declared, "I am afraid there may be some truth in what Brother Hotel has said. Brother Echo has been found dead in his apartment from an apparent murder-suicide."

Again, the room exploded into chaos with shouts of disbelief and Moses had to employ the gavel extensively to regain order. "I have no further details on the matter except that Brother Echo was found dead in his home from poisoning, along with a young black woman who had been shot in the head. It is presumed by the police that Brother Echo shot her and then killed himself.

"It is my belief that this resulted from the failed operation in Mexico to which he would have been connected. The fact that Brother Echo was a closet Nazi certainly would have been sufficient to call for his dismissal from this August society."

Zevi then called for the right to speak, "Brother Alpha, I am curious, as I am sure the others here are. How you could have come by this information. I was under the impression that we were to be anonymous to each other."

"Yes, of course, Brother Hotel. But at least one of us must know the identities of the others in order to take care of matters such as the one tonight. How else would we know if a member were compromised or merely on vacation? I, as the Alpha member, have dossiers on all of you." Damn him, Zevi had forced him to reveal information that he had hoped he would be able to keep secret.

"Would being a closet Zionist be sufficient reason to dismiss a member?" asked Brother Bravo, the second highest-ranking member.

"Yes, certainly it would. Our mission is to raise all of humanity to an enlightened state. This would of course, preclude setting any one people as the dominant race. That is why it was decided to use a mercenary company to carry out the operation. No ethnic group could claim power or responsibility in this way."

"Then, Brother Alpha, who contacted the Army of the Golden Dawn and informed them about the Ark and its location? It could only have been someone in this room. I believe we can eliminate Brother Hotel, since his people were there and failed, as well as Brother Echo, in as much as he was an anti-Semite. I can only vouch for myself since I can honestly say that I am not a Zionist, nor am I Jewish," said Brother Bravo.

"Since you possess the dossiers Brother Alpha, perhaps you could tell us who might be responsible," remarked Zevi. "I admit that I am Jewish, but I am not a Zionist, so who does that leave?"

"I will not answer that question Brother Hotel," answered Moses. "But I will look into this matter fully and make a report at our next meeting. That is all for tonight gentleman." Moses made his exit quickly by his private door which none of the others could open and leaving them all to wonder if there were more to this meeting than had been revealed.

The rules stated that once the Alpha member left there was to be no further discussion, but Brother Bravo broke this rule tonight. "Watch yourselves brothers, we may have a killer among us."

Outside, on a nearby rooftop, an Eagle kept vigil upon the abandoned building at 109 Bixby Avenue, waiting for his prey to emerge. Finally, the grate in the sidewalk opened and a solitary figure emerged, looked around, and then quickly moved off into the dimly lit street in search of transportation.

Finding his car, he got in and quickly pulled out into the caterpillar line of traffic hoping to be lost in the mass of moving steel and rubber. Overhead, the Eagle had no trouble keeping up with the late model Bentley, since there were no others of its kind on the road, and traffic was moving slowly. Once he reached his destination and parked in his private garage, he felt safe to enter his sanctum sanctorum.

The Eagle made note of the address, then went off in search of something more fulfilling; something with four feet and fur.

CHAPTER 36

Jason was hosting a cookout that evening as I pulled up on my bike. The parking lot of the restaurant had been roped off on one side just for us. Everyone was there, even some of the prisoners. Dakota came up to me as soon as I shut the motor off, handed me a soda, and an I-missed-you-a-lot kiss. I don't know which tasted better, but I knew which one I wanted seconds on.

We joined the rest of the group and, after hugs, we settled down to some serious gustatory work. Jason had ribs, brisket, sausage, and burgers, along with 'tater salad, ranch beans, coleslaw, and plenty of cold pop. After we put away a cow, a couple of hogs, and several cases of soda, Jason raised his hands and called for everyone's attention, " Brothers and sisters, I have an announcement."

As he spoke he lifted up a 'cycle jacket that looked a lot like mine, which I had not been able to find after waking up.

"Gunny-Sergeant Tom Harper, front and center," he called out.

I stepped up coming to attention and he held out my jacket with the Gideon's patch on the back. I slipped my arms into the sleeves, shrugged the jacket over my shoulders, and then Jason spoke again, "I present you brother with the colors of our organization and I ask you others to step up and bless him in the name of our savior."

The others had put their jackets on too and they formed into a circle and began to pray a blessing on me, as well as on our whole group. "Lord, we ask that you would bless us and keep us from all harm, that we might ride our motorcycles for your glory and you would aid us in our struggle against the Evil One and his servants. Let us be a blessing to others and never bring reproach on your name, on each other, or on this emblem of our brotherhood. Amen."

We broke up then with congratulations all around and plenty of hugs. I worked my way over to Bill who was talking to Bob. As I walked up Bob said, "Got some news for you Nephew."

"Those numbers you gave me had some interesting names behind them: Zevi Cohen, Maximilian Von Rhome, and Moses Goldman, all out of Santa Fe. Also, the one named Rhome is dead," said Bill, who went on to fill me in on Max's death and then it was Bob's turn.

"I went to have a look at this Moses guy on the wing. He went to an address on Bixby Avenue and disappeared down a trick grate like a scene out of 'Get Smart.' The building is supposed to be abandoned, but a records search shows the 'Industrial Lighting Corporation' of Geneva, Switzerland owns it. That company is a paper tiger though, no physical address that I could find. It claims to be a consulting think-tank, but an answering service was all I could reach.

"Anyway, I followed the guy home. Here's his address. There were at least ten other men who went through the grate as well and my senses told me that there were others living inside. I also saw Zevi there. I would say they are both Illuminati."

"Sounds like we should watch these people, they may decide to come after us. Let's not forget General Carter either. I don't think his intentions were altogether honorable.

"We need to find a place to hide the Ark where it will be safe. Any suggestions?" I looked at Jason when asking this question, since he knew the area intimately.

"There is no place that is one hundred percent safe, as was proven at Area 51 a few days ago Tom. But we can hide it so that it will be very difficult to find. I know of some caves that would be pretty safe and we should limit knowledge of the place to only a few of us."

"Okay Jason, I agree. It's not perfect, but it will do until we put the present danger behind us. I say we limit that knowledge to just the two of us."

"A good suggestion little brother, let's get busy on it tomorrow. Tonight we enjoy our victory."

Amen to that I thought and sought out Dakota who was busy helping the other ladies to clean up. I came up to her from behind wrapping my arms around her waist and kissed her on the neck. "Guess who?"

"Oh Jason, stop. Tom will find out," she said with a giggle and twisted around in my arms to face me.

"I love you Dakota, like I've never loved another woman in my life." I reached up brushing her cheek with the fingertips of my right hand and kissed her again. "We will be going out tomorrow to hide the Ark and to track down the people responsible for the mess in Mexico. I will truly be glad when this is over so we can spend more time together darling and I can make you forget Jason."

"It's okay Tom, we'll have plenty of time; the rest of our lives."

"That's what I'm talking about."

Zevi Cohen exited the Illuminati headquarters building feeling some fear in his gut. Echo was dead and Alpha seemed a little too knowledgeable about it for his comfort. The Nazi connection through Echo and, he suspected, the Jewish connection through Alpha, meant that his life could be in danger as well. This had started out as such a simple plan, how could it have gotten so out of hand? Perhaps it would be better to pull out all together before his motives were uncovered.

As he approached his parked car, he stopped in sudden panic. What if there was a bomb in his car? Could Alpha be that ruthless? He began looking the car over, searching for something he probably would not recognize anyway and finally, in frustration, he stood off some distance and pressed the alarm button to unlock the doors.

The beep the car made as the alarm turned itself off startled him, even though he had heard it a hundred times before. He carefully climbed in and, leaving the door open, turned the ignition switch. He could not quite remember what happened next, but there was a sensation of extreme pressure and heat, followed by a peculiar flying feeling.

Later he would remember seeing his car rear up like a metal black stallion pawing at a landscape set ablaze. The next thing he knew he was laying on a gurney with sirens wailing out their soul wrenching song as a man worked over him trying to keep him alive. He couldn't really feel anything; there was no pain, but rather a sense that he was dreaming.

He passed out again and the next time he awoke; there was pain. It felt like someone was trying to pull his skin off by sliding a dull knife under it and at the same time pouring acid over his body. Somewhere he cold hear screaming, like the sounds of the damned, but there was total darkness around him so that he could see nothing. He heard a voice saying, "Give him a quarter grain of Morphine, IV STAT." The pain began to ease; the screaming was silenced, as he was carried away on the night ship of Morpheus to a place of strange dreams and nightmare alleys.

With sunrise, General Carter began to feel the need for sleep. It had been at least twenty-four hours since he had so much as a nap. The girl was sleeping next to him even though the four-by did not have a very smooth ride and the road was more like a test track for tanks.

He spotted a clearing in the forest where the truck would not be seen from the road and pulled off. There was a creek where he was able to wash and check the wound he had running across his ribs.

It was not deep, but it was painful; possibly having cracked a rib. The girl walked up to him, knelt down dipping a piece of cloth in the water, and gently washed the blood away. Afterward, she wrapped his ribs with a bandage from a first-aid kit she had found in the truck. During all this, she had said nothing and neither had he.

Feeling the bandage under his left arm, he looked at her and said, "Thank you, Miss?"

"Tracy, but Handlebar always called me Bubbles. He said it was because I like champagne so much."

"Hum, well," stumbled Carter. "Thank you Tracy. Is there any food in the truck? I don't know about you but I am starved."

"There was some, I'll see what's left." She got to her feet and headed for the truck, thankful that the old man had said nothing about her soiling herself the night before. All the shooting and Shauna getting killed right next to her had been too much for her. He had been nice though, letting her clean up and burying Shauna like he did.

She knew that Meronek would have left her in the bushes for the buzzards and beat her for crapping her pants, or worse. She found some tuna, potato chips, and crackers in the back-end so they had a little picnic. Afterward the old man stretched out on the back seat and went to sleep and, after a few minutes, she did the same.

The sun was high in the sky when he woke up feeling sweat running down his face and his clothes clinging to him. The buzz of insects in the cabin and the smell of blood drying in the back was a bit too much and he had to get out of the truck. He went to the creek plunging his face under the water, feeling its coolness refresh him, then looked up and around like some feral animal scenting the air for predators.

There were the usual sounds of the forest, crickets, cicadas, birds, and—chainsaws? They were distant, but too close for comfort. He went back to the truck looking for the girl who was still asleep in the front seat.

He found a bucket in the rear and used it to wash the blood out of the bed. The girl woke up while he was cleaning and went out into the bushes to relive herself and wash up. Coming back to the truck she stood watching the blood-colored water run out the back with a sad expression on her face.

"You wanna help clean up?" he asked her as he threw another bucket of water in the back.

"Maybe we should pull out the carpet. It might be easier that way," she offered.

He could see the sense of that and asked, "How do we do that?"

She showed him how and once the rug was out, the cleaning proceeded quickly. He decided to leave the rug out since it was too hard to get clean and it wasn't needed anyway.

"Get in Tracy," he directed. "We need to get going."

While he drove, he thought about what he would do when he got back. Getting the Ark back was his primary concern, second was his military career. After what had happened, he would be lucky if they didn't bust him down to airman and lock him up in Leavenworth for a hundred years. Getting the Ark back from those damn Gideons would not be easy either, but maybe he could ingratiated himself with them; maybe even join them. He might be able to pull himself out of this yet.

He looked over at the girl who smiled at him nervously and then went back to his driving. It would probably take another full day to get to the border and he had no money. He would have to find a way around that soon, since the gas tank was getting close to empty.

The sound of chainsaws was much louder now as he came to a sharp curve in the road. On the other side were three Federalie vehicles and several uniformed officers all pointing their weapons right at him.

"Just not my day I guess," he said.

"Just be cool old school," Tracy said. "We're just a couple of tourists that got robbed and lost in the jungle. They'll believe us. Tell them I'm your granddaughter and we were on our way to see some temple ruins when we got separated from the tour group by bandits. It happens all the time down here. They will take us back to the city and we can escape from there. It's cool."

He could see no other choice and it might work, so he pulled up and shut down the engine.

While I waited for Dakota to get out of the bathroom I was looking through an old book on demons for anything I could find on the one named Faustus. The book was on the Internet in the Vatican Library. Using my limited computer skills, I asked for a search under that name and found myself looking into the face of a handsome individual with an article attached. Faustus was a demon of high order, just below Lucifer himself. According to the article, he was responsible for giving witches their power and played a part in the downfall of many men and women over the ages. It also stated that if you could learn his real name, you would have the power to command him.

Dakota came in wearing her Sponge Bob pajamas and sat down in my lap planting a kiss on my mouth. "What'cha got there cowboy?" she asked indicating the article.

I told her about this demon and how I believed he was the one I had seen at Blavatsky's cabin.

"Sounds like someone to avoid," she said.

"I don't think we can, he is too powerful, and has too much at stake. Balvatsky belonged to him and we killed her. I don't think he is going to forgive us. He doesn't seem the type."

"Yeah, probably not." She got up and headed for the kitchen. "Anything you would like honey."

"No thanks darlin', I think I'm going to get some sleep. You go ahead."

She came back with some coffee and sat down next to me. "You play with him and you'll get burned. Stay away from him."

"Much as I would like to Chica, I don't think that is possible now. Did you find out anything on that jewelry?"

"Not much. It's definitely old though. I scanned it and let some antique dealers look at it. They said the ring was definitely Middle Eastern and probably over a thousand years old. The necklace was from the Middle Ages, German, and made around the 1200's or so, as well as the other stuff. All of it was made from silver and worth quite a bit if we were willing to sell; especially the ring."

"Yeah, the ring seems to be the most important. There was some sort of fight between Meronek and Blavatsky concerning the ring. We will have to question him about that tomorrow. He should be recovered enough by then to talk." Meronek had not really been hurt, but he had been hysterical ever since being loaded onto the plane. We both kicked back on the couch planning the future until we both drifted off to sleep.

A sky more blue than I had ever seen before, with high, fluffy white clouds, gently taking on fairy tale shapes. Tall grass waving in the gentle breeze for as far as I could see. Dakota standing next to me, beautiful, dressed in Native American buckskins and turquoise jewelry.

"How did you get in my dream babe?" I asked.

"What makes you think it's your dream?" she answered.

"Stay close to me darlin', I get the feeling this is not an ordinary dream." I looked down at myself and saw I was wearing typical cowboy clothes of the mid 1800's, except I had no gun.

A mounted rider was coming toward us from the North, a bad omen in Indian medicine. "If this is who I think it is, be prepared to call upon the Lord to save us, but let me see if I can learn anything useful from him first."

"Okay love, but be careful."

"Amen to that."

He pulled up hard in front of us, the horse dropping on his haunches and skidding in the grass to a stop, with the rider jumping off to stand in front of us. Except for the buckskin vest and breech-clout, his appearance was the same as his picture in the Internet article. There was a faint odor of brimstone coming from him and the horse.

"Faustus, I presume?"

"You know me? I was not aware we had met." He seemed genuinely surprised that I recognized him.

"We haven't, but I know of you and your friends."

"You mean Guzman?" he asked.

"Yes, and Meronek too."

"Yes, they were poor servants at best, but they belonged to me. You have destroyed poor Carmine and made Meronek a prisoner. What ever shall I do with you?"

"May I suggest going back to the pit you came from and leaving us alone."

"Very funny Mister Harper. No, I'm afraid I can't do that. However, I am willing to make you an offer. Listen to me before you make up your mind."

Stalling for time was all I could do and maybe he would reveal some weakness.

"You have proven yourselves to be very clever and I would like for you to come over to my side. I can make you rich and powerful. You can rule entire countries if you want. All you have to do is bow down to me, claim me as your master, and all your desires will be met."

"What would I call you? I know you are called Faustus, but I don't think that is your real name. I know the legend of Faust: the man who made a deal with Mephistopheles for power and wealth. Do you claim to be him?"

He began to laugh then, "I said you were clever, but I am not stupid either. I will not give you my name so easily."

"It was worth a try," I said.

"I will let you think about my offer for a few days, but not too long. Make the right choice, the wrong one could cost you your life; and the lovely ladies." His eyes turned an evil red as he made the threat and the smell of brimstone became intense.

His attention shifted to Dakota then and he said, "Wear the ring and the rest of the jewelry as my wedding present. It will look good on you."

I squeezed Dakota's hand to keep her from answering and said, "Thank you Faustus, we will consider your offer."

He mounted the horse then and rode North where he had come from

"When Hell freezes over!" I added, as he grew small in the distance.

✝ ✝ ✝

The sun was up when I woke with a feeling that the house had been invaded during the night. Dakota was curled up next to me looking very vulnerable and childlike in her P.J.'s. I got up and started the coffee, then moved quietly around the house looking for the source of my discomfort, but everything seemed to be on order. I checked outside as well making sure the dogs were all right and then returning to the kitchen. I made myself a cup of coffee, then sat down across from her and considered how nice it would be to have this lovely young woman as my wife.

The phone started vibrating on the table and I grabbed it up to answer. It was Bob, so I stepped out back before speaking so as not to awaken the sleeping princess. "Yeah Bob, what can I do for you so early in the morning."

"Hey Nephew, I know it's early but this is important. Zevi Cohen was hit last night. Somebody made a human pop-tart out of him." He went on to fill me in on the details and we decided to look in on Mr. Cohen as soon as possible.

I told him about our double vision with Faustus the night before as well.

"We will have to talk about that Nephew. You aren't ready to face a demon of his caliber yet. Get down here to the restaurant ASAP. By the time we get to Las Vegas whoever was trying to kill Cohen will know they failed, and may try again."

I hung up, turned to go back in the house, and there was Dakota looking very frightened. "What's the matter hon," I asked, giving her a hug and a kiss.

"I woke up and you were gone and I remembered this terrible dream with a demon and a horse and I was scared and you wouldn't answer when I called and I was so scared." She was trembling and crying, so I wrapped her in my arms and held her tight, telling her it was all right.

"I'm sorry hon, I didn't want to wake you. It was Bob on the phone. Zevi Cohen was attacked last night and he wants me to go to Las Vegas with him to talk to him. Don't be scarred hon, I won't let Faustus or anybody else hurt you. I could not live with that, it would kill me."

She stopped trembling after a few minutes and we went back inside. She fixed a cup of coffee for herself, while I took a quick shower and dressed for the trip. Back in the kitchen, I found her staring out the window into the back yard.

"What's the matter hon, what do you see?"

"A single black crow has been sitting there staring at me since you went into the shower."

I stepped out back and walked up the crow saying, "In the name of Jesus Christ I cast you out of this place you demon spawn. Be gone in the name of the Living God."

I threw a rock at the animal and actually managed to hit it right in the chest. With a squawk, he lifted up from the top of the utility shed and took off away from the house leaving only his trademark squirt of feces on the ground. I was about to walk away when I saw movement in his excrement. I bent for a closer look and saw it was full of maggots. This confirmed it was demonic.

I went back into the house to Dakota, "Just a sleepy crow hon, nothing to be concerned about."

The look in her eye said she didn't believe me though. "Go and get dressed babe and come down to the restaurant where you will have company." Where you will be safe, is what I was really thinking.

"Okay, just give me ten minutes." She went off to her bedroom and I poured myself another cup of coffee. More like thirty minutes was my guess.

Zevi was in the intensive care unit of Lions Burn Care Center in Las Vegas where he had been transferred with burns over forty percent of his body. The doctor said his prognosis was good though and he should be able to talk by now. "Don't push him to hard though please," she said. Her name was Dr. DeeDee Sherman and I was sure Zevi Cohen had to be in bad shape, because one look at this woman would have raised Lazarus from the grave.

She walked out leaving us alone with Zevi and all the beeping machines, blinking lights, and dripping IV's. His head was bandaged so we could not see his eyes and most of his injuries seemed confined to his arms, legs, and head.

"Zevi, can you hear me? This is Tom Harper, Zevi. We met a few days ago and I talked about the Ark with you. Do you remember me Zevi?"

"Yes—I hear you—I remember," came a hoarse whisper from the wrappings.

"Zevi, do you know who did this to you?" I asked.

"No—yes—no."

"What do you mean Zevi, yes or no?"

"Let me," Bob suggested. "Zevi, was it Moses Goldman who did this? We know you are with the Illuminati and we know that he is too."

"I don't know his name," Zevi mumbled. "Don't know each others names or faces. Only Alpha member knows everyone."

"Moses Goldman has a mole in the middle of his chin. Does Alpha?"

"Yes," he replied.

"Okay," I said. "That's all we need for now Zevi. You rest now. We will have you watched so Moses can't get to you, okay?" I patted his bed gently and we left him.

"Shall we go visit Mr. Goldman Uncle?"

"Yes, nephew, I think we should."

✝ ✝ ✝

Moses Goldman lived in a mansion in an exclusive downtown enclave in Santa Fe where getting in without an invitation would require a search warrant or the skills of someone like Murph the Surf, AKA Jack Murphy, to break in. Of course, the fire department needs no such invitation.

A simple grass fire was all we needed, besides a couple of fireman's uniforms that we 'borrowed' from a station downtown. Once we were in, we went directly to his address and rang the bell. After a short wait, I suggested we let ourselves in.

"No need to Nephew. I know his car, we can just wait until he comes home and jump him before he gets through the gate."

"Might work, but what if he's not planning on coming home?"

"Good point, Nephew," Bob said as he broke out his lockpicks and proceeded to work on the lock while I picked up a large potted plant next to the door and picked up the key lying there.

I tapped him on the shoulder and presented him with it. "All right Nephew, nobody likes a smart-ass."

I opened the door and we both rushed in with guns drawn to an empty house. Bob went to the alarm panel and did something to the keys there, playing a little tune on it. The alarm remained silent. We went through the place quickly, looking for any sign of Goldman, but he was not there. His car was in the garage and we could find no luggage in the master bedroom. The drawers and closet had been rifled as well. We could find nothing to indicate where he might have gone so we locked the house up and let ourselves out of the compound.

"We will have to make a search of airport records though he probably had enough sense to use a phony ID," I said as we headed back to our rental car.

Bob looked at me like a poor, backward relation. "Nephew, this guy has his own plane."

"Touché uncle. You got me there, what do we do?"

"We go see if he filed a flight plan and whether he stuck to it."

Jason, David, John, and Peter had gone out into the desert taking the Ark with them to hide it. Everyone but Jason, of course, was wearing a hood so they would not know the location and so could not reveal it even if they wanted too.

After driving for two hours, mostly in circles, Jason pulled over and checked the sky in all directions looking to see if they had been followed by any kind of flying creature. Satisfied they were alone, he got back in the truck and continued onward to a place considered sacred by his ancestors.

Driving slowly, because of the rough ground, Jason entered a area known to his people as the 'Canyon of a Thousand Caves' and drove until a group of large boulders blocked the way.

Jason had everyone remove their blindfolds and exit the truck. They had all purified themselves according to Talmudic tradition before leaving that morning so they could safely handle the Ark.

They took up the poles that were already in place on the Ark, lifted it, and continued into the canyon for another hundred meters until they came to an opening in the wall leading gently downward. Jason allowed them to set the Ark down for a short break. It was not very big, but all that gold did make it heavy. Also, he wanted to check the cave to make sure it was safe to enter.

They took up the Ark again once Jason was sure the way was clear and, tuning on the lamps they had strapped to their heads, they marched forward into the heart of the Earth. The cave angled downward gently for fifty meters where they came to a pool of stagnate water. The water was a half-meter deep, very cold, and stretched about eight meters wide. The path led upward from there with an occasional side tunnel leading away into Stygian darkness.

The walls of the main shaft were decorated here and there with pictographs hundreds, perhaps thousands of years old, representing the people and animals that once inhabited this land. The ground was littered with stones, bones, and other detritus collected over the millennia and they had to pick their way carefully.

Peter asked, "Any bats in here Jason, I gotta tell ya man, I hate bats."

With Peter's voice still echoing down the tunnels, Jason answered in a whisper, "Yes, there are bats in some of the tunnels, though I have never seen any where we are going."

Not wanting to hear his own voice again in this unnatural place, Peter remained silent for the remainder of the journey.

After they had traveled what seemed like a quarter kilometer they came to a narrow side-tunnel which Jason led them into. There was barely enough clearance for the Ark so that they had to carry it from inside the poles with Peter and Jason moving backwards in front and struggling with the effort. After another thirty meters the shaft opened up into a cathedral-sized room. They set the Ark onto a natural alter toward the back of the room, then rested from their labors for a few minutes.

Jason led them in prayer before leaving, asking the Lord to keep the Ark hidden from those who would use it for evil and to bless them in their effort to fight the servants of darkness.

As they continued to pray, a golden light began to glow between the wings of the Cherubim on the Ark lighting the room and warming them with its glow, imparting a feeling of love and peace they had never experienced before. They left the caves returning to the harsh light of the world outside feeling blessed.

All of them were silent for the trip back to the restaurant and everyone there sensed they had undergone something very special that day.

Moses got off the plane at a secret airstrip in the Negev desert leaving the pilot instructions to continue on to Paris and finally back to the U.S. A black Mercedes limo picked him up and drove him to a large concrete building that had no windows and few doors. The building was located just outside Beersheba at a secret military base. The only designation on the structure was a golden sun disk. The driver of the Mercedes spoke into a microphone in the partitioned cab and a garage-size door opened to allow them in. Once they were stopped a soldier in desert camo and gold colored beret opened the door for him.

"Welcome back Aluf mishne(Colonel) Goldman, if you'll follow me sir, I will take you to the others," said the young Rav turái rishón(corporal).

"Thank you," was his simple reply.

They walked to an elevator where the soldier used an electronic key to call the car and then they waited. Moses made no attempt to engage the corporal in conversation and barley seemed to take notice of his surroundings. The car arrived and his escort motioned him to enter first, then followed him making certain that no one else was allowed to join them.

Using his key once again, the escort pushed a button labeled Admin in Hebrew, then waited as the car descended the eighty meters to its destination. When the doors opened again another escort was waiting to take him to his appointment.

"Welcome back Aluf mishne Goldman," said the new escort. "I hope you had a pleasant journey."

"Thank you Rav seren(Major) Silverman, it was very agreeable. Have they got the firing squad ready yet?"

"I don't think it's quite that bad Aluf mishne, but they do seem somewhat upset by the failure of our expeditionary force."

"As am I Rav seren, as am I."

They made their way through the maze of passageways until they came to a set of double-doors guarded by a pair of soldiers armed with Uzi sub-machine guns. The two guards came to attention at their approach holding their weapons at Port Arms position and turning in order that the two of them could open the doors to enter.

Inside was a standard military conference room holding a central table that would seat fourteen people. On side tables located at each end were samovars containing coffee, with cups and pitchers of cold water provided as well.

On the walls were pictures from the Six-Day war (1967) and the Yom Kippur (1973) war, as well as pictures of the leaders of the Jewish state, past and present. There were a number of men already seated carrying on conversations, drinking coffee, smoking cigars, and all of them stopped what they were doing as soon as Moses Goldman entered.

"Good afternoon gentleman, though it is difficult to tell this far underground," said Moses in a vain attempt at humor.

There were greetings in return, but not from everyone. There were several faces in the group that were openly hostile, but Moses had expected that. Several of them would blame him for the loss of the one object that was more precious to them as a people than any other on Earth.

The men moved to their seats at the command of one man who was wearing an epaulet bearing the insignia of a Tat aulf(Brigadier General). A gold olive branch with a gold sword on a black field. He directed Moses to a chair at the end of the table.

"Gentleman, this meeting is called to order," said the man, whose name was Tat aulf David Ben Gurion. He was a man of singular bearing; just over two meters tall with the broad shouldered physique and trim waistline of a much younger man. At sixty-two years he was approaching retirement and wanted the Ark to return to Israel on his watch.

He took his seat at the head of the table and said, "Seren(Captain) Sharon, please proceed with the after-action report."

"A total of two UH-1H Huey helicopters, one Apache attack helicopter..." the litany went on, including names of the men lost or captured, leaving Moses feeling even more insecure as to the outcome of this inquiry. The captain finally fell silent with his report complete and General Ben Gurion spoke again. "Moses, can you explain what caused the failure of this operation?"

"Yes General, at least in part." He went on to list his excuses for failure and the steps he had personally made to avenge the men whose lives had been sacrificed so nobly. "We can still salvage this operation General, if you will allow me to outline a course of action."

The General considered a moment. "Go ahead Colonel."

"The Gideon's hold the Ark at the moment and they are only a meager paramilitary group. We can watch them easily enough and take the Ark back from them as soon as we find out where they are hiding it. These are not sophisticated men sir and there are only a few of them, no more than twenty."

General Ben Gurion leaned forward, elbows on the table, fingers forming a steeple and spoke, "You will get the Ark back for us Colonel Moses or you will not return to this facility. I will assign a special op's group to you for the operation; do not abuse them."

The captain who had given the action report stepped over to Moses and said, "Colonel, if you will follow me, I will introduce you to the people attached to you for the duration of this assignment."

Leaving the room, Moses understood that he was probably walking the halls of this facility for the last time. He had screwed up the operation in Mexico by allowing Zevi and Max to execute separate actions. He had hoped that they would destroy Meronek and each other, leaving his people to take possession of the Ark, but the Gideons had blown the whole affair with their interference. Now, he would have to win this battle or die trying, because General Ben Gurion would tolerate no further failure.

The captain led him into another smaller, briefing room where six people sat waiting.

"Colonel Goldman, this is your team. They are all specialists in their fields and are veterans of several actions. You will have one hour to acquaint yourselves before transport will return you to the airfield. Whatever weapons and equipment you will need you will have to procure in the U.S. Good luck, shalom."

Left alone, he looked his group over. "Please introduce yourselves and tell me something about your specialty. Let's start with you soldier." He indicated a young woman.

"My name is Zeva Brandon," she stated. She was five feet six inches tall, one hundred thirty-five pounds with the dark hair and eyes common to Semitic people. "I am expert in languages and weapons."

Next was a young man of six feet with sandy brown hair and average looks. Now that he looked closer, he noticed they were all of average appearance and probably chosen for that reason.

"David Mayer, computer systems, and alarms."

"Solomon Shlomo, also alarms and communication systems." He was five feet ten inches with red hair.

"Karl Getz, with a K. Radio systems and surveillance equipment." He was five feet eight inches tall with dark kinky hair and dark skin. Except for the hair he looked like an American Indian, thought Goldman.

Next was, "Lenny Haim." Five feet nine inches, average weight and the joker in the group. "Surveillance and Medic."

"Mary Magda," She was five foot six inches, one hundred forty pounds, blonde hair, violet eyes, and a figure that would stop traffic on Fifth avenue in New York.

"Computers and Medic." She wore an expression that said she would rather not be on this assignment.

This would be his team; the people his life and his future would depend on. He was already considering bringing in some mercenaries of his own. There were those South African's he had met two years ago...

✝ ✝ ✝

Carter and Tracy arrived back at the border town of Gordo Mendoza to find they were out of food, gas, and money. They were not going any further unless he could come up with something.

"I could turn some tricks tonight when the home boys come over to party. That would get us enough for gas and food until we get over the border," Tracy suggested.

The general knew that would work and probably wasn't something she hadn't done before, but he still didn't like the idea. For some reason he had grown fond of this little girl over the past few days and did not want to see her do that, especially for him. He would find another way, all he had to do was think. First, he had to find a phone though.

He turned toward the cantina and nearly walked right into Juan Mendoza, the man Meronek had bought the truck from.

"Where you going viejo?" Mendoza asked.

"I was going to see if I could find a phone to call someone in the states."

"What seems to be the problem? Where are all your rude friends? The ones who have no courage?"

"They were not my friends. I was their prisoner and they are all dead or in jail now. I don't know which and I don't care."

"The one who kiss my burrito, he is dead?"

"I don't think so, but he is a prisoner."

"He was a pendajo grandé, I think. I tell you what Señor, you sell me the girl and I give you two hundred Yankee."

"That is very generous Mr. Mendoza, but I could not do that."

"I was not asking Señor." Mendoza hit Carter on the jaw staggering the much smaller man. Carter came back swinging a blow at the mountain of flesh before him, sinking his fist into Mendoza's gut several inches. Mendoza only laughed and back-handed Carter, knocking him to the ground. Tracy jumped in begging Carter to stop; that she would go with the big Mexican. "It ain't no big thing General, please."

However, Carter was not the type to give up and jumped back into Mendoza again, raining blows on his head and shoulders, while kicking him in the knees with a lot of fury, but not much effect. Mendoza punched Carter again, knocking him to the ground on all fours. He slowly raised up, blood running from his nose and lips, but defiance still in his steel-gray eyes.

Mendoza looked at the little man and asked, "What is she to you gringo? Is she your mija? Your hija?"

On his feet again, somewhat unsteadily, Carter answered. "No, I only met her a week ago. She belonged to the bikers, but now she is under my protection. You will have to kill me to stop me."

"Whatever you wish amigo," Mendoza said as he pulled out an ancient revolver. Tracy stepped in front of Carter and said, "You'll have to shoot me too."

Mendoza looked at the two of them for a moment, then muttered an oath under his breath. "You Yankees are mue loco." He turned to one of his men and said, "Fill his tank and let them go. I admire a man of courage. You are not like the other one. You would die for what you believe and I respect that little hombre. Via Con Dios."

Carter and Tracy got back in the truck where she helped him to clean up while the Mexicans filled the truck's tank. Mendoza came out of the cantina and handed them some bowels of Carné

Asada and tortillas. Tracy thanked him while Carter sat wondering at the sudden turn of events.

Juan looked at him and said, "This is my village Señor, and you
have acted like a man of honor, a man of respect. You are welcome
here anytime."

Carter replied, "Thank you Mr. Mendoza, I appreciate your
help. I may have to take you up on your offer. That idiot Meronek
may have made it impossible for me to stay in the states. You are
also a man of honor sir." The little general saluted the big man
and then drove off into the night headed for Mom's restaurant
and whatever the future held.

CHAPTER 37

Bob and I rolled into the restaurant parking lot about six in the evening, burnt from the sun, dirty from the road, and hungry enough to eat road-kill. We went in through the back door where Dakota wrapped herself around me, kissed me, turned up her nose, and pointed toward the shower. "I love you too darlin'," I said. "Order up a Double Cheeseburger and fries will you hon?" I asked as I made my way to the shower.

When I got out, Dakota had a place set for us, since she was eating too, and plenty of questions about what we had found out that day.

"Eat first woman, then kill dinosaur," I grunted, in my best caveman impression.

She thunked me on the hand and reminded me to give thanks before diving in. "That's what I keep you around for darlin', to keep me straight." I leaned over and gave her a big P.D.A. kiss.

After dinner, I got together with Bob and Bill to discuss Moses' flight plan. Bill said he would make a search but noted, "Is there anything in particular I should look for?"

I thought about it for a moment then said, "Yes. Israel."

"Why Israel?" Bill asked.

"Because I am betting that's where the Army of the Golden Dawn is headquartered and that he is connected with them."

Jason came over and asked if we would join him in interrogating Meronek.

"I would rather miss the Texas-O.U. game than miss that," I answered.

Ten minutes later we had Meronek in an old shed out back under a bright light and duct taped to a wooden chair. His appearance was haggard: cheeks sunken, dark circles aunder his eyes, and a dullness in his speech.

"What's wrong Meronek," I asked. "You act like you've lost everything dear to you. We probably saved your life, you know. That black widow Guzman was going to suck the life out of you so she could become human again."

"Tom's right Steve. She was going to kill you after she got what she wanted. There is no goddess, no three wishes—that was all B.S. to get you to steal the Ark. The power is in having it, because other people believe in the power of the Ark. She and Faustus just wanted it so they could use that power to rule the world."

"She would have been mine, I would have made her give me the ring man. That was the secret—the ring. But you broke it up, all of you, and now she's dead. Faustus will kill all of us for screwing up his plans. The Ark would have been his and he would have given her to me, but that asshole came and messed it all up."

"Who are you talking about, who messed it up?" asked Jason.

"That guy Rogers, that's who!"

I had almost forgotten about Rogers. We had not found him among the dead, or the living, which meant he had gotten away, and that reminded me of the crow that morning at Dakota's place. He was still around somewhere and would have to be added into our plans.

"Look Meronek," I said, in a more gentle voice. "The only thing she wanted was your soul and the only thing Faustus wants is power. You can offer him nothing and she only wanted what you could not give her. If she didn't kill you, Faustus would have. She belongs to him, that's where she got the ring. She is married to him. She could not give you that ring even if she wanted to."

Tears were running down his cheeks. "I killed for that bitch! I let myself be humiliated for her!" he cried.

"Then get even Meronek, tell us what we want to know. How do we find her house?"

His world had collapsed like a house of cards around him and there was no more resistance left in him. He took paper and pen offered to him and began to draw us a map to Guzman's house. Of course, in a real sense her house wasn't here, but only a shadow of it. We would have to search for the part that was here and destroy it in order to destroy her place in the spirit world. Once that was done, she would no longer be able to enter this world.

Jason led me to one side away from Meronek and spoke softy so as not to be overheard. "He's going catatonic again Tom, we may have to have him committed."

"It would be kinder just to kill him I think," I answered.

"Kinder maybe, but we can't put ourselves above the law Nephew," added Bob.

"I agree, but I can't help feeling we will regret allowing him to live. He still belongs to Faustus and I don't think he's done with him yet."

"I believe you are right little brother, but as Bob says, we must follow the law. With all the things he has done, it is not likely he will ever get out of prison."

"No doubt," I agreed. "But Faustus may be able to find a way. However, it would probably be easier to find a replacement for him. Let's turn him over to David and he can formally arrest him and take him in. The charge of killing that trooper is enough to get him the death penalty. Do the same with the others too, except the one called Preacher." I was looking at the Sun Disk that had been found around his neck. "I think he knows more that he is letting on about the Illuminati. Let's lock him up in here and talk with him this evening after he sees the rest being handcuffed and led away."

"Right nephew," agreed Bob.

Meronek was released from the chair and led back to where the others were being held. David placed him and the rest of Hardcore's people under arrest as I pulled Preacher out and led him away to the shed.

"Sit in the chair," I instructed him.

"Sure man, anything you say. You ain't gonna beat me are ya bro?" he asked.

"Depends on you, but we might, just for fun," I said only half joking.

After he was secured, we left him and went back into the restaurant to have some coffee. With everyone present, except David, I brought up the subject of what we should do next. "The forces of evil are not done with us by a long shot. Faustus came to Dakota and me both with an offer of riches, power, and glory if we would bow down and worship him.

"The Army of the Golden Dawn and the people behind the Army of the Fourth Reich are not done either. We are pretty sure that Moses Goldman escaped to Israel and it can only be a matter of time before they mount an operation to recover the Ark. As far as we have been able to determine, Max Von Rhome was acting alone, but was a member of the Illuminati, and someone will likely step in to fill his position quickly.

"Along with guarding the Ark, I feel that we should mount an expedition to seek out Blavatsky's cabin and render it useless to her spirit and that of her master, Faustus. I suggest five of us to take care of the cabin—all volunteers, of course. The rest will stay here to guard our headquarters and the Ark.

"Any further suggestions or discussion?"

"Should we try recruiting more members?" asked Peter Gault.

"Yes, by all means," replied Jason. "The more of us there are, the better our chance of success."

"We will have to draw up a charter and rules for membership then," added Bob.

"We should elect officers too," pitched in Bill.

"That's right," I said. "But right now we need to concentrate on fighting the battle we are in. We can do all of that as we find time. Agreed?"

Everyone was in agreement and moved on to the business of picking out people to take care of Blavatsky's cabin. We decided that Bob, John Little Bear, Brian Daniels, Charlie Lyons, and I would make the ride to California while the others would continue operations here.

I grabbed Jason, suggesting that he take someone with him, and go question Zevi Cohen some more concerning the Illuminati and their possible plans. Then I spent some time with Dakota.

The trip back to the states was not the luxury he had become used to. A ride in the back of a cargo plane as far as England and, as though that weren't bad enough, a five day cruise in a specially prepared cargo container. This was quite possibly the worst week of his life and certainly the most humbling. None of the others complained and he soon learned they had no patience with his grumbling. After all, he was responsible for making the trip necessary in the first place.

After a rough trip by rail and finally truck, they heard the sounds of the locks being removed and dummy cargo being shifted to gain access to their hidden compartment. The smell of fresh air was like a reprieve to a man about to be executed and the sunshine like balm to a leper.

"Colonel Goldman, Captain Judah Zebulon, I will be taking care of your transportation and accommodation for the time being." The captain was dark haired, and very Semitic in appearance, but could pass as an American Indian—which made him invisible in Clovis, New Mexico.

They went directly to an old cabin outside of town where they were all able to bathe, get a change of clothes, eat, and check out their new inventory of weapons.

"You will be limited to hand weapons for the time being, at least until you find the location of the Ark," Captain Zebulon informed them.

Zeva was busy going through all the weapons, settling on a Glock nine millimeter for herself, and passing out to each what they preferred. Moses took a Smith&Wesson 9mm because it fit well into his smaller, more feminine hand.

The captain then produced maps and aerial photos of the area around Moapa. "I also looked into the man named Zevi Cohen for you Colonel. He did not die in the explosion. He is being treated at the Lions Burn Care Center in Las Vegas. I have people looking for him, bit I suspect the Gideons have moved him somewhere since I can find no record of him there."

"Cohen knows nothing about us, he will be useless to them."

"Perhaps about us, but he knows quite a bit about the Illuminate. That could complicate matters, especially if they decide to move in and try to silence him. I expect they will be looking for you too, since you have betrayed them, and he does know you."

Moses had not thought about it in those terms. He had betrayed the Illuminati and they would not take it lightly. It might even be them who had spirited Cohen away. This game was getting very complicated.

The next morning they set out for Moapa and Mom's restaurant.

Jason, Peter, and Simon set out the next morning for Las Vegas to look in on Zevi Cohen and see about moving him to a safer location. When they got to his room Jason immediately noticed that his police guard was missing and rushed in to find a man dressed in a white lab coat about to inject Zevi with a syringe full of clear liquid.

Jason moved quickly to stop the man while Peter leveled his gun at him and Simon blocked the door preventing escape. The man, seeing he would be unable to make his delivery, turned the syringe toward Jason who simply batted it away. Disarmed, with no escape route, and staring down the barrel of Simon's Glock, he chose door number three—going out the sealed window. That they were on the eighth floor did not seem to matter to him as he plunged to his death without even a sound. He had died in the service of his masters and his only regret was that he had failed in his primary mission; the death of Zevi Cohen—traitor.

Jason looked out the broken window at the body down below on the covered parking roof, pulled back and said, "Where's the cop that was supposed to be on duty? Find him!" he ordered the other two men.

As they went in separate directions in the hall, he looked into the bathroom and, seeing it was empty, turned his attention back to Cohen. His eyes were still bandaged, but he had heard everything that had transpired and he was scared.

"You've gotta get me outta here, they'll kill me. Please you gotta help me who ever you are."

"My name is Jason Long Bow, I am one of the Gideon's Warriors, and that is why we have come. It looks like we were just in time too."

"Found him in the doctor's lounge Jason. Looks like he was drugged—couldn't remember how he got there. He said he drank some coffee brought by a Candy-stripper and that was the last thing he remembers," reported Peter.

Simon came in trailed by Cohen's doctor, "What is going on here?" she demanded as she surveyed the broken window and armed strangers in her patients room.

"The security here just failed doctor. Can this man be moved?" asked Jason.

"No, certainly not, moving him would kill him."

"In that case doc, he's gonna have to die," pronounced Jason.

A battered old Chevy four-wheel drive pulled into the parking lot of Mom's and General Carter and Tracy Collins got out. Road weary, dirty, and hungry, they entered through the front door with

Tracy half carrying, half dragging the old man. "Please help," she cried to anyone who could hear and Dakota heard.

She rushed up to the pair and asked, "What's wrong with him honey?"

"I don't know, he started getting light-headed and real pale about ten miles from here. He said this is where we were going and we could find help here. Please help him."

"Okay honey," said Helen. "We'll help him. Couple of you big strong men get over here and carry this man to the back room." Joseph Long Bow and his grandson Gabriel helped the general to the cot in the back room. Sam Conner, sometime tracker, and full time E.M.T. was having lunch in the back and offered his help.

After looking Carter over, he ordered some Gatorade and a large bowel of ice cream. Looking at the concern on Tracy's face he said, "Don't worry missy, he's just dehydrated, and his blood sugar is a bit low. Help him drink this and eat the ice cream and he will be fine. How do you feel? You look like you been rode hard too."

I came back from looking in on Preacher and recognized Carter despite a week's stubble and several bruises. "This is General Alois Carter, former commander of Area 51 folks. And you are?" I asked the girl.

"Tracy Collins, I was one of Handlebar's girls."

"Are you still one of his girls?" asked Dakota.

"No, I hope I never see that bastard again," she said with anger in her voice. She was mopping Carter's forehead with a damp cloth and the sort of look one usually sees with young lovers.

"Here honey," Dakota offered. "Let me do that. Helen, why don't you show Tracy to the shower and help her get cleaned up."

Tracy looked at Helen for a moment and said, "He's really gonna be okay?"

"Yes honey, he'll be just fine now," answered Helen.

I stepped over to the other side of the general and sat down saying, "We missed you Carter, looks like you've had a rough time."

The old man tossed back a healthy shot of Gatorade and said, "Got any brandy? I been out of cigars for a week too. That's the worst of it." He got down some of the ice cream then demanded coffee.

When Tracy got back, we got an account of the past few days and the general's heroic, self-sacrificing action with Juan Mendoza. Joseph spoke up about Juan, "He is a good man believe it or not. He was probably angry about the way Meronek acted and was not sure whether you were part of his gang. He might have robbed you and beat you to a pulp, but he would not have killed you."

"Well, he still managed to beat me to a pulp," Carter said.

"I don't think so," returned Joseph. "He barely touched you."

"Well, I'm glad you think so." The old man looked at the girl then and you could see the lines soften in his face and his eyes take on a twinkle. "She saved my life," he said. "She stepped between Mendoza and me when he pointed his gun at me. Told him he would have to shoot her first."

Joseph chuckled a little at that, but decided not to tell Carter that Mendoza never loaded the old six-gun—it was just a prop gun John Ford had given him when he was a kid and had a part in one of his westerns.

I went out back to the shed to question Preacher taking Charlie and Brian with me. It was hot in the shed by now, over 110°, and Preacher was sweating buckets. I offered him some water and waited until he was through drinking it before going on.

"Look man, it ain't necessary to cook me, tenderize me, or steam me. I'll tell you whatever you want to know."

"That's good Preacher," I said. " Let's start with your real name."

"Sure man, Carl Holdman. See how easy that was. How 'bout cutting me loose now man, this tape is really making me itch."

I pulled out the Sun Disk emblem, set it down in front of him, and said, "Tell me about this."

He was silent for a moment then said, "Some chic gave that to me man. It was a gift, that's all."

"Okay," I said. "You want to lie to me, I got time. Just so you know, it gets cold our here at night and the snakes, rats, and other critters like to slip in here looking for a warm spot."

We got up and turned toward the door to leave when he said, "You don't understand man. These people don't forgive or forget. They will hunt me down and kill me. I can't talk to you."

I looked at him, fingering the Sun Disk in my hand for a moment, then said, "We know about the Illuminati Carl. All we are interested in finding out is their level of interest in the Ark. How bad do they want it?"

"I don't know, but I'll tell you what I can since you already know that much. Not everything, but what I can."

"Okay, we'll see how that works then." I had Brian cut him loose and give him some cold Gatorade to start him talking. "Who sent you on this job?"

"I was reporting to Moses Goldman, but I think he is a traitor to the society."

"Why do the Illuminati want the Ark?"

"I'm just a low-level grunt man, they don't tell me that kind of stuff. I was told to join up with Meronek's group and keep tabs on them. I was to tell Moses everything they did and where they went. That's all man. I don't even know if it was really the Illuminati that wanted it or if it was just Goldman. I have never been contacted by the central committee."

"Your saying that Goldman recruited you for this job," said Bill. He had just come in holding some papers in his hand.

"Goldman is the only one from the Illuminati that I have ever talked to," answered Carl.

Bill handed me the papers and I began to look them over. They were phone and text histories from Carl's cell phone. There were several calls to and from Moses, as well as calls to an overseas number that came back as the 'Industrial Lighting Corporation' of Geneva, Switzerland. Most of the traffic was obviously in code as well. I glanced up at Preacher who looked wary; trapped.

I handed him the report and asked, "Care to explain this. They came from your phone." He had rabbit written all over his face as he reached for the papers and just as he was about to take them he bolted for the door. We were ready though and he didn't even get close.

When he came to, he found he was taped to the chair again. I looked at him and said, "It's Déjà vu all over again man."

We left him there, locked the shed, and went back into the restaurant. Jason was back by now and I wanted to talk with him. "Did you find out anything bro?" I asked.

He filled me in on what happened and told me in conclusion, "I decided we would let it be reported that the assassin was successful, but killed himself rather than be captured. Meantime, we moved Zevi to a different room under a phony name."

"Good work, Jason."

"I left Pete and Simon to watch him until we can get them relieved."

"Okay," I thought over this information for a moment. "This Illuminati organization must want the Ark very badly if they are willing to kill their own. You continue working on Preacher while we're gone, okay?"

"Will do, little brother. I see Carter has returned. How should we handle him? I know the Air Force is looking for him."

"I don't know yet. Let him get his strength back a little and let's see what decision he wants to make."

I took Dakota by the hand and led her outside where we could have a moment alone. She was worried about us making the trip to Blavatsky's cabin and said she wanted to go along. "After all, I have a patch too, ya know."

"Yes honey you do, but it's gonna be a long drive and the passenger pillion isn't real comfortable. I would like you to come along though."

"I will then and if I have to, I will catch a cab or something."

With the trip decided, we just held hands and enjoyed the desert sunset and each others company.

Moses took in the little town with its quaint western stores hawking souvenirs and clothing, as well as Indian crafts. How different it would have been if those goyim had not ruined his plans. He would make them pay for that. His handlers back in Israel had reported to him that the Illuminati were turning over every rock looking for him and would probably kill him if they got the chance. He had read in the newspaper that they had gotten to Zevi at the hospital, which was good; it would save him the trouble of doing it himself.

Up the road ahead he saw a truly garish establishment with a huge sign bearing the logo, 'Mom's' and a big pie with the smiling face of someone's mother depicting what was supposed to be a welcoming message proclaiming 'EAT HERE' in ten foot high letters.

'And die from food poisoning' he thought to himself.

The parking lot was crowded though, mostly pick-ups and four-wheel drives that shouted 'trailer trash', and 'red neck' spoken here. He would love putting a little Jewish lightning to the place then shooting the rats as they ran out.

"Oh well, business first, pleasure later," he mumbled to himself.

The others glanced at him, but said nothing. They were already getting used to the idea that Colonel Moses Goldman was probably not all there anymore, if he ever had been. He would show them just how right they were.

They found a parking spot on the truck-stop side of Mom's, away from all the motorcycles and went in trying to look as much like tourists as they could. The others did a pretty good job of it, but Goldman took a seat and sat looking like a Mossad hit-man on holiday.

He watched as the Gideons drank coffee and talked, having a good time. The sight of them only served to inflame his anger and make him look even more out of place.

A big Indian stepped up and asked him for his order telling him that the days lunch special was beef stew and fry bread. Rather than telling the idiot that he would rather eat pig and hold hands with Yasir Arafat, he settled for some of the swill they euphemistically called coffee.

He did notice the man's name tag though—Jason. Over in the dining room he also saw a pretty, blond shiksa holding hands with a man she called Tom. These were the two men most responsible for his failure and it was all he could do to restrain himself from pulling out his gun and shooting all of them.

The others gathered in a booth to order from the non-Kosher menu of swill this place dispensed and he turned his attention to his coffee. Taking a sip, he found that it was actually pretty good and, though he hadn't noticed before, there was a small kosher menu in the lower right hand corner of the big menu which read, 'FOR OUR VALUED JEWISH CUSTOMERS'.

When the little waitress came around to refresh his coffee, he asked about the kosher foods.

"Our friend, Rabbi Goetz supplies everything for us. What we don't use gets turned back to the local food bank. My dad does it because our Lord was a Jew, ya know?"

"That's very considerate of him, uh, Ruth, is it?"

"Yes, my dad is Jason, he owns the place," she said pointing out her dad who was serving a middle-aged couple at a booth.

He decided not to ask why the place was called Mom's and instead, ordered Salmon cakes and bagels with sour cream. He did not notice that several of the Gideons were observing him now. It did not even occur to him that he had just pinned a big yellow Star of David on himself here in the house of his enemy. When he and his operatives left in their van they didn't notice they were being followed.

CHAPTER 38

A meeting was taking place inside a cottage in the Black Forest of Germany. Present were ten men of various background, but one purpose. They were discussing the loss of men and material on the botched Ark expedition. The man at the head of the table was Hans Bettendorf and wore the title President, since Führer still carried a negative connotation.

"Gentleman," Bettendorf was saying, "we must try to recover this Ark. With it under our control the mud races of the world will have no choice but to accept us as their rightful masters." Bettendorf was a striking figure at six-four, two hundred forty pounds, blond hair, blue eyes, everything Aryan that Hitler had not been. "Have a plan put together immediately for its capture. Also, I want someone put in place to spy on these Gideons. Heir Dorfman, that will be your responsibility."

Dorfman was the groups spymaster. "Yes Heir President, I will take care of it before the day is over." He knew just who to send. He was a parody of his leader; short, fat, and wore thick glasses that made him look nerdish. He made a note to call Olga and give her travel orders to America.

"Karl, I want you to arrange a business trip to America. You will visit the area where these Gideons operate under the cover story that you are thinking of building some sort of factory there. Take who ever Erik assigns as well."

Karl Betz would be happy to do this. A man of elegant taste, he loved everything American. Of average height, he was considered handsome, and a very eligible bachelor. "As you wish mine President," he responded. "How long shall I stay?"

"For you," Hans considered. "No more than a week—for Erik's spy—as long as necessary to locate the Ark.

"Stephan, you will accompany them in case they are in need of your talents."

"Ja, mine President," responded the fortyish graduate of Spandau prison where he had majored in theft, murder, extortion, and other illegal pursuits. At six-two, two-hundred-eighty pounds, shaved head with many scars, several piercings, and enough ink to cover a city sidewalk, Stephan Von Himmler was what polite society called a career criminal—less polite people just called him a psycho.

"Keep in touch through regular channels and be careful. These men may be amateurs, but they have been very successful."

† † †

The sky was full of stars, bright little points of incandescent light poking holes in a tapestry of black velvet. A fire crackled in front of me, competing with the music of the night: crickets, coyotes, and the spirits of those who haunted the plains in darkness. A lone pair of yellow eyes approaches the edge of darkness resolving into the muzzle and gray fur of a coyote. He comes up to me and sits down waiting.

"I seek your wisdom old one, tell me what to do. How do I defeat the spawn of evil who calls himself Faustus and his human agent Guzman? How do I protect myself, as well as the one who has given her heart to me?"

"You can not protect either of you by yourself, but you should know this already," was his enigmatic answer. "Only with the armor of the Creator can you withstand the arrows of this demon. 'Stand your ground, putting on the sturdy belt of truth and the body armor of God's righteousness. For shoes, put on the peace that comes from the Good News, so that you will be fully prepared. In every battle you will need faith as your shield to stop the fiery arrows aimed at you by Satan. Put on salvation as your helmet, and take the sword of the Spirit, which is the word of God' (Eph. 6:14-17)."

"I try do these things every day old one, but he is powerful and crafty. I fear he may harm those close to me in order to hurt me."

"You are wise to be wary of this one, he can only be overcome through prayer and fasting."

"How can I learn his real name old one? To have his real name would give me power over him. I have not even been able to learn your name."

"Command him in the name of Him who is over all the angels and he will not be able to resist."

"Who are you old one? Are you the Lord? Or one of His angels?"

"Yes," and then he turned, trotting off into the darkness and leaving me alone to consider his answer.

✝ ✝ ✝

I woke shortly after the dream. It was still dark and I was damp from sweat, so I made my way to the kitchen and started a pot of coffee. It was 0430 as I went to the shower and cleaned up, got dressed, and started breakfast. At a little after five, Dakota came out and put her arms around me, holding me tight.

"What's the matter babe, bad dream?" I asked, giving her a kiss on the forehead.

"No, not that I remember. I just felt like I was being watched by that demon Faustus and woke up. I smelled the coffee and knew you were awake so I came out."

I kissed her again for re-assurance and said, "Let's eat darlin', we've got a long ride today."

"Okay, just lemme go potty first."

I went out and checked the bike over one last time, checking, oil, lights, gas, nuts and bolts. There's nothing that turns a trip into a bummer faster than having a wheel fall off at seventy m.p.h. Satisfied, I started back into the house when, out of the corner of my eye, I spotted movement in the bushes. I went on in, grabbed my Colt, and went out through the backdoor. I went over to where I had seen the movement, but there was nothing there. There were tracks though, from shoes that were on the small side; maybe a woman's.

Back in the kitchen, Dakota was having a second cup of java and while she worked on that I grabbed my saddlebags and loaded the traveling necessitates—rain suits, tools, first-aid kit, and extra ammo.

We met up with the others at Mom's and after prayer we set out for Guzman's cabin.

"Where can they be going so early?" asked Zeva Brandon. "Should we follow or stay here?" she asked Solomon who was the only other person in the van.

"We stay," he answered, "until we get orders otherwise from our glorious leader."

Zeva was already tired of this assignment. Bad food, worse coffee, and that megalomaniac Goldman had her ready to rip somebody's head off. "What if they are going to the Ark? Somebody should follow them."

"They are on motorcycles Zeva, they could not carry the Ark if they wanted too. No, they are going somewhere else. We will stay here and watch the others as we have been commanded to do by the colonel."

"I need to pee," Zeva spit out and exited the van.

"That one will get us all caught," mused Solomon Shlomo— even if she is hot.

The airport at Las Vegas was like so many others; clean, bright, and sterile, thought Karl Betz. There were decorations in the mezzanine area and slot machines in every open spot. The requisite souvenir shops with their cowboy hats and Indian jewelry as well as restaurants catering to every taste. When he had time, he would have to buy a few trinkets to impress the fräuleins back home. "Go ahead to the car rental Stephan and pick up our vehicle, meet us at the exit, ya?"

Obediently, the Butcher of Munich left to carry out his assignment while he and the beautiful Olga Steiner made their way to the baggage area. There was the usual delay as they waited for their bags, but they finally arrived and with the help of a skycap, they were loaded up and rolled out to the car where Stephan waited patiently. Acting as their chauffeur, Stephan opened the trunk for the luggage and the doors for Karl and Olga.

With everyone loaded into the Crown Victoria, Stephan pulled out onto the road following the directions on the G.P.S. and they headed for Moapa.

We made a practice of stopping every hundred miles for gas and to stretch our legs, so it took a bit longer than usual to reach the little town of O'brian, in the Redwoods of Northern California. It had taken us about twelve hours traveling on I-80 to Sacramento, then north on I-5 until we reached our destination. It was beautiful and we were all looking forward to the drive back.

Dakota made no complaints along the way and really seemed to enjoy the experience. I could tell though, by the way she walked when she got off, that she had a major case of monkey-butt.

We spent the night at a little motel called 'The Redwood Rest Stop', which was run by an English couple who had fallen in love with the area back in the seventies while on vacation and never left.

Next morning we set out in the crisp, clean morning air for the cabin, which was at the end of a road called Drury Lane. We missed it the first time and had to double back, finding it only by faint ruts in the ground, and old sign that was barley legible tacked to a tree.

We were able to drive in, but the going was slow with us having to dismount several times to remove fallen branches and other debris from the trail. Finally, we spotted the broken down cabin, parked the bikes, and went the last fifty meters or so on foot.

It was probably a nice place at one time, but years and weather had taken a toll. The roof had holes in it and had collapsed over part of the porch. The swing had fallen on one end and crashed through the floor of the porch. The windows had been broken out by vandals or storms and the furniture was broken or simply rotted in place. It was hard to imagine Meronek coming here and not seeing the place for what it was, but that was the nature of Guzman's power and his lust.

Dakota crowded up next to me, grabbing my hand and holding on. I could see no evidence of Guzman's remains or even a grave on the site, but I knew her body had to be here somewhere—it was the only way she could maintain her power here.

"Everybody pair up and look around for a grave or a shrine of some sort. She has to have left something here," I directed.

"Honey," said Dakota. "Wasn't she always in the swing on the porch."

"Yeah, she was Chica." I walked around to the side of the porch to have a closer look at the spot. I tore away some of the boards that had been used to enclose the porch and keep animals from getting under it.

With a screech like a tortured soul from hell a juvenile cougar came tearing out of the hole I had just made and, with tail twitching wildly, ran for the protection of the deep forest. Dakota was trying to climb up on my head, while I was trying to get on the roof of the cabin at the same time.

It took several minutes for both of us to calm down and even longer before Bob and the others managed to stop laughing and get up from the ground where they had fallen from laughing so hard.

Bob came over at last and asked, "You two okay? I thought both of you were going to jump on the roof you were so scared."

"Ha, ha, Bob," I answered. I turned to Dakota who was still a little pale and said, "You alright honey?"

"Yes, I think so. What was that anyway?"

"A young cougar," Bob answered. "Lucky for you he was more scared of you than you were of him."

"I would not bet my life on that Robert Harper," said Dakota with menace in her eyes.

"You better find someplace to get, Bob," I said with a snigger. "This cat has bigger claws."

"Roger that, Nephew," chuckled Bob as he wandered out into the woods in search of Guzman's grave.

"Sometimes Tom, I feel like I could skin him alive," said Dakota.

"I know the feeling babe, patience is a virtue; with Bob it is a full time job."

Using a flashlight, I had a look under the porch and spotted what looked like bones protruding from piles of leafy detritus. Rather than crawl under, I used a long forked branch to drag the debris toward me. Once out in the sunlight we were able to separate out some ribs, some arm bones, a thighbone, and some vertebrae. Digging around a bit more, I found the skull, jaw, and most of the rest of the bones, along with some rotted bits of clothing.

Bob came over and broke out a small metal detector to look for any items of metal, but found only a few silver hairpins and a broach. These were defiantly Carmine Guzman's remains though, just where she had fallen years ago. It was difficult to pin down the circumstance of her death of course, but there was a breach in her skull that looked a lot like a bullet hole. It was just above the left eye, but we could find no exit wound or slug inside the skull.

A search of the grounds in the direction that I saw Faustus come from turned up nothing but an old outhouse. Working on a hunch, I knocked the old privy over and started digging with a shovel that had been in a tool shed next to the cabin.

Twenty minutes later, we had a bronze bust of some sort, which was far to encrusted to identify. There were several other items of interest as well: glass bottles, coins, some porcelain dolls, a pistol of civil war vintage, and several items that looked like they may have been used for casting spells.

It was looking like Madame Guzman had been executed for witchcraft. There was an old leather-bound book hidden inside the house behind the bricks in the fireplace as well. We would have to deal with it later under better conditions though or it would fall apart. For now, we put it in a sealed plastic bag.

We took her bones, placed them into the pit left by our digging, and would have burned them if it had not been so dry. There was an area wide burn-ban in effect and a simple wooden cross on top of the grave would have to do.

I was pretty sure the items we had found had constituted a shrine to Faustus and the book had contained her spells. With some luck, though a blessing would be better, we might be able to find his real name in it.

I talked with Jason on the phone when we got back to the motel and he said he would arrange with a friend of his, who was an archeologist, to clean up the items we had found. He also said the Jews we had spotted in the restaurant were still watching from the van parked across the street. He mentioned too, that some Germans had come into town claiming to be looking for land to build a factory, but wouldn't say what the factory was for. Seems that his two assistants did not 'feel' right either. The man, Stephan, was just muscle and the woman, Olga, seemed more interested in our group than in the available land. They didn't seem to know much about local land values either. I reminded him that they could be legit, but to keep an eye on them just the same.

"We'll be home tomorrow Jason, Lord willing. Then we can try tackling some of these new mysteries.

† † †

Dick Rogers, wearing a disguise, came up to the white van and knocked on the door. "Open up in there or I'm calling the cops!" he said, in a loud voice. He heard movement inside, but the door did not open, so he decided to try a different approach. "The eternal rays of the Golden Dawn will bring you out sooner or later."

The door opened and the pixyish face of a young lady, suspended over a Glock, looked out at him. "Who are you, speak quickly," she commanded.

"I am Captain Dick Rogers and you need to let me in." He was not really a Captain in the Golden Dawn, but they would not know that and it would take them to much time to figure it out. So he was safe for the moment.

The door opened to reveal two occupants, the cute girl, and a rugged young man who asked, "Who sent you?"

"No one sent me exactly. I have been on this operation from the beginning. Are you two aware that the Gideons know of you and are watching you?"

"They can't be, we just got here two days ago. We would know if they were aware of us."

"You are?" asked Rogers.

"Sergeant Solomon Shlomo, this is Corporal Zeva Brandon, and I must ask again. Who are you?"

"I am working for Moses Goldman, have you seen him lately?"

The girl made a face that said she had. "Yeah, his highness is sleeping in the Motel 6."

"Call and let him know I am here please."

"I'll give you the phone Captain and you can call him yourself," the girl said with some rancor. That would have to do he surmised; Goldman had obviously worked his charm on these people as well.

"You better have a damn good reason for waking me up!" growled the voice on the other end of the phone.

"Good evening Colonel Goldman, since you would not return my calls I decided to come visit you."

"Mmm, yes," responded Goldman. "Mr. Rogers isn't it? How are things in the neighborhood?"

Dick let the weak humor slide and said, "About to warm up. They know your watching them Moses. They are watching you in return. Get rid of the van and try to dress like you get your clothes at Walmart not Neiman Marcus. I'll be around so don't try to find me, I'll find you. If I locate the Ark, I'll get back to you."

He hung up the phone, looked at the two sitting in front of him and said, "Good luck, you'll need it with Goldman in charge."

Dick did not like Moses and did not like Faustus forcing him into working with the old fool. He would do what he had to though and if that meant leading Goldman to his Waterloo, then so be it.

✝ ✝ ✝

We put our kickstands down about eight in the evening and it was good to be back. The ride had been uneventful, but very pleasant. We were a little saddle-sore from the long ride, but everyone was in good spirits. The gang came out to welcome us, then we went in for food, drink, and conversation. Jason sat across from me and filled me in on the events since we had left. Dick Rogers had visited the people in the van, the Germans had been acting like tourists, and Preacher was beginning to hallucinate out in the shed.

In turn, I reported on what we had found at the cabin and Jason said the archeologist, Drew Paulson, would come by the next morning.

After dinner we went out to see Preacher who was mumbling to himself and obviously suffering from the heat. "Preacher, tell me about Rogers."

"Mister Rogers? Would you be my neighbor? Great show; he died though didn't he? Yeah, I'm pretty sure he's dead." He was rambling, but still cogent.

"The man who crashed the ceremony down in Mexico, that Rogers." I reminded him.

"Oh, that dude. Never seen him before man. I don't think he is Illuminate—could be. Secrets upon secrets man. Their so secret they don't even know who they are."

He was obviously not completely lucid, but he was answering questions. "How long have you been with the Illuminati?" I asked him.

"Since I was ten years old man. They adopted me, raised me in this orphanage in Switzerland."

"What do they want Preacher?" asked Jason.

"They want to rule the world, just like all the others. 'Cept they want to make the world some kind of Utopia, ya know? Everybody living in peace and harmony; with them at the top, of course."

"If they had the Ark, do you think they would use it to kill?" I asked.

"Why not man, they would kill me now if they could find me. They've killed before, they even ordered me to kill anyone I had to in order to take the Ark. They told us all about how humanitarian they was, but they're just killers like all the rest."

"Tell us what you know about their headquarters in Santa Fe. Tell us how to get into the building."

He was tired and willing to answer our questions, but this one brought him up short. "You don't wanna do that man. They would send every operative they have to destroy you and everyone connected with you. They would not rest until every one of you was dead. I will tell you what I can about them because you are the only ones that don't seem to be interested in using the Ark for your own gain, but stay away from their headquarters man."

"Okay Preacher," I said. "I'm going to let you go now and give you a little freedom. If you take off they will probably kill you, so stay where we put you, okay."

"Sure man, thanks. If there's anything else I can do just ask."

Jason's boys took him out to the reservation and put him up in an empty room in one of the houses and we moved on to other business. "Where are the Germans now" I asked Jason.

"They are in the Motel 6 along with Goldman and the rest of his people. It's really the only place to stay for people used to four-star accommodations."

"You really think they're here looking for the Ark? Why?" I asked.

"They wont say what kind of factory they want to build for one thing. Also, the two people this Karl Getz has with him just aren't right, like I said. They have been cruising around areas where there is no water or power, but plenty of caves. They are looking for something, but not factory sites."

"Okay then, let's keep a close eye on them, but not interfere for the time being."

The next morning the archeologist, Drew Paulson, came by with her mobile lab and we turned over the artifacts we had recovered. She looked them over and told us, "The bust will have to soak for a few days, but I believe it is a bust of Hecate who was the Queen of the witches.

"The other items here could have been used as spell binders, especially the dolls. What will be of greatest interest will be the book. If I'm not mistaken this is a book of demons and spells which is hundreds of years old."

"Possibly from the thirteenth century," I asked

"Yes, the twelfth or thirteenth at least—very rare and extremely valuable. If she was killed for being a witch, I am surprised they did not burn it. The pages are made from vellum and would have resisted rot very well. We will have to be careful in handling them though: they will be very fragile."

"It was hidden behind a space in the fireplace which is why it probably went undetected." I said. "Is there another copy somewhere we could look at in the meantime?" I asked.

"There are a couple of copies, but they are all in private collections. I do have a copy on disk though, if you want to see what it contains. I could make you a copy."

"That would be great."

"I will have my assistant e-mail a copy, if that would be faster."

"Even better. Bill can give you our address, thanks."

I left her to her work and went into the war-room to tell Bill that I wanted to have a look at that copy as soon as it was available, then I went into the dining room to get some coffee and Danish. The German woman was in the front checking out the jewelry and the gegaws.

Seeing me, she came over and asked, "Iz zis stuff really made by ze American natives or do zey buy it from China as I have heard?"

"I know some stores get their stuff from China, but Jason gets all of his from craftsmen on the reservation. You can trust that ma'am."

"Ach, ya, zis is goot," she said in accented English. "I vant somesing, how you say, genuine, ya? People are alvays trying to take advantage of tourists, ya?"

Like many foreigners, she had a habit of ending her sentences as a question. I got the impression though, that this woman could speak flawless English if she wanted too. She was trying to seduce me right in front of Dakota and the others. "Everything in here is genuine ma'am."

"Ya, I bet zat it iss," she said, with a slight bedroom tone in her voice.

"Tom," called Bill from the war-room. "I've got that download for you if you want to check it out."

"Okay bro," I answered. "I'll be right there."

"I am so sorry," she purred like a housecat. "I have taken too much of your time my friend. Please excuse me." She walked away with her rear end moving like two cats in a burlap bag, fully conscious of what she was doing.

I turned back toward the war-room to see Dakota dong a slow burn, approaching meltdown. I grabbed her hand and told her to come with me. I was afraid at that moment she might go after Olga.

"Don't kill the Nazi spy just yet honey. It wouldn't look good on your resume. She's only trying to seduce me as any good operative would. Don't lose your temper. She has nothing I want, you are the one I love, and the only one I want. For her it's just business; divide and conquer. Don't let her get under your skin; that's what she wants."

"Okay Tom," she said, looking somewhat contrite. "But if she lays a hand on you I will skin her alive and feed her to the dogs."

I was actually flattered by her jealousy, I had never had a woman show so much concern for me before. "That's my domestic little cougar," I said and gave her a kiss. "Now, let's have a look at this book of demons."

I sat down at the computer and opened the file. The book was rich in illustrations and the artwork depicting the demons was lifelike in the tradition of renaissance artists. There were hundreds of minor demons, but they were not pictured. Only those of major importance were described, along with instructions on how to summon them.

I could not find one called Faustus though and a physical description was useless since they could change that. Their true appearance was also useless, since they were creatures of spirit, not flesh. The only thing to do was take down all their true names and hope that Guzman's book would reveal who she was serving.

Out in the dining room came sounds of an argument. I went out and found Olga and a large German man involved in an altercation with someone. They were arguing in German and appeared to be ready to come to blows. I couldn't understand much of what they were saying, but I did catch a few words. The man they were talking to was Jewish according to them and a pig or dog—or both. He was calling them fascists in return.

I walked up and sat down on a stool to watch. After a few moments we had a crowd gathered, but using hand signals I let everyone know to watch; but do nothing. Olga began to catch on and grabbed Stephan, pulling him toward the exit. The man they had been arguing with began to follow them, but I had Jason and Brian interject themselves between them.

The man then made the mistake of putting his hands on Jason to push him out of the way. Jason grabbed him, carried him back to a stool, and sat him down not to gently and held him there.

"Moses Goldman I presume," I said standing in front of him to keep him from getting up. I motioned Jason to search him, but he just smiled and showed me a Smith&Wesson which he had purloined from the Germans while they had been arguing.

Jason took it from him and put it behind the counter.

"Very cute trick Mr. Goldman, where did you learn that?" I asked.

"On the streets of Jerusalem," he replied.

"Try to behave yourself, Mr. Goldman."

"I don't know who you are talking about," he shot back. "My name is Arthur Brooks, I have ID to prove it too."

"I got ID to prove I'm Clark Kent," said Brian. "You can buy 'em at the drug store."

"Glad to meet you Mr. Kent," retorted the man.

"Mr. Goldman," I continued. "You think you have been clever, but you must remember having eaten here two days ago? We got your fingerprints from your water glass and matched them to your records at the D.M.V." I waited to see what he would say next, but he only remained silent. "You are wanted for murder and attempted murder in Santa Fe Mr. Goldman. Very serious charges I'm afraid."

"My name is Brooks, Arthur Brooks. I don't know any Goldman, but those Nazi's thought I was him too."

"Easy enough to find out. David, if you would check his prints for us."

Brooks was taken into the war-room where his prints were taken electronically. He had not expected to be checked right there and then.

"First, check against the print from his last visit here, then run it through C.O.D.I.S. and Interpol," I said.

"I'm telling you I am not Moses Goldman. I am Arthur Brooks, retired from the Israeli army. I was a Major in intelligence."

"Gunny," said Bill, getting my attention. "He's not Goldman."

His passport picture from immigration came on screen confirming his identity and his prints did not match the prints from the glass either. "Bring up the photo we took of him at the lunch counter," I asked Bill.

The picture came up and Bill put them side-by-side for comparison. "Are you aware of having a twin Mr. Brooks?" I asked. He was staring at the pictures himself and having a hard time believing what he was seeing. Goldman's hair was slightly longer and he had a scar on his chin, but other than that, the resemblance was striking.

"Who is this Goldman?" he asked.

"Good question sir. We have been trying to figure that our ourselves for several days now. I will tell you what we do know of him. Please sit down. Were you going to order something? It's on the house," I offered.

"Mighty free with my money there Tom," said Jason.

"Oh," I replied. "Now it's Tom, not little brother. I see how you are."

Jason only laughed and then pointed out the kosher menu for Brooks who ordered salmon cakes and matzo ball soup while I filled him in on Goldman's history; as far as we knew it.

"I was raised in an orphanage in Israel," he told us over coffee. "I was told my parents had been killed in the '67 war. There was never anything about me having a brother."

"Do you know anything about The Army of the Golden Dawn, sir," I asked.

"There have been rumors, yes," he answered. "Like many secret societies I suppose. The Illuminati, Skull and Bones, the Masons, and so on. If they exist, I have never come into contact with them knowingly. I was in intelligence you know, but we were only interested in military stuff, how many SCUD missiles, how many tanks, planes, and troops. There was talk now and then about this Golden Army, but I supposed it was just gossip, you know."

"Tell us what you did hear sir, it could be important now," Jason asked.

"Supposedly, they go back to the time of King Solomon, and the Masons. They were formed by one of Solomon's generals to protect the treasures of the Temple.

"According to the legend, they carried the Ark away after the breakup of the kingdom in 900 B.C. or so when civil war broke out. The war became so terrible that even the army became involved, so the high priest and a handful of loyal men took the Ark and fled to the land of the Phoenicians. We don't know where that land is exactly though and apparently they left no record of how to find the Ark.

"The Golden Army fell into disfavor and went underground after that. If they still exist they can not be much of an army."

"Interesting," I said.

"Excuse me," said Joseph, Jason's father. "I remember reading somewhere that the Phoenicians were a sea people who lived on the coast of Canaan and their name meant 'Red People', isn't that correct?"

Bill queried the computer and it confirmed Joseph's statement.

"So the Phoenicians could have been the ancestors of the American Indians," I concluded.

"That is one theory," confirmed Brooks. "But America is a big country and if they hid the Ark here it cold stay lost forever."

"No, probably not," said Jason. "The people would have kept a record of such a valuable artifact, but it may have been lost if the people caring for it were wiped out because of some tragedy."

"Somebody bring General Carter here please," I asked.

"He's at my house," said Jason. "He and Tracy needed some rest. I got John checking on how the Air force is feeling about him as well."

"Okay, let's call him then." Bill picked up the secure phone, called Jason's house, and had Carter on the line in minutes. "General Carter? Tom here, how are you doing? Good, good, and Tracy? She is doing well too, I hope. Good, listen General; I need to ask you some questions about the Ark. Do you know where, when, and how it was found?"

"Yes, I do," he answered. "But I wont say over the phone. I'll have someone drive me over there."

I decided to yield to his wish, after all it would take no more than twenty minutes or so for him to make the trip.

"Who's on the Germans?" I asked.

"David is following them. Do you want to bring them in?" Bill asked.

"No, not yet," I answered and turned back to Brooks. "What was the argument about? Who started it?"

"They started it—the man did. I guess he thought I was Goldman. He told me I served a bunch of losers and that we were all pigs. I could not take such an insult silently, I thought he meant the Israeli army, but I guess he meant the Golden Dawn. He never called me Goldman, but he did say I was stupid to openly show my face. The woman tried to shut him up, but he would not, of course."

Bill had been running some facial recognition software while were talking, trying to run down the German's faces. He spoke saying, "Stephan Von Himmler, late of Spandau prison, where he was a guest for a long list of offenses. His record starts at age ten when he killed and old man and burned down his house, because the man had called him an idiot.

"He has also been convicted of armed robbery, extortion, racketeering, rape, and murder. He was doing life for the last two, but somehow got a pardon. It also states that he became a member of a Neo-Nazi gang in the unit and held the position of enforcer for the gang. He is suspected in the deaths of several inmates, but it was never proven. That seems to be the end of the record on him; he has been under the radar for the past three years."

"Sounds like he found some friends in powerful places," I said. "I don't like the idea of this psycho running around here free." I was thinking of Dakota. "He is dangerous and these people are obviously using him for his muscle, not his brains. I don't wish to see those talents used on any of our people."

"Tom's right," John pitched in. "They would not have brought along a man like that unless they intended to use him to hurt someone."

"Okay, suggestions on what we should do with him?" I asked.

David spoke up, "I could arrange something that would get him put away behind bars for a few days—maybe weeks."

Brooks made a suggestion, "If you don't mind gentleman, that would not help. The people he serves would have him out within hours and it would only make trouble for you. You must use other means with a man like this. Perhaps send them on a wild duck chase."

"Goose chase," interjected Bill. "Sorry, the phrase is, wild goose chase."

"Yes," Brooks went on. "Let them think they have discovered the hiding place, but be vague enough that they will spend several days looking before they discover they have been duped."

"No," I said. "They might decide to take a hostage, one they might torture or kill. They may try anyway."

"Tom's right," said Jason. "We need to put this man, and the others, somewhere that they wont be able to hurt anyone and then send them back where they came from—maybe a little worse for wear."

"That's probably the best course under the circumstances. Let's keep an eye on him for now, and talk with this industrialist tomorrow." I went over to Dakota, gave her a kiss and told her, "If you see this Stephan guy around, don't hesitate to get somewhere safe and call for help. Keep yourself armed at all times and don't be afraid to shoot him if you have to. The world will not miss him a bit if you do."

"Okay, Tom, I promise. I don't like him either, he gives the creeps a bad name."

General Carter came in through the back door and was directed to a seat in our little group. He looked at Brooks for a moment then asked, "What's he doing here?"

"Have you seen this man before?" I asked.

"He tried to get into a site where we were working about four years ago. Said he represented The Native American Bureau of Antiquities or some such tripe. There was no such thing and I had him thrown off the site."

"Would that have been the site where you found the Ark General?" I asked. "Because this is not the man you spoke to. This is his twin brother."

"No shit?" exclaimed the General. "Sorry, 'scuse my language, but you're sure?"

"Yes," I said. "We got Goldman's fingerprints and this man's prints are not a match."

"Okay," Carter went on. "Yes, it's where I found the Ark. It's about four miles north of the base, but still on government prop-erty. I can take you there. We found it as a result of a plane crash. The impact opened a cave up and one of my men had to go in to retrieve some of the planes parts. What he saw brought him back out quick. There was more than the Ark you know. All kinds of stuff: scrolls, them menorah things, plates, all of 'em looked like they were made of gold too."

"There were scrolls?" inquired Brooks. "What happened to them?"

"We left them there. I guess I should say, I left them there. I knew what the Ark was, so I had it loaded up and taken out as part of the wreckage. I couldn't bring out the rest without too many questions being asked, so I had a dozer cover the hole and left it. I figured I could always come back for it later. Never did though; got so wrapped up in dreams of ruling the world that I forgot all about that stuff."

"We must get all those artifacts out as soon as possible," demanded Brooks. "If there is a Torah there, it could be the oldest ever discovered. Its value would be immeasurable."

"I know Mr. Brooks, but they will be safe for a few more days. It would be a good way to throw off the bad guys though, get them to looking in the wrong direction."

"Yes," said Brooks. "But these are dangerous people and they might damage some of the artifacts if they discovered us at the site in their haste to find the Ark. They could use those items to hold the Ark hostage, in fact."

"True Arthur," I said. "We wont deal with those things right now. We need to take care of the problem we have in front of us."

"How did knowledge of the Ark's presence in the hanger get our Carter?" asked David.

"I'm not sure, but I guess it must have been one of the people on the recovery team. All I could do was swear them to secrecy you know. I did try to keep them all on base, but a few finally finished their enlistment and left. Who knows for certain."

"Mr. Brooks, what are your plans for the immediate future?"

"I'm hoping you will let me stay and help to recover these priceless objects for Israel."

"We can certainly use your help, but for obvious reasons I think we will need to put you in disguise for the time being. Dakota?"

"Yes, a little hair dye, different glasses, maybe some padding. I'll see what can be done.

"Okay hon, I leave you to it.

A circle of light in a place of darkness so complete that nothing could be seen beyond the knife-edged corona. This was the extent of his world. Out of the darkness, a voice called to him, "Jack Shepherd, called Hardcore?"

"Yes master, I am here."

`"Do you still serve me?"

"Yes master, you know that I do."

"Then listen to me and do what I tell you, that you might live and prosper."

"Command me master, I will do as you say."

"Find the one named Meronek and free him. I have use of him yet."

"I will need your help master. Give me one of your own."

"Meronek will be moved soon, I will tell you where and when. Be ready to strike."

"Meronek, on your feet dirtbag you're being transferred."

Steve got up from the hard mattress, which covered the steel bunk, put on his cheap Chinese deck shoes and gathered the few possessions he had: a tooth brush, toothpaste, bar of cheap soap, and one unbreakable comb.

He was pulled out and handcuffed to a man who was black as midnight and possible the biggest man Meronek had ever seen. He was seven feet tall, three hundred twenty pounds of muscle, bone, and attitude. In silence they were herded out to a Bluebird bus, along with a half-dozen other miscreants, and took a seat in the front of the bus because Midnight, that was what he called himself, would not fit anywhere else.

They pulled out heading for the maximum security unit in Carson City in the northwest part of the state near Reno. He was considered too dangerous to be kept anywhere else.

With a voice like the distant rumbling of canon-fire, Midnight informed him, "You be ready to move white boy. We's gonna bust outta here."

Meronek believed this man could rip open the bus with his bare hands, but asked anyway. "How we gonna do that?"

"Hardcore's gonna help after we has a little accident."

A few miles down U.S. 95 on a desolate stretch of highway the bus was suddenly thrown sideways by an eighteen-wheeler as it performed a pit-maneuver on it. As the bus spun around Midnight braced himself with an arm to the ceiling, locking himself to his seat. Meronek braced himself with his feet to the cage and his free arm to the side of the bus.

For a moment that lasted an eternity, everything was in chaos. Bodies were flying around helplessly chained to each other as the bus filled with screams of pain, cries of horror, the sounds of metal grinding against pavement, glass shattering, and finally silence, as the bus ground to a halt.

There were the overpowering odors of blood, feces, and gasoline, as Meronek found himself trapped underneath the body of Midnight, as well as the bodies of two other men jammed against his back. The guards, one in front, and one in back, were trying to make sense of what had just happened to them when they were silenced forever by the thunderclap of twelve-gauge shotguns.

A much louder bang at the back of the bus opened the door and a man wearing a Devils Angels patch stepped in over the once pretty, blond haired guard with some bolt cutters to open the cage door. Meronek felt himself jerked into motion as Midnight headed for the freedom of the open rear gate.

Rather than have his arm torn from the socket he scrambled over the moaning and broken bodies of his fellow inmates in an effort to keep up with the big man. Men screamed curses at them as they trampled broken limbs beneath their hands and feet in their haste to exit the bus.

Meronek grabbed the dead guards 9 mil Glock on the way out staggering in the bright light of day and coming up short to face of Hardcore staring at him out of the driver's window of a Dodge Windstar van.

"Get in," Hardcore ordered the two of them while someone else set a torch to the gas tank of the bus. Safely in the van, with the black and orange gasoline fireball behind them, Hardcore floored the accelerator and headed off toward the safety of Las Vegas and its thousands of nameless faces.

"Meronek!" shouted Hardcore.

"Yeah, boss," answered the younger man.

"Faustus had me break your sorry ass out of prison, so don't get the idea this is a mercy mission. He wants you to do something for him, so pay attention. Midnight was sent to help you. Don't piss him off, understand?"

Looking up at the big, grinning face of the black man, Meronek decided to take Hardcore's advice.

"I understand boss. You got any dope man? I need a fix bad, I feel sick."

This was one part of Meronek that Shepherd did not like. He did not like addicts because they were undependable. He had tried to make this point to Meronek when they were in San Quentin, but Steve just kept coming back to it. Shepherd felt like kicking him out of the van without stopping, but Faustus wanted him and Faustus always got what he wanted.

Hardcore nodded at a girl in the passenger seat and she pulled a loaded hypo out of her purse, along with a rubber hose and handed them to Handlebar who made quick use of them. Looking at the girl as the dope eased his pain Meronek realized it was Kelly 'Lips' Hermann. "Hey Lips, how's tricks? Come on back here and make me happy baby."

"Knock it off Meronek," barked Hardcore. "We got more important things to do right now."

"Like what Hardcore?" whined Meronek. "We got plenty of time, she can do my friend Midnight here too."

"You don't speak for me dirtbag," rumbled midnight.

"He can't get it up on smak anyway," Kelly said.

Meronek tried to grab Kelly for that, but was restrained by the immense bulk of Midnight who was quickly taking a real dislike to him. "Why don't you sit still little man," warned Midnight. "You beginning to piss me off." One hand, measuring fifteen inches from thumb to little pinky, closed all the way around Meronek's neck threatening to pop his head off like a seed from a grape.

"Okay, big guy," Handlebar nervously laughed. "Don't get yer undies in a wad, I was only foolin' man."

"Try to be quiet 'til we get to the house Meronek. I'm already putting more on the line than your sorry ass is worth."

The heroin kicked in and Meronek sat in his own little world for the duration of the drive into Vegas. When he had parked the van in the garage, Shepherd let the giant, along with his Siamese partner, out the side-door and led them into the house where he used a key to separate the disparate twins.

I was sitting in the war-room with Dakota having some of Helen's Pecan pie and coffee when the news about the crash of the inmate bus came on the TV. Due to the fire, ID's were not immediately available, but the count was three officers dead and eighteen inmates with two survivors and two missing.

I saw David pick up a phone and make a call, but I already knew that Meronek would be one of the missing.

"Who could do such a thing," asked Dakota in a tone of disbelief.

I could tell her of a lot of people who could, but left it at, "Probably Hardcore's people, helped by that demon, Faustus."

David got off the phone and came over to say, "Everyone's accounted for but a huge black guy named Maurice 'Midnight' Johnson and the guy he was cuffed to—Steve Meronek."

"No surprise there bro," I remarked. "They're probably long gone by now too."

"Yeah, no sign of them. This was a professional job. Looks like they used a pit-maneuver to flip the bus, blew through the back door, and shot the officers. They'll get the needle for this one sure," said David, his voice choked with emotion.

I looked over to Jason and asked, "Any movement on the Golden Dawn or the Germans?"

"Nothing so far. The Germans are still out at the airport seeing Karl off and the G.D.'s are still spying on us from across the street in their invisible white van."

That left Shepherd and his Devils Angles. "John?" I called out.

"Yeah Tom," came an answer from behind one of the computers.

"See if you can get ahold of Jake Holland and find out if Shepherd had anything to do with this please."

"On it Tom, had the same thought. Hope he's alright; no answer yet. I'll keep at it though."

I went out back and sat down on a chair thinking about all those lives lost and found myself crying and praying for the first time in my life for a bunch of people I didn't even know. I felt a pair of arms close around my neck and I pulled Dakota down in front of me, wrapped my arms around her, and hugged her to me. I held her tightly for a long time soaking her shoulder with my tears and she mine until she finally asked me, "Why are we crying hon?"

"Because twenty-one people are dead and all I had to do is kill that son of a bitch to stop it."

She reached up wiping away my tears saying, "You followed your conscience honey, you did what was right."

"I know darlin', shut up and hug me."

She did.

✝ ✝ ✝

Dick Rogers sat watching a house in a seedy neighborhood of Las Vegas, waiting until the time was right. The sun would be down soon and he would be able to slip out and take care of his master's business. Normally he would be against this kind of job, but this time would be different.

The garage door opened and a dark blue van with heavily tinted windows pulled out into the street. He could see a woman's face as it pulled away, probably going out for food or booze, but an opportunity for him. He let himself out of the Toyota Corolla and quickly moved across the street. As he approached the garage door he dropped to the ground and rolled under the lowering door just making it in before it closed.

He came to his feet pulling his .45 Colt long slide, with the suppressor already attached, and went through the inside door. He found himself in the laundry facing another door and through that one, the kitchen. There was a bar in the kitchen that looked into the dining/living room area where Hardcore and two of his men were sitting and waiting for Kelly's return. Midnight and Meronek were busy in the bath and bedroom respectively.

Rogers raised the .45 and let it whisper death to Shepherd and his two companions as they sat drinking their last beer and smoking their last joints. Rogers didn't like killing people, but this time was different. Hardcore had betrayed his master by not completely following his orders. He was supposed to have released the men in the bus which would have kept the cops busy chasing all those escapees and making it easier for Meronek and Midnight to escape. Now the cops would leave no stone unturned until they found those responsible for the massacre.

Midnight came out of the bathroom and seeing Rogers asked, "What you doing?"

"Our master's business. Get Meronek and let's go."

"Hey Tom," called John. "I got Jake on the line."

I kissed Dakota one more time and went back into the war-room wiping away the lipstick and tears on the way. "What'cha got John," I answered.

"He says he's coming in 'cause it's getting to dangerous any-more. Anyway, he also said that Hardcore took out early today in a van along with some guy driving a tractor—had some of his muscle with him too. He would not say where he was going, but it looks like he's good for the bus job. I got a description of the tractor and the van, which I'm forwarding to the police."

"Okay, good." I said. "Have Jake come here if he can, this will be the only safe place for him for a while."

"Right Tom, he's on his way over now."

I went back out front and sat down in one of the booths, think-ing about all that had happened over the past few weeks. Too many people had died, but I had made some wonderful friends and found a woman I had fallen in love with. I would not take it back for anything or change one part of it, except the innocent lives that had been taken. These people had become my family and I loved everyone of them.

"Mr. Harper?" asked a voice as smooth as silk and somehow at the same time, sibilant as a snake—it was Olga looking like a dimestore cowgirl.

"Yes ma'am," I drawled, sounding Texan even in my own ears.

"My name is Olga Steiner, Mr. Harper and I was hoping I might speak with you a moment."

"Well, I don't think it will hurt anything ma'am. But you best be careful of my fiancé 'cause I don't think she likes you."

"Really, I don't know why. I have done nothing to her. I only want to talk to you about land. I am told you know a man named Jason Long Bow, I would like an introduction to him please."

"I suppose I could do that, wait here a moment."

I went into the kitchen to find Jason who was on the phone with his wife and waited for him by sampling some of his cooking. Dakota came in looking somewhat aggravated and it was not hard to guess that she had seen Olga.

"What's that Teutonic tramp up to now Tom?"

"Claims she wants to speak to Jason about land, but judging from the way she's dressed, I'd say she is trolling for information."

"I'd say she is trolling for a lot more than that," was her caustic comeback.

"Yes, she is testing us to see if anyone will trade information for her favors," I said.

Who is she talking to now?" she asked.

"No one, she's just standing around looking available."

There was no doubt that Dakota would like to set up Olga, but I felt it would be safer to keep her away from temptation for the time being so I suggested, "Hon, why don't you help out in the war-room until she's gone. I know you don't like her, but we need to use her to catch her boss."

"I know Tom," she answered. "It's just hard for me to deal with her. I'll behave though."

I could see that she was struggling with feelings of low self-esteem, so I reached over and pulled her into my arms and said, "You are much prettier and way more sexy than she will ever be darlin'," and kissed her, giving her a pinch on her little bottom.

I must have pushed the right button because she squealed like a schoolgirl presented with a prize Toad at the school picnic and ran off into the war-room.

"I think you are going to have to marry her Tom," said Jason. "It would kill her now if you didn't."

"I know Jason, it would kill me if she said no."

"You don't have to worry about that little brother, she is waiting for you to ask."

"I know Jason, but I think we really need to wrap this business up before we try getting married you know."

"I agree with you Tom, and I think you are right to wait. Just don't wait too long."

Good advice I thought.

"Olga is out front looking for you. She says she wants to talk to you about land. Maybe you could sell her some of that land were they set off one of the A-bombs—serve her right."

"Yes it would Tom. But we both know she is not looking for land."

Jason went out to talk to her and I followed him out to watch. As they talked, she would look at me, smile and bat her lashes to show interest. She was like something out of a bad spy movie from the forty's, like Mata Hari. I went back into the war-room to see how things were going there and ran into a guy wearing a suit, a very large guy wearing a suit, who was talking to John.

"Tom, this is Jake "Bones' Holland."

"Good to see you again bro," I said. "You look a little different than you did last time."

With a big smile and a warmhearted laugh he said, " Yeah, it's nice to clean up a bit. I was really getting tired of the beard."

"You okay with leaving Hardcore? I know you put a lot of time into that operation."

"It was time to get out Tom. Shepherd was becoming more and more unstable. He hasn't come back since the bus hijacking and no one has heard from him. He had one of Meronek's women with him, Kelly 'lips' Hermann. We have a B.O.L.O. out for her and the van, but nothing yet."

"You know of any safe houses he may have had in Vegas? He seemed to be headed that way. Probably knows it would not be safe to go to his house." asked John.

"I know he had one, belonged to his wife, but I don't know the location. We've got people working on it; I should know something within a few hours."

"Okay, cool," I said. "Keep us posted."

"I would like to join your club Tom, if it's alright." asked the big man.

"You would be welcome with us brother," I said and gave him a hug.

"Thanks, Helen is working on a patch for me. You have no idea how much I wanted to be rid of that Devils patch."

✝ ✝ ✝

Meronek came into the living room looking like he had just shot up an armload: because he had. Seeing Hardcore sitting on the couch with the dime-sized hole in his forehead, along with the baseball sized hole in the back, brought him to a stop.

"What the hell happened man," he asked Midnight who was standing in front of Rogers. He stepped away revealing the other man who said, "Sorry man, I know he was your friend, but Faustus ordered him hit and I had no choice."

"I knew him a long time," Meronek said, "but he was never my friend. You should'a let me whack him." Meronek began to laugh, then he stuck his index finger into the hole in Shepherd's forehead, pulled it out, and tasted the blood on the end of his finger. Still laughing, he walked away picking up Hardcore's Glock that was lying on the floor and slipped it into his belt.

"Okay," said Rogers, more than a little sickened by what he had just seen. "Let's get out of here."

"What about Lips, let's wait for her. She's a lot of fun."

"I'm afraid she's not on the passenger list Meronek and we've got work to do. If you want to talk to Faustus about it, I'm sure he'll change his mind—just like he did with Hardcore here."

"Okay man, but she'll come back here and freak out when she sees this. She'll think I did it man."

"So what," Rogers shot back. "She knows to keep her mouth shut. This ain't her first rodeo."

They went out and got into the Corolla, which listed slightly to the side that Midnight was on as they pulled away. Three blocks down the road they passed the van which was corralled by a half-dozen police cars with Kelly handcuffed in the back of one of the units. Meronek locked eyes with her for a moment as they passed, then sunk down as far as he could in the seat hoping the police would not see him. There was not much they could do about Midnight, who was lying across the back seat unable to sit upright anyway.

Fortunately for them, the police were too busy searching the van and questioning Kelly to notice them and they made their getaway. Rogers took them out of town and headed back to Moapa and the destiny that awaited them there. On the way, Rogers told Meronek the plan of action that Faustus had given him.

CHAPTER 39

Moses got in the van, along with the rest of his crew, and handed out bags of bagels to everyone as though he were giving out four-star meals. The two that had been on duty remained at their positions in front of telescope and electronic eavesdropping equipment while Moses and the others made themselves more or less comfortable.

"Okay," said Moses. "What was so important that I had to come out here?"

"I think we picked up a lead to where they have hidden the Ark," said Lenny Haim, the surveillance expert.

"Go on then," Moses prompted. "Tell us what you have found."

"The one called Jason had a phone conversation an hour ago with one of his family members. Seems that Olga was poking around out near some sacred caves used for burials back in prehistoric times. He became excited about this and said he would have some of his people out there right away to escort her off the reservation. What alerted me was that his wife said, 'she is getting to close to it.' Her exact words Colonel."

"Okay, good. Let's get moving then. You still have the G.P.S. lock on their vehicle?"

"Yes Colonel," Lenny replied. "I have laid out their route here on the map. This appears to be where they were forced to turn around. It is very rugged terrain sir, you may want to consider a four-wheel drive instead of this van."

"We will need some additional equipment as well sir," added Karl Getz. "We will need torches and possibly some ropes."

"I have already taken care of these things," Moses replied. "You will find them in the motel room along with a four-wheel drive Chevy Blazer out front. You two stay here and keep watching the restaurant. Report to us if anything happens we should know about. We will go tonight when it is dark and use night-vision to find our way."

Having been escorted all the way back to the hotel by the reservation police, Olga and Stephan were certain they had found the hiding place of the Ark. As they pulled into the parking lot, Olga saw Moses loading some equipment into a Chevy Blazer.

"There is that kike again," said Stephan. "It looks like he is going somewhere too, ya?"

"Ya," replied Olga. "But what is he looking for?"

They parked and went to their rooms. After a few minutes, Stephan let himself into her room and waited until she came out of the bath, surprising her in his purple boxers, which were emblazoned with red hearts.

"Darling," she cooed. "You are so primitive."

He took her in his arms and for the next hour they explored each others flesh until neither of them had places left secret. Finally getting up, Stephan looked outside to see that the Blazer was gone. "It is time for us to leave Olga," he announced.

"Tom," called David. "L.V.P.D. just called. They found the van. They also found Shepherd and two of his gang. Somebody blew their brains all over the walls. No sign of Meronek or Johnson, but they were there."

"Any idea who did the shooting?" asked Jake.

"No, but they said it was a .45; probably silenced since no one heard anything. One neighbor said he saw three people get into a Toyota Corolla and one of them was the biggest African American he has ever seen. The coroner puts the T.O.D. at 2030 hours, about forty-five minutes before they were found. The only description I got on the other two was that they were white, one skinny, the other average. Although the witness said it was kind of hard to tell how big the white guys were next to Johnson. He made them look like little kids, ya know."

"Right," I said. "They've got an hour and a half head start on us."

"That's about how long it would take them to get here Tom," said Jason. "Somebody go check on the Germans and Moses. David you come with me," I said.

"I got the Germans," volunteered Jake.

We went out the front and crossed the street toward the van Moses had positioned to spy on us. I pulled open the side door and Lenny fell out onto the pavement—a bullet hole through his neck. Solomon Shlomo sat slumped over his telescope with half his face blown off. I checked his carotid where I found a weak pulse and there were sucking, gurgling noises coming from his throat to show that he was still alive.

"David call 911, get an ambulance here A.S.A.P. This one's still alive!"

As David made the call, I pulled out my phone and called Jake to let him know that he might be walking into an ambush. He answered to say that Moses and the Germans were gone, but someone had paid them a visit. Both of their rooms had been broken into and ransacked. Since there was no sign of the perp's, we had to assume they had moved on in search of the others.

Our trap was now drawing all three players into the snare and it was time for us to go and check on the bait.

At the restaurant, we left a small guard consisting of Jake, Dakota, Helen, and David to protect the place. The rest of us grabbed our weapons and headed out to Snake Canyon where we had led Olga to believe the Ark was hidden.

David Mayer was driving, Moses was riding shotgun, Zeva, Karl, and Mary were in the back. The ride was rough, especially since potholes, rocks, and other bumps were almost impossible to pick out with the night-vision goggles. Sometimes it was difficult just to tell where the road left off and desert began. They had been following Olga's trail for thirty minutes and were approaching a high-walled canyon.

Moses was already feeling the praise of Israel as they bounced along. They were about to enter the mouth of the canyon when a lone coyote suddenly appeared in the road before them. David jerked the wheel sharply to the right to avoid running over the yellow-eyed canine and went off into the ditch bringing the Blazer to a sudden stop.

Pulling his face out of the dash and cursing his driver's lineage all the way back to Abraham, Moses shouted, "Why did you do that? Now we are stuck."

Of all the places they might have gone off the road they had done so where the wheels of the left side were no longer in contact with the ground and on the right, they were buried in soft sand. They would need their winch to get out, but there was nothing to tie it off to. They were on foot now, like it or not.

✝ ✝ ✝

Stephan was piloting the Jeep Bronco and trying not to get wedged in between the boulders that lined the canyon floor. They looked like some giant child's marbles that had been carelessly thrown down in the bottom of his toy chest.

Olga spoke saying, "We may as well stop Stephan. We could be right on top the cave and we would not be able to see it. We must wait for light, ya?"

Stephan shut off the motor, killed the lights and said, "Ya, you are right frau. I need to get out for a moment anyway and inspect the tires."

"Ach, they are not flat are they?"

"No leipshin, I must make water, ya?" Stephan stepped out walking a few feet to the rear of the Jeep where he began to water the rocks. When he finished, he turned and found himself face to face with two glowing yellow eyes that were growling at him like a rabid dog. Unable to see anything, he froze waiting for what would happen next. He was not familiar with the animals of the South-Western United States, so he did not know it was only a coyote standing atop a large rock, and not a large wolf intent on making a meal of him.

He backed away from the glowing eyes, reaching for his Glock, but before he could clear the holster the coyote jumped at him using muscles that had been coiled tighter than the spring of a cheap watch. The animal bounced off his shoulders coming so close to his face that Stephan could smell his hot rancid breath, which stank of desert mice and left a trail of urine across his face, marking him like territory.

Stephan cursed in his native German, his eyes stinging from the yellow water, and fired several shots at the disappearing animal; his bullets harmlessly striking the rocks and making lost-spirit sounds as the ricochets echoed off into the night revealing their location to anyone for five miles.

Olga had opened the door of the Bronco waiting for Stephan to return, but when he started shooting she tried her best to get under the nearest rock for cover. She felt something bite her on her cheek, just under her left eye, and jerked back rolling away without seeing what it was.

Stephan had regained his footing and was nervously cursing and laughing at his own foolishness as he walked back toward Olga.

"Stephan, I think that something has bitten me!" she exclaimed.

He flicked on his flashlight shining it on her face to see the unmistakable twin holes made by the strike of a pit viper. He knew they had no anti-venom and it was more than an hour to the nearest clinic. If he left now they might lose the Ark to the

Jews and Erik would be angry with him, but if he did not, she would probably die. He decided that the mission would be more important to Eric than the life of this silly woman.

"It is nothing leipshin, you will be fine."

"It burns Stephan, it is more than nothing."

She knew that it was bad; she could already feel the venom burning across her face like hot liquid metal flowing under her skin. "We must go back Stephan. We can always come back later you know. Erik will be cross with you for letting me die out here. Take me back now and I will live."

Stephan was tempted. After all, she had had sex with him, and done things most women would not without calling him sick or a pervert. In turn, he was not so sure about his encounter with the coyote. What if it had rabies? Could he catch it from being peed on?

"Alright then, let's go." He helped her back to the Bronco and was reaching for the door when the scene was flooded in sudden, brilliant light.

"Hold it right there asshole or I put a hole in you and your pretty fräulein," came a voice from the darkness behind the light. "Take his gun Meronek, but don't hurt 'um yet."

A shadowy figure came up and took his gun, then frisked Olga in a way that was very familiar. She called him a pig and tried to slap him when he put his hand between her legs, but he brushed her slap aside and laughed as he stepped away. "Wouldn't mind tapping that partner."

"You better be quick then, because she has been bitten on the face by a snake," said Stephan.

Leaning in for a closer look, Meronek whistled low, stepped back and said, "He's right bro, got her right on the cheek. Too bad man, she's nice looking ya know?"

The voice in the darkness said, "Tell us why you came out here. If you tell the truth, I may let you go."

Olga spoke with panic in her voice," Ve heard zer vas treasure in zees caves ya? Ve vas only looking for zat ya? Some silver or gold ya?"

"Very good Olga," replied the voice. "But the wrong answer."

"Their goddamn Nazi's man," blurted out Meronek with rabid hatred in his voice. "Kill 'em, kill 'm both. If you wont, gimme the gun and I will."

"Calm down Meronek, I know what they're looking for. You're looking for the Ark. What has lead you to believe that it's hidden here? Speak or you will die here."

Rocks began to splinter around them and the rear window in the Jeep exploded with a shower of glass spraying everywhere. Rogers doused the light and dropped for cover behind the rocks, as did Meronek, Stephan, and Olga.

Rogers could see the strobe-light effect of automatic fire, as well as single shots coming from the mouth of the canyon. He was not sure who it was though; the Jews or the Gideons. He decided it had to be Goldman's crew, as Tom would not have opened up without giving them a chance to surrender.

He returned fire shouting at Meronek to retreat behind cover. Stephan and Olga did not wait, but took off up the canyon at a run. From the rocks above the sustained single fire of a large caliber rifle began to seek out targets in the canyon mouth silencing the automatic fire immediately and within moments the other fire ceased as the shooters scrambled for cover.

During the respite Rogers and Meronek scrambled into the canyon after the Germans in an effort to find better positions to defend themselves. Coming behind some large boulders that formed a natural fort they stopped and prepared to return fire at their pursuers. Rogers felt arms wrap around him from behind in a bear-hug that threatened to squeeze his heart out of his mouth.

Meronek was having his own troubles with Olga who was trying to scratch out his eyes and reduce his manhood to mashed potatoes with kicks from her booted feet. He smashed his pistol butt into her jaw knocking her onto her back unconscious and then turned his attention to Stephan.

Rogers stomped sharply on the arch of Stephan's foot causing the big man severe pain, then followed it up by slamming his head into the mans jaw and twisting around enough to break his grip, dropping him to the ground. Meronek ended the fight by pumping six rounds from his Glock into the big German, bringing his nefarious career to and end.

"You okay man?" Meronek asked Rogers.

"Soon as I get my breath back. That s.o.b. was strong."

Shooting resumed from the mouth of the canyon, but was being directed toward Midnight on the upper wall.

"Get up on the other side where we can get them in a cross fire Meronek."

"Would love to help man, but I'm outta ammo, less you got some extra nines."

Rogers was carrying his .45 so he could not help. As he was scrambling toward the wall of the canyon he called back, "Check the dude for ammo, look for his gun."

"Yeah," Meronek shouted back as he was pulling down his pants and said in a lower voice, "I got some other business to take care of first."

✝ ✝ ✝

Zeva lay on the ground with her head propped up on a rock as Mary Magda tried to stop the blood spurting out of the femoral artery in her right leg. The 7.62 round had torn her flesh badly and Mary was having a hard time stopping the flow because she could not see in the poor light.

"I think I have shit my pants Mary," Zeva said weakly.

"Don't you worry Zeva," replied Mary as she applied a tourniquet above the wound. "We will get you through this."

She tied off the bandage and as she reached for her medic bag her head exploded like a watermelon with an m-80 stuck in it, splattering Zeva with brains, skull, and blood.

Zeva began to scream hysterically as Mary's body slowly fell over and hit the dirt with a quiet thud. Her screams did not last long though, as the last of her life's blood soaked into the thirsty desert sand.

Moses realized too late that Olga and Stephan were not the only ones in the canyon. Someone was near the top of the canyon wall sniping at them and had already killed Zeva and Mary. He was feeling an overwhelming urge to get away from this place with its smells of burned gunpowder, blood, and bowel. Karl was shouting at him from a few yards away for orders, but he could not make his legs move or form words with his mouth.

He felt as he had when he was a child and some older Arab boys had jumped him, taunting him with shouts of 'dirty Jew', 'all Jews are dogs', and 'you will all die Jew pig.' He lay there on the ground in a fetal position with his pants wet and full of his own feces afraid to move until an old Palestinian had come along and frightened the boys away. His adoptive father shamed him further by calling him a coward and a sissy. Only his mother had shown him any comfort and to this day, even with all of his successes, his father showed him no respect.

David Mayer finally called to Karl to move up on the right flank, he would take the left, and get the sniper in a crossfire. He shouted at Moses to provide suppressing fire.

Finally, Moses came out of his fugue and began to fire at the last position he had seen for the sniper.

He realized now that he should have waited for daylight or at least gotten enough night-vision glasses for everyone. Now they were stuck here unable to go forward and no vehicle to retreat with.

He ran out of bullets and stopped to put in a fresh magazine just as David called out that he had been hit and needed help, but there was no one left to help anymore. Both medics were dead and there was only Karl left. He could see only one course of action he could take at this point, so he turned his back on his people and ran as fast as he could toward the highway proving his father had been right about him.

Karl heard Moses running and turned to see where he was going which caused him to lift his head far enough for Midnight to take off the top of his skull. It took Karl several minutes to die and he used the time to pray for forgiveness and to curse Colonel Moses Goldman to the deepest pit of Hell.

The shooting stopped and the desert returned to an unnatural silence as, off in the distance, a dozen or more lights like fireflies trapped in a child's Mason jar, slowly snaked their way toward the canyon.

With the gunfire from the canyon's mouth silenced, Rogers made his way back down to the floor of the canyon and found Meronek still engaged in sex with Olga, even though she did not appear to be conscious. "Meronek, get your sick ass up and let's get out of here. Is she still alive?"

"I don't know boss," Meronek replied in a belligerent tone, "Why don't you check for yourself. She's still warm."

Rogers was truly disgusted by this canker on the ass of the world and pushed him away as he reached down to check her carotid artery. She still had a pulse, but it was weak and rapid. She would be dead soon without medical help.

Midnight came up and rumbled, " People coming, looks like at least a dozen."

"Okay," Rogers acknowledged. "Let's get out of here."

"What about her and the Ark?" asked Midnight.

"Leave her," he replied. "She's good as dead. I don't think they hid the Ark here. I think this was a trap to draw these idiots out. We will just have to wait and see what they do when they get here."

They slipped out of the canyon and made their way to their car which was hidden some distance away without taking time to check the bodies of the soldiers of the Golden Dawn to see if any were still alive.

CHAPTER 40

We stopped when we got to Moses' Blazer and I had Brian 'Merc' Daniels check it out. Finding nothing, we went on into the canyon where we found a scene of carnage like I had not seen since leaving Iraq. "Fan out and look for survivors. Be careful, the shooters could still be here," I directed.

Jason, Charlie, and some others went into the canyon with me where we found the German's Bronco with Stephan and Olga lying among the rocks, just as Rogers had left them. Jason found them first and called me over.

"Looks like she's been raped, but it also looks like she's been snake bit on her face."

"Is she still alive?" I asked.

Checking her pulse again, Jason replied, "Yes, but not much longer without immediate help. Better call for an air-ambulance. I've got some anti-venom for rattler's, but we don't know what kind of snake it was, and she's in bad shape."

Jason went to work to help her and I called for the life-flight, which would take about twenty minutes to arrive from Vegas.

Sam Conner, the tracker, came over to say, "I've found fresh sign leading away. Three men, one very big. They are headed to the east."

"Okay," I said. "I'll get some men and we'll follow." I grabbed Charlie, John, and Simon and we set off following the tracks carefully.

"You think they may set an ambush?" asked Charlie.

"No," I answered. "I don't. I think they've already left. They figured out this was a trick and took off before we could catch up with them."

"Figures," said Charlie. "What do we do if they left something behind, know what I mean?"

I knew what he meant and the same thought had crossed my mind, "Charlie's right ya'll, keep your eyes open for trip wires. You too Sam."

"Don't teach your grandma' to suck eggs sonny," was his impertinent reply.

Using hand signals, I deployed John to my right, Simon to the left, and followed the tracks to where their vehicle had been parked. There was nothing there now but tire tracks leading off into the desert toward town.

"I got a bad feeling," I said. "Let's get back to the restaurant ASAP."

Rogers parked their stolen Land Rover in the back of the restaurant lot and instructed Johnson, "Midnight, you and Meronek stay here with the van, I'm gonna see about getting us some leverage on these Gideons."

He got out, headed to the back of the restaurant, and entered through the back door holding his silenced .45 Colt at the ready. Inside, he saw Helen, Bill, and Dakota sitting at the computers.

Pointing his gun at them he said, "Nobody moves, nobody gets hurt. Okay? You two," indicating Helen and Bill, "get on the floor face down and no trouble."

Helen locked eyes with Rogers and demanded, " What do you want this time, you Judas?"

"I just want the Ark. I don't want to hurt you people so don't do anything stupid, okay? Just tell me where it is and I'll be on my way."

"We don't know," said Dakota. "They didn't tell us where they put it so we couldn't tell anyone in case something like this happened."

"I believe you Dakota, which is too bad." Rogers came over to Dakota and put his gun to her neck, grabbed her arm and began to force her toward the back door. "Don't struggle Dakota, just do what I tell you and I promise you wont get hurt."

"Harm a hair on her head Rogers," said Helen, "and there wont be any place on this whole world where you can hide. We will track you down even if you hide on the lowest level of Hell."

Rogers had a feeling she meant every word of that threat as he steered Dakota toward the door. The door to the restaurant opened just then and he found himself looking at Jake, whose very large hand nearly concealed the Desert Eagle .50 which was leveled at his face only five feet away.

"Don't do it cowboy," said Rogers. "We don't need no heroes tonight. I get what I want, you get her back. I'll call in thirty minutes, make sure Tom is here to answer okay?"

"He'll be here Rogers," said Helen.

"One question before you go dude," said Jake.

"Go ahead big guy," replied Rogers.

"What do you want on your headstone?"

"Here lies the King of the World," laughed Rogers as he backed out into the night.

I knew something was wrong as soon as we pulled into the parking lot of Mom's. Helen, Jake, and Bill were in the lot with expressions of horror on their faces. Helen came running up to me with tears running down her cheeks and I suddenly felt as though I had been dropped off a tall building without a parachute.

"Tom, oh Tom," she was saying. "Rogers took her Tom. He says he's going to call. I'm so sorry Tom. There was nothing we could do, he had a gun on us before we knew he was there."

"Slow down Helen. Did he hurt her? Tell me exactly what he said."

"No Tom," said Jake. "He did not hurt her. I would have killed him if he had. He wants to know where the Ark is. He took off in a late model Land Rover. It looked like a dark color, but I couldn't tell because of the darkness."

"He's going to call any minute Tom," said Bill.

I headed into the war-room where we would be able to trace the call and record it. Jason was trying to calm Helen down because she was becoming hysterical. I stepped over to her, put my hands on her shoulders and said, "Psalm 23 Helen, repeat with me: 'The Lord is my Shepherd, I shall not want, he makes me to lie down in green pastures, he leads me beside still waters, he restores my soul. He guides me in paths of righteousness for his name's sake. Even though I walk through the valley of the shadow of death, I will fear no evil, for you are with me: your rod and your staff, they comfort me, you prepare a table before me in the presence of my enemies. You anoint my head with oil; my cup overflows. Surely goodness and mercy will follow me all the days of my life, and I will dwell in the house of the Lord forever.' Amen."

She was much calmer now and so were the rest of us as we waited for Rogers call.

"This ones even prettier than the kraut," Meronek said reaching toward Dakota who shrank back saying, "Touch me and Tom will kill you so slowly it will take a week for you to die."

"Meronek, I will let Midnight break all the small bones in your hands and then I will cut off your equipment and feed it to the dogs if you touch one hair on her head, got it?"

Pulling his hands back, more afraid of Midnight than he was of Rogers, Meronek said, "Okay man, no problem. The kraut bitch took care of me good anyway man."

Rogers drove west until he found an abandoned strip mall where he could park out of sight. Dakota spoke after they stopped, saying, "Tom is not going to tell you where it is you know. If you hurt me in anyway he will find you no matter where you go and you know what he is capable of doing to you when he finds you."

"Yeah, I know Dakota, but my boss wants the Ark and I am far more afraid of him than I am of you or Tom, understand?"

"Walk away Dick, that's all you gotta do. God will forgive you."

"Maybe," Rogers said "But I am not really interested in being forgiven. I would much rather have the reward my master has promised me. Now be quiet while I call my old Gunny Sergeant."

Rogers pulled out his cell phone and punched the number for Tom, then waited.

"Bob," I called. "Get over here uncle, I need your help."

"What'cha need Nephew?"

"I need you to shape-shift and go find Dakota. We know Rogers headed west from here, but I don't think he's going to go very far, not yet. Not until he gets the location of the Ark."

"Okay, I'll go out looking. What are you going to do?"

"I'm going to tell him where it is. There are only three of them and by the time we get out there, you guys will be waiting for them."

"What if they decide to take Dakota with them for insurance?" asked Jason.

"I'm counting on it. I am going to trade her for me. No deal otherwise."

"Okay," Jason went on. "I will set out now with the others and prepare a welcome for them."

"No Jason," I said. "He will be expecting that, I will have to go alone. He will know if anyone leaves here. I'm sure he has someone watching this place."

Jason looked at me a moment and I could see in his eyes that he understood.

"Jason, I do want you, Charlie, Brian, and Jake to cover the mouth of the cave after we go in, but wait until we get there to move out. If they come out without me, do what you have to, but stop them."

"Hope you know what you're doing Tom," said Jason. "We'll be waiting."

Me too, I thought, as we sat down to wait for Rogers call.

Moses was soaked with sweat by the time he had jogged to the highway and stood panting at the side of the road. Looking to the right he saw a deserted strip mall about two hundred meters away. Gathering up what strength he had left, he turned and began to jog again.

In the back of the mall he started looking for water and found Rogers Land Rover instead. He slipped back out front and went on about two hundred more meters to a convenience store where he was just in time to find a couple of teenagers jumping out of their beat up old Willy's jeep to enter the store.

He took this as a sign that he was living right, because the idiots left the keys in the ignition and the motor running. He ran up and jumped into the drivers seat, threw the transmission into reverse, and tore out into the darkness. He parked not far from the strip mall and waited for Rogers to make his move.

While he waited, he checked his Smith&Wesson and made some calls looking for backup, but the people he had left in the van did not answer. He even placed a call to those merc's in South Africa again.

"Yeah Rogers, you got me," Tom said answering the phone.

"You know what I want Tom, just tell me where it is and I will see to it that your little squeeze doesn't get hurt."

"Sorry Dick," I answered. "But I can't agree to that. I will take you there though, if you let Dakota go."

"I don't like that idea Tom, maybe I'll just turn Meronek loose on her."

Tom felt that falling feeling again, "Do that, you bastard, and not only will you never get the Ark, I'll use some of those nasty tricks we learned from the Taliban on you when I find you. And I swear by Heaven and Earth that I will find you Dick!"

"I'm not really worried about that Tom and you shouldn't be either. I don't want your little army following me for the rest of my life, so what do you want to do?"

"I will meet you out by the city limits sign going west out of town. You follow me until we get to the canyon. We will have to walk in from there. You let Dakota go and I will lead you to the Ark."

"Okay Tom," Rogers responded. "We'll do it that way, just make sure you're alone."

I hung up, headed out for my bike putting my .45 in the tool bag hanging from the triple tree, and hid my knife down inside my boot. I also hid a smaller folding knife in my hatband. Then I held hands with Bill and a few others to ask God's protection on all of us, as well as a successful outcome to the mission.

Even the old general joined in the circle and asked a blessing over us saying, "This young lady," indicating Tracy, who was under his left arm protectively, "has awakened my sense of fatherhood and you people have made me aware of how foolish I was to think that I could rule the world.

"When I lost my wife and daughter I blamed God, even though I knew it was my fault for drinking and driving. I could not forgive myself, so I decided to hold God hostage by keeping the Ark locked away in that hanger. I tried to make a bargain with him—his freedom for my family. You people have shown me the love of God and Jason's father showed me that God does not live in a box, but in the hearts of people. I must forgive myself and I am asking you to forgive me if you can. If I can be any help Tom, just ask."

"I know something of what you have gone through, I have had a hard time forgiving myself for the things I did in Iraq General, but I know now that he has forgiven me and I am sure that he has forgiven you too. Thank you General Carter."

I fired up Gideon, folded up the side stand, and roared off west into the gradually brightening sky. I did not want to think about what might be happening to the only woman I have ever loved, so I directed my thoughts into prayer instead. I am no Bible scholar by any means, but as I prayed, I began to feel a sense of peace that I had never known before. I would swear I could hear another Harley beating out its soulful song next to me as I cruised along even though I was alone on the road. Maybe Jesus did ride a Harley and, hopefully, a few of his angels too.

Moses sat patiently watching as a lone beam of light approached from the east to be joined by twin lights pulling out from the parking lot of the strip mall. Starting up the jeep, he fell into line as they passed without even noticing the Eagle that flew high above.

It would soon be light and that would be a problem for Moses, so he began to fall back hoping they would be too preoccupied to notice him.

When their taillights left the road, he turned off his lights and slowed even more. From now on he would have to be careful since it would be very easy to lose them. There were a lot of trails out here, he had found out last time, from all the off-road vehicles that came out to play. He would have to stay close enough to keep them in sight, but far enough away not to be seen.

The dark mass of the mesa walls was growing in front of me, rising to block the stars in the black velvet sky. I opened the throttle a little in order to get some distance between Dick and myself, because I wanted to have a moment to prepare when we got there. The road was pretty rough for me, so I knew it had to be giving Rogers and his crew a real pounding, which would slow them down. Time I could use to read the ground and send a message to the others.

They began to fall behind until I judged there was enough of an interval to give me the time I would need to prepare. I parked and then pulled out my phone to read the message that Jason had sent. The call of an Eagle announced Bob's presence overhead so I knew that Jason was not far behind.

Rogers pulled in raising a great cloud of dust as he locked the brakes of the Land Rover and skidded to a stop. He got out, walked over to me, and said, "Hey Tom. Glad you decided to co-operate. Hope you don't mind, but I will need to check you for weapons."

"I do mind Dick. I want to see Dakota before we do anything else."

"Okay Tom," he answered. "Bring her out," he ordered the other two in the car.

Meronek came out pushing Dakota ahead of him and causing her to stumble to her knees. I stepped forward to catch her, but Dick caught me and held me back. Midnight struggled out of the car like a clown in a circus act, unfolding himself until he could stand fully erect, then knocked Meronek to the side so he could help Dakota to her feet, saying in his rolling-thunder voice, "Sorry ma'am, but that fool got no manners."

Seeing an opportunity for an ally, Dakota responded, "Thank you Midnight, it's nice to know that there are still gentlemen in the world."

The big man was obviously embarrassed by this praise, as he awkwardly turned away mumbling, "It weren't nothin'."

I took advantage of the moment to close the distance between us and enclose Dakota in my arms. "Are you okay darlin'?"

She looked up at me with fear in her eyes and held me tightly. "Oh Tom, I'm okay now."

"How touching," interjected Dick. "I'm almost brought to tears."

"Shut-up Dick," I snapped. "Keep your end of the deal and let her go."

"Okay bro," he returned. "Don't get yer panties in a wad. I think we will take her with us though. Wouldn't be right to leave her out here in the dark by herself. I don't want to hurt you Tom— or her. I could have killed both of you on several occasions, but didn't. I just want the Ark and then we'll go."

There was no point in arguing any further and it was true that Dakota would be safer staying with me. "Alright Dick," I said. "If you're ready, let's go."

With Bob flying overhead, we turned toward the mouth of Lost Souls Canyon and set out. The night was clear, the moon in half-phase lighting the way. Crickets, cicadas, and locusts beat out their nocturnal symphony as we picked our way among the rocks and brush. To my right, I saw a pair of yellow eyes slinking along, keeping abreast of our passage, and knew that we were not alone in this battle.

"No matter what happens hon, you stay close to me, okay?" I said to Dakota.

"Don't worry about it cowboy, I'll be closer than your own skin."

"If you don't mind," said Meronek. "Shut-up and keep walking. All this sweet talk is making me sick."

To emphasize his point he shoved his pistol into my back in an effort to move me along, but being much smaller than me, it had little effect—except to make me angry.

"Little man," I said in a tone of voice that only dead men had heard before, "I am gong to enjoy ripping your arm off and beating you to death with it."

Dick had heard me talk like that once before in Iraq after capturing a Taliban soldier that had just tortured a Marine to death using knives and fire. Nobody was ever able to prove anything since he disappeared without a trace, but hearing me sent a chill down his spine. He knew what happened, he had been there.

Inside the canyon we picked our way along moving slowly in the shadows of the cliff walls to avoid snakes and other critters. Also, I wanted to give the others time to move into position so they would be ready to act when the time came.

We finally came to the cave's entrance and I went in saying, "Wait here, I'll make sure we don't have company, unless you would rather go in first Meronek."

Emotions flickered over his sallow face in rapid succession, fear, revulsion, anxiety, and back to fear again. Dick decided for him by saying, "Both of you go in and remember Tom, I got your girl here with me."

I flicked on my flashlight as we entered, Meronek doing the same, and made a quick search back to the water pool. I called out to Rogers to come on in, then we waded through the ice-cold waters of the pool coming out on the far side and heading up the incline to the main tunnel.

✝ ✝ ✝

Jason and the others took positions on the mesa overlooking Lost Souls Canyon. No one would enter or leave without coming under their field of fire and Jason began praying for the Lord's intervention and protection for everyone until he could feel great beads of sweat running down his forehead. He could not remember praying this hard for anything for a long time now. It felt good to be in the power of the Spirit once again.

He could feel that great forces were gathering here and there would be a battle that would encompass far more than the physical world. There would be a battle this day that would take place in the unseen world and, in his mind, there was no doubt of the outcome.

His cell phone began to chime letting him know he had an incoming text message. He fumbled it open and read the glowing screen: NORA—NAME IS TIRHAKAH—HOPE IT HELPS.

Jason forwarded the message immediately to everyone, especially Tom.

✝ ✝ ✝

Dakota was shivering next to me and I pulled her closer to give her warmth. "You want my jacket hon?" I asked.

"No," she replied. "I'm more scared than cold. I don't like caves or bats."

"Keep moving," admonished Dick.

"Yeah, keep moving," commanded Meronek, pushing me along from behind once again.

After a long walk during which most of us were silent, except Meronek who kept babbling about what he was going to do when he was King of the World, until Dick finally threatened to blow his head off if he didn't shut-up, we came to the side tunnel that led to the cathedral room.

The Ark was just where we had left it, silent and patient as the Sphinx. Jason had told me of the God-light he and the others had experienced when they had left the Ark in the cave, but now there was only the Stygian darkness.

"Set up the lights," commanded Rogers.

Midnight began setting up several battery-powered work lights that he had been carrying in a duffel bag, placing them around the room and turning them on, revealing the splendor of the Ark. The golden Cherubim spreading their wings across the top of the mercy seat seemed to be watching and waiting, to see whether we came to worship the God of all Creation, or to bring dishonor upon his name.

Dakota and I backed up to the wall nearest the entrance to prepare for a quick exit if necessary and I whispered in her ear, "Whatever happens do not look at the Ark hon. Be ready to run on my command and don't look back no matter what happens, okay?"

"Okay Tom," she answered. "I love you."

"I love you too." I promised her I would kiss her so hard when this was over, that her grandmother would feel it. Then I returned my attention to Rogers and company. He was chanting some sort of invocation as he approached the Ark, while Meronek stood to one side, and Midnight blocked the entrance.

"What are ya doing?" Meronek demanded of Rogers. "We ain't got the sacrifices or nuthin' to call the goddess out."

"Don't be stupid," rumbled Midnight. "There ain't no goddess. He's calling out Lucifer."

"Whoever he calls out, the power is mine," Handlebar shouted; now feeling cocky once again. "I been through too much and I ain't sharing it with nobody, ya hear."

Meronek began threatening Rogers with his pistol and anyone else who dared to stand between him and his ultimate quest for power. In anger with this fool that he had been ordered to bring along, Rogers finally rebuked him saying, "You're going to get what was promised to you Meronek, just shut-up and let me finish the summoning. After our lord appears, you will receive your reward."

There was a definite glow about the Ark, as though it was filling itself with tremendous energies. I whispered into Dakota's ear, "Turn to the wall hon and get on your knees. Pray that God will spare us and bring destruction on these men."

We both turned, got on our knees and silently began to pray, asking the Lord to send his angels to intervene with these wicked men and show his Glory to us.

Having mollified Meronek for the moment, Rogers turned back to the Ark and his incantations, but Meronek continued to grumble.

A ball of incandescent blue light began to form above the mercy seat of the Ark, between the Cherubim, growing and crackling; discharging enormous energies like a Tesla coil in an old horror movie. In my prayer, I began to entreat the Lord to bind over Lucifer's demon, Tirhakah, to that place of darkness where there could be no escape.

I heard Midnight call out, "He know your name, we is lost master."

At that moment, the energies contained in the Ark burst forth in a pure white light so bright it was like looking into the sun. Even with my eyes closed and my back to the Ark it seared painfully into my brain. With one hand to the cave's wall and the other around Dakota I headed for the exit hoping Midnight would be too blinded to notice us.

I pulled Dakota out of the exit without making contact with the dark-skinned giant and headed to the right toward the exit. There were sounds coming from the room that never came from human throats, sending a chill of fear through my gut such as I had not known since my first baptism of fire in Iraq.

Squinting my eyes against the light, I pulled Dakota into the first side passage we came to, threw her down in front of me, and covered her with my body to protect her from the furies released in the cave. I called out for Jesus to protect us, hearing Dakota do the same, until after what seemed like hours, but was only seconds, the light disappeared as swiftly as it had come and we were once again in darkness as silent as the tomb. I started to get up and asked Dakota, "Are you okay honey?"

"Yes Tom," she answered with a slight waver of fear still in her voice.

A scream, like a child suffering from some terrible nightmare, came from within the cave followed by the sound of running footsteps that passed our position heading toward the exit. I flicked on my torch and ventured out of the passage telling Dakota to sit still while I investigated.

She informed me in no uncertain terms, "Tom Harper, you are not leaving me here alone, even if I have to lock my arms and legs around you."

I shined my light into the cathedral room where the Ark still stood with a faint afterglow to it and the smell of ozone permeating the air. There were definite scorch marks on the floor and ceiling where bolts of God-fire had struck. There was no sign of the three men who had been there moments before.

I pulled out my cell phone hoping to contact the others, but the screen was dark and it would not power up. The energies discharged by the Ark had rendered it useless, so there was nothing to do but head for the exit.

"Try to stay as quiet as possible Dakota, so we can listen for the others. If they got out they may be hiding in one of the side passages."

"Okay Tom," she said and pulled my face to hers kissing me so hard I felt the enamel coming off my teeth. "Whatever happens now, I at least know that the two of us are truly saved."

"Amen to that darlin'."

CHAPTER 41

Just outside the mouth of the canyon Moses waited, hoping that the others would secure the Ark for him, thus saving him the time and trouble of carrying it out to where the vehicles were parked.

He was startled by a sudden brilliance of light inside the canyon that lit up the whole area like a phosphorus shell. Along with the light was a sound that sent chills up his spine and took the metal out of his legs. He could not remember hearing anything like it in his life, the only thing close was the terror stricken voices of those who had been caught in a murder-bombing at a theater in Tel Aviv. He knew that somehow the Ark had been activated and the only question now was whether the fools had survived or not.

He crept as close as he dared to the cave that Rogers had ventured into, not knowing that others arranged above him on the cliff walls were observing him. Then he heard the sound of a man approaching his position who had obviously witnessed something that had broken his mind. His screams revealed more than unbearable pain in the flesh, but also some terrible wound to the soul.

Meronek came out of the cave entrance into the long shadows of early morning light revealing a parody of the human form. His hair was burned away with smoke still rising from his blistered scalp and this was only the beginning of his injuries.

His head twisted this way and that as his eyeless skull surveyed a landscape he could no longer see. His clothing was mostly burned away, showing places where strips of flesh and muscle were falling away from bone. The heat he had been exposed to had been so great that his body had cooked like a brisket in an oven. The apparition before him collapsed to its knees expelling one last plea, "Mama," then fell forward onto its face with the entrails bursting out, and lay silent.

Moses approached the corpse, trying to avoid the pungent stench of burned human flesh, to make certain that this pile of excrement that had once been Steven 'Handlebar' Meronek really was dead. Satisfied that he had ceased to share existence in this world, Moses stepped over the remains and entered the cave.

The sound of someone else approaching from inside the cave threw a supernatural chill up his spine and Moses turned away running as fast as his legs would carry him, not stopping until he had reached his stolen jeep.

From his vantage point atop the cliff, Jason watched the 'Savior of Israel' drive off toward town as fast as the old jeep would carry him, then Jason and his companions began to descend into the valley below, praying to find Tom and Dakota unhurt and still alive.

✝ ✝ ✝

As we approached the pool room near the entrance, the smell of scorched hair and flesh was becoming overpowering for both of us. At one point, the fragrance was particularly concentrated and I had to stop while Dakota was ill. Once she was okay again, I thought I heard a voice from somewhere deep in the cave, but it may have been only bats or some other cave dwelling creature. If Rogers or Midnight had survived, there was no indication.

I helped Dakota up and we waded through the pool, where we washed our faces in the cold water and came out into the morning light to find the smoldering remains of Meronek.

"Don't look hon," I warned her and turned her away from the sight of the wretched corpse. "It's Meronek and it looks like the fires of Hell have come early for him."

I led her past his remains toward the canyon's exit then stopped at a hail from Jason and the others who were just reaching the floor of the canyon.

"Has anyone else come out Jason?" I asked.

"No little brother," Jason called back. "But Goldman was here. After seeing Meronek die, he started to enter the cave, but turned and ran away like the Devil himself was on his tail. I guess he heard you coming out and got scared you were a demon."

"Okay," I answered. "Let's get Dakota back. Charlie, Brian, you drive her using Rogers Land Rover." I kissed her again as she joined Charlie and watched her walk away to the mouth of the canyon.

"Jason, Midnight and Rogers are still in there somewhere, unless they were vaporized. If they are still alive, we need to find them. Any suggestions?"

"Yes," replied the big man. "We will have to get a few more men out here first though. What happened in there little brother?"

I explained how the plan to leave Dakota outside had failed and what followed in the cathedral room.

"So you think they could still be alive after that?" he asked.

"I heard something, I just don't know whether it was human or not. Is there any other way out of that cave?"

"I don't know Tom," he answered. "I have not fully explored these caves, but I know someone who has. My sons Gabriel and Jr. mapped much of these caves as a school project last summer. I will call them and get them to come out with their maps."

"Let's get some people to relieve us here, get some food and rest, and be back about 1300 okay."

"Sounds like a plan little brother."

Moses did not stop until he had put a good twenty miles between himself and Lost Souls Canyon, finally pulling over to let the rest of the shakes wear off. He sat there wondering what had frightened him so much back at the cave.

However, Moses had never been one for introspection and was soon distracted by a passing state trooper. He was reminded that he was sitting in a stolen vehicle, so he got out and headed toward a honky-tonk bar just up the road. It was aptly called the Dry Gulch Saloon and had a handful of cars parked out front. They were either left from the night before or else belonged to a dedicated group of drunks looking for an early start. He decided it was the former since the doors were locked and there was no sign of anyone inside.

He turned his attention back to the parked vehicles and chose an old beat up GMC truck that looked like it would be easy to hot-wire. God was favoring him he decided when he found the door open and the keys in the ashtray. The old truck was a little loud as he pulled out and left a cloud of blue smoke that could have hidden a fleet of battleships, but it would get him back to his motel and safety. Once there he would call those South African merc's and secure their help in getting the Ark back, but this time it would be for him—not Israel.

There was still the matter of the Illuminati to take care of and the Golden Dawn. Without the Ark to protect him, he knew he would be a dead man soon.

The sun setting behind the mountains and trees of the Black Forest traced shadow lines on the table in front of Hans Bettendorf. His spymaster, Erik Dorfman, sat to his left and the industrialist, Karl Betz, to his right. The look on Heir President's face was one of frustrated anger and controlled rage. "What do you mean you have not heard from them?" demanded the erstwhile Führer of the Fourth Reich, referring to Olga Steiner and Stephan Von Himmler. The question was aimed at Dorfman who had been placed in charge of the operation to recover the Ark.

"They have been out of touch for forty-eight hours now Heir Bettendorf. According to reports from the local police, one body matching Stephan has turned up at the local morgue. There is no word from Olga and nothing has turned up about her from any law enforcement or hospital agency."

"We may assume then," Heir Bettendorf continued, "that she is either dead or captured. The operation is kaput!"

"I can not be sure of that mein heir," replied Dorfman. "But it would seem so."

"Have we anyone else in the area that can give us a report?"

"Ya," answered Betz. "There is a man near the place they call Area 51. His name is Karl Stotz, but goes by the alias, James Aubrey. He has been reporting to us for several years about black projects in the American military."

"Ya, okay," said Bettendorf. "Tell him to get over there and report on what he finds."

"Ya, heir Bettendorf," replied Betz.

Bettendorf dismissed Betz, then turned his attention back to Dorfman. "Put together another team. This time choose from our best trained Shock Troops and get them ready to go. I must warn you Colonel Dorfman, failure this time will not go unpunished."

"Ya, heir Bettendorf," Dorfman answered. "I will not fail you this time." Dorfman got up flourishing a stiff armed Nazi salute and hurried away from his master.

Left alone, the Supreme Commander of the Fourth Reich sat contemplating the snifter of brandy on the table before him and studying the report that he had just received via confidential courier. The heading on the folder said, 'Army of the Golden Dawn'. If only Hitler had relieved him of these troublesome Jews.

CHAPTER 42

In the artificial light of his spacious office eighty meters below ground General Ben Gurion contemplated the report in front of him, as well as the grim expression on Captain Judah Zebulon's face as he stood across from him on the other side of his oversize desk of Lebanese cedar.

"All of them?" inquired the general in grudging disbelief.

"Yes sir," the equally grim reply of the captain. "There were no survivors sir. There has been no contact with Colonel Goldman, but we have no reason to suspect he is dead. His body was not found with the others and there is no report of any bodies matching his description."

"Very well," said the general. "Have our people in the U.S. keep us informed and notify me at once if Goldman surfaces."

"Yes sir," the captain replied. "Will there be anything else sir?"

"Yes Captain Zebulon," the general answered, looking as though the last few minutes had aged him ten years. "Have Major Silverman come to see me as soon as he is free please."

With a salute, the captain left the old man to consider the report and the disappearance of Moses Goldman.

General Gurion thought back over the years that he had known Moses; starting with the brash young lieutenant he had been in nineteen eighty, infiltrating the Syrian city of Damascus. His mission had been to spy out the leadership of Hamas and either kill, or set up for execution, a man who had ordered the assassinations of several Jewish politicians. Goldman had succeeded in marking the man's car for an aerial mission, but it was rumored that he had been unable to pull the trigger himself.

Goldman was ambitious though and soon had himself taken out of the field and placed behind a desk, which came as some relief to many field officers. He had proven competent as an information officer, translating and deciphering coded missives from Arabic sources, but had taken a sudden and unexplained interest in the secret society of the Illuminati a little over ten years ago.

He had requested a transfer to the United States to be close to the fabled Area 51 to keep an eye on the rumored stealth aircraft being tested there. Since it would get him out of his hair the general approved his transfer. Had he known of what was actually happening with Moses he would have recalled him long ago. He had reported on something that he hinted would be World changing, but was not specific as to what it could be.

He thought it had something to do with secret weapons systems in the United States and only learned six months ago about the existence of the Ark. By then Moses had worked his way into a high-level position with the Illuminati, which in itself seemed strange now that he though about it. It seemed very likely to the general that Moses Goldman's waters ran far deeper than the surface would indicate.

A knock at his door announced the arrival of Major Silverman, head of foreign operations, and a highly decorated officer of the Mossad. The fact that he also worked for The Golden Dawn represented no conflict of interest in this country of small population and divers enemies.

"Come in Major," grunted the old man as he got up to refill his coffee cup, musing how handy it would be if he had an Elijah to fix it so that his pot would never be empty and started preparing a fresh pot.

Major Silverman walked in wearing a plain khaki uniform, bereft of insignia or name tag, and said, "Sorry for the delay David, I was sitting in on the interrogation of Mamoud Ali."

The crisp English accent always threw people off when meeting the swarthy major. He had studied at Oxford on a Rhodes scholarship and could speak six languages as though they were his native tongue.

"Quite alright Ben," Gurion replied as he motioned to the coffee mess. "Cup?"

Recognizing that he would probably be here a while, he always was when David offered refreshment, he moved to the coffee mess, poured a cup of the French roast and asked, "What's up David, you look upset?"

The general filled him in on the events of the operation, which the major had been unaware of to this point, including his feelings concerning Moses Goldman. "We need to salvage this operation Ben and get the Ark back to Israel." The general stopped there, knowing Ben would understand what had not been said.

"Let me look into it David," the major replied with his brow furrowed in deep thought. "I will go to these Gideons and talk with them, maybe we can get it without further loss of life."

With Gurion's blessing, Major Silverman left, made arrangements for travel, then went home to pack a few things and give his wife the usual mysterious goodbye that she had grown accustomed to over the two decades of their marriage.

✝ ✝ ✝

The aroma of eggs, bacon, and coffee brought me out of a dreamless sleep, as well as gentle kisses on my lips, cheeks, and ears. I reached up wrapping my arms around the warm, firm body of the woman I had come to know and love over the past few weeks, pulling her down on top of me with squeals of delighted outrage.

"Time to get up Gunny Sergeant Harper," she ordered. "It's a little after noon; brunch is ready and you best get moving if you are going to meet up with the others at Lost Souls Canyon."

"Okay darlin'," I answered, "but just for a moment I want to hold the woman I love." I kissed her again, then turned her loose, and watched her walk away. I noticed that I did not feel the lust I had felt the first time I saw her, though my desire for her had grown in other ways. My emotions were changing, maturing in a way that was entirely new to me and not unwelcome. I washed up and made my way into the kitchen where Dakota was sitting, crying softly into a dishtowel.

She got up as I entered, wrapped her arms around me, and held me like a lost child found in the woods after a scary night alone. She pushed away after a moment, wiping her nose, and commanded, "Eat, I'll be right back."

She went off into the bathroom closing the door behind her to leave me wondering whether I had said something wrong, or something right. So is the mystery of woman.

Bob called on the phone as I was finishing my eggs to let me know that Goldman had checked out of the motel and headed south towards Mexico. I sat thinking about whether we should bring him in for the murder's of Von Himmler and the attack on Olga, but Bob counseled me to let it go for now, as it was very likely that both the Illuminati and The Golden Dawn were after him, as well as the police and possibly the Mossad. He would have problems enough to deal with and we probably would not see him again for a while, if at all.

CHAPTER 43

In the cool darkness he could not distinguish up from down, leaving him in an uncomfortable state of vertigo. The pool of cold water he had stumbled into had at least given him some relief from the excruciating burns on his body. The sounds of someone screaming, suffering the tortures of the damned, had only subsided when he realized they were coming from his own throat.

He had passed out prostrate in the pool soon after stumbling into the room, and had no idea how long he lay there. Other than the occasional faucet drip of water landing in the pool, he could hear nothing but the sounds of his own labored breathing being echoed back into his ears.

He remembered looking into the Ark's brilliance and seeing the faces of the Cherubim turning to look at him with expressions of happy, child-hood innocence. He had begun calling his masters name, the way Faustus had told him too, but that damn Tom and his bitch began cursing the name of Faustus, binding him in the name of the God of Heaven and suddenly—the faces of the Cherubim began to change.

There was unfathomable rage now, where innocence had been, and power began to flow outward from the Ark, striking Meronek first, picking him up like a child's rag-doll and slamming him against the cave wall where he began to boil right in front of his eyes. His hair burst into flame, his flesh bubbled as the fat turned to liquid, and blue God-fire danced over his body in a parody of St. Elmo's fire.

Behind him he heard Midnight screaming like an Alpine avalanche as he too, became engulfed in the supernatural pyrotechnic discharge.

He saw Tom and Dakota slip out the exit and decided that, since he had been trying to run from God most of his life, now would be a good time to revisit his old vocation.

He charged toward the exit feeling the power of Heaven playing over his body and coursing through his entire being. He could not remember feeling pain at that moment, just overpowering fear. His master had left him to face the Most High all alone and the only thing he could think of now was to find the deepest darkest hole he could and hope it would be enough to hide him.

He felt for his watch, finding it melted into his wrist and useless, leaving him no clue how long he had been unconscious. With no idea where he was or which direction to go, he decided that all directions were equally valid. He drank some more of the water he was lying in and began to crawl in the direction he had been traveling when he had collapsed.

Now he began to feel pain. He could not remember feeling such excruciating pain before in his life. It was even worse than the time, in Iraq, when an I.E.D. had gone off next to the Hummer he had been riding in. His right arm, right leg, and three ribs had been broken. He had suffered third-degree burns on his face and hands from which he still bore scars.

All that had been nothing but a splinter in his finger compared to what he felt now. It was as though every nerve in his body was working overtime on steroids with no relief in sight. To stay was to die and Marines don't quit, so he put forward another hand, then another knee, and made his way forward into the black velvet that surrounded him leaving bits of himself behind with each painful move.

He crawled in this way for what seemed like an eternity; his only company the sounds of his body dragging over water-smoothed stone and his labored breath loud in his ears. He felt something under his hand, soft and squishy. Fearing that he had come across some cave dwelling creature, he drew back looking for signs of life, but there was only the unbroken silence.

He moved slowly forward, exploring the object in front of him until he had identified it. It was the body of Midnight; cold and still in death's embrace. Checking for signs of rigor, he judged the man to have been dead for several hours, giving him some idea of how long he had been unconscious. Not that the information was much help to him as he moved around the body to continue his journey into night.

He felt something long and tubular under his hand and recognized it to be a flashlight. He fumbled for the switch until he heard it click and found he still had the capacity to feel even more pain. The light flooding out was so bright to his eyes, now accustomed to darkness that, for a moment, he actually thought he might have suffered a stroke. The reality of the light was worse than the darkness, because he could now see the extent of his injuries.

He could see muscle where skin had once been and in a few places, the white of bone showed through. As bad as he looked, Midnight was far worse. That the man had managed to get out of the cathedral at all was a miracle.

A miracle was what Dick Rogers needed at that moment if he was going to survive and a sound began to bubble up out of his throat, soft at first, coming from somewhere deep in his primal soul and crawling its way up and out of his fleshly tomb, seeking release for all the pain he had suffered or caused. Release only came when he finally collapsed into unconsciousness once again.

There were enough bikes gathered at the mouth of the canyon to have a rally. Dakota climbed off the back and we headed toward the crowd milling about near the entrance of the cave. At our approach, Jason and Bob broke away to join us.

"You're just in time Tom," spoke the big guy. "We were just about to split up into teams."

"Good Jason," I replied. "Any news on the German woman?" I had almost forgotten about her with all that had happened in the last twenty-four hours.

"You must have read my mind Nephew," said Bob. "I just got a call from the hospital. The doc says she will live, though she will not be pretty anymore, not without a lot of reconstructive surgery. She lost her left eye and most of the skin and muscle where the fangs hit her. She is going to have a rough time."

I heard Dakota draw in a sharp breath at this news and felt her hand close more tightly around my own. "That's too bad," I commented. "I think her beauty was all she had to define herself. I will try to see her when we get some time. Dakota, would you come too?"

Dakota looked up at me with many emotions competing across her face. She finally settled on compassion saying, "Yes Tom. I think we should."

Jason and his boys began to hand out maps of the cave along with balls of twine, which were to be used to keep from getting lost, along with flashlights, and radios.

Dakota and I teamed up with General Carter and Tracy Collins. We went in as far as the cathedral first to check on the Ark before beginning our search. It still sat as we had left it. I felt a sudden urge to pray and invited the others to join me.

As the four of us got on our knees, I began the prayer, first thanking the Lord for sparing us and delivering us safely out of the cave, then for Meronek and all the others who had died these past weeks whether innocent or not. I felt, in that moment, a wellspring of emotions like a dam bursting under millions of tons of pressure. I fell on my face unable to speak words and let go instead with a wail of grief, pain, and finally—joy. From somewhere I heard that voice again saying, "Well done my faithful servant. You have learned the true meaning of the cross."

I don't know how long I lay there feeling the afterglow of those words which were like a balm to my spirit, but it was not

---

long enough. The spell was broken by a sound like a tortured soul in Hell, made more eerie by the reverberations of its passage through the tunnels of the cave. I got up and ran into the main passage trying to pick up the last echo in hope of identifying the direction it had come from. The general came over wiping away tears that ran down both his cheeks and asked, "Could you tell where it came from Tom?"

I saw that everyone was wiping away tears, including my big bad-ass self. "I'm not certain, but I think it came from this main passage on the left."

I looked at the map Gabriel had given me which showed that passage to end in a room with a deep pool. "Come on," I told the others, "we'll check it out."

I anchored the free end of a ball of twine and the four of us started off down the passage. As we walked along, I began to see blood here and there on the walls forming hand prints. One set very large, probably Midnights, and a smaller set, which would be Rogers.

After fifty meters, we came to a pool about a foot deep that had bits of charred clothing floating in it, as well as bits of meat that insects had started dining on. There was no doubt we were on the right trail. The only question now was: What would find at the end of that trail? Dakota turned her head at the sight of the charred flesh Rogers had left behind as he crawled out of the pool searching for an exit.

"Tom," she said with her voice unsteady, "this is awful."

"Yes darlin', and it's going to get much worse. Maybe you and Tracy should stay here."

"Yes Tracy," the general agreed. "Stay here until we come back for you. This is not something you want to see."

"As a matter of fact," I continued. "Why don't you two go back to the entrance, tell the others that we have found them, and guide them here."

There was no argument in Dakota's eyes this time as she gave me a kiss and turned back. She was a little surprised to see that she had to wait as Tracy was kissing the general.

When the two girls had left the old man looked at me and seeing the grin on my face, he said, "I know, I'm way to old for her, she'll get over it."

"Maybe, maybe not Al," I answered. "You're not that old."

"Like hell I'm not," he grumbled, but I saw a smile that went with it.

I took the lead and the two of us set off keeping silent in order to listen for any sound of our quarry. Another thirty meters brought us to Midnight's corporal remains. I was glad we had sent the ladies back, it was not the worst I had ever seen, but it was bad.

It looked like the flesh had been stripped to the bone on his face and chest, leaving a macabre skull staring at us like some Halloween Voodoo mask. The rest I wont describe because it was just to awful. It was something that would haunt me for years to come. We moved on knowing there was nothing more we could do for him, except to bury his remains.

Twenty meters further we entered the pool room to find Rogers lying on his back at the water's edge, barley alive. I knelt down calling his name, afraid to touch him. He was so badly burned and missing so much skin, that I was not sure he was still able to answer.

He eyes flickered open and his voice rasped, "Who's there? Is that you Tom?"

"Yes Dick, it's me," I answered.

"I'm gonna die ain't I," he croaked.

"It don't look good Dick," I answered, deciding it would be best to be honest with him. "You might want to get right with the Lord while you can."

"Tom's right," said Carter. "He's giving you a last chance Rogers."

Dick's eyes closed and I could hear air bubbling in his lungs, which were filling with fluid from heat damage. Soon he would drown without medical attention and, probably, even with it.

"Who's with you Gunny?" he asked.

"General Carter," I answered. "He's given up on ruling the world and come over to our side."

"You was always a charmer Tom," Rogers choked out. "Guess that's why I was always so jealous of you man."

"Jealous," I said surprised. "You were always the ladies man Dick. You had nothing to be jealous of bro."

"Yeah I did," he said, then coughed a bit. "Men followed you without being asked Tom. You commanded loyalty, but never demanded it. You got the mark on you Tom; always did."

I could see he was serious, but I had never thought about it. The years as quarterback and team captain in high school just came easy to me, not because I asked for it, but because people just seemed to want it. I had never realized that people would envy me, but now that I thought about it, I could remember other kids that would avoid me for reasons I could never figure out.

"Maybe I do Dick," I answered at last. "But you're paying a heck of a price to get even. It's not too late Dick, confess Jesus as Lord and you will be forgiven."

"No Tom," he replied, then coughed some more. He was beginning to shake with pain and loss of body heat, his breathing becoming shallow and labored. "I made my choice and I'm gonna stay with it."

Again, his body jerked as he went into a coughing spasm, plasma spraying out of his mouth, and running down his chin. Then one final breath, running out with that rattling sound I had become so familiar with over the past few years and Dick Rogers, Corporal, U.S.M.C., Silver Star, made the final march to Fiddlers Green.

I brushed away the tears staining my cheeks, as much for the passing of a man I once thought my friend, as well as a fellow warrior fallen in battle.

General Carter put his hand on my shoulder and said, "You tried Tom, but he made his choice. There was nothing more you could have done."

Footsteps announced the arrival of Jason, Arthur Brooks, Moses' twin, Jake, and Brian Daniels. Taking the scene in, Jason came over, squatted next to me and Dick saying, "You okay little brother?"

"Yes," I answered. "I'll be okay, I just wish I could have brought him to the Lord first, that's all."

"Tom," Jason went on, "it ain't up to you. You don't bring people to the Lord, the Lord brings them to you. All we can do is tell them the message of the Gospel. Sometimes, no matter how hard you try, or how much you want it, they just won't answer, because they aren't called."

I looked at him and I must have looked confused because he said, "You can't save anybody Tom. That is Jesus' job. Tom, Romans 8:29 & 30 says, 'For those God foreknew he also predestined to be conformed to the likeness of his Son that he might be the firstborn among many brothers. And those he predestined, he also called; those he called, he also justified; those he justified, he also glorified.' You did your part Tom, the rest was up to him."

"Tom," Jake interjected. "It's up to some of us to plant the seed, others will come along and water it, and still others to bring in the harvest (1Cor. 3:5-9). Don't try doing it all bro. Just do your part and let the Holy Spirit do the rest."

"Try to remember the parable of the four soils," said Jason. "It's in Matthew 13:1-9. 'A farmer went out to plant some seed. As he scattered it across his field, some seeds fell on a footpath, and the birds came along and ate them. Other seeds fell on shallow soil with underlying rock. The plants sprang up quickly, but they soon wilted beneath the hot sun and died because the roots had no nourishment in the shallow soil. Other seeds fell among thorns that shot up and choked out the tender blades. But some seeds fell on fertile soil and produced a crop that was thirty, sixty, even a hundred times as much as had been planted. Anyone who is willing to hear should listen and understand.' Thing is Tom; Dick just wasn't good soil."

I had to admit he was right, but I still felt bad for my brother in arms. "Let's get him out of here, Midnight too, and call it a day."

As I walked out Jason caught up with me and said, "You did all you could little brother, you will be blameless where Dick is concerned."

"I know Jason, but he was a Marine and a good soldier."

I made my way back to the cathedral room where I sat down and cried like a child over a broken toy, until there were no more tears. Then I sat in silence with the Lord until Dakota came in, sat down next to me, and held me like my mom had when I was a boy.

The flight had been long, boring, very uncomfortable and Benjamin Silverman could only hope that these Christians would be reasonable and give the Ark back to the rightful owners, that is, Israel. After collecting his one piece of luggage, he would have been reimbursed for more, but hoped he would not be here that long, he picked up a Crown Victoria at the rental agency and headed toward his hotel.

The agency had wanted to assign him a driver/bodyguard from their Las Vegas office, but felt that might make things look too official. The on-board navigation system smoothly led him to the Holiday Inn not far from the airport, where he checked into his room, took a shower, and was able to get something to eat before Shabbat. He would be here until at least the following evening, since he could not travel during the Sabbath, and decided to take in some of the city's famous sights.

He had seen Vegas on TV before of course, but it was far more impressive seen with his own eyes. He would not have believed there could be so many lights in one place or that they could all be turned on at one time, flashing in a hundred colors, advertising every sin ever thought of since The Garden of Eden.

Because it was Sabbath, all could do was look, he could not gamble, could not drink, could not seek any of the pleasures that Vegas so amply offered. Just where the navigation system said it would be, was the Or-Baridbar Synagogue, nestled between the drive-through marriage kiosk and the twenty-four hour Genie car wash. Inside he found only a handful of faithful and was only mildly surprised to find that there were no slot machines along the walls.

He introduced himself to the Rabbi, a man of middle years, moderate girth, and joyful features. His name was Ariel Cohen and turned out to be quite a good cantor.

After the service, they gathered around a little table with pastry's and coffee, which Ben helped himself to, finding that he was hungrier than he thought. Most of the others present were travelers like himself, some on business, and some for the pleasures that Vegas offered.

It was getting late, so he made his goodbyes and went back out into the hot dry air that Nevada was so famous for. There was a hint of honeysuckle in the air, along with the smells of fresh-cut grass, auto emissions, and cooling pavement. Other than a few working girls the streets were empty as he made his way back to the hotel and, he hoped, a good nights sleep.

CHAPTER 44

Moses Goldman had decided that Mexico was perhaps a nice place to visit, but not the place he wanted to live. By spreading his money around, he had been able to move into a small hacienda and hire a cook, maid, etc. He also arranged for security with the local patron, who was involved in the usual border occupations—moving illegals, drugs, guns, whatever there was demand for.

This was fine, but it was not going to get the Ark into his possession. The man he had spoken with in South Africa had said he would be there in two days with thirty men. Including vehicles, weapons, and men, it would only cost him a quarter million up front and twenty-five K a day. This was not out of reach for Moses, as long as the Illuminati, or anyone else, did not find and freeze his assets.

He sat down at the desk in his office to look at the map of the area where the Ark was hidden for perhaps the hundredth time in the past few days. This time there could be no mistakes; he would either emerge as the master of the Ark or die trying.

He could not believe the bad luck he had had against these amateurs. They had managed to defeat him, the Germans, Zevi's mercenaries, and the bikers without taking so much as a single casualty. Maybe God was showing them favor, in which case he was doomed, but damn it, he was a Jew, a direct descendent of Moses himself, and if anyone deserved to lead the Jews into the New Kingdom, it was him.

The phone rang and he let his Mexican maid answer. She turned to him and said in her broken English that it was Kreig, the S.A. merc.

"Moses here," he said into the mouthpiece, "What is it?"

Good news, the mercenaries were in-country headed his way, and would be there on time. Now it was time to make the proper sacrifices and purify himself. Now he would become the Deliverer.

✝ ✝ ✝

The next morning I met with Dakota at the restaurant. I had spent the night with Jason and the other men in our group at a Kiva, praying and asking the Lord what he wanted us to do with the Ark. It had also been a time for us to let go of the emotions that had been pent up over the past few days. Many of us had worked long hours and been under a lot of stress, so a campfire session really helped.

I met Dakota in the war-room giving her a hug, as well as a very passionate kiss, before checking the wires to see what had transpired during our absence.

"There was a message this morning babe," said Dakota. "From a guy named Benjamin Silverman. He said would like to talk to you and if you would call him back. He sounded British and the call came from Vegas."

"Okay hon, I'll give him a call in a few minutes, I want to check with Bob first. Have you seen him?"

"Yeah," answered Helen who was banging a keyboard a few feet away. "He's out front working on some of Ruth's Huevos Rancheros Tom. You look good hon, last night must have gone well."

"Yes it did," I told her, " I feel much better this morning." I bent down and gave Helen a kiss on the cheek, then went out into the dining room in search of Bob and some coffee. I found both in a booth.

"Hey Uncle, how's it going? Heard anything good?"

"I don't know how good it is Tom, but Zevi Cohen died last night from complications. Some kind of pneumonia that was resistant to treatment."

"Too bad," I commented. "I am sorry to hear that."

"Yes," Bob went on, "when you dance with the devil, the devil doesn't change, you do."

"What do you mean by that Bob?" I asked.

"The devil uses people Tom, but he does not care about them. When he's finished with someone he does his best to kill them, like Shepherd, and the woman Reaux."

"Yeah, I guess your right Uncle," I replied, "how's the German woman?"

"She's healing Tom," he answered, "but the doc says she still has a long way to go. She has a hole in her cheek the size of a silver dollar. I have been getting reports of a German industrialist making inquiries about her. No name on him yet, but we should know more soon. I get the feeling Nephew, that we aren't finished with the Nazi's yet."

"Or the Golden Dawn and the Illuminati either," I said, telling him about the call from Silverman.

"Why don't you call him Tom, I'll wait here until you get back."

I went back into the war-room and picked up the secure phone, dialed the number and waited for an answer. "Ben Silverman here," answered a cultured British accent. "With whom am I speaking please?"

"Tom Harper here, returning your call sir."

"Yes sir," he went on. "I would like to get together with you and your people to discuss the future of the relic in your possession."

"That may be possible," I said. "Who do you represent, if I may ask? There have been a number of interested parties, if you know what I mean."

"I do indeed sir," I could almost feel him standing ramrod straight while he spoke. "I represent a Jewish organization that wishes to see the artifact returned to its rightful owners."

"Do you know where to find us?" I asked.

He replied that he did, but due to the travel restrictions on the Sabbath, he would not be able to get here until ten or eleven in the evening. I told him that would be fine; someone would be here to greet him unless an emergency came up. I hung up and turned my attention to Dakota who was desperately in need of it.

Jason come over with some hot fry bread, setting it down in front of us with a cheerful, "When you two gonna get married anyway?"

"As soon as he gets around to asking me, I recon," quipped Dakota.

"Now don't rush me gal," I drawled. "This mustang ain't never had a bit in his mouth ya know."

Jason laughed his hearty laugh and sat down with us. I picked up a piece of the bread tearing it in half, offering Dakota the other and said to Jason, "Brother, on a some what more serious note. I need to ask a question."

"Go ahead little brother," he replied. "I will answer if I can."

"Thank you," I said. "There was something Rogers said about me having a mark on me and it reminded me of the little girl back at your place that said I might be THE ONE. What did she mean by that?"

"Oh yeah, that," Jason answered and slipped into thought. "My great grandfather, Kicking Horse, had a vision when he was on his first Vision Quest. He saw a white man who would bridge the two worlds: the world of the red man and the world of the white man.

"He would be a man of great spiritual power, blessed by the Great Spirit to fight against the evil spirits of the world. He would lead his chosen people into a great battle and restore the balance between the spirit would and the physical world.

"It is also said, that he would be a man of great humility and inner strength. He would be blessed with great wisdom."

"Sounds like my kind'a guy," said Dakota with a smile. "Where can we find him?"

"Amen to that," I replied. "I don't think that sounds much like me bro."

Chuckling a little, Jason went on very seriously, "Little brother, it sounds a lot like you."

"Your right Jason," concluded Dakota. "It does sound like my man." She looked into my eyes and I saw that she was not only serious, she was completely devoted to me. It left me feeling very humble and very speechless.

I decided not to tell them about my dream of the two armies facing each other in the valley. I believed what I saw, but I did not want to set myself up as some sort of prophet. If it came true, I would deal with it then.

I told Jason, instead, about the call to Silverman and we decided it would be a good idea to have people stationed around the restaurant as guards, even though we probably would not need them. Then I said I was going to go take a nap, since I had not had much sleep for the past few days. Dakota insisted on taking me to her place where I could rest without being disturbed—too much.

I was in a forest by a pool of beautiful blue water; the trees were Oaks and Quaking Aspen, full of fall colors. Ferns grew a meter tall and the ground was spongy from a layer of leaves and moss. The breeze was gentle on my face, smelling of mushrooms and humus. In the distance, a waterfall splashed into the pool sending gentle waves in my direction to lap up on the shoreline. This was a paradise the likes of which I could not remember ever having seen except in pictures, but I knew I would not mind spending a few lifetimes surrounded by such beauty.

"It is restful isn't it?" said a voice from behind me, breaking the tranquility. I turned to see who was speaking, expecting the wily old coyote, but saw an old man with long white hair tied into two braids, a white flowing beard, and wearing buckskins. His eyes were gentle, brown in color, and set above high cheekbones.

"It is unlike any place I have ever seen before old one," I said.

"Listen carefully Tom Harper, there are important things I must tell you about the forces closing in on the Ark."

"Yes old one," I answered, "But please tell me who you are. Your voice is not that of the Lord, which I have heard. I only wish to know who your serve."

"I am the voice of one crying in the wilderness Tom, and that is all I will tell you now (Isaiah 40:3)."

"Yes old one, thank you."

"The forces of the one called Moses Goldman are closing in and you must discourage him before he grows in strength. The Germans will come against you soon as well, but they are weak. The Illuminati are strong, but have no army of their own. Do not let Israel have the Ark yet; their time has not yet come.

"You are doing well my son, keep to the path you are on."

"Do I have the Lord's blessing to marry Dakota?" I asked.

"Yes my son," he answered with a smile. "She will be a good wife for you."

"Thank you old one, for all your help."

"It is my pleasure Tom Harper. Be at peace in this place."

There was a splash in the pool and I turned my head to look. When I turned back he was gone, of course—suckered me again. I did stay in that place for a while longer though, enjoying the peace and stillness.

✝ ✝ ✝

I woke about three in the afternoon still feeling the peace of that special place. Dakota was outside taking care of chores which she had neglected over the past few days. I got a cup of coffee and stood at the backdoor watching her putter about and thinking how blessed I was to know this beautiful, Godly woman. I resolved to ask her the big question as soon as I could arrange the right setting.

I also decided to call my family back in Texas and let them know how things had been going as well. I would have to let dad know it was safe to visit now and tell him about Bob as well. That was going to be harder than telling them about Dakota. Well, finish my coffee, give Dakota a hug, and make the call in that order.

"Oh honey," I called. "Your man is awake and needing a hug."

At 2230 hours, Benjamin Silverman entered the restaurant and stood looking around the place in that calculating way that military men develop as a habit. Everything is taken in at a glance: how many people, how many exits and their locations, potential combatants and non-combatants.

Ruth went up to him and asked him if she could show him to a seat. He replied that he was expected and introduced himself, so she escorted him to the back and had him sit down in the rear booth. She let him know that we would be out to see him in a moment and would he like some coffee while he waited? He ordered tea of course: "Earl Grey and cream, if you please."

I watched him from the kitchen through the order window. He struck me as the sort who would fight all day and still insist on wearing his old school tie to dinner and everyone else as well.

After he got his tea, I walked out and introduced myself, "Gunnery Sergeant Tom Harper, late of the U.S.M.C. sir. You are Major Silverman, I presume?"

"Yes, Israeli intelligence. Good to meet you sir. Please sit down Mr. Harper, tea?"

"No thank you Major," I answered. "I prefer coffee and please call me Tom or Gunny. We are not quite so formal here."

"Very well, uh, Gunny," he said, somewhat uncomfortable with such informality. "To be fully honest I should tell you that I also represent interests in the Army of the Golden Dawn."

"Yes," I answered. "We thought you probably did. Moses Goldman was with the Golden Dawn wasn't he?" I asked it as a question, but it was really a statement. I only wanted to see if he had an interest in finding Goldman.

"Indeed he was, uh Tom. We would like to find him if possible, but that is not why I have come here."

"No," I said. "I know why you have come and what for. However, I am willing to give you Goldman, no charge. He is guilty of a double murder in Santa Fe, as well as other crimes committed here while trying to steal the Ark.

"As far as returning the Ark to your government or organization, I am unable to do that at the moment. I have been advised against any such action at the present time."

"May I ask sir," queried the Major, "who the source of this advice may be?"

"You may ask sir," I responded, "but I am not at liberty to reveal that source at the present time. Suffice it to say that I have already consulted him about this matter and his response was that we cannot turn it over until he is ready."

The Major sipped his tea and nibbled at a biscuit while he considered my answer, then said, "I don't suppose the source was the Almighty?"

I considered his question at some length while munching on a doughnut. I did not wish to be a 'nut' case and tell him that 'Yes God told me' or come off being arbitrary and let him think we were keeping the Ark for ourselves.

"It did not come directly from his mouth to my ear, but yes, it comes from him. The messenger identified himself as 'the one crying in the wilderness', which I believe is a reference to Elijah or John the Baptizer."

"And this came to you in a vision?"

I wondered what he was getting at. Was he simply trying to gauge my sanity? After the past few weeks all I could say was, good luck.

"Yes," I answered. "In a vision as I was taking a nap this morning. I know who you represent and what you want, so I sought God's will concerning the matter. This was not the first time this person has appeared to me and, I hope, not the last."

I stopped there to gauge his reaction. "Perhaps," I went on, "if you were to remove Goldman he would change his mind. I don't know, I only know that there are several other organizations intent on taking possession of the Ark and we have no intention of letting that happen."

The mention of other organizations drew a reaction from the major in the form of a slightly raised eyebrow and a quick flick of his eyes. "Do you know who these other organizations are Gunny?" he asked.

"Yes," I answered. "We do." I left it at that though. He turned my answer over for a moment, and then said, "Perhaps we could be of some help to your organization Mr. Harper."

"Perhaps you could," I said, seeing a way to keep them occupied for a while somewhere else. "An organization calling itself the Fourth Reich is one of the players Major Silverman. They are based somewhere in the Black Forest, in Germany, as far as we know. We have had dealings with some of their people of whom there is a single survivor. She has been in no condition for questioning, but should be sufficiently recovered by now. She showed up here with two men, one called himself Stephan Von Himmler, and the other was Karl Betz. Have you ever heard of these people?"

After a moment the major decided to answer, "Yes, we know of Betz and his fascist leaning, but we did not know he was with the Fourth Reich. We have been watching their leader Hans Bettendorf for several years now. He believes he is the successor to Hitler, but is not as charismatic as the Führer. We do not consider him more than a minor threat, but perhaps we could discourage him from any further activity as our contribution to having the Ark returned."

"I can't tell you that would help any Major, but it might. I got the impression from the messenger that he wasn't ready for Israel to have the Ark at this time. When he is, we will turn it over, rest assured."

"I believe you Tom, and I will relay your message to my superiors. In the meantime we will do what we can to help you without interfering."

"Thank you Major," I said, standing as he got up to go. He stopped at the register where Ruth was waiting and told her, "Very good tea young lady and thank you for the biscuits as well."

He handed her a five, turned back toward me, and said, "We'll be in touch Mr. Harper."

"Call me in the morning Major and I will give you Goldman's whereabouts. If you wish, I will take you to see the German woman as well."

"Very good Mr. Harper, I will call you tomorrow."

I was sure he would.

✝ ✝ ✝

Moses had just gotten off the phone with the South African merc and was feeling better than he had in weeks. They would be delayed twenty-four hours due to transportation problems, but was assured, they would arrive ready to carry out the mission.

Out on the verandah he was enjoying a snifter of brandy, as well as a good Cuban cigar while watching the sunset in his little Latin paradise. Out beyond the porch by the tree line he saw movement in the bushes that lined the perimeter of the property. As he watched, a coyote poked his gray head out and seemed to look at him, even making eye contact. Maria came out to see if there was anything else he needed before she went home and, seeing the animal, she quickly crossed herself. Moses spoke fairly good Spanish and understood her superstitious prayer, but asked, "Why do you pray Maria, it is only a coyote."

"He is a spirit Señior, some brujo has sent him."

Moses was amused by this idea and asked, "You believe that someone can take on animal form Maria?"

"Si Señior," she answered. "They do this to listen in or to follow someone. They are like a witches gato."

He thanked her and sent her home, assuring her that it was only an animal looking for food. After she left he looked back to where the animal had been, but it had disappeared back into the brush leaving only its haunting yip's to remind him that it had been there at all.

When he got back to his hotel room Ben Silverman made an international call to General Ben Gurion, filling him in on what he had learned so far. The general agreed that force against the Gideons was not in their best interest at this time. The Ark had been lost for more than three thousand years and at least now they at knew where it was. Patience was a virtue the Jews had learned from God after forty years in the wilderness—they could afford to wait a little longer.

He also informed the general about the Nazi's sudden interest in the Ark and, he agreed again, that Bettendorf's interest in the artifact would have to be curtailed. But it was the news of Moses Goldman that most interested Ben Gurion. He had taken Moses' failure and defection personally. He gave the major the order to find Moses and capture him if possible—terminate him if he could not.

After hanging up the phone, he sat thinking about this brash young Texan and his friends. Could this man truly be a prophet? Did God speak with him or was he just another lunatic who has been out in the desert sun too long without a hat? He would have to find out more about this man before he made any further decisions. He did not wish to find himself guilty of stoning another of the Lord's prophets, as so many of his ancestors had.

Besides, he found himself rather liking the young man, he did not have the fevered look of a zealot and those around him were not empty headed followers, as he had seen with others in the past. He did not express a desire for power—just the opposite in fact. He would find out more in the morning.

✝ ✝ ✝

The next morning I was having breakfast with Dakota and some of the others when Silverman showed up. I had Ruth bring him over to sit with us at our booth.

"May I recommend the bagels Major, they are kosher," said Ruth.

"Thank you," the major replied, "and coffee—black."

I had seen Bob earlier and he had hinted at knowledge of Goldman's location so, as she was about to fill the major's order I asked Ruth, "Please tell Bob to join us, I believe he is in the kitchen with your dad."

She smiled as way of an answer and headed for the order window shouting 'Order up' as waitresses have been doing for all of recorded time.

"Major," I said. "This is Dakota Walsh, my fiancé."

"Pleased to meet you Miss Walsh," he said.

"Just call me Dakota, please. Everyone does, it keeps me from beating them senseless," she replied with her most endearing smile.

"I shall keep it uppermost in my mind, Miss Dakota."

Bob came out of the kitchen and joined us, introducing himself to the major. "My Nephew tells me that you may be interested in the location of Moses Goldman."

"Yes sir," the major answered. "We would like to return him to Israel to stand trial for various charges, including desertion."

"You can find him at Rancho Villa Rosa about five klick's south of Nogales. He enjoys the protection of the local patron, but I don't think your people will have any real problem getting him out. If you don't get him, we will for the double murders in Santa Fe."

"We will get him Mr. Harper," the major assured him. "He has much to answer for back home. If you don't mind, I will take care of the matter immediately as Moses is not likely to remain in one place for any length of time."

"Of course," I said. "Good hunting Major. Here is the location of Olga if you still wish to speak with her." He took the slip of paper and left without further comment.

After the major made his exit, I asked Bob to stick around for a minute. I turned to Dakota and handed her a small box telling her to open it. As she did so I got down on one knee and said, "Dakota Walsh, I pledge my life and my love to you, if you will accept my proposal of marriage."

I swear that was the closest I ever came to wetting my pants. Even though I knew she was gong to say yes, I was terrified that she would change her mind for some reason and refuse. For a moment that stretched into an eternity, she just stared at the ring as though she had never seen one before, and then said, "Tom Harper, I thought you would never ask. I would be honored to be your wife."

With tears running down both her cheeks and mine too, Helen said, "If you two don't kiss each other right now, I'm going to have Jason throw you both out."

As I kissed her, we joined in a way I had never experienced with anyone before. I felt her feelings, both physical and emotional, and she in turn felt mine. We had become one flesh in that moment.

Then a familiar voice from behind me said, "Well, it's about time son."

"How about introducing us to the young lady," said the voice of my mom.

After the introductions had been made I looked around for Bob. "Dad there is someone else you need to meet." The two of them stood looking at each other for a moment and then I saw a torrent of emotions flow across my father's face ending in a look that broke my heart. It was the look of betrayal, as though Bob had played some cruel joke on him.

My dad suddenly turned away and walked out of the restaurant saying only, "Come on Rae, we're leaving," to my mom.

I caught him in the parking lot, getting between him and the car and said, "Wait up dad. He didn't mean to hurt you, it was for your safety and mom's."

There was a flash of anger in my dad's eyes like I had never seen before and he hit me on the jaw. Maybe not as hard as he could, but hard enough. I bounced against the car door in surprise, because he had never hit me before in his life and I said, "Hit me again dad."

I stood there with blood running from my lip down my chin, looking into his eyes and seeing the pain he was feeling. Then I stepped up to him and threw my arms around him saying, "Dad it's okay, it's okay. You're right to be mad, but today you have your brother back and all the guilt you have been feeling all these years can be washed away. You are free dad, forgive yourself and forgive Bob. At least listen to his story and find out why he did it."

My mom came up echoing my sentiments and reminding my dad that this should be a happy day. His son had proposed to a beautiful young woman and he had found his brother, who had been dead to him for thirty years.

My dad pushed me away from his car and opened the door. He looked at my mom and said, "Get in Rae, we're leaving."

I had not seen my mom stand up to my dad very many times, but she did now saying, "No, I won't run away. I am staying here with Tom."

My dad's face went pale with this double betrayal. It was too much for him to handle in one day; he started the engine and drove away, leaving us in the hot Nevada sun.

Bob came alongside us on his Chief and said, "I owe you one Nephew," referring to the shot to my jaw. "Don't worry, I'll catch up to him and talk with him, he'll be okay."

He roared off in pursuit of my dad and I turned to my mom who had taken my arm and said, "He'll be okay Tom, don't you worry. It's just too big a shock for him; too much to take in at one time. Let the two of them have some time together and I'm sure they'll be back in no time like nothing ever happened."

I took my mom's arm and walked her back to the restaurant with Dakota on my other arm. We took a seat in the back and then I told mom what had happened to Bob all those years ago, because dad had never told her the whole truth.

It was noon, siesta time on this side of the border, when all activity stopped until the sun had passed its zenith. Moses sat in his office with the ceiling fan blowing warm air over his head, as it made a monotonous clacking noise, like a car with one bad valve, due to being slightly out of balance. He was going over his maps and reviewing his battle plans, so he did not notice the figures in jungle camouflage approaching his hacienda.

There were six altogether, closing in an ever-tighter circle. Had he been paying attention, he would have noticed that the compound had gone completely silent minutes ago. There were no barking dogs, no sound of insects, only the ticking of the fan overhead.

He nearly crapped his pants when he saw the muzzle of the Uzi pointed only inches from his face and heard the odd British accent, so out of character in this place, ordering him: "Come with us Colonel Goldman."

He was about to protest when someone rudely turned out the lights.

Dad drove until he came to a little bar on the other side of town called Billy's. The parking lot was full of the usual redneck specials—pick-ups, mostly with flaking paint jobs and a few old cages thrown in. He walked in and found himself a stool at the bar where Billy, a middle-age dishwater blond with a bosom only slightly larger than her ample waistline, served him a Bud light, then went back to her friends at the other end of the bar.

Sunlight broke the spell of darkness again only moments later, as Bob came in and took a seat next to Joe and waving at Billy to serve up two more brews. The two of them sat in silence nursing their beers until Bob finally began to tell his story of escape, survival, and redemption.

For his part, my dad sat silently and listened, mostly as he put it, out of guilt for hitting me in the mouth. Four beers and an hour later my dad got up and took a swing at Bob, but missed. Unfortunately, he did not miss the stocky little Indian who had been sitting next to him happily eavesdropping on their whole story and knocked him off his stool into the thirty-something cowboy wannabe with an oversize belt buckle and equally oversize beer gut.

After bouncing off the cowboy the Indian stumbled back and fell over a table where two young men from Nellis air base were plying two underage local girls with beer and lies of being war heroes, upsetting both the table and their licentious hopes for the evening.

Beer bottles and punches began to fly in all directions including that of Bob and Joe. Belt buckle took a swing at Bob, knocking him back against the bar, so dad hit the man just above that buckle causing him to double over, then followed up with a knee to the jaw, dropping his opponent to the saw-dust covered floor.

Bob fended off one of the girls from the table who, in very unladylike fashion, was aiming a beer bottle at the back of dad's head, saving him from serious injury. From that point on, the two of them took on all comers until the local cops arrived and took them all away to the Gray-bar Hilton.

Moses came to consciousness aware that he was no longer in his Latin paradise. His hands were duct-taped to the arms of a sturdy Oak chair, and his ankles to the chair legs. A dark hood was over his head admitting only sparse light, but he could make out shapes moving around him. He could hear whispers in the room, so he knew he was not alone. He remained still, hoping to learn who his captors were and maybe something that would be useful in dealing with them.

The hood was jerked off his head and he saw in front of him, a dapper dark-haired man who was smoking some kind of European cigarette, probably British judging by the stink of its tobacco. The man had a document folder in his hands pouring over the contents, which seemed to be not inconsequential.

He held a photograph up as though comparing the likeness to his face and then said, "Colonel Moses Goldman, Army of the Golden Dawn, Mossad, and it would seem, traitor to the state of Israel. What do you have to say for yourself sir?"

The Oxford accent was all Moses needed to hear to know that he had fallen into the hands of Major Ben Silverman. This man had been a thorn in his side since the Damascus operation and that wet-job he was supposed to carry out on the Hamas leader. He had never given an adequate explanation for not killing the man when he had the chance.

How could he explain to his fellow officers that he simply did not have the stomach for killing up close and personal. To kill a man with a knife, to watch the life go out of his eyes, the heart vibrating wildly in its death throws against that steel intruder was something he could not bring himself to do.

He had left field work after that, but Silverman had never let him forget the incident. They had to send in a helicopter gun-crew to do the job and though it had been a success, it had cost the life of one man on that chopper. A young man named Joseph Silverman Jr., Ben's older brother.

"Shalom Major Silverman," Moses said, preferring to keep things professional. "Why do you call me a traitor Ben?"

"You were sent here to recover the Ark for Israel and instead I find you living in luxury at a hacienda in Mexico. The squad of six fine Israeli soldiers assigned to you, we found out are lying in a morgue in Nevada. The Ark is still in the possession of the goyim and you wonder why I call you a traitor. Moses, I knew you were a coward, but I have never called you a fool until this day."

Moses tried to think; what could he say? "The Gideons are very good Ben, but they were not the ones who killed the squad. That was done by and Bettendorf's Nazis."

He spat this out hoping the hated word would have some mitigating effect on Silverman. "They ambushed us as we were going to the cave where the Ark was hidden. Them and that crazy biker gang. We never had a chance. They were shot down and picked off by sniper. I only got away because I was flanking the group and had cover."

This was not the truth of course, the Nazi's had been murdered by Meronek, but Moses was desperate and the truth was his first victim as usual.

Ben stared at him for what seemed an eternity, then closed the document folder and put it into a standard courier's pouch. He steepled his fingers together in front of his face and seemed to consider some choice he was making. "Moses, I find that I need to make a choice concerning you. Take you back in disgrace to Israel or leave you here to stand trial for murder in Santa Fe. In Israel you wont face the death penalty, thanks to our politicians, but you will in New Mexico. Which would you prefer?"

This was no choice at all; he would not be executed in Israel, but that did not mean he would not be killed. He had no illusions about his odds of survival in a military prison. "I will not make your choice any easier for you Ben." Then he fell silent.

"Put him in the cell," Ben told someone behind Moses as he left the room. The bag went over his head once again, so he would see nothing of where he was taken, then he was lifted bodily and carried into another room where the door was slammed, leaving him in total darkness. Things were not going according to plan—again.

CHAPTER 45

David came over to us while we were having a late lunch and pulled me off to the side to say, "Sorry to tell you bro, but your dad and your uncle are in the city jail for busting up Billy's bar. I just heard about it man."

"Any idea what happened?" I asked.

"Seems your dad took a swing at Bob and hit somebody else and one thing led to another until they wound up whipping everybody in the bar. I can get them out, but they will have to pay Billy for the damages."

"Okay," I answered, "how much?"

"Billy says fifteen hundred will cover it. Some chairs, tables, broken bottles, you know."

"Can you take me down there? It may be better if I don't take my mom."

I made my excuses to Dakota and mom, then we left for the short drive downtown. A lot of things went through my mind on the drive there; mostly I was worried that dad would not be able to forgive Bob. I started looking through my little pocket Bible for all the scriptures dealing with forgiveness that I could find, but I knew it would be a hollow gesture. Right now my dad's blood was up, I would just have to wait and see how much damage was done.

The two of them were sitting on a bench inside the booking room looking for all the world like two kids that had been caught looking through their dad's Playboy magazines. Billy was at the desk waiting for us as well. I walked up ready to make apologies, but she turned to me, threw her arms around me, and bubbled, "So you're the man gonna tie down Dakota Walsh."

"Yes ma'am," I managed to squeeze out. "She did say yes only a couple of hours ago."

"I have known Dakota since she was in diapers. Me and her mom go way back, lemme look at you, uh humm. If I was a few years younger I would go after you myself ha, ha."

She was a very jovial person and probably a lot of fun to be around at a party. She looked over toward dad and Bob and said, "These two sure know how to fight. They cleared out my bar in record time. I should press charges, but I know what their story is and it being a special day for you and Dakota I'm just gonna let it drop. I do expect you two to pay for the damages and clean up the mess though, okay?"

Dad and Bob agreed to the conditions and my dad said, "Son, I'm sorry I hit you, it wasn't your fault, please forgive me."

"Okay dad, as long as you pay for the first round. Let's get over to Billy's and clean up so she can get back into business and we can celebrate."

By the time we got back to the restaurant dad and Bob were acting like nothing had happened. Mom and Dakota were both waiting with dinner and the knowing smiles that women have welcomed back their men with since we got put out of the Garden.

Karl Betz was beginning to feel his years, even though he was only fifty-four. He still felt he was in good condition, though his doctor told him he should lose a few pounds—about fifty to be exact. He was returning to his house in Dresden from a week-end with the Füehrer and some of the high-ranking officers. He was feeling good, especially since he had bagged that big-boobed, frau Helga. She was Dorfman's very young secretary and quite a treat, much better than his fat aging wife, Brenda.

As he walked in through the back door of his two-story, twelve-room house, he was suddenly thrown into darkness as a hood was pulled over his head. Hands gripped him from either side and carried him along to a chair where he was forced to sit while his hands and feet were secured into painful immobility.

"What is going on? Who are you?" he sputtered, praying that the thugs just wanted money. Kidnapping had become a national pastime in Europe, as it had in so many other parts of the world, and it would be alright as long as they didn't kill him.

He heard his wife crying in another room and voices commanding her to be silent and she would not be hurt. For the first time in their many years together, she actually followed orders. Then a voice spoke to him in good, but accented German, "We don't want your money Nazi, we are not here to rob you. We are from the Army of the Golden Dawn. You and your organization will leave the Ark alone, if we have to come back, we will not be so polite, verstehen?"

It was not a question: it was an order. He was not sure who the Golden Dawn was, but he was determined now to find out. After several minutes of silence, he began to call out to his captors, who remained silent. He pulled the hood off his head after working his hands free of the simple restraint put on them by strips of duct-tape.

On the table in front of him were two simple items—a military knife laying across a Star of David.

Moses found himself in a place of infinite space; there were no walls or ceiling that he could detect; nor any surface that would define his location. He sat within a circle of light waiting for something, but he was not sure what. He began to hear a voice saying something over and over, but it was far away and he could not make out what it was saying, like when he had been a child and the doctor would talk to his mother on the other side of the door about his bed-wetting.

The voice grew louder and he thought, closer, until he could make out what it was saying, "Moses, Moses?"

Her voice was throaty, resonant, beckoning like the sirens of Odysseus. Frightened, but desperate not to be alone, he called out, "Here, I'm over here."

The voice continued calling his name, coming closer and closer until it sounded like it was only a few feet away from him.

"Moses will you serve me?" the voice asked.

"How can I serve you," he answered. "I am a prisoner, I will never see freedom again."

"Ha, ha, ha," laughed the voice, "that is no problem Moses. I can slip your bonds easily enough, but you must swear to serve only me."

"Okay," he said, since he had nothing to lose. "Let's talk. Who are you?"

"You may call me Carmine, Moses, and I can make your dream a reality. You and I ruling the world, isn't that your dream Moses? Meronek failed because he was a fool, but I sense you are no fool Moses. With the Ark in our control, no power on earth can stop us. What do you say Moses, or should I say, King Moses?"

She walked into the circle of light at that moment and Moses gave up any apprehension he may have had.

✝ ✝ ✝

Late that night after many toasts and wishes of blessings on our marriage, Dakota and I finally found a few minutes of privacy. We talked about what we would do after marriage. I told her she should go on with her job and I would apply for a position in law enforcement. With my background, it would be no problem, especially with Jason and David to vouch for me. That would also leave me free to work in the motorcycle ministry I felt the Lord was calling me to.

"What about the Ark though Tom? Has he said anything about what to do with it?"

"No," I answered, "he hasn't. I have been thinking about getting Carter to take us out to where he found it and see what else is there. Might be a good place to leave it since it took about three thousand years to find it the first time."

"That would be a good idea Tom, I know Arthur would like to see what's in there." That reminded me to ask Bill about the background check I had ordered on Arthur. Everything was looking good right now and I just prayed the Lord would give us peace for a while.

Mom and dad sat at the next booth talking, laughing, and having a good time with Bob. I was so glad to see them together. Bob looked as though some great weight had been lifted off his shoulders and my dad's eyes had lost some of the emptiness that had lurked in the background for so many years.

Dakota nestled into my arm, putting her head on my shoulder, and was soon asleep. I prayed over her then, asking the Lord to bless us coming in and going out with long life, great joy and many children.

CHAPTER 46

The next morning was bright and clear, holding great promise. Bill brought the background check on Brooks and I read it while having my breakfast of eggs, Texas toast, bacon, and oatmeal.

It was pretty much as he had told us: Twenty years in the Israeli army, decorated for meritorious service, and retired with honor. I called him over to the table and after a few minutes, Carter and Tracy joined us.

"General, what have you heard from the Air Force?" I asked to get things started.

"They were not happy about losing the artifact, as well as the bloody action at the base, but they have been unable to place the blame on me or anyone else. We did what we were supposed to do; by the book. They have offered to let me retire and call it even. I said I would accept."

So, the general would get his benefits and full retirement and the Air Force would avoid public exposure over the contents of Hanger 10. Everything was working out well.

"That's good General, real good. How would you like to lead us out to that secret stash in the desert? I know Arthur would like to see what's in there and so would the rest of us."

"Sure," answered Carter, "we'll need at least a couple of trucks and a bobcat."

"I think we have everything we will need out at my place," offered Jason. "I've got a flatbed and David has a box truck."

"I think we should leave this to Arthur since this kind of dig will have to be supervised by some university or maybe the National Geographic Society."

"Yes Tom," Brooks said. "If we go in there we may damage something. I will arrange it with the authorities, that way no one will be able to claim rights to the contents. Except Israel of course."

While Arthur did that, we set about making the Ark secure in its new hiding place. We used a cave in the same general area and left a guard to watch it. Everything seemed to be settling down and Dakota and I were able to sit down and make plans about the wedding.

He had been wandering around the desert for the past three days taking on any form he could: rabbit, coyote, crow; whatever presented itself. They weren't as satisfying as a human host, but as yet, he had had no calling. Then came her voice, the one who served the master. She pointed him toward a host with promises of pleasures he had not tasted in a very long time. The black man should have been better, more fun, but the Ark had put and end to that host before he had been able to enjoy the pleasures he offered.

He arrived at the house and shed his animal host in order to enter the new host inside the structure that he would need to carry out the directions he had been given. The one called Preacher lay in his bed asleep as he hovered over him, seeking his point of entry. Finding it, at the man's navel, he entered in and made himself comfortable. He was surprised that this host was empty as there were indications of a previous possession. No matter, it was his now, and if need be, he could invite others to help control him.

Preacher woke with a start, as if from a bad dream. He got up, went into the bathroom for some water, and stopped to look in the mirror. He was aware that something was different, but was unable to put his finger on it. The demon flowed into his consciousness, bringing a smile to his time-weathered face. He had felt this way before, but not in a long time.

Now it would be time to party.

He got dressed in his black leather jeans; black engineer boots, black t-shirt with Black Sabbath emblazoned on it, and then let himself out into the hall. He debated whether to kill the others in the house or not before leaving. The taste of their blood and fear would be good; it would give him strength for what he was about to do. He was stopped at the bedroom entrance, unable to go in because of a crucifix with the Lord's Prayer affixed to the door. With a muttered curse he turned away and went outside to where his '45 knucklehead patiently waited.

The others in the house woke up at the staccato burst of straight pipes and the barking of every neighborhood dog for two miles to find Preacher gone; his parole broken.

The wind in his face, cool and sharp in the early morning felt so good he had to let out a howl that was absolutely primal. The thundering vibration of the old V-twin between his legs was as reassuring as a binky to a baby. The road stretched out before him, lost beyond the single vibrating cone of light projecting from his headlamp. He was going to need money for gas and supplies, so he started looking for someplace that would be easy and quick to rob. Then it was on to Santa Fe and his appointment with destiny.

The phone woke me at 0500: it was Jason telling me that Preacher had taken off from his cousin's house where we had put him up. That was bad news; the worse news was that he had armed himself with a sawed-off shotgun and a box of shells.

The second call came an hour later from Dave to tell me that a man matching Preacher's description had robbed Billy's bar. He had left with the night's receipts, but not without shooting the place up first. Billy was badly wounded, Belt Buckle was dead, and one of the young girls that hung out there had been forced to go with him, presumably as a hostage. He was headed south when last seen.

I could not imagine what had brought this on, Preacher had been doing well, had been receptive to the gospel, though he had not received Jesus yet, and seemed genuinely trying to turn his life around.

Dakota had been listening from across the table and said it sounded like he had been possessed, like in the scripture of Mat.12:43-45. 'When an evil spirit leaves a person, it goes into the desert, seeking rest but finding none. Then it says, "I will return to the person I came from." So it returns and finds its former home empty, swept, and clean. Then the spirit finds seven other spirits more evil than itself, and they all enter the person and live there. And so that person is worse off than before.'

I had to agree that it sounded like something had possessed him, I had not taken him for a killer, and he had no record for armed violence, but he was a life-long one-percenter and certainly capable of it.

Since I had been responsible for his parole I felt it was up to me to go after him. I gave Dakota a long kiss, with a promise to come back safe, and headed out on his trail while it was still light. At least so far, it was not going to be very hard to find him, all I had to do is follow the trail of bodies.

CHAPTER 47

Moses was more scared than he had ever been in his whole miserable life, even more than he had been when some older classmen at the Academy had threatened to force him into having sex; as the catcher of course. Silverman had been quiet, saying only that they might be catching a plane in Tucson. He had chosen to ride in the lead vehicle, leaving Moses in the company of four strong-but-silent types. Two in the front of the Navigator and one on each side of him in back, and no amount of chattering on his part would induce them into conversation. They sat as silent and inscrutable as the Sphinx.

They were on a deserted stretch of two-lane blacktop that Silverman thought would be more secure when a lone figure in black began to slowly grow in the rear-view mirrors. The driver's head turned slightly taking notice of the lone intruder in this desert wilderness and quickly dismissed him as a threat. It was only one guy on a motorcycle and they were eight men in two large hunks of rolling Detroit iron. A sad miscalculation on his part, as they were about to learn: the hard way.

The lone rider pulled up alongside and passed the SUV carrying Moses, then pulled in front of them, placing himself between the two vehicles. In quick order he pulled a shotgun from his lap which, by means of a string, opened a bag hanging under the taillight releasing a hundred or so sharpened jacks that made quick work of shredding the tires of the Navigator and sending it careening out of control at over eighty m.p.h.

Preacher pulled alongside the lead vehicle, leveled the twelve-gauge at the driver, and pulled the trigger releasing its load of deadly shot like a horde of angry bees. The driver was only wounded, but lost control of the big Lincoln, sending it off the road into the soft sand of the desert where it began to roll like a child's toy—the doors flying open and bodies ejected to bounce like rag dolls in the sagebrush.

The driver of Moses' vehicle struggled desperately to bring the huge beast under control, but with all four tires ripping themselves apart it was a losing battle. They went sideways and began to tumble like a baseball in a dryer, eventually coming to a stop in the soft sand of the road's shoulder.

Through some miracle, Moses had remained conscious, perhaps because the men on either side had him wedged in so tightly that he had hardly been able to move. They had come to a stop upside down and it took him a moment for his head to stop spinning.

There were two loud pops from the passenger-side window and he watched with some curiosity as blossoms of red and gray erupted from the heads of the men in the front seat, spraying brain-matter all over the passenger compartment and splashing him with the gore.

An equally gruesome deluge quickly followed from the men on either side of him. Somebody was screaming, but he could not tell where it was coming from. He could feel blood and other more solid matter, dripping from his face and head. Then a knife appeared in a hand covered in a black leather glove releasing him head first onto the cars bloody roof. Only when he hit did he realize that the screaming was coming from him and he began to fight back nausea that threatened to empty his stomach all over his rescuer. Then the smell of all the blood, mixed with gasoline, overcame him and he began to spew all over the ground where he lay face down.

There were more sounds of gunfire coming from the direction of the other vehicle while he lay gagging and trying to get control of himself. Carmine had kept her promise; he really was being set free. Now, if only he could get to on his feet and get away from this place.

I pulled up and stopped as close as I dared to get to the still burning vehicle. Looking around I did not see anyone moving and could not hear any calls for help. There were four dead in the first car, so I moved on to the next, which was not burning. I found the first body just short of the SUV. Too many of his limbs pointed in impossible directions, leaving no doubt he was dead. There was another underneath the Navigator, I assumed, since only an arm was visible. One other body had been churned to mush in the cargo section and I could see no sign of anyone else.

I spotted a few vultures about a fifty meters away that were fighting over something hidden by the sagebrush and cactus, so I walked up chasing the ugly carrion eaters off with well aimed rocks.

Major Ben Silverman lay unconscious with at least a broken arm, judging from its unnatural angle and blood from many cuts staining his khaki uniform. I bent down and felt for a pulse at the carotid on his neck and, finding one, I called for emergency help.

While I waited for the ambulance, I bent over him to keep the sun off his face and hold him still if he came too. After a couple of minutes, I heard him moan and he opened his eyes.

"Lie still Major," I said. "Help is on the way. Can you hear me Major?"

In a barley audible whisper he said, "Yes Tom."

"Hold on man," I said, then I started reciting Psalm 23 over him and watched as his lips moved silently in sync with mine.

The chopper arrived and the medics took over his care with looks that said they did not have much hope for the major's survival. I went back to my old panhead, Gideon, and looked out across the black snake of pavement wriggling into the heat haze of late afternoon and said, "This time its road-kill Moses, but damn you to Hell, next time you wont get away!"

THE END